Steven Morrisy drove along M Street, passing the closed shops and open pubs lining the main district of Georgetown. Behind them flowed the Potomac River. He stopped in a parking lot lit by old fashioned street lamps that cast more shadow than light and shut off his engine.

"Now, we wait," he told Carla after sweeping the lot for other cars.

"Steven, it's not too late to get out of here," she said, looking around nervously. "Coming back to Washington was crazy and—"

She stopped speaking when two black Mercedes pulled into the lot. The cars drove slowly past them and parked twenty feet away. A few seconds later, three men emerged from the first limousine, two men from the second. They conferred briefly before one of the group broke away and walked to the darkest spot along the abutment on the river.

"Cover me, but do not leave the car," Steven said, scanning the lot quickly then, getting out of the car. He took a deep breath in the cold night air, then walked over to the man. Stopping three feet away from him, he bowed from the waist. The Ambassador of the People's Republic of China did the same.

Without further amenities, Steven said, "I am going to ask you a question. The only answer I want is the truth. Without it, both our countries may perish."

"Please Mr. Morrisy, I have come [illegible] sked. There is no need fo[illegible]

"I can assure yo[illegible] am wanted as a spy, a[illegible] FBI. And, someone is tr[illegible] ady killed two of my fri[illegible]

The ambassador [illegible] dark river, then after a bri[illegible] moment, said, "How can I help my country?"

AS PEACE LAY DYING

DAVID MILTON

PINNACLE BOOKS
WINDSOR PUBLISHING CORP.

PINNACLE BOOKS

are published by

Windsor Publishing Corp.
475 Park Avenue South
New York, NY 10016

First printing: March, 1990

Printed in the United States of America

For Alana Sarah

Acknowledgements

It is with appreciation that I offer my thanks to: The infallible research of Leslie O'gwin-Rivers; and, Vietnam veteran Henry Dassler, for his help with *The Nam*.

Prologue

Her knuckles turned white on the door handle. Cold air rushed across her fingers. She breathed in short gasps which puffed rapidly outward in misty clouds.

"Please," she whispered, her voice catching.

"Out," the driver said, his voice as menacing as the tip of the knife pressing into the underside of her jaw.

The car was pulled off the side of the road. A three-quarter moon illuminated the icy lake, twenty feet distant.

She opened the door farther. Her fingers cramped with tension. A shrieking horror reverberated through her, paralyzing her with the knowledge of what was going to happen.

Tell him what he wants to hear! her mind screamed. Tell him anything!

She wanted to turn to face him, but the knife prevented any movement.

"It's not too late," he said. "It doesn't have to be this way."

She heard the lie in his words. Strangely, it gave her the strength to accept what was happening. She turned to him, ignoring the bite of the knife. "It won't work."

The pressure from the knife lessened. She felt a flicker of hope. Then he back-handed her, the force of the blow knocking her against the door. Her head hit the glass. Pain turned the night amber. She lost her grip on the door handle and fell to the frozen ground.

With a desperate cry, she scrambled to her feet. But her muscles were stiff, disobeying. She used her hands to push herself up. Her right hand caught on a rock. Two nails bent back and snapped off. The pain cleared her head, momentarily. She slipped wildly on the ice-crusted snow of the embankment, floundering and fighting her way to the blacktop. She knew that the drugs he'd been feeding here were slowing her.

She reached the blacktop, sensing him close behind her. She stumbled blindly into the night, fear acting as her guide. Behind her came the sound of footfalls.

Oh, please, no, she prayed, refusing to look back, reaching for the strength to keep on running.

Pain seared her abdomen. Her lungs screamed against the air that was a freezing razor blade slicing through her with every breath. Her mind was mired by the fear pounding at her temples.

The road curved to the right. Tall evergreens lined the side of the road. She knew she had to get to them. They were her only chance for sanctuary, for life.

She angled toward the trees. Her legs ached, her feet were numb. Her right foot sank in the snow as she left the road for the trees.

And then, with safety looming close, an intense pain exploded on her scalp. Her head was snapped back. Her feet flew out from beneath her. For an instant, her body floated parallel to the ground.

She was slammed down, her back and head hitting at the same time. She felt consciousness slipping away. She fought against it, unable to move yet unwilling to give up.

The man was above her now. His face was obscured by the dark.

He scooped her into his arms and carried her back toward the car. But he did not go to the car; he worked his way down the snow-covered embankment until he was at the lake's edge.

The ice was thin at this point. The lake was long and deep. There were a few places along its shoreline that were shallow enough to wade in. This was not one of them. Inches from where he stood, the water was five feet deep. A few feet farther out, the bottom dropped thirty feet.

It suited his plans perfectly.

Placing her on the ground, he saw that her eyes were closed. He looked around, spotted a large rock, and hefted it. He went to the water's edge and, going to his knees, slammed the rock against the ice. It shattered into a spiderweb of cracks. He struck again and again. The hole widened, the broken pieces of ice reflecting diamond-like in the moonlight. He stopped only when the opening in the ice was large enough to satisfy him.

He looked down at her. She was beautiful. But she had looked where she should not, and had learned things she could not be allowed to talk of.

He took off his right glove and caressed her face. His fingers traced her high cheekbones, moved to her mouth, and then followed the smooth curve of her lips. He sighed and put his glove back on.

He lifted her and kissed her mouth. "Goodbye, Eleanor." He thrust her away from him.

Her body arched through the air, striking the ice and water at the exact spot he had prepared. She hit hard, broke the remaining ice, and sank quickly.

The water's biting coldness snapped her back to full consciousness. Her eyes opened as the water swept over her head. Terror moved her muscles. She flailed her arms and opened her mouth to scream. Water flooded in, choking her. She fought, spitting and kicking toward the surface.

Her head broke free. She gasped for air. Suddenly a hand was on her head, pushing her down. She saw his contorted face. He pushed her down, but not before she had a chance to take a breath.

Panic overrode her when she failed to break his grip. Then, with the sudden clarity of someone who knows that there is only one possibility, she acted.

She stopped fighting and hung limp. She exhaled half her air in one forceful push. A few seconds later his hand was gone.

She kept herself under, her heart battering her ribs until her lungs rebelled and she could no longer feel any sensation in her legs.

Be gone, she prayed, holding her panic at bay when the top of her head broke the surface. Knowing that if he saw her she would never get another chance, she rose higher. The instant her mouth was out of the water, she took a deep breath.

Then she saw the lights. Two bright circles in the blackness. Someone. Help me! she tried to yell, but no sound emerged from her frozen larynx.

The lights came closer, moving fast.

The headlights wavered, bounced, and then straightened as the car moved inexorably toward her. She pushed back. Her head hit the ice, momentarily stunning her.

Then the car slid sideways and hit a tree. A glimmer of hope rose, only to die when she saw that the tree had only slowed the car a little and it was still coming toward her.

Before she could send herself under the water, the right front fender of the black Pontiac came hurtling down on her head.

Steven Morrisy drove along M Street, passing the closed shops and open pubs lining the main district of Georgetown. Behind them flowed the Potomac River. He stopped in a parking lot lit by old fashioned street lamps that cast more shadow than light and shut off his engine.

"Now, we wait," he told Carla after sweeping the lot for other cars.

"Steven, it's not too late to get out of here," she said, looking around nervously. "Coming back to Washington was crazy and—"

She stopped speaking when two black Mercedes pulled into the lot. The cars drove slowly past them and parked twenty feet away. A few seconds later, three men emerged from the first limousine, two men from the second. They conferred briefly before one of the group broke away and walked to the darkest spot along the abutment on the river.

"Cover me, but do not leave the car," Steven said, scanning the lot quickly then, getting out of the car. He took a deep breath in the cold night air, then walked over to the man. Stopping three feet away from him, he bowed from the waist. The Ambassador of the People's Republic of China did the same.

Without further amenities, Steven said, "I am going to ask you a question. The only answer I want is the truth. Without it, both our countries may perish."

"Please Mr. Morrisy, I have come as you asked. There is no need for melodrama."

"I can assure you that this is no melodrama. I am wanted as a spy, a traitor, and murderer by the FBI. And, someone is trying to kill me as they have already killed two of my friends."

The ambassador turned to look out over the dark river, then after a brief moment, said, "How can I help my country?"

Chapter One

The phone rang. Startled, Steven Morrisy glanced suspiciously at the instrument. There were only half a dozen people who knew where he was. Two of them had left a few hours earlier and would have no reason to call now. The others would only call him at this hour if it was an emergency. Steven, legal counsel and advisor to one of the most powerful senators in the country, was not a man to play games with.

Steven put down his pencil, picked up the receiver, and said hello.

"Why didn't you call me? What the hell happened?"

The voice of Arnold Savak, the senator's chief of staff, was unmistakable. "I haven't called because nothing's happened," Steven said.

"You— Oh my God, you don't know."

"Know what?"

There was silence. Then Savak said, "Steven, there's been an accident."

An inkling of dread turned Steven's voice skittish. "What accident? The senator?"

"No, not the senator. It was last night. Ellie's car went off the road, into a lake."

Ellie's car went off the road, into a lake. The statement

was so simple, so easy to say, and so hard to hear. He looked at the window across from his desk. An elongated vee of Canada geese crossed the horizon.

"Where the hell is there a lake in D.C.?" he asked, holding back his growing panic.

"Not in Washington. Her car went into Lake Pompton last night. That's why—"

"Here?"

"What the hell happened?" Savak asked.

Steven felt cold. "I haven't seen Ellie since last Monday, when I dropped her off at the office."

"But the note she left on Pritman's desk last Monday night said she was coming to Greyton to meet you."

"I don't know what you're talking about, Arnie. What hospital is she at? Greyton?" Steven demanded, as a vision of Ellie, hurt and desperate, filled his mind.

"Yes. I just got the call. Steven, she's in critical condition."

He slammed down the receiver, his mind mired in fear.

And then the pain hit.

For years he'd kept himself immune from such pain. But loving Ellie had made him open up.

The pain diminished slightly, replaced in part by a growing numbness. He reached for the phone, his first thought to call the hospital. No, he decided, he would go to the hospital instead of wasting time on the phone.

Still, he made no move to stand.

Why? It made no sense. Ellie wasn't the type to surprise him by just turning up in Pennsylvania, especially now, when she knew how important it was that he be able to work undisturbed. And, she certainly wouldn't have come last night, knowing that he was scheduled to be back in Washington today. Something was wrong, terribly wrong.

He shuffled the papers into a neat stack and put them into the waiting attaché case. He locked the case and went into the front hallway.

Steven was zipping up his parka when the phone rang again. In his need to get to the hospital, he almost ignored it. Changing his mind at the last instant, he picked up the living room extension. "Yes?"

"Steven, it's Chuck. I didn't know about the accident until I got in, a little while ago. Steven, I'm sorry."

Chuck Latham was the head of emergency medicine at Greyton Memorial. Chuck, Arnie Savak, and he had grown up together. "I'm on my way, Chuck. Arnie just called. How is she?"

He felt the weight of Latham's pause. "Not good, Steven."

Perched on the corner of his desk, Arnold Savak glanced at the clouds massing over the nation's capitol. ". . . I'm afraid so, Senator. I have reliable confirmation that it is Ellie. I don't have all the facts as yet, but the preliminary report is that she lost control of the car and skidded into the lake."

"How badly is she hurt?" Senator Philip Pritman asked. His normally deep voice was made tinny by the speaker phone.

"They don't know if she'll make it."

"Dear Lord. Have you spoken to Steven? Is he all right?"

"He didn't know about it until I called him."

"But she was with him."

Savak hesitated before answering. He stared across the room, at a man sitting on the couch, and said, "Steven says she wasn't with him. Senator, can you do without me for a day or two? I want to fly to Greyton. Steven will need me."

"Of course," Pritman said. "Perhaps I should go as well?"

"Absolutely not." A third voice said strongly, "Sir, you must not involve yourself in this. Not yet."

"Simon, is that you?"

"Yes, sir," the senator's press secretary replied. "I'm sorry, Senator, but until we know more about the circumstances of the accident, I must caution you against personal involvement."

"I'm afraid I must agree with Simon," Savak said. "Steven wouldn't want it either. And you have appointments," Savak reminded him as he opened his desk calender and ran a finger down a page. The notations, in his secretary's handwriting, leapt out at him.

"You've got the Foreign Relations session this afternoon and dinner with Speaker McDonald tonight. Senator, you must get his support for the new arms bill. He's the key man. Tomorrow you have the meeting with Harold Gibbons in Langley. Senator, you simply can't go to Pennsylvania."

"I suppose," Pritman said uncertainly.

"I'll extend your sympathy to Steven."

"Keep me posted on this, Arnold. Any time, day or night."

"I will," Savak promised before shutting off the speaker phone. He stood and walked to the window. His thin frame and five-foot-eleven height were accentuated by a royal-blue pin-stripe suit. Savak ran his hand through thinning light brown hair before turning to the man sitting on the couch. "Well?"

Simon Clarke, Pritman's press secretary, wore a crisply pressed suit and fresh shirt. In contrast to his clothing, Clarke's face was unshaven, evidence of his haste to get to the office after receiving Savak's call.

"I'll make sure the senator has a statement prepared," Clarke said. "One of those 'we are saddened by . . .' if she dies, or an 'our hearts are with her . . . tada tada,' if she makes it. But you've got to get back to me fast. This sort of thing can turn into a nightmare. If the press is already there, you'll have to do something to get around it."

Savak stared at Clarke, a look of distaste settling on his features. "It was an accident, Simon. The media won't be there. Greyton isn't Washington."

"Neither was Chappaquidic. Arnie, Ellie is the senator's personal assistant. Steven is the second ranking staff advisor as well as the senator's legal counsel. Can you really take the chance that some hotshot reporter who's looking to make a rep won't hear about the accident? A hungry reporter can turn this into something it isn't. With the rumors of Pritman's announcement forthcoming, don't think it couldn't happen."

"This isn't political," Savak said, rubbing the side of his sharp nose.

"I'm sure it's nothing more than an accident," Clarke said. "But Arnie, we've spent too damn many years getting to this point to leave anything to chance. The least little thing can trip us up and it's all over." He snapped his fingers. "Poof, just like that."

Savak stared out the window, his hands clasped behind his back. "All right, Simon, I'll make sure all our bases are covered in Pennsylvania."

"Arnie, I don't want to be a hard-ass about this. I know how close you and Steven are—"

Savak turned suddenly, riveting the press secretary with an intense glare. "You don't know the half of it," Savak stated.

"Yes, I do, along with most everyone else around here. We know what the two of you have been through together. But it's my job to make sure that the media is good to Senator Philip Pritman, nothing more, nothing less.

"So, Arnie," Clarke added, standing to face Savak, "I'd suggest you find out why, if Ellie said she'd be in Pennsylvania with Steven, he says she wasn't there. That worries me. We can't afford an uncontrolled situation."

Chapter Two

Steven pulled into a parking space. The four-story brick structure of Greyton Memorial Hospital, built bold and modern twenty years before, loomed menacingly before him. He tried not to think about what awaited him inside.

He got out of the vehicle and locked it, catching his reflection in the tinted glass. His dark hair was messy. His eyes were shadowed by the missed night of sleep. He shrugged and went to the back of the Bronco to make sure that his attaché case could not be seen.

Because of the early hour, the lobby was quiet. He walked past the closed gift shop and rows of empty chairs. At the reception desk, a middle-aged woman entered figures on a sheet of paper.

"Eleanor Rogers' room, please."

Without looking up, the woman turned to her computer console and entered Ellie's name. A moment later she glanced at him from over the rim of her clear plastic glasses. "Are you a relative? Her husband?"

"No. My name is Steven Morrisy."

"I'm sorry," she said, her face evincing professional sympathy. "Miss Rogers is in neurology ICU. She's permitted no visitors other than immediate family."

"Doctor Latham is expecting me."

"Oh yes," she said, tapping a pink memo slip on the white formica desk. "I'll call Doctor Latham."

While he waited for Chuck, he paced the confines of the lobby, his mind filling with unwanted scenarios. Just as his patience came to an end, and he started toward the bank of elevators, Chuck Latham emerged from a stairwell.

An exclamation mark of straight blond hair hung over Latham's left eyebrow. His features, set in a cherubic face at odds with a tall athletic body, were tainted with what Steven thought to be foreboding.

"Chuck, is she—"

Latham, the head of emergency medicine at Greyton, put a hand on Steven's shoulder. "It's touch and go. Ellie's been in a coma since they found her."

"I want to see her," he said, starting toward the elevator.

Latham's grip tightened. "Not yet." He drew Steven away from the reception desk. "I need to talk with you first."

Steven pulled free. "I don't want to talk. I want to see her. Chuck, what the hell's going on?"

"That's what I have to find out," Latham said. "Steven, what happened between you and Ellie?"

He was surprised by Latham's reluctance, and nonplussed by the unexpected question. "Nothing's happened, Chuck. Now, will you tell me just what the hell is going on?"

Latham's eyes clouded. "She wasn't with you last night?"

"The last time I saw Ellie was a week ago in Washington. And now, if you're finished playing twenty fucking questions, I want to go to her."

"Steven—"

"Damn it, Chuck, why are you doing this to me?"

Latham's expressive face altered again. The intensity left his eyes; the furrows on his forehead cleared. "The next twenty-four hours are crucial. If she survives them, and remains in stable condition, there's an excellent chance for recovery."

Latham's words were like a hand closing around his heart. His anger drained; the doubts raised by Latham's earlier words disappeared. His neatly ordered world was falling apart around him.

Like a blind man trying to cross an unfamiliar street, he let Latham guide him across the lobby and into a waiting elevator.

"And the coma?" he finally asked.

Latham rubbed his palms together in a nervous gesture. "Let's wait until we're upstairs. The neurosurgeon can explain it better than I."

They got off on the fourth floor. Latham took him directly to the ICU section of neurology, five windowed double rooms surrounding a central nurses' station. There, Latham introduced him to Daniel Skolnick, the neurosurgeon who had performed the emergency surgery on Ellie.

Skolnick was a short man, with a high forehead and brown intelligent eyes. After shaking hands with him, Skolnick said, "About Miss Rogers condition—"

"I'd like to see Ellie before we talk," Steven said, cutting off the neurosurgeon.

"Of course," Skolnick agreed.

The two doctors accompanied him to Ellie's room, but hung back when he went to the side of the bed.

He stared at her for a moment, trying not to believe that the bandaged shape in the center of the bed was Ellie. Just looking at her hurt more than he could ever have imagined. Her head was wrapped in overlapping bandages. All that was visible of her face was a small pale oval beginning under her lower lip and ending a half inch above her eyebrows.

Her eyes were closed, the left eye was swollen purplish black. Three jagged scratches marred the surface of her left cheek. A narrow, white line of teeth showed between her pale lips.

The tube of a clear plastic oxygen line ran upward from her nose. Three IV bottles hung from a stainless steel pole, their contents blending into a single line that ended at her right arm. A bank of monitors was set on the wall. Wires ran from the machines to Ellie's head and chest.

She was so still that if he hadn't seen the slight movement of her chest pushing against the covers, he would have believed her dead, no matter what the instruments above the bed claimed.

He was numb, lost. He was afraid for her, and for himself. He reached for Ellie's hand. Behind him, Latham and the neurosurgeon waited.

Steven pressed Ellie's hand between both of his. Her skin was cool, her hand unresponsive. Still holding her hand, he turned to face the doctors. "Tell me."

"She was in the water about twenty minutes," Latham said. "Luckily, she wasn't fully submerged. When they brought her in, they were able to stabilize her before surgery."

Steven focused on the surgeon. "The surgery?"

"Was successful," Skolnick said, his voice professionally unemotional. "We were able to clean out the bone fragments imbedded in her brain. We joined the break in her skull and the bone will knit together nicely. But I'm afraid there's no way to judge fully the severity of the physical damage to the brain."

"Which means what, exactly?"

The neurosurgeon met Steven's stare. "Barring death, and utilizing what knowledge we have of the human brain and its abilities to regenerate and compensate, I believe that when Miss Rogers emerges from the coma, the likelihood will be that she will have no long-term or short-term memory. Random fragments of memory at best, nothing more."

"Amnesia?"

Skolnick shook his head once, sharply. "Only in the broadest sense. The trauma Miss Rogers suffered was caused by more than just a simple blow to the head. Some small bone splinters were driven into the brain, destroying quantities of brain tissue. In Miss Rogers's case, it will affect her memory, and possibly some motor functions."

Steven's vision blurred. He tightened his hold on Ellie's hand. "Are you positive she's lost her memory?"

"As certain as I can be. I've had a great deal of experience in this area of trauma. Mr. Morrisy, I'm truly sorry."

Steven massaged his temples with his left hand. "I won't accept that."

The surgeon grasped Steven's shoulder and pressed gently before leaving the room.

"I wish there was some way to say it isn't true, but it is," Latham said after Skolnick was gone.

There was a knock on the door, followed by a nurse calling Latham's name. "I'll be back."

Steven looked at Ellie. But he didn't see the Ellie who lay in the hospital bed, comatose; he saw the Ellie he had always known, the Ellie he loved.

He looked down at her hand. Her emerald engagement ring was missing.

"Steven," Latham called from behind him, "Sheriff Banacek wants a word with you."

"In a little while."

"It has to be now, Steven."

Caught short by Latham's curt tone, he turned to his friend. "Why?"

Latham shifted his feet uncomfortably, his troubled

expression deepening. "I'm sorry, Steven. Where were you last night?"

Steven's breath whistled from between his lips. He was no longer able to dismiss the subconscious warnings he'd been ignoring since Arnie Savak's call. He stood to face Latham. Anger controlled his movements.

He took a step toward Latham. "You son-of-a-bitch. We've known each other since . . . since we could walk. You're supposed to be my friend."

"You know damned well I am." Latham retorted, red-faced and defensive. That's why you have to answer me."

He stared at Latham, but saw another person, a shadow out of his past. "I was home."

"Can you prove it?"

"Don't push me, Chuck. Not now."

"Damn it, Steven. Latham swore loudly. "Haven't you worked it out yet? Don't you understand? Ellie wasn't in an accident. She didn't end up in the lake because her car went off the road. She was put into the lake. Steven, someone tried to kill Ellie last night."

Steven recoiled. The thought of someone trying to kill Ellie sickened him. He sucked in a ragged breath before saying, "I was home all night, working. I was alone, except for a couple of hours when Sam and Larry came by."

"Lomack and Londrigan?" Latham asked, the tension draining from his features.

Steven jabbed a forefinger into his friend's chest. "I want you to tell me what the hell happened to Ellie. I want to know all of it."

Latham went to Ellie's side. He pulled the light covers down to her knees and raised the hospital gown, exposing her from mid-thigh to below her breasts.

A large gauze bandage covered her stomach, held in

place by micropore tape. Latham glanced at Steven. Their eyes locked, and Steven thought that Latham was trying to tell him something without speaking. Then, slowly and carefully, Latham began to peel the tape from her skin. A muscle pulsed on the side of Latham's jaw.

Steven was surprised to see Latham's fingers trembling as the doctor drew the bandage down. But the instant the first angry red line came into view, Steven knew what it was that Latham had tried to tell him with his eyes.

Bile flooded his mouth. He wished he was somewhere else; but he made himself look at Ellie's abdomen. Some of the cuts were short and precise lines not more than an inch long. Others were slashes that ran for several inches. One went from hip to hip, curving like a nude model's gold chain. She had been cut dozens of times.

He closed his eyes. His mind was spinning backward, leaping over the years to a past he had spent over a decade trying to forget. He smelled rot and decay, and felt the lice crawling over his skin. And then a scream began to build in his mind.

His eyes snapped open. He wiped a hand across his lips, wanting a drink of water to wash away the foulness in his mouth. In the background, a code blue issued from the loudspeakers. He heard the rattling of a crash cart, and the quick cadence of rushing feet. He grabbed onto the sidebar of Ellie's bed and held it tight to help him keep his balance.

"A razor was used on her stomach," Latham said. "We found salt residue on her skin. She was tortured, Steven."

Steven stared at the hideous red lines criss-crossing Ellie's stomach. He wanted to turn away, to hide, but he was caught in a grip of such horror that he could only continue to look at the violation of Ellie's skin.

"I'm sorry, Steven," Latham said, replacing the bandage and covering her.

"Her stomach, Chuck. It's just li—"

"I know," Latham said sharply, while casting a warning at him. "The sheriff will explain it to you. We can use my office."

Steven shook his head. He wouldn't leave her alone, not yet. "Send him up here."

"It would be better in private."

"Here."

Latham gestured toward the window facing the nurses' station. A warning prickle at Latham's unexpected movement raised the hackles on his neck. He looked through the observation window and saw a large man in a khaki sheriff's uniform.

"He's been out there all this time?" At Latham's nod, Steven glanced at the two-way speaker above Ellie's bed. He looked back at Latham, feeling betrayed by his closest friend. "He heard us too, I suppose."

"Every word, Mr. Morrisy," Sheriff William Banacek said when he entered the room.

Banacek was a bear of a man, gray-haired and slightly past middle age. He stood well over six feet and had a barrel chest and wide shoulders. His full features, ruddy complexion, and sharp eyes bespoke Slavic ancestry. Steven knew Banacek by reputation only. The sheriff was said to be a decent man.

"I heard what you had to say, Mr. Morrisy," Banacek continued, his gaze heavy on Steven. "And as Doctor Latham has already explained, Miss Rogers was not supposed to be in this hospital bed. She was supposed to be in the morgue."

Steven remained silent, keeping his questions, and his pain, to himself.

"I spent two hours at the scene last night. I went

back when the sun came up. Our preliminary findings confirm that Miss Rogers was in the lake before the car went in."

"There's no reason for anyone to want her dead," Steven said at last. But the cuts on Ellie's abdomen could not possibly have come from an automobile accident. They were the proof that Banacek and Latham were right. "Why?"

"There usually is a reason, Mr. Morrisy, even if we don't know what it is," Banacek said, his gaze shifting momentarily to Ellie's face. "And there are a lot of crazy people in this world."

"You think a psycho kidnapped and tortured Ellie?"

"I don't know who did it," Banacek said bluntly. "But even before we knew about Miss Rogers's wounds, we were certain it wasn't an accident. As I said, Miss Rogers was in the lake before the car went into the water. My deputy found her hanging onto the passenger-side mirror."

Steven stared at Ellie's bruised and discolored eye while he listened to the sheriff. He used his anger at what had been done to her to give him the strength to keep listening.

"The initial fingerprint dusting picked up only her prints, and primarily on the passenger side of the car," Banacek continued, "but forensics dug up a second set. The technician found grain patterns left by leather gloves. The same prints were found on the driver's side of the car, the emergency brake, and the steering wheel. Miss Rogers wasn't wearing gloves."

"Which doesn't mean much," Steven said. "She could have been thrown out of the window, or the door could have come open."

"There's always that possibility in an accident, but it's not what happened. Whoever tried to kill Miss Rogers was pretty sure neither she nor the car would be found until next spring. The section of the lake where Miss Rogers was found was not only deep, but the ice was conveniently thin. Mr. Morrisy, the driver's window was rolled two-thirds of the way up. There's no possibility that she could have been thrown through it. The door was locked and secure."

Banacek raised his hand to stop Steven's objection. "I know. Freak occurrences are within the realm of an accident. But even if she was in the driver's seat, and she had somehow been thrown out the window, how did she manage to shut off the ignition?"

"She didn't," Banacek answered himself. "There wasn't a single one of her fingerprints on the steering wheel. However, there were lots of her prints on the passenger window and door handle.

"Did you know her car had one of those ignition locks? Sure you do. All cars have them nowadays, ones that lock the steering wheel when the ignition's turned off."

Banacek scratched absently at the stubble on his jaw, producing a sandpaper sound. "Which brings up another interesting detail. The tires were dead straight, but the tracks in the snow, leading from the edge of the road, curved at one point."

"Which means what?" Chuck Latham asked, speaking for the first time since the sheriff's entrance.

"The car was driven off the road and onto the embankment. Then the driver maneuvered it into a position that pointed toward the lake. The front wheels were straightened so that the car would track directly to the water. The ignition was purposely shut off so the steering wheel was locked into place. Then the emergency brake was released."

"But something went wrong," Steven said, the ethereal sense of calmness, underscored by a gripping tension, held firm. He remembered feeling this way in

Nam—just before going into action.

"Which was lucky for Miss Rogers. And for us. Because of the embankment's incline, and the ice and snow, the car slid. Its rear fender hit a tree, slowing it enough for the back tires to get hung up on the old roots leading into the lake. The car ended up on an angle, the front end in the water. Instead of disappearing into the lake, Mr. Morrisy, where the blood on the fender would have washed off, it got hung up. Which gives us the evidence we need to prove attempted murder.

"There was no blood inside the vehicle, but there was plenty of it on the fender which struck her in the head. The passenger-side fender, Mr. Morrisy. That's how we knew she was in the water first."

Steven's gaze strayed beyond the sheriff's shoulder to the nurses' station. Two women in pale blue uniforms chatted. On the wall behind them was a chalkboard filled with patients' names and room numbers. He saw Ellie's name and number.

"Why was she out alone last night?" the sheriff asked.

He stared at Banacek while trying to figure out a reason for Ellie's presence in Greyton. He couldn't come up with one. "I don't have an answer for you, Sheriff. Ellie shouldn't have been in Greyton at all."

Banacek looked from Steven to Latham and back. "Why is that, Mr. Morrisy? I was under the impression that Miss Rogers had been with you all week."

The sheriff's words lingered in the silence of the room. Anger again clouded Steven's logic. His lips compressed into a thin line. He spoke slowly and carefully. "You're the third person today who's told me that Ellie was with me. She wasn't. I thought she was in Washington."

"What about you? Why are you here?"

"I live here, Sheriff."

Banacek tilted forward on the balls of his feet. "You used to live here. Now you just visit. You live in D.C."

"Greyton is my legal address. I came here to do some work. I needed the quiet."

Banacek nodded slowly. "Let's say that's true for now."

Steven held his anger in check, refusing to be baited.

"I overheard what you said to the doctor about Sam Londrigan and Larry Lomack," the sheriff continued without acknowledging the interruption. "How long were they with you?"

"They showed up around ten-thirty and left about one."

"You were together all the time?"

"Except when one of us took a piss," he snapped. "After they left, I went back to my work."

"You're sure about the times?"

"I'm sure. Look, Banacek, I don't like the implications of your questions."

"I'm not taking any pleasure in asking them, Mr. Morrisy, you can believe that. And I intend to speak to both of them and see if they back you up."

"You do that. And Sheriff," Steven added, his voice low, "I'll say this once, and only because you don't know me: I love Ellie. I wouldn't hurt her. Now, if you don't mind, I'd like a little privacy."

Banacek's eyebrows rose fractionally. He made no move to leave. "I'm sorry, Mr. Morrisy, but I'll need you to come to the station with me."

"For what?"

"A statement, initially."

"Initially? Are you planning on arresting me?"

"Let's not get ahead of ourselves. Let's just say you're coming in for a statement."

"You're out of your mind, Sheriff."

"Mr. Morrisy," Banacek said wearily, "you're a lawyer, and a damn good one from what I hear. Please don't say anything else. Not yet."

Steven fixed Banacek with a cryptic stare. "Don't do this, Sheriff. The ramifications go further than me, or Greyton."

"I know how high they go. All the way to the Senate, right? I may be a bit of a redneck, but I'm not stupid. And I'm trying to keep this as quiet as possible. I'd suggest you do the same. The best way to do that is by coming to my office and getting the preliminaries over with. For what it's worth, Mr. Morrisy, it's the circumstances that point to you, not any physical evidence. But until I can speak with Lomack and Londrigan, I don't really have a choice."

Banacek's unerring reasoning helped to temper Steven's anger. He went to Ellie's side, bent, and kissed her cheek. Then he looked down at her hand. "Chuck, where's Ellie's engagement ring?"

"All jewelry is removed in the ER and put in a safe. It'll be there with any other jewelry she was wearing. I'll get it for you if you want."

"She never wore much jewelry, only her ring. Sometimes, she would wear simple earrings, but nothing else. Is her purse there too?"

"My deputy couldn't find her purse, Mr. Morrisy," Banacek said. "It must have gone down in the lake."

Steven frowned. "How did you identify her?"

"From the license plates on the car. When we learned that the car was leased to Senator Pritman's office we called the feds for an ID. But it was Doctor Latham who recognized her when he came on duty."

Steven turned to Latham. "Why did you call Savak, in Washington, if you—"

"Steven, I'm sorry," Latham said, his face apologetic

as he cut Steven off. "When I realized the patient was Ellie, I must have panicked. I don't know why, but for some reason I didn't even think about calling you here. I called you in Washington. When there was no answer, I called Arnie. He told me you were here. Steven, I . . . I just didn't think. I'm sorry," Latham repeated.

Steven gripped Latham's arm. "It was a natural reaction. I usually call you when I'm in town," he said, understanding what had happened. Steven turned to Banacek. "All right, Sheriff, let's go get my statement taken."

Downstairs, Steven and the sheriff left Latham by the lobby elevator. They were halfway to the front entrance when two men entered. The taller of the two took off his hat, revealing short-cropped dark hair. When his brown eyes swept across Steven and Banacek, he nudged his companion.

"Sheriff Banacek?" the man called, advancing on them.

Nodding, Banacek stopped to wait for the two men.

The man in the lead pulled out an ID case and flipped it open. "I'm Inspector Everett Blayne, FBI. This is Special Agent Grodin," he added, tilting his head at the second man.

"Yes?" Banacek said, slowly drawling out the word.

"We're here on the Rogers' case."

Silently, Steven sized up the two agents. Blayne was the shorter, about Steven's six-foot height. He was in his mid-thirties. He wore a dark gray suit, white shirt, and an unpatterned blue tie. His neatly conventional looks were marred by hard eyes and thick lips.

The second agent appeared to be about twenty-eight. He was blond-haired and blue-eyed and a couple of inches taller than Blayne. His hair was longer and his lips thinner. His clothing was more modish in style.

"The Rogers' case? You mean the accident, don't you?" Banacek asked.

"No, I don't," Blayne said. "And since Miss Rogers is on the staff of a United States senator, we'll be taking jurisdiction in the case."

"On what grounds?" Banacek asked, his voice turning hard.

"The National Security Act," Blayne stated smoothly. "We're here to take Steven Morrisy into custody. That is you, isn't it, Mr. Morrisy?" Blayne asked, shifting his gaze to Steven.

Chapter Three

"Not so fast," Banacek said, holding his hand palm-outward and stepping between the inspector and Steven. "As far as jurisdiction is concerned, Miss Rogers's accident occurred in Greyton. Mr. Morrisy is a resident of Greyton, and as such, he is under my jurisdiction. So, unless the rules have been changed, I think you boys are forgetting something in the way of constitutional legality—like a warrant?"

"I'm not trying to force the issue, Sheriff, but if it's necessary, I'll have a warrant drawn up."

Blayne then favored Banacek with a forbearing look. "Because we came here as soon as we got your query, we didn't have time to get the warrant. But Sheriff, Miss Rogers is a United States senator's personal assistant. We have ample reason to believe that her accident is not what it appears to be."

"That may be so, but it still seems a bit unusual, your being here so soon," Banacek remarked, "seeing as I haven't even filed a report yet."

Blayne nodded. His smile warmed. "As I said, it was your ID query which brought us to Greyton. Was it an accident?"

Banacek glanced at Steven before saying, "Well, I guess you'll find out soon enough. No, it wasn't an accident. It was attempted murder."

Steven followed the brief exchange of eye contact between Blayne and Grodin. "In that case, Sheriff, I must insist on your letting us take Mr. Morrisy with us. It's imperative for the sake of the country."

"Oh, I think not. You guys come riding in here on your high horses, spouting national security but not showing me diddily shit to back yourselves up. So I guess you'll just have to get that warrant. Mr. Morrisy is entitled to know what he's being charged with, and national security sure sounds like espionage to me. Is that what you re saying?"

"No," Blayne responded quickly. "There are other charges we can bring out."

"Make them very specific, 'cause if I don't like the way that warrant reads, there ain't a chance in hell I'll let you take Mr. Morrisy out of my jurisdiction."

"That wouldn't be a smart move, Sheriff. Your career isn't worth it," Special Agent Grodin said.

Steven heard Banacek's sharp intake of breath. The sheriff glared hotly at the brash young FBI agent. "My *career* isn't at issue here. You just bring your paper to the station. We'll talk further there. And son, don't think because you carry federal tin that you can intimidate me. More important people than you have tried. You understand what I'm saying?"

Without waiting for a reply, Banacek motioned to Steven and walked past the two men. When they reached the police car, Banacek opened the front passenger side door for him.

When Banacek got behind the wheel, Steven said, "Why?"

Banacek turned and favored Steven with a long stare. "Because they used the wrong charge. I know a little of your history, Mr. Morrisy, and after what you went through, there's no way you would be a traitor."

With that, Banacek drove out of the hospital's curved drive and into the light flow of traffic.

On the two-lane highway that doubled as Greyton's main street, Steven continued to watch Banacek. "Greyton is my home," Banacek said suddenly. "I've been on the force for thirty-five years. I was a deputy when you were going to high school. I remember you from the football games. That was one hell of a team we had with you, Latham and Savak, and Londrigan and the others. We had two state championships, right?"

Steven nodded, wondering where Banacek was leading with his innocuous dialogue. "When the war came, you and the Savak boy and Doctor Latham made this town damn proud."

"I thought you didn't consider me part of Greyton any longer?"

Banacek gave him a half smile. "That was part of my job. I was looking for a reaction. But regardless of what I said in the hospital room, you are one of us. You may live in Washington most of the year, but you're there for us. And no FBI man wearing a three-hundred-dollar pin-striped suit and spouting bullshit legalities is going to take you out of my jurisdiction before I've made sure you've been cleared. Greyton has always looked after its own."

Steven was still reflecting on Banacek's words when they passed the high school. Lights showed in almost all of the windows. The American flag fluttered in the breeze; the Keystone state flag hung beneath it.

Steven remembered back to when he and Latham and Savak had returned from Southeast Asia. Unlike other towns and cities in the country, Greyton had treated the three of them to a hero's welcome.

But their shared resentment of what had happened in Southeast Asia had made Greyton's homecoming reception a bittersweet event. After the welcoming festivities, the three friends had decided to donate their medals to the high school. Today, the medals rested in a glass-encased wall unit just inside the high school's main entrance.

"My only alibi is the two men who were with me last night," Steven said when they had passed the school. He looked at his watch. It was almost ten-thirty. Three and a half hours had passed since Arnie Savak's phone call. He felt as if it had been a lifetime.

Seven minutes after leaving the hospital, Banacek turned into the parking lot of the sheriff's station. He shut off the ignition but made no move to get out. Banacek drummed thick fingers on the steering wheel, and then said, "Mr. Morrisy, this isn't Washington. Once we go inside, whatever you have to say will stay there. There are no press leaks here, and no games. Now," Banacek added, opening his door, "we might as well get this over with."

Inside the station, Banacek paused at the duty officer's desk. "Have Helga come into my office with her machine," he told the man whose name tag read O'Bannon, before taking Steven into a large office with a single glass wall that looked out on the rest of the station.

The office was plain, with utilitarian furniture and randomly placed plaques on graying white walls. The sheriff motioned Steven to an old caster-legged armchair and told him he'd be back in a minute.

Through the glass wall, its venetian blinds drawn up, Steven watched Banacek go to O'Bannon's desk and say something to the duty officer.

When Banacek returned, he was followed by a middle-aged woman whose salt-and-pepper hair was wrapped in a prim bun. The sheriff went to his chair, while the woman set up her steno machine.

When the woman was ready, Banacek said, "Helga, please note that Mr. Steven Morrisy is making a statement of his own accord, and is showing a willingness to help speed along our investigation on . . ." He stopped talking to look down at his desk. He shuffled through several papers before he found what he was looking for. ". . . Case number AZD6196. Put in the date and time. Also add that Mr. Morrisy is here acting as Miss Eleanor Rogers's next of kin."

Looking from the stenographer to Steven, Banacek said, "Shall we begin?"

Steven held Banacek's gaze for several seconds, trying to judge the man and find a sense of who Banacek was. He thought he saw openness in the sheriff's dark brown eyes, a willingness to trust him. Steven felt an ebbing of the doubts and anger that had been growing since the sheriff first appeared in Ellie's hospital room.

Then, before the sheriff could ask his first question, the intercom rang. As Banacek listened, Steven saw his eyes narrow.

When the sheriff hung up, he regarded Steven thoughtfully. "Sam Londrigan went to West Virginia. Lomack is with him. They went to a car auction. Flew there in Londrigan's private plane. Took off about two hours ago and won't be back until tonight or tomorrow. Did you know about this little trip, Mr. Morrisy?"

Steven met Banacek's inquiring stare. "Sam didn't mention it. I guess he didn't know I'd need an alibi."

"I imagine," Banacek agreed, unperturbed by Steven's sarcasm. "When did you see Miss Eleanor Rogers last, Mr. Morrisy?"

Hearing the subtle shift in Banacek's tone, and the formality of the question, Steven answered in kind. "On Monday past, January twenty-eighth, just before I left Washington for Greyton."

"And under what circumstances did that meeting

take place?"

"We had spent the weekend together, as we always did. After breakfast on Monday morning, I drove Ellie to work. I dropped her off just before nine and . . ."

Helga closed up her machine at eleven twenty-five and left Banacek's office. Cradling a cup of coffee between his palms, Steven said, "I'm still trying to figure out those circumstantial facts you mentioned. All I can come up with is that Ellie is my fiancée."

"There's much more than just that," Banacek declared. Holding up his left hand, he unfurled his index finger. "One: You and Miss Rogers work for the same person. Two," he said, flicking up his second finger, "as the senator's legal advisor and aide, you've got to stay squeaky clean—"

"That's a necessity, not a fact."

"Which means that if you've done something that might affect the senator, and Miss Rogers found out about it, she could have been blackmailing you."

Banacek brought up his third finger. "Which leads us to fact number three: The possibility that she was about to go public with whatever it was she found out when you learned of it and you decided to do her in."

Banacek's words triggered a disgust that Steven was hard pressed to contain. "That never happened."

Banacek cocked his head to the side. "You asked me what makes you a suspect. I'm answering you, Mr. Morrisy, not accusing you. The fourth fact," Banacek continued smoothly, bringing up his little finger, "is the location of the 'accident.' Everyone from around here knows that Lake Pompton is fed by an underground stream. Hell, that's why the kids who play hooky from school in the spring swim at the north end of the lake. Water's warmer. During the winter, the ice is thinner there. But the real question is, with all the shoreline available, why pick that exact spot?"

"Coincidence?"

"Or the knowledge that it insured privacy and a damn good chance that the body wouldn't be found until spring thaw. No one is around there from December to March. The weekenders and vacation people don't use their places in the winter. And even when there's an occasional resident who wants a few days alone up there, they let us know. But populated or not, we patrol it twice nightly. Once at eleven p.m., and again at three a.m. It was on the return from the eleven o'clock patrol that my deputy spotted the reflection of taillights down in the lake.

"So you see," Banacek said, lowering his hand, "there's ample reason to suspect you."

"Suspect him of what?" Arnold Savak asked as he entered the sheriff's office.

"I'm sorry, Sheriff, I tried to stop him," a harried-looking O'Bannon said from behind Savak.

Banacek waved the duty officer away. "Come in, Mr. Savak."

Savak nodded to Banacek, but spoke to Steven. "Are you all right?"

"I'm fine," he said, relief washing over him with his friend's unanticipated arrival. "But Ellie isn't," he added as he stood and embraced Arnie.

After they stepped back, Savak took off his overcoat and sat in the chair Helga had recently vacated. "I still can't believe what happened. And this garbage Chuck told me about—that it wasn't an accident—it isn't true, is it?"

"It is," Banacek said.

Savak met the sheriff's eyes. "I understand the FBI wants to question Steven."

"They want more than to question him," Banacek

said, leaning back in his chair and absently rubbing his chin with the flat of his thumb. "You seem pretty well informed for just having gotten into town."

Savak stared at Banacek for a moment. Then he smiled easily. "Sheriff, I landed in Greyton field forty minutes ago and drove straight to the hospital. Chuck Latham filled me in on everything that's happened, including the argument you and Steven had with the FBI agents. He also told me that you suspect Steven of . . ." Savak stopped and turned to Steven. "At least you have Sam and Larry to back your story. That should take care of any questions."

"When the sheriff can get hold of them." At Savak's blank stare, Steven explained about the two men's sudden trip to West Virginia.

"But," Banacek said, "I may have to hand Mr. Morrisy over to the FBI before then. Judging by that inspector's attitude, he'll be along pretty soon with his warrant. I think you should wait here until then, Mr. Morrisy. They won't play their games with me."

"A warrant?" Savak asked, his face going rigid. When the sheriff nodded, the muscles on each side of Savak's jaw knotted. Then came the characteristic double stroke of his bent finger against the side of his nose. Savak turned to Steven, his gray eyes dancing. "Which will give me all the time I need."

"For what?" Banacek asked.

"To get this stopped before it goes any further. Sheriff, if the media gets wind of this—" He cut himself off, shook his head, and said, "I'll need a phone, and some privacy."

Inspector Blayne and Special Agent Grodin showed up two hours later, not one as Banacek had predicted. They were armed with a federal arrest warrant, which

Blayne smugly presented to Sheriff Banacek.

For his part, Banacek didn't bother to look at the warrant; he handed it to Steven.

"It's all in order, Mr. Morrisy," Blayne said.

When Steven read it, he experienced another painful jolt. The charge was kidnapping. He felt his anger grow. He looked at Blayne coldly, while trying to discern exactly what it was that the FBI inspector was after. "What happened to all that bullshit about national security? Wasn't that what you were so damn concerned about at the hospital? There's no way you're going to make a kidnapping charge stick."

"It'll do for now."

"I'm afraid it won't," Savak said in a low voice as he stood to face Blayne. "My name is Arnold Savak, Inspector. And your warrant has been rescinded." Extending his hand, Savak held out a white business card. "Call the number on the back."

Blayne matched Savak's hard stare for several seconds before looking at the card. When he did, a flicker of doubt crossed the FBI agent's features. He scowled at Savak, and glared at Steven. "May I?" he asked Banacek, nodding toward the telephone on the sheriff's desk.

Banacek waved him to the phone. A few seconds after he dialed, he said, "This is Inspector Blayne." He was silent, and then, "I understand."

Hanging up, Blayne turned to Savak. "You hot-shot political pariahs are all alike. You think you pulled a fast one on us, don't you?"

Savak stiffened, his eyes narrowed, but his voice was calm. "Not at all, Inspector. You see, we're all very much aware that the present administration will do anything in its power to interfere with Senator Pritman's nomination, should he decide to run for office. And the Bureau . . . Well, it is common knowledge that in the past few years, the administration has looked with undeserved and ah . . . shall we say partisan favor upon the Bureau."

Steven watched a vein on the agent's forehead pulse angrily before Blayne pivoted from Savak to face him. The inspector's face was flushed. His eyes were dark with anger, and his lips were tight and bloodless. "This won't change anything, Morrisy. Your friends have just bought you a little time."

After hours of worrying about Ellie, and of listening to the accusations about him, Steven's control snapped. He shot from the chair and closed the space between himself and Blayne.

He grabbed Blayne's shoulder before the surprised agent could react, and found the nerve endings near the collarbone. He dug sharply into Blayne's muscles, immobilizing the man, and eliciting a startled grunt of pain.

From the corner of his eye, Steven saw Blayne's partner start toward him. The FBI agent's right hand slid into his jacket, going for his pistol. Savak stepped calmly in front of him, a tight and thin smile turning his face hard.

Steven held his punishing grip on Inspector Blayne for three more painful seconds before releasing him. Then he stepped back and, in a soft and barely audible voice, said, "The woman lying in that hospital bed is going to be my wife. Don't threaten me and don't get me any angrier than I already am, Inspector. You won't like the results."

Blayne's arm dangled limply. He used his left hand to knead circulation back into his shoulder. "That was a mistake."

"Yes. Yours," Steven said before he walked out of Banacek's office, Savak at his heels.

He felt Blayne's hot and angry eyes follow him all

the way to the front door. In the back of his mind, he knew that Blayne wouldn't let it end here.

But Blayne didn't matter right now, only Ellie mattered.

Chapter Four

A team of doctors surrounded Ellie. Daniel Skolnick stood at the foot of her bed, holding an aluminum medical chart. Steven, drained from his experience at the sheriff's office, leaned against the door frame and listened to the neurosurgeon lecture the students.

In a strange way, Skolnick's well-measured cadence of medical jargon was reassuring. If Ellie was still in critical condition, the neurosurgeon wouldn't be lecturing over her, or so Steven believed.

A moment later, a nurse came up to him and placed a gentle hand on his arm. "Grand rounds," she explained. "They'll be finished in a few minutes. Would you like to wait elsewhere?"

He thanked her, but stayed. The teaching session ended a few minutes later. The troop of doctors-in-training filed out. Skolnick trailed, pausing long enough to tell Steven that Ellie was not only stabilized, but doing much better than expected.

Steven smiled his thanks and entered the room. He closed the door part way, and pulled a beige plastic chair close to the bed. He was finally alone with Ellie.

Ellie appeared to be in a light sleep. Her chest rose and fell rhythmically. There was a little more color in her face, which he took as a good sign.

A black and consuming despair swept over him, inundating him with feelings of loss and inadequacy. He put a hand to his face, squeezed his eyes shut, and found himself remembering their times together. He could hear the softness of her voice, and smell the scent of her skin after they'd made love. Suddenly, his mind opened onto the past, and he felt himself being carried back to relive the day he had given Ellie the engagement ring.

The sun was bright overhead, warm and soothing on that late March day. The crowds of tourists who would swarm over the Washington Mall, surrounded by the stately buildings of the Smithsonian Institution, had not yet arrived in force.

In the near distance, the Washington Monument stood needlelike against the cloudless blue sky. The cherry trees were just starting to bloom. Soon, the trees would blossom, heralding the start of spring.

Ellie sat across the plaid blanket from him. They had just finished a light picnic lunch she'd prepared, when Steven reached into his jacket pocket and withdrew something. He took her hand, brought the soft skin of her palm to his lips, and kissed it. Before releasing her hand, he placed a small box in her palm and closed her fingers over it.

He saw her eyes cloud and her lips grow taut. "Steven . . ."

"Open it," he ordered with a mock gruffness he realized was not as false as he'd intended.

Her lips quirked in a fleeting grin. She pried up the top of the black velvet box. Her eyes widened when she saw the square-cut emerald. "My God, Steven. It's so beautiful. But I . . ."

"Don't say anything yet, just listen to me. We've talked about the future. We've never said when. I know you're not ready to get married yet. And I'm not trying to push you. But what I would like you to do, if you love me, is to put on the ring. We'll let the future take care of itself."

Ellie stared at him, her eyes searching his face. "Are you sure, Steven? You really don't know me that well."

"I know that I love you."

She tried to blink away the tears forming in her eyes, but the tears came anyway. Without taking her gaze from his, she wiped beneath her lower lids with the back of one finger. And then she took the ring out of its velvet box.

She smiled, hesitantly, and said, "I do love you, Steven. More than I have ever loved before. After the job is . . . after the elections, we'll get married if you still feel the same way."

He drew her to him. Kissing her gently, he tasted the moist warmth of her mouth.

When they parted, she said, "I promise I won't ever let you go, Steven. No matter what, I promise you that. But . . ."

"But what?" he asked, ready for another argument.

"When you get the wedding band, make sure it's the right size," she said, laughing lightly while she struggled to push the emerald over her knuckle.

"I can have it resized."

"Not today," she said quickly. After moistening her finger with her tongue, she worked the ring over her knuckle. Holding her hand out at arm's distance, she tilted her fingers slightly up so that the ring would be directly in the sun.

"It's beautiful," she whispered, her voice catching.

* * *

Chasing the memory away, Steven opened his eyes and stared at Ellie's bruised face. In the eleven months since he'd given Ellie the ring, she had steadfastly refused to take it off and have it resized. She had told him that she would do it after they were married.

"Oh, Ellie," he whispered, bending to kiss her unresponsive hand.

He breathed deeply. Suddenly his self pity was changed to rage directed at the unknown person who had done this terrible thing to her and to him.

Steven focused his attention on Ellie, and on the possible reasons that had put her in this hospital bed. He thought back to what the sheriff had said, sifting through Banacek's excess verbiage, going for the core of the sheriff's explanation.

But all of Banacek's explanations had seemed to be guesses and suspicions.

Why was she here? When he'd left Washington, she'd been deluged with work.

Someone had tried to kill Ellie. That same person had tortured her first. Could it have been a psychotic? Banacek didn't believe so. Neither did he.

He heard the soft padding of a nurse's rubber-soled shoes come up behind him. "Would you like something to drink? Water, coffee?" she asked when she reached his side.

Morrisy looked at the nurse. She had a young face but her eyes were old with experience. "No, thank you."

"No, thank you," he said.

She left, taking with her the whooshing sound of nylon pantyhose rubbing against her cotton uniform. He thought back to the last time he'd seen Ellie, a week ago today. He searched his mind for the memory, as he had so long ago trained himself to do.

He was gifted with the rare ability of total recall. He had a photographic memory. Now he put that ability to use by seeking a memory switch, a trigger that would unlock a particular memory path. When he found the release, the memory returned so swiftly that he could almost smell the light scent of her perfume.

As he had already told Banacek, he'd been in his car, dropping her off at the office. She had been calm and relaxed. There had been nothing in her face or carriage to suggest something was wrong. They'd talked about Pritman's scheduled trip to Los Angeles, as the guest speaker for the annual L.A. Press Club dinner. She had been looking forward to going to California with Pritman and Steven.

He explored the other possibilities. Banacek had mentioned one: Ellie might have found out something about someone on Pritman's staff that had almost cost Ellie her life.

Whatever it was that she had uncovered, it had to have happened on that day. It was the only plausible explanation for the note. She must have tried to come to Greyton to find him, and to warn him about what she'd discovered.

But why torture her?

Steven understood the basic use of torture. It was to gain information. Someone had tried to learn if Ellie had told anyone. "Told what?" he asked aloud.

And why had the kidnapper waited a week from the day she disappeared from Washington before deciding to kill her? Was there another purpose for the attempt on Ellie's life to have happened in Greyton, on the night before he was due back in Washington?

And just what the hell were the FBI doing here? Why did they want him in custody?

This enigma made him look in a new direction. He

had to consider the possibility that what happened to Ellie had been done to discredit Steven, and thereby cast doubt on the man they both worked for, Senator Philip Pritman.

On the surface, it was much too obvious. Steven was a good enough judge of character to recognize that Blayne's anger had not been an act. Blayne was a dedicated man who took his job seriously. Steven had seen the look in Blayne's eyes on other people committed to what they considered to be a higher purpose.

He swallowed a groan. There were no answers, not yet.

"What is it, Ellie?" He looked at the bank of monitors and contemplated the green phosphorous lines tadpoling across the screens.

Why here? Banacek had shown how all the circumstantial evidence pointed to Steven; but that was because Ellie had not died in the lake.

He exhaled loudly. Could that be it? Was it all planned to look like a botched murder attempt? If Ellie had died, it would appear that her killer had failed to hide the evidence of the crime. Again came the ugly notion of scandal.

He tried to clear his mind. It was important that he think straight. But there were too many unknown elements for him to be able to find a reason for what had happened.

Leaning back in the chair, and, in an effort to not think at all, Steven took Ellie's hand in his and listened to the variety of sounds unique to a hospital.

An hour later, Helene Latham came into the room. Chuck Latham's wife hugged Steven and offered him a strained smile along with her regrets. Helene, an elementary school teacher with green eyes and wavy blond hair, was a pleasingly handsome woman with a gently maternal nature that she shared with the world.

After releasing Steven, she drew another of the plastic chairs across the room, and set it next to his. "I don't understand why anyone would want to hurt Ellie."

Steven, his gaze fixed on Ellie, shook his head.

"I've never seen Chuck so upset. He . . . he told me a little about her wounds. He said it was just like—" She stopped herself, and took a deep breath. "Who could do something like that to another human being?"

Looking into Helene's soft green eyes, Steven saw fear and doubt. He moistened his lips, started to speak, and then stopped himself. There was no explanation; the kind of person who could carve another's flesh into a raw and bleeding mass had never been a part of Helene Latham's world. No, that kind of person was from a world buried in Steven's past.

Instead of words, Steven simply shook his head again and then turned back to Ellie.

Helene remained for another half hour, holding his hand, and lending him silent support. When she left, and he was again alone with Ellie, he submerged himself in his memories of their times together.

At seven, Savak and Latham put a stop to his bedside vigil. They brought him to the almost-deserted cafeteria, where the three friends ate a quiet dinner.

When they finished, and were having coffee, Steven saw Savak cast a signalling glance to Latham before saying, "Steven, I know all of this just happened, and that you're going to argue with me, but I want you to think about coming back to Washington. Chuck and I have been talking, and—"

"I'm not leaving her alone," he stated, his tone carrying a warning to drop the subject.

Shaking his head quickly, Savak reached across the table and gripped Steven's hand. His touch was firm, the warmth of his hand important. "I'm sorry, Steven,

I wasn't making myself clear. I meant that I want us to bring Ellie to Washington."

Steven exerted an answering pressure before withdrawing his hand from Savak's. "It's too soon."

"No, it's not. We can have her transferred to Georgetown University Hospital. She'll get the best care in the world there, won't she, Chuck?"

A momentary flash of anger crossed Latham's features. "This is a damn good hospital, Arnie."

"It is, Chuck, but I'm thinking about what's best for Ellie. Georgetown is a better-equipped hospital. We both know that."

"What I know is that you politicians have seen to it that the hospitals in Washington are better equipped than in less important areas of the country," Latham shot back.

"Jesus, Chuck," Savak snapped, "we've been down that road enough times. We're not talking about allocations, we're talking about Steven's fiancée—about our friend! You and I spent half the afternoon talking about this. An hour ago you agreed with me, but now you—"

Annoyed at the childish byplay, Steven leaned forward and cut them off. "Both of you, listen to me. We're not going to argue about this. I'm going to do what I feel is best for Ellie."

Latham turned from Savak to favor Steven with a searching gaze. "You're right. And so is Arnie," he admitted, grudgingly. "Georgetown is better outfitted for long-term coma care, and it really won't make any difference if Ellie is here, or in Washington. She isn't aware of who is or isn't with her. It's doubtful that she even knows who you are."

Refusing to acknowledge Latham's last remark, Steven picked up his glass and said, "Right now, the most important thing is for Ellie to get better, not which hospital is better."

"The decision to transfer her has to wait," Latham stated. Steven and Savak looked at him, waiting. "For Ellie to be moved, we have to make sure she'll remain stable. And," he added, holding Steven's gaze, "we have to wait for Londrigan and Lomack to back you up."

Fifteen minutes after sundown, a white-and-silver Cessna landed smoothly at a small airport outside Fairmont, West Virginia. Two men got out of the plane and strode purposely to the single structure that served the private airport in all capacities from control tower to pilots' lounge.

While the two men were inside, the Cessna's pilot went about getting the plane refueled. It took ten minutes for him to round up what passed for a ground attendant: A shaggy-haired gas jockey wearing faded jeans and a grease-stained Grateful Dead denim vest.

After the plane was fueled and parked on a side apron in preparation for take-off, the pilot leaned casually against it, waiting for his passengers.

When they appeared a few minutes later, the taller of the two, a man with iron-gray hair and dark brown eyes, called Anton, said, "The plane is on the south apron. Twin-engine job with a blue-and-white undercarriage. White-and-blue wings." His slight accent was all but unnoticeable.

The second man withdrew a leather satchel from the plane's cabin. Then the three men walked across the darkened runway to the south apron and the line of small planes anchored along its length.

They spotted a blue-and-white Beechcraft, and checked the FAA registration number. Then, with the pilot keeping watch, Anton and the other man went to work. Thirteen minutes and twenty-eight seconds later, the white-and-silver Cessna lifted from the runway.

At nine-fifteen, Sam Londrigan started the engines of his plane. As usual, Larry Lomack was bitching. This time it was about having to leave the two women they'd met during dinner.

"With your luck, you'd probably end up with the clap," Londrigan said, studying the instrument panel.

"That's why they invented penicillin," Lomack informed Londrigan as he extracted a silver flask from his pocket. "Want a drink?"

"You want to make it back to Greyton?"

"I don't really give a shit."

Londrigan glared at his friend, but knew it was useless to say anything when Lomack was in one of his dark moods. Instead he turned on his radio and contacted the tower.

Approval and instructions for take-off came a minute later. He eased off the brakes and manuevered the small plane to the foot of the runway, revved up the engines, and started forward.

He brought the plane to the proper ground speed and pulled back on the control. He was rewarded by the Beechcraft's instant response.

The light plane lifted smoothly off the runway. As always, Londrigan experienced the special thrill of breaking free of the ground.

At a thousand feet and climbing, he followed the control tower's instructions to bank away from Fairmont. At five thousand feet he changed course to his approved flight plan.

An instant later there was a loud snapping in his ear. "What was that?"

"What was what?" Lomack asked, his flask hovering an inch from his mouth.

"Nothing," Londrigan said, belatedly realizing that his headset had gone dead. He tapped the earpiece ineffectually and then leaned forward to try a different frequency.

The headset remained dead.

As his hand came away from the dial, an unexpected vibration rippled through the plane. He immediately identified it as coming from the left engine. He looked at the wing and saw a sputter of flames. An instant later the engine was engulfed by fire.

He turned to Lomack, about to speak. Before the words could come out, the right engine burst into flames.

Lomack followed his wide eyed stare, and saw the right engine being consumed by flame. "Ohfuck."

The two words, coming out like a single strangled gasp, were enough to snap Londrigan out of his daze. He shuddered, turned to the instrument panel, and scanned the gauges.

Then, surprising himself with his calmness and remembering everything he had been taught, Londrigan shut down both engines and maneuvered the plane into a wide turn.

"What the hell's happening?" Lomack shouted, unable to tear his eyes from the fireball on the wing.

"We've got problems," Londrigan understated, his voice shaky. "But I think we can make it back to the airport."

But, halfway into the wide gliding turn, an explosion destroyed the stabilizer and aileron cables.

The blood drained from Londrigan's face. His knuckles turned white as he fought the controls. And then, when he was unable to make the plane obey him, his calmness shattered.

Londrigan sat paralyzed by the horror of the onrushing ground. The low moan building deep in his throat was squeezed off by the tentacles of dread winding tightly about his chest. His heart beat wildly, his bladder voided, and then the Beechcraft struck the ground.

Larry Lomack screamed once.

Chapter Five

Steven and Arnold Savak arrived at Steven's house at ten past nine. After turning on the lights and putting his attaché case on the desk, Steven started toward the kitchen.

He stopped dead in the center of the living room. A feeling of apprehension sent his internal alarms clamoring. He looked around and saw things out of place. Not by much, but just enough to tell him that something was wrong. Two of the trophies on the fireplace mantel were in the wrong positions. "Someone's been here."

He went into the master bedroom. The signs of a search were more evident. Two drawers of his cherrywood bureau had been left partially open; the closet door was ajar.

"FBI?"

"Who else?" The feeling of having been violated grew stronger when they went into the kitchen. The visible evidence of a search became even more blatant. It was as if the men who'd searched the house had gotten angry that they'd found nothing.

"What were they looking for?" Savak asked.

"How the hell do I know?" he snapped. Then he held himself still in an effort to calm down. "Sorry,

Arnie, this whole thing's getting to me. Drink?"

"I'm long overdue for one. So are you," Savak replied. Savak took two glasses down from a cabinet over the sink and put ice into them. "The scotch still in the same place?"

"If the feds left us any," Steven said as he looked around the disheveled room.

"Come on," Savak prodded, leading Steven into the living room.

Steven followed obediently, his thoughts troubled. After Savak poured three fingers of Haig over the ice, he handed Steven a glass and went to the couch.

"You come up with any ideas?" Savak asked once they were seated.

Steven took his time, weighing each word carefully. "A few things have crossed my mind, but I can't be sure without more information. And there's something else that doesn't fit. Why is the FBI involved?

"They talked national security, but came up with a kidnap warrant which makes no sense at all. Then those sons-of-bitches searched my house, looking for what I can't even begin to imagine."

He sipped his drink, rolling the scotch over his tongue before letting it slide down his throat. "What would happen to Pritman's campaign if it's shown that one of the senator's upper-echelon staff tried to murder another member of his staff?"

Savak double-stroked the side of his nose with a knuckle. A thoughtful frown tugged at the corners of his mouth. "It could create a scandal that would knock Pritman out of contention, if it's not handled properly. But there are ways of dealing with that kind of a situation."

Steven wagged his finger. "Only one way. If I resigned from the senator's staff and predated the resignation to last Monday. Then the senator would announce that my resignation had been asked for because of erratic behavior. Oh, boy, wouldn't Simon Clarke have a field day citing all the cases of post-war stress syndrome while showing the public that Senator Pritman was so much the people's candidate that he filled his staff with Viet vets."

Steven saw the angry flaring of Savak's nostrils. "Pritman would never do that to you. And I sure as hell wouldn't let it happen."

"He'd have to," Steven countered, his voice low and without anger. "And you'd have no choice but to go along with him. I couldn't let it happen any other way. He, and you, would have to use my Vietnam background to its best advantage, by showing that he was sympathetic to veterans by having hired me in the first place. But that's not what I'm getting at. Discrediting him is an assumption we have to consider."

"No, it's too damn soon. He hasn't made his announcement yet."

"It's an accepted fact at this point. Why the hell else would he be doing fundraisers and benefits all over the country? If the opposition can throw enough dirt at him now, they'll stop him before he really gets rolling."

Savak leaned forward, his eyes burning bright with inner knowledge. "That's not how the game's played. Besides which, you've already come up with a way to keep Pritman clear of the situation. No, if it was planned by the opposition, the evidence would have been indisputable."

Steven shrugged. "It was a thought. And without any information, all that's left are assumptions. But Arnie, there are a lot of things that don't add up. Things that no one has brought into focus."

"Like her stomach," Savak said in a scratchy whisper. "Jesus, Steven, I . . . When I heard about it, all I could think of was Nam."

Steven watched the subconscious movement of Savak's left hand rubbing across his abdomen. "Yes, the torture is part of it," Steven agreed. "But nobody seems interested in knowing about the other factors—like where was Ellie last week?"

Savak shook his head, his hand still on his stomach.

Steven finished his drink, set the glass on the table, and said, "Arnie, why was she here?"

Savak picked up his glass and rolled it between his palms. The remnants of the ice cubes clinked together. "She was coming to you, obviously. But I don't have the answers we're going to need to clear up this situation. And I don't think we'll find them here, either. But in Washington, maybe. Steven, we have enough contacts and friends to get a quiet but full-scale inquiry going."

"I'm staying with Ellie."

"We both are," Savak stated. "But you heard what Chuck said. And, Georgetown is better equipped to handle long-term coma patients. Steven, if Ellie has a chance, the doctors and equipment at Georgetown will increase that chance."

"We still have to wait until she's out of the critical period."

"When Chuck and I were talking, earlier this afternoon, he said that she was doing well under the circumstances. If she remains stable through the night, we can move her as early as tomorrow afternoon. Steven, please, let me make the arrangements to get her to Georgetown."

He tried to come up with a sensible argument but realized that Savak was right. He could do as much for her here as he could in Washington. He studied his friend's face, and saw within the stoic's mask he always wore, Savak's own personal agony of the situation. Suddenly, Steven realized that Savak was hurting as much as he was.

"All right do what's necessary," he said at last. "And, Arnie, thank you."

A half-smile formed on Savak's lips. "Don't go maudlin on me. We do for each other. That's the way it's always been." Savak stood abruptly, saying, "I have to call Pritman and fill him in. I might as well get the ball rolling to have Ellie transferred. I'll use the phone in the kitchen."

When Savak started for the kitchen, Steven went over to the fireplace.

"I can hold off a bit if you want to talk," Savak said from the doorway.

Steven shook his head. "I don't know what we'd talk about, Arnie. No, make your calls."

He started to turn back, but hesitated. "Arnie," he said, "how did you get that warrant jerked?"

Poker-faced, Savak said, "It was all kind of roundabout. I called a friend at Justice, who called someone high up in the Bureau to explain that there are certain lines that shouldn't be crossed without having properly analyzed *all* aspects of the situation."

Steven knew better than to press Savak for a clearer explanation. His friend had contacts and influence that few people in Washington could match. "Thank you."

When Savak disappeared into the kitchen, Steven consigned himself to the mindless job of cleaning the fireplace. He spent ten minutes on the task, and then went about preparing a new fire.

Once the wood caught, he returned to the couch. He sat back, resting his feet on the coffee table. The muted tones of Savak's voice filtered in from the kitchen and mixed with the sound of the wind tugging at the trees outside.

Listening to the confluence of sounds, he found that

so much had happened in the space of a single day that his mind was completely jumbled. He'd been up for almost forty hours, and was emotionally drained by the events of the past fourteen.

He blamed himself for what had happened to Ellie. If he hadn't decided to come to Pennsylvania, Ellie wouldn't be at Greyton Memorial. If he hadn't wanted to be alone . . .

Steven stopped his taciturn mood swing, and looked across at the fireplace. The history of his life was neatly laid out across the mantel. His high school picture showed twenty-three smiling kids who were about to step into a world on the edge of havoc. With hindsight, he didn't think anyone graduating school in the early sixties could have foreseen what was to come. How could they? There'd been no preparation for it.

The late fifties and early sixties had been a perfect time to grow up. Rebelliousness was channeled into rock and roll, hot rods, and back-seat sex.

War was something that was in the history books and comic books. Vietnam was a country very few people had ever heard of. Football and baseball, sock hops and pep rallies were what made up a high school student's life.

He smiled thinly, thinking about the special group of friends who had known each other from childhood. Sam Londrigan had wanted to become an electrical engineer. Instead, he'd ended up owning the largest automobile dealership outside of Philadelphia and Pittsburgh. He'd married, had three kids, and gotten divorced all within a decade and a half.

Larry Lomack, another of the Greyton High School football team of '63, had never gone to college. He'd joined the Air Force, seen the world, and after the war had come home a distant man who drank more than he should and smiled less. He worked for Londrigan as

Sam's manager.

And then there had been the unholy trinity—himself, Arnie Savak, and Chuck Latham. Steven moved his gaze to the picture set between two gilded trophies. It was the Greyton High football team the year they'd won the state championship. In the center, all within an inch of the same height, was himself, Arnie, and Chuck.

The three of them were the backbone of the team. The quarterback, end, and halfback. When the three played together, they were infallible. Savak was the strategist, instinctively knowing which play would work when. Steven was the logical one, spotting weaknesses and faults and feeding them to Savak. Latham was their secret weapon. His long fingers and sure hands always knew where the ball was and when it would float down to him.

And now Chuck Latham's sensitive hands were being put to the best possible use. A doctor isn't what Chuck had started out to be, it's what he'd grown into. Like Arnie Savak and himself, Chuck's early visions of the future had been altered by the same events that had affected Steven and Arnie.

Arnie and I, Steven said to himself, we were the only ones to leave Greyton. And Arnie had been the only one of the group who'd left Pennsylvania for college. He'd gone to American University to study political science. A subject none of the others had been the least bit familiar with.

Arnie Savak had wanted to enter the diplomatic corps. But after Nam, he'd turned his ambitions from the international arena to the domestic, and to Senator Philip Pritman. For fourteen years Arnold Savak had devoted his career to the senator. Ten years ago he'd begun to run Pritman's staff as the senator's top advisor.

It had been Savak who had talked Steven into leaving his fledgling legal practice in Greyton to join the senator's staff. Together, they'd worked to bring about the changes they had dreamed of and planned following their time in hell.

He leaned back, closed his eyes, and pictured Eleanor smiling at him. Azure eyes sparkled mischievously. Her mouth, both seductive and innocent at the same time, pouted invitingly. She was the part of him that had been missing for too many years. She was the perfect foil to his seriousness. And she was the one who had broken through his carefully nurtured guards to make him want to set aside the pain of the past and love again.

Steven shifted his gaze from the mantel to the glove-leather attaché case resting by the far wall, a present from Ellie. Within its locked interior was the future. The case's contents had been the reason for his coming to Greyton. He had wanted the solitude he felt was necessary for absolute concentration. Time was running out. The final version of Senator Philip Pritman's international policy proposal, and the plank he was determined to set into the party platform, had to be ready when he won the party's nomination for President of the United States.

It was ready now. A dozen years of preparation, and two years of constant brainstorming with the premier minds of international politics, had been translated into forty pages of theory, legalities, and proposals. And every day of those years had been well worth the effort.

Steven and Savak had designed the proposal to accomplish two important objectives. The first was to put Senator Philip Pritman into the White House; the second was to use the proposal as a tool to help stop the accelerated nuclear weapons buildup that was reaching disastrous proportions. In its present form, it would give Pritman the ability to bring the super powers to a conference table and force them to reach a binding agreement on arms control.

If it's used right. That was the catch-phrase as well as the other aspect of his job, to assure that what he and Arnie Savak had created would not be misused.

"It's all taken care of," Savak said.

Steven looked up. "What is?"

"Georgetown. Pritman's pulling a few of his famous strings. He's confident that Georgetown will accord Ellie full VIP status. They'll be able to help her to recover, Steven."

"The neurosurgeon says Ellie won't have any memory."

Savak worried at his lower lip. "His opinion isn't gospel. He's a neurosurgeon, not a mindreader. No one can know whether Ellie's lost her memory while she's in a coma. And we both know that Ellie's a tough lady. She's a fighter. She'll get her memory back."

Steven looked at his friend, and saw all the Arnie Savaks he'd known throughout his life: The little boy who became the high school jock; the army captain who evolved into a senator's chief advisor. "It's not amnesia, Arnie, her memory was physically destroyed."

"They think it was destroyed!" Savak shouted, his face unexpectedly showing the strain of the day.

"But," Steven continued, ignoring Savak's outburst, "even if she doesn't remember, I'll be there to help her because I remember." He paused, another thought slipping into place. "Has anyone notified her sister?"

Savak nodded. "I tried her before I left DC. All I got was an answering machine. Simon Clarke said he'd keep after her."

"It's funny," Steven said, feeling detached again. "In all the time I've known Ellie, she's hardly mentioned her sister. I've never even met Carla."

"Some people are like that. Not everyone has a story book relationship with their family."

He glanced sharply at Savak, who had been estranged from his family since before joining the army. Nothing had changed in the years since. He'd never told Steven what had caused the break, and Steven doubted if he ever would. Even as a boy, Savak had always been intensely private.

"Arnie—"

"Forget it. What about the Entente proposal. Is there much work left?"

Steven pointed to the attaché case. "It's finished. All I need to do is have the final draft typed and incorporated in the rest of the platform. Three days should be enough time to get it into Pritman's hands."

"And the problem areas?"

"Are fine now. But it's not the semantics of the proposal that worries me. It's being able to get the right people to understand its intricacies."

"Which is what Pritman does best," Savak reminded him. "It will be on his shoulders to make sure that his backers not only understand it, but believe in it. Without them, it's a dead issue."

"No. Whether or not they understand its power and the consequences, they'll believe in it because it's their passport into the White House after too many years of playing second best. But Arnie, it has to be handled very carefully. If it isn't—"

"Enough!" Savak said, hitting his thigh with the palm of his hand. "We've been over this a hundred times. We both know that any radical shift in foreign policy will be met with hostility by those who don't understand it. And we've both had enough experience in and out of politics to know that to gain anything worthwhile, risks must be taken.

"I think Entente is worth every bit of that risk! And deep inside, so do you. Steven, we have an opportunity to make sure that the madness we were a part of can never happen again. I have no intention of losing that chance."

"Why didn't you ever marry?" Steven asked, not sure why he had changed the subject.

Savak blinked. "I guess I didn't have the time."

A log popped in the fire, hurtling a glowing ash against the wrought iron encased glass guard. "Not good enough, Arnie."

"Perhaps for the same reason as you."

"But I am getting married," he said quickly. And just as quickly, he felt the pain of his carelessly spoken words. An image of Ellie lying helpless in the hospital bed grew strong, forcing him to see the truth of the situation. And the reality was that he no longer knew if he was getting married, or if the woman he loved would even know who he was.

He braced himself against his fears. "I want an answer, Arnie, and not the bullshit that you haven't found the right woman yet."

Steven saw his friend's reluctance to speak written clearly across his features. Then, Savak exhaled slowly. "I guess I never married because of what happened to us in Nam. For me, marriage means children. How the hell can I bring a child into the world knowing that the same people who sent us to that prison camp are still in charge?

"No," he reiterated, "I won't bring new life into an old world. But I'll do my damnest try to make it a better place for those who do. Isn't that why we went into politics? To help guide the right man into the right job? Isn't Entente the fulfillment of our plans?"

"I thought it was," Steven said truthfully. "But now . . . I'm not so sure. Ever since we put it together I've been thinking about its ramifications. If the Soviets or the Chinese get wind of our plans before they're set in motion . . ."

He took a calming breath. ". . . or if they learn about Entente in the wrong way, it could destabilize the world political balance. God help us, Arnie, we could end up panicking the Soviets into a war."

Savak put his palms on the coffee table and leaned toward him. His eyes narrowed and his voice turned passionate. "What it will do is exactly what we've designed. Entente will make them deal with us in a way that they've been avoiding for decades. This isn't some hare-brained scheme you and I cooked up overnight. Look at the people we chose to construct the proposal. Theodore Hammel is this country's leading expert on Soviet affairs in the private sector. He gave us the backbone."

"He also has visions of becoming Secretary of State," Steven reminded him.

Savak made a dismissing gesture with his hand. "Hammel will be more than satisfied with a seat in the NSC. But that's not the point. Hammel, and everyone else who's contributed to the project, agrees that it will work in the way we intend."

"What they agree about," Steven corrected his friend, "is that their contribution to the project will work. They don't know just how much of their individual theories will work as part of a much broader plan."

"It will work," Savak said in a fervent whisper.

"Will it, Arnie? Or is our vision of Entente a fantasy we dreamed up in Nam?"

"A fantasy . . . for what?"

"Revenge."

Chapter Six

Steven pulled off the side of the road. He stared through the windshield, down to the lake. The sky was cloudless. A myriad of stars sparkled in the black heavens. The three-quarter moon shone brightly; its light shimmered iridescently on the ice-covered lake.

Logically, Steven knew he shouldn't be here. But he'd had no choice. Shortly after Savak had pleaded fatigue, and gone to bed, Steven had been gripped by an urgent need to drive to the lake where Ellie had almost died.

Why? he asked himself. To look for a clue to Ellie's assailant? If there had been something of significance, he was certain that Banacek would have found it.

Nor did Steven doubt that the FBI agents had searched the area as thoroughly as had Banacek. Yet his need to be here was too strong a force to ignore.

Leaving the ignition on, Steven stepped out of the Bronco. He stood in the cold night air, wondering where to start and what to look for. Finally, he walked toward the embankment.

When he reached the edge of the road, he looked down toward the lake. Directly below him was where the car had gone in. The moonlight illuminated the rippling water contained by the jagged hole. Even from a distance of thirty feet, Steven could see small pieces of ice forming on the water's surface. Soon, the hole would disappear.

Steven started toward the water's edge. The snow crunched beneath his boots as he searched the ground around him. He saw the curving tire tracks that Banacek had told him about, and was able to understand Banacek's observations of the accident.

By the time he reached the water's edge, and saw the deep gouges on the thick roots of the old tree, Steven's anger at what had happened to Ellie returned.

After staring into the dark water, he walked back to the road and leaned against the Bronco. He tried to build a scenario of the previous night, but could not.

He looked from where he stood down to the lake, following the tracks of the car. Ellie should have been in the car, not in the water. What did that signify?

"She was conscious," he said aloud. And, he thought, she had tried to get away. It was the only really logical explanation. If she'd been unconscious, she would have been left in the car when the car had been sent into the lake.

He went toward the curve in the road, when he glanced at the tall pines across from him. They stood like giants, guarding the gates of a dark sanctuary.

He stared at the trees. If he was right, if Ellie had been trying to escape, he knew where she would have tried to go. Into the pines, and into the refuge of darkness that was offered by the thick copse of trees.

He crossed the blacktop, and slowly walked toward the curve in the road. He focused on the old hard snow, looking for footprints and knowing that the possibility was slim.

A hundred feet from where he had begun, he stopped dead. There was a single footprint. It was deep, showing that all of the person's weight had been put onto that foot. Someone running heavily would make that deep an impression.

The shoeprint was small and narrow. Ellie's feet were

small and narrow. Steven knelt by the print. He looked farther on, but saw no other prints.

He sensed that this was the spot where her torturer caught up to her. This was the spot where her fate had been sealed.

He stared at the thick pines. His stomach knotted. His hands curled into tight fists.

She had been five feet from safety. Five feet too far.

To the uninitiated denizens of Washington, the nondescript government building situated on Pennsylvania Avenue appeared deserted. The workers and administrators who populated the building for up to eighteen hours a day had gone home.

All of the building's entrances were locked and alarmed, except for two: The front entrance, with two security guards on duty, and a little known doorway that opened into a basement room from a tunnel that ran thirty-nine feet beneath Pennsylvania Avenue. The tunnel and the door leading from it were hooked up to a separate security system. Both the entrance to the tunnel and the exit were guarded by Marines who had served in combat. The doors were four-inch carborundum steel, sealed with air-tight gaskets, and locked with an intricate series of computer-relayed locking devices.

Despite the building's deserted appearance, and without the main entrance security guard's knowledge, six men were inside the building. Three of those men sat in a large windowless and soundproofed office.

A fourth man sat at a desk in the outer office, attentive not to what was happening behind the closed door, but to any eventuality that might occur in the hallway. A clear plastic receiver was in his left ear. On the desk, near his right hand, was a nine-millimeter pistol. A clip holding nine rounds of parabellum ammunition was in place. Beneath the man's blue pin-stripe suit was the most advanced form of body armor available in today's world. He wore the vest not selfishly, but to keep him alive long enough to protect one, if not all, of the men in the office.

A small black box, with green glowing lights and a curved increment gauge, was in the center of the desk. The electronic sweeper would detect hidden bugs or recorders within two hundred feet. There were none.

Two more men were in the hallway. One was near the center stairwell; the other was in place by the elevators. These men, like the solitary man at the desk, carried modified nine-millimeter weapons.

In the soundproof inner office, tension charged the air like the ozone crispness preceding a thunderstorm. Two men sat on a brass-trimmed leather couch. The third man was ensconced behind a large oak desk. This man, his features wreathed by lines of age and worry, gazed pensively at the men across from him. "You're absolutely certain it's no one on my staff?"

"Yes, sir," said the man seated on the left side of the couch. "And I no longer see any need to conduct our meetings here. We've also narrowed the suspects down to a certain few."

"And those are?"

The man, a green-eyed grandfather with a round face, cradled the bowl of a meerschaum pipe between thumb and forefinger. Julius Axelrod, while in fact the grandfather he appeared to be, was the director of the United States Secret Service.

"I'm sorry, sir," Axelrod said, "but I don't believe you should have that information. It could prove detrimental to your office if things don't go as planned."

The President shook his head, exhaling sibilantly. "Does anything really go as planned? No, this time, old friend, I must overrule your wishes. I want to know who is trying to make this country impotent."

Axelrod exchanged glances with the third man in the office. General Amos Coblehill, USMC retired—tall, lean, bald and sixty, with critical eyes and a caustic wit, was the current director of the National Security Agency.

"Very well, Mr. President," Axelrod said, thoughtfully tapping the black stem of the meerschaum on his other wrist. "We're within ninety-percent probability that the leak is coming from Senator Philip Pritman's office. It's either Pritman himself—"

"Impossible," the President interjected. "I've known Philip Pritman for almost twenty years. We may not see eye to eye philosophically or politically, but he's no traitor."

"God only knows what happens to people, sir," Coblehill stepped in, taking the onus off Axelrod. "However, both our agencies have independently reached the same conclusion. The information is either originating from the senator, or from a member of his staff."

"How is it even possible for Pritman to become privy to this sort of information?"

Axelrod slipped the now cool pipe into his jacket pocket. "It's not really that hard, sir. There are ways. Someone within the bureaucracy who might have been reached; or, logical assumptions from unguarded conversations. Christ, Pritman's on more committees that deal with foreign relations and intelligence than a Washington hooker has clients. All it really takes to put together the bits and pieces of information Pritman comes away with from those meetings is a world-class political strategist."

"And," Amos Coblehill added, "Pritman wouldn't even know he was giving up vital information. All it would take is a discussion with an aide after an intelligence session. And the man keeps notes, prodigiously. They're in a locked file which he believes is secure. We know better."

"Do you both still believe it's tied into that Entente nonsense you learned about?" the President asked, fixing his gaze on Axelrod.

"It seems to be, Mr. President," Coblehill answered for them.

"Stupid. We can't move overtly against them. Everyone knows that it's only a matter of weeks before Pritman announces his candidacy. Any actions we take will be construed as a political ruse to discredit Pritman. The minute anyone gets scent of it, Pritman will announce."

The President wearily pressed his forefingers to his temple. "All right, take whatever steps are necessary to find out who the leak is. But it must be done quietly and it had damn well better be discreet."

"We understand, sir," Axelrod said. "And we've anticipated your needs. We've taken additional measures to watch Pritman's staff people. But we can't do the same with Pritman, too chancy for obvious reasons. Something will turn up soon, indicating who it is. Especially with this latest business in Pennsylvania. Sloppy work," he added with a shake of his head.

"How can anyone high on Pritman's staff be a Soviet mole? How is it possible?"

"It's happened too many times before." Axelrod's voice was a flat and unemotional statement of a fact that everyone knew but no one wanted to admit.

"I still think we should have Mulvaney check with his sources in Moscow," Coblehill advised.

"No," the President said forcefully. "I want no CIA involvement. Not while they're being put through the ringer with that goddamn Central American investigation. And we can't take the risk of letting the Soviets know we're on to them. Julius, you were the one who brought that bugaboo up," he reminded Axelrod pointedly. "And you're right. If they think we've got even a little whiff of their scheme, they'll send the mole so far back under we'll never know he existed."

"Then as a last resort," Coblehill interjected, "we'll have to leak the information about the woman to the papers and brew up a scandal for Pritman. It's got all the ingredients: A woman found in a frozen lake, her body mutilated, her fiancé the number-two man on a United States Senator's staff . . ."

The President looked down at the back of his right hand and studied an old jagged purple scar. "I'd prefer not. Those things have a way of coming back at you. Give me your best guess. I want the name."

Again, Axelrod and Coblehill exchanged glances before Axelrod said, "If I had to choose right now, I'd say it's Pritman's number-two man, Steven Morrisy. Everything points to him, all the way down the line."

"Morrisy? Good Christ, man how the hell can someone who's been through what he has do this to us now?"

"Sir, you know—"

"All too well. I also know that this situation cannot be allowed to continue." Standing, the President looked at the men who rose respectfully with him. "I want to thank both of you for clearing my staff. It means a lot to me, having my trust in them justified."

The President walked ponderously to the door, put his hand on the brass knob, and then turned back to the two directors. His eyes went hard. "Use whatever methods you deem appropriate, but put an end to it. I want you to get that bastard! For me, personally!"

Chapter Seven

Steven woke with a headache. He pressed his palms to his head to help ease the incessant throbbing in his skull. It was only when he sat up that he realized he'd fallen asleep on the couch.

He remembered returning from the lake, sitting on the couch, and suddenly feeling so physically drained that he hadn't been able to summon enough energy to go into his bedroom. He'd lain back on the couch but hadn't been able to fall asleep.

He'd called the hospital around three. The duty nurse had said that Ellie's condition was still stable. Sometime after that his mental circuits had shut down. He didn't remember falling asleep.

With a low groan, he looked at the clock. It was seven-ten.

He was groggy. His bladder was full. But before going to the bathroom, he called the hospital and learned that Ellie's status had not changed.

In the bathroom, he peered at his reflection in the vanity. He didn't like the strained lines bracketing his mouth. The two-day growth of beard accenting the dark half-moons beneath his eyes didn't help his self-image either.

He showered and shaved and donned fresh clothes. Twenty minutes later, the throbbing in his head had settled into a dull ache centered behind his eyes.

He made coffee and then stuck his head into the second

bedroom. Savak was lying in bed, his eyes open. "Coffee's on."

Savak sat up, wiping at his eyes. "How you doing?"

"I'm okay. I called the hospital. Ellie's stable, no changes. I left a clean towel out."

When Savak stood, Steven stared at the scars on his upper torso. "You'd think that after all this time they'd be gone."

When Savak shrugged, Steven left him at the bathroom door, returned to the kitchen for a cup of coffee, then walked outside.

He sat on the porch bench, his parka on but open, staring out at the distant mountain ridges. The sun was partially obscured by clouds. Steven wondered if it would snow. There hadn't been a heavy snow in the week he'd been here. He liked the soft feel of newly fallen snow.

Has it only been twenty-four hours since Arnie's phone call? he asked himself, surprised at the rapid passing of time.

He thought about the lake, and how, if Ellie had made it into the woods, she would be here now, with him, and not comatose in the hospital.

The sound of a car intruded on his thoughts. A few moments later a Greyton patrol car crested the hill and turned into his property. Banacek was behind the wheel.

He sipped coffee while waiting for Banacek to park and come up onto the porch.

"Morning, Mr. Morrisy," Banacek said in casual greeting.

"Morning, Sheriff. Coffee?"

Declining, Banacek said, "Didn't really expect to see you up this early."

Steven's smile went tight. He met the sheriff's open stare, and said, "Then why are you here?"

"I haven't gotten a whole lot of sleep lately. I've been pretty well bothered by what's happened to Miss Rogers."

"Welcome to the club. But I have a feeling you didn't come here looking for a cure for insomnia."

Banacek chuckled. "No. Mr. Morrisy, what kind of friends do you consider Londrigan and Lomack to be?"

Banacek's question sent the ache behind his eyes climbing up the decibel scale. He regarded Banacek silently while waiting for the throbbing to pass. "I've never thought about it. Comfortable friends. Sam more so than Larry. It's an old friendship that's made it through a lot of years. We grew up together, played on the football team together."

He took another sip of coffee. The steam rising from the cup momentarily blocked his sinuses. Then the delayed impact of Banacek's question registered. His resentment mounted. He looked past Banacek, at the snow-capped mountains. "Sheriff, if you think that they'd lie for me, and give me an alibi for the other night, you're way out of line!"

Banacek lifted his jacket's fur-trimmed collar against the cold January breezes. "I wish to God that was all it was."

Staring at Banacek, Steven tried to analyze the odd inflection in the sheriff's voice.

"There's been another accident," Banacek said, looking directly into Steven's eyes. "Sam Londrigan's plane crashed last night. Sam and Larry were killed."

Steven's vision blurred. The mountain vista became unglued.

"The fuel tanks were full," the sheriff continued, "the plane exploded when it hit the ground. It took almost fifteen minutes for the first fire truck to get to the scene. There was nothing left of them. They were just . . . ashes."

The pounding in Steven's temples grew louder. "Do they know why the plane crashed?"

"I spoke with the Fairmont police, and then the FAA. It may take weeks of sifting through the debris to find out the cause of the crash. But it must have been sudden. Londrigan never radioed that he was in trouble."

Steven stood and went to the railing. "Do you think the

crash was an accident?"

Banacek pulled a hard pack of Camel filters from his pocket. He extracted one cork-tipped cigarette and slipped it between his lips. He lighted it with a disposable butane lighter and inhaled deeply.

Releasing the smoke, Banacek took the cigarette from his mouth and held it cupped in his hand. The sheriff's gaze was fixed on the cigarette's tip when he said, "I've got no reason not to think it wasn't an accident, do I, Mr. Morrisy?"

"That depends on whether or not you believe I tried to kill Ellie."

Banacek nodded. "I've been working real hard on that."

Steven kept silent, sensing that Banacek had something to say that he wanted Steven to hear.

"I spent some time last night at the *Greyton Standard.* I dug out those old stories about you and Savak and Latham. I read every last one of them. I learned a lot about you from what was written . . . and even more from what wasn't."

Banacek took another drag of the cigarette. "I think I came away with a good character sketch of you. I learned that you're a damn smart man, Mr. Morrisy. You graduated college cum laude. And between you and your two friends, you've got enough medals for a battalion.

"So, to answer your question, no, I don't think you tried to kill Miss Rogers. In fact, I'm pretty sure that if you wanted her dead, she wouldn't be in the hospital now. You don't survive the kind of war you were in—and not know how to kill someone. I know you've had the kind of training that isn't in the rule books. You showed me that yesterday, with Blayne."

"A prosecutor would tear you apart in a courtroom."

Banacek nodded solemnly. "It has to get that far first."

"What about Sam and Larry?"

"There's not much I can do unless the FAA inspector finds evidence that the crash wasn't an accident."

"You don't think it was, do you?" Steven asked, aware that he was forcing the issue.

"It does seem to be a funny coincidence. Without those men, the case against you is a whole lot stronger, strong enough, in fact, for a prosecutor with an eye toward a big career to consider going for an indictment."

With Banacek confirming Steven's own thoughts, the disorientation clouding his mind disappeared. The events of the past twenty-four hours fell into a sequence that was as logical and clear to him as it was terrifying. "It's all been spur-of-the-moment, ever since your deputy found Ellie."

Banacek's thick eyebrows lumbered upward. "What has?"

"Yesterday you implied that whoever tried to kill Ellie was counting on the fact that her body wouldn't be discovered until spring, if ever. But not only didn't she disappear, she's still alive. Don't you find it curious that the only two people who could have proven I was at home that night died in a plane crash?"

"In my line of work, we call it suspicious, not curious."

Steven ignored the remark, saying, "To add to the confusion, it was only an accident that Sam and Larry came here that night. No one was supposed to know I was here. I came here so I could work without any interruptions. But Sam's secretary saw me at the convenience store that afternoon and told him. That's why they came out to visit."

Steven paused, took a deep breath, and looked away from Banacek. "And I think that maybe that's why they died."

Banacek took a last drag from the cigarette and flicked it away. Both men watched the butt arc slowly, turning end over end before coming to rest on the frozen ground.

"Sheriff, I've got another question for you. Where was Ellie for the six days she was missing?"

Banacek shrugged. "All we know is that she left Washington on Monday night and showed up in our lake Sunday night."

"No, you don't. All you know is that a note was left in Washington last Monday night, saying she was going to join me. But I wouldn't take odds that she wrote it. And her stomach, Sheriff. . . She was tortured. And those wounds weren't inflicted Sunday night."

"Obviously. And if she'd stayed in the lake until it thawed, her body would be decomposed enough so that it's doubtful if the razor cuts would be recognized for what they are. Which," Banacek added, his eyes narrowing until all that could be seen were two dark dots encased in folds of flesh, "brings out another interesting aspect: If the murder had gone the way it was intended, and if Miss Rogers's body was found in the spring, you'd be the prime suspect. Especially when it's discovered that the last time anyone saw Miss Rogers, she was coming to Greyton to stay with you."

Although he had been working along the same lines as Banacek, and had come to almost the same conclusion, hearing the sheriff put thoughts into words rocked him.

He looked away from Banacek, following the upward slope of a distant mountain. "Which means, if you're right, that whoever tried to kill Ellie had planned to make it appear that I was responsible, whether she had been found now or in the spring."

When the police car's engine became a distant echo, Steven's sadness grew stronger. During the time Banacek had been talking, Steven had kept his emotions under tight control. Now he allowed them to be free.

He felt a deep anguish building within him. He had grown up with Sam and Larry. He'd known them for over thirty years. They were his friends, and as much a part of his life as was Greyton itself. He would miss them.

Why? Was the plane crash an accident, or was it tied

into what happened to Ellie? Had they died because they had been with him that night?

The implications of his thoughts stunned him. If Lomack and Londrigan had been killed because of what happened to Ellie, it spoke volumes about the killer's resources and abilities.

But that wasn't important now, he realized; he would think about those facts later.

Drawing in a breath of cold mountain air, Steven wiped his eyes and went inside to tell Savak about their friends.

He found Savak in the kitchen, dressed, his hair still damp from the shower. He waited for Savak to fix himself a cup of coffee and sit down across from him before he spoke.

Savak's surface reaction was exactly what Steven had expected. A flickering of his eyelids followed by a curtain of detachment falling across his features.

He knew Savak too well to be fooled by appearances. Since Nam, Savak had mastered the outward control of his emotions. But Steven was able to see beyond his friend's false front to the pain in Savak's eyes, and the knotting of the muscles in his friend's neck.

After several long and silent seconds passed, Savak said, "That's bad for us, Steven. They were your only alibi."

He stared at Savak, his hands trembling. "I don't give a damn about that. What I can't help thinking is that they're dead because of me."

"What the hell are you talking about?" Savak shouted, this time failing to keep his features under his usual tight control.

"I think that what happened to Ellie *and* Sam *and* Larry is being directed at me."

"Jesus Christ on a fucking cross! Listen to yourself. You're talking conspiracy. You've been in Washington too long, Steven; you've been to too many cocktail parties."

He shook his head, once. "It fits, Arnie."

"Don't even think it, much less say it," Savak warned.

"Everyone pleads conspiracy. For your own good, and for Ellie's, don't bring it up again."

The phone rang, interrupting their argument. He answered it and listened to an unfamiliar voice ask for Savak. Handing Savak the receiver, Steven sat back down and stared at the sediment in the bottom of his cup, trying to calm his frayed nerves.

When Savak finished his brief conversation, he said, "That was the duty officer at Andrews. Georgetown has cleared Ellie's transfer with Greyton. A medevac chopper is scheduled to reach Greyton at three. It will return to Andrews with you and Ellie. An ambulance will be waiting."

Fifteen minutes later, Steven went from room to room, carefully shutting off the lights and securing the windows. Then he turned off the boiler and closed the gas petcock.

When Steven was satisfied that the house was properly shut down, he and Savak loaded their bags into the car and opened the garage door.

Steven backed out of the garage, and used the remote to close the garage door. Then, before driving into Greyton, Steven looked back at his house. He had a strange premonition of a coming doom that made him wonder if he would ever be back. He pushed the feeling aside and drove off.

They were halfway to town, passing Walt Higgens's old Gulf station, abandoned during the gas crunch, when Savak broke their silence. "I'll take the attaché case back to the office today. I'll also make the arrangements to have your car driven to Washington."

"Arnie, I—"

"For Christ sake don't thank me again," Savak interrupted, his voice rough-edged with emotion. "Let's just get Ellie settled into Georgetown. Once that's taken care of, and if you feel up to it, come into the office tomorrow and go over everything with Pritman. But," he added quickly, "let's take it one step at a time. First Ellie."

Steven nodded, grateful for his friend's understanding. A moment later, he thought about Lomack and Londrigan again. "Arnie, why don't you come back with Ellie and me? You can have one of the pilots at Greyton field take your plane home."

In the ensuing silence, Steven felt Savak's studying gaze. He turned slightly and saw a half smile on Savak's mouth. "That wasn't even a good try. No, Steven, I'll fly myself home. But thanks for worrying about me."

Steven gripped the steering wheel tightly. "I've lost enough friends today."

"You won't lose me," Savak said in a low voice.

Silence fell again, broken only by the air slipping over the windshield and the tires rumbling on the blacktop. A quarter of an hour later, Steven left Savak in the hospital's lobby and went upstairs.

The neurosurgeon, with a nurse in attendance, was examining Ellie's sutures. When the doctor finished, and the nurse rebandaged Ellie's head, Skolnick said, "She's doing much better, Mr. Morrisy. There's no sign of infection and the swelling is down well below the danger point. I don't foresee any problems with the transfer and, I've already spoken with the neurology people at Georgetown. They'll take very good care of her."

"I hope you don't resent—"

"Not at all," Skolnick said, dismissing Steven's words with a casual wave. "I only wish our equipment was up to Georgetown's caliber."

"I appreciate all you've done for Ellie," he said, shaking Skolnick's hand.

Skolnick held Steven's hand in a tight grip while staring intensely into his eyes. "Just remember that when she recovers from the coma, she'll be in a very delicate emotional and mental state. I can't even begin to imagine what it would be like to have no memory. Can you?"

When Steven replied, his voice was thick with emotion.

"There have been times when I've prayed for just that. I have a photographic memory."

"Complete and instant recall?" Skolnick asked, finally releasing Steven's hand.

"Basically," he said. "I have to use memory triggers. With the right trigger, I can remember anything that I've seen, read, or heard since my third birthday."

"That can be very beneficial for her. Your memories of shared experiences can help give her back a little of herself," Skolnick said, his eyes bright.

"The coma? How much longer will it last?"

The neurosurgeon's expression changed. "I'm afraid that's something we have no way of knowing. Aside from external causes, a coma is also a mechanism the body uses to help heal itself. So pinpointing a time when Miss Rogers will emerge from the coma is impossible. Only nature, and God, can know," the neurosurgeon admitted before leaving with the nurse.

Alone, he sat next to Ellie. He glanced at her left hand and remembered the missing ring. He lifted her hand, separated her fingers, and saw what he hadn't seen yesterday.

Putting her hand down gently, he caressed her soft and unresponsive skin before going to the nurses' station. He asked the young nurse with the pretty face and experienced eyes to call Chuck Latham. While she dialed, he looked up at the clock on the wall behind her. It was ten o'clock.

"Doctor Latham's in the ER," the nurse informed him after she hung up. "He'll be up as soon as he's free."

When he returned to Ellie's room, he was seized by a wave of fatigue. He sat down heavily, waiting for the tiredness to pass. He knew that the four hours of sleep he'd gotten weren't nearly enough.

The clarity of his thoughts grew indistinct. Briefly, he was transported backward in time. He began to live the nightmare of his past, to smell again the scents of the jungles, and to hear the cries and the . . .

He grasped Ellie's hand, holding it tight in an effort to anchor himself in the present. He knew that stress and exhaustion were responsible for triggering the unwanted flood of memories.

All of them—himself, Latham, and Savak—had learned to deal with the past in their own ways. Savak's method was to remember everything so that he might eventually be able to expunge the guilt he bore—and the rage that had come later.

Latham had dealt with his past by funneling his energy into creating a new and different life. After his discharge, he'd returned to college and then gone on to medical school. Medicine had become his salvation. Healing others helped him to heal himself. Latham had been the first to come to terms with the past, and the first to marry.

Steven had the perfect escape. He simply didn't choose to remember.

Only it wasn't working anymore.

He bent forward, closed his eyes, and pressed his forehead to the back of his hand. He tried to hurl the memories back to the hidden part of his mind. But he was no longer the same Steven Morrisy who had been able to choose to forget.

He'd fallen in love with Ellie and changed.

"No!" he whispered, stopping himself from thinking about the war, and the prison camp.

Then Steven felt a presence in the room. He pushed aside the fuzziness and lifted his head. Blinking, he focused on Chuck Latham.

"You okay?"

"Fine, just a little trip down memory lane."

"I understand," Latham said, looking from Steven to Ellie and misreading Steven's comment. "You wanted to see me?"

Steven pointed to Ellie's hand. "Her ring. It's still not on."

"I know. I checked the safe and talked to my ER staff. She wasn't wearing it when she was brought in."

"What about the paramedics?"

"I checked with them as well. They don't remember seeing it."

"They could be lying."

Latham shook his head. "I know the two men who were on duty Sunday night. They aren't lying. And beside the fact that I trust them, they wouldn't risk their careers or their reputations to steal a ring."

"She wouldn't take it off, Chuck."

"She was in freezing water, Steven. Skin contracts. It could have fallen off."

"The damn ring was too small. She put it on when I gave it to her. And she struggled to get it on. It hasn't been off since." He grasped Ellie's hand and lifted her ring finger. "Look at her knuckle, Chuck," he said, pointing to the gouges low on the sides of her knuckle.

Latham bent to examine Ellie's ring finger. When he stood up again, Steven saw the knowledge surfacing in Latham's face long before Latham said, "Someone forced it off. But not in the last few days."

Chapter Eight

"This thing has got me so damn wound up I can't think straight," Steven said.

They were gathered in Latham's office, drinking coffee and waiting for the medical helicopter's arrival. He'd been chased from Ellie's room so that the medical preparations for her transfer could begin.

"I keep thinking about Ellie's stomach, and then I start to flash back to Nam. Jesus, when I think about that, I—we were so . . ."

"Gullible?" Savak offered.

"Stupid," Steven amended.

"We weren't stupid," Latham said, looking up from the file on his desk. Steven saw a specter of the past fill Latham's eyes. "We trusted them," Latham continued. "We needed to believe that we were on the right side. We were the apple pie boys who grew up on World War Two movies, and were taught that our ideology was infallible.

"But man-oh-man did those army shrinks sure know what they were doing! We were together again. And because we were, we knew we could pull it off. We always did the impossible when we were teamed up."

"Yeah," Savak agreed sarcastically. "We were three times as gullible and idealistic as anyone else."

"In a way," Steven agreed thoughtfully. "And you're right too," he said, looking at Latham, "about how we were brought up. We accepted certain things as intrinsic. Even when we knew the war had become something it never should have, we couldn't embrace a philosophy that made what we believed in wrong.

"Which was the reason you re-upped for the second tour, wasn't it?" he asked Latham suddenly. "Do you remember the night before we crossed into Nam, when Arnie asked you why you volunteered for another tour?"

"I said it was because I wasn't ready to go home yet," Latham answered quickly. Too quickly, Steven thought, for it to have been very far from his everyday awareness.

"But it was more than that, wasn't it?" Steven's voice was rough, his throat dry. "You were too filled with guilt about what you had seen and what you'd been a part of to go home without trying to rectify it, at least in your own mind."

Latham's round face showed strain. "I felt dirty. I'd go out on patrol, day after lousy day, and we'd hit the villages the intelligence reports said were NVA controlled. But most of the time we didn't find Charlie. We usually didn't find men of fighting age. Just old men and kids and women.

"But we couldn't take a chance because the women usually had weapons under their clothing. And those little kids . . . they'd smile at you and, a minute later, pull out a grenade and blow the brains out of the men nearest to them. So we'd react before we could be killed. And you know what hurts so damn much about that?"

From the corner of his eye, Steven saw Savak's pale face mirroring his own emotions as Latham talked.

"They didn't think they had any choice!" Latham shouted. "They'd heard Charlie's propaganda about how the American devils were killing everyone. And what's worse was that those women and kids weren't on one side or another. I really believe that all they wanted to do was to grow their food and live the way that had for the last thousand years or so.

"But they'd been so filled with half-truths that they were scared that one of our patrols would slaughter them. And it had happened enough times for their fears to be real," Latham finished, his eyes challenging each of them in turn. "Yes," he said, finally. "I felt dirty and guilty and needed to make up for it so I signed up for another tour."

Steven broke off Latham's intense stare. "We all had our rationales for taking the mission. But beneath all the bullshit, it was pretty much the same. Each of us wanted to be able to go home and to not be ashamed."

Latham picked up a pink memo slip from his desk and began to shred it in neat quarter-inch strips. When a little more than half the paper was piled on his desk, he said, "And that's the pathetic part, isn't it? What we wanted was so simple. What we got was so damn . . ."

Steven sensed that none of them would ever find the exact words to describe their innermost feelings. Then he wondered if there were any words to convey the depths that they had been cast into, in Vietnam.

"This is getting sick!" Latham said, glaring at them. "All we're doing is bringing things up we don't need to think about. It's long over. For God sake, drop it!"

After Latham fell silent, the anger in his eyes vanished and his voice took on that uniquely professional air reserved for doctors. "It's two-thirty. The copter will be here soon. I'll go check on Ellie."

Steven started to rise. Latham waved him back. "We don't need you getting in the way."

When the door closed behind Latham, Steven continued to stare at it. "I didn't mean to get him upset."

"It happens," Savak said, his words rough-edged and uneasy.

"What about Ellie's sister?"

"Didn't I tell you?" When Steven shook his head, Savak explained that he'd called the office earlier and

Simon Clarke told him that he'd tracked her down. "Carla Rogers is a GS-14 statistician at Treasury. But she's on vacation and no one seems to know where she went."

He picked up his coffee and took a sip. "He left word in case someone hears from her?"

"Of course he did," Savak said as he shifted in his seat. "Steven, once Pritman gets the nod, do you think Clement will withdraw?"

Steven ran a thumbnail down the side of the styrofoam coffee cup. Little white flakes of plastic sprayed outward. "Are you trying to keep my mind occupied?"

Savak shrugged, then he grinned. "I thought that was what friends were for?"

Steven felt a rush of warmth for Savak. It wasn't a new feeling, but it was one he hadn't felt in a while. He returned Savak's smile. "No, Arnie, I don't think Clement will pull out. He's always been after the nomination, and he's got a decent share of party people behind him."

"Which will change once the people who matter hear what Pritman has to offer. They'll grab at it. They'll have no choice."

"They may just as conceivably believe Pritman's lost his mind and give him the boot."

Savak's right eyebrow lifted in response to Steven's remark. He double-stroked the side of his nose, and said, "Never happen, m'boy. They'll listen and analyze and make their decision. But they'll never point him to the door. They can't. The Senator is the only viable candidate. No one else has Pritman's degree of public acceptance.

"In the last two years, the President has had every major foreign policy issue derailed. Every diplomatic effort the administration has dreamed up has failed. America's foreign policy is a patchwork of half-ass stopgap measures.

"Look at the mess in Honduras," Savak said with a single shake of his head. "That gambit cost us an enormous amount of credibility in the world community. Honduras was the single most important aligned Central American country we had."

Watching Savak, his face carved into pensive lines of concentration, Steven knew that he was seeing a different Arnold Savak than ever before. The Arnold Savak seated three feet from him would soon be, if things went according to plan, the second most powerful man in the country. Savak would be *the* man behind the President; *the* person closest to the chief executive, and *the* one whose guidance and advice would always be listened to.

If Pritman was nominated and got elected.

Not for the first time, but with more clarity than ever before, he saw just how closely his own destiny was linked to Arnie's. One day he too would be standing behind the President, wielding the kind of power and authority many people dreamed of but few attained.

He curbed his thoughts and made himself pay attention to what Savak was saying.

"Given all the administration's problems, and if you've smoothed out those last few snags in the proposal, the men at the meeting will see Entente for the tool that it is—strength without war. How the hell can there be a war, if no one knows *who* they're supposed to be fighting?"

"In theory, Arnie," he said as a knock sounded on the door and Sheriff Banacek entered the office.

"Mr. Savak, Mr. Morrisy, good afternoon," the sheriff said, turning toward Steven. "I got a message you wanted to see me?"

Steven nodded. "It's about Ellie's ring. It's still missing, and Chuck says it was never receipted in and put in the hospital safe."

"You think someone here stole it?"

"Chuck says not and I'll go along with him. But the scrapes on her finger seem to indicate that the ring was taken off forcefully."

"You think that whoever tried to kill her stole the ring?"

"Do you have a better idea?"

Saying no, Banacek asked Steven for a description of the ring. After writing it in a small spiral note pad, which he tucked carefully away in his jacket pocket, Banacek promised he'd do what he could to find the ring.

"Any word about the plane crash?" Savak asked.

"Nothing yet," Banacek said without taking his eyes from Steven. "I understand you're accompanying Miss Rogers to the hospital in Washington?"

"Is there a problem? Or am I a suspect again?"

"I'm sure you understand the position I'm in," Banacek said, his eyes telling Steven that he knew Steven Morrisy, attorney-at-law, comprehended the situation perfectly.

Steven did. If he left now, he would be out of the sheriff's jurisdiction. Should Banacek decide to bring charges, the sheriff would have to go through the immense amount of red tape involved in an extradition proceeding. "But I'm not the one you're after. We both know that."

Banacek hitched up his belt, shifted the well-worn leather holster an inch to the back, and said, "When I found out about your plans to return to Washington with Miss Rogers, I had to speak with the county prosecutor. He said that because of who you are, and the implications that would be attached to Senator Pritman should you be detained, he was not averse to leaving the crime report on open status."

"However?" Steven asked, knowing that there had to be a quid pro quo.

Removing an envelope from his pocket, Banacek

handed it to Steven. "The prosecutor drew up an agreement of cooperation between you and the county."

Steven extracted the folded agreement and began to read as Banacek went on. "It says that you agree to return to Greyton, to offer testimony, within twenty-four hours of his office contacting you."

Savak rose from his chair. "This is getting ridiculous!"

Steven waved off his friend's objection and went to Latham's desk. Using a standard hospital-issue clear plastic Bic, he signed the letter of agreement. When he returned it to Banacek, he said, "Thank you, Sheriff. And if anything comes up, you'll notify me?"

"You can count on it," Banacek promised.

As Steven shook Banacek's extended hand, the office door opened again and Latham came in. "Time to go, Steven. The medevac's coming in."

Banacek, who had started toward the door before Latham had spoken, paused. "Mr. Morrisy, can I give you some advice?"

Steven nodded slowly, wondering if some Pennsylvanian homily was about to be offered, when Banacek said, "Watch your back."

The medevac helicopter was a self-contained flying hospital, so far removed from the old troop and medevac copters of Steven's past that he couldn't find an accurate parallel.

The medical compartment was quieter than he'd expected. Ellie lay on a gurney clamped to the floor. Monitoring wires ran from her head and chest to the instruments on the wall. An IV continued to drip into her arm, and oxygen was fed through the familiar nose tube.

Steven sat in a webbed chair next to Ellie. Two other men occupied the compartment with him. A uniformed medical technician sat before a bank of instruments, keeping a constant check on Ellie's readings; the other man wore white overalls, without insignia, and was sitting across the gurney from Steven. He appeared to be either in his late twenties or early thirties.

When Steven had entered the copter, and glanced at the man, he'd felt a twinge of recognition. But the sensation had faded as quickly as it had come. And he was grateful for the man's silence as he buckled himself into the seat.

The thought of Savak, flying his private plane back to Washington, sat heavily on him. He forced himself not to think about Sam Londrigan's fatal crash.

"Almost there," said the man across from him, speaking for the first time. "Half-hour should do it; another half-hour from Andrews to the hospital if the traffic isn't too bad."

Steven nodded.

"They're among the best in the world at Georgetown," the man added. "If she's got a chance, it'll be there."

When he met the other man's eyes, he sensed that the man wasn't speaking simply to get him into a conversation. "They have to," Steven said in a low voice.

"Automobile accidents are the worst. It's always the wrong person who gets hurt." Taken by surprise at the intensity in the man's voice, Steven could only stare at him. "Mr. Morrisy, I know that whatever I might say may not help, but I've seen a lot worse come through."

Steven gazed at Ellie, feeling his muscles knot with hatred for the person who had done this terrible thing to her. "She didn't deserve this."

The silence resumed, intensified by the whine of the turbine. Five more minutes passed before the technician spoke again. "You are the Steven Morrisy who works for Senator Pritman, aren't you?"

"Yes," Steven said without taking his gaze from Ellie.

"My name is Joshua Raden, sir. I . . ."

Steven's head snapped up. He realized the familiarity he'd sensed earlier had been brought on by the well-defined contours of the man's face. "Raden?" When the technician nodded, Steven shook his head in denial. "You're too old. You couldn't be—"

"His brother, not his son. You wrote to me and my mother after you got out."

Raden's words turned him mute. He tried to speak, but could only manage a weak and strangled grunt. And then it started again. His mind began to slip from the present and slide into the past. He fought back the pain and anguish, refusing to be beaten.

"The sergeant was a good man," Steven said at last.

"I hated the war with all my soul. My father died shortly after we got word of Jeremy's capture. My mother went through hell. When your letter came, it helped her to cope. Lana told us that you had also written to her."

Steven blinked at the mention of Raden's widow.

"I was twelve when my mother showed me the letter," Raden went on. "She made me read it over and over until I understood. It helped change my perspective of why my brother, and the others like yourself, were over there."

"Is that why you became a medical tech?"

"I'm not."

Puzzled, he started to speak, but Raden stopped him. "I'm a neurologist, on staff at Georgetown."

Raden explained how he had schemed his way onto the medevac when he'd found out who Ellie was, and that Steven was going to be traveling with her.

"I wanted to come on this flight," Raden added, "so that I could tell you who I was, and let you know that I'll do everything in my power for Miss Rogers."

Raden looked down at his hands, which he rubbed

together absently. "A long time ago you went out of your way for my mother and myself, by writing to us and telling us the truth. That meant more to us than those medals the army awarded Jeremy. As you asked in the letter, we've never said a word to anyone."

Behind Joshua Raden, the medical technician glanced over his shoulder. "We're on final approach, Doctor. The ambulance is waiting."

When the copter landed, Raden personally supervised Ellie's transference. Once she was in the ambulance, Raden waved Steven inside.

Because of an accident between a truck and several cars, the traffic was heavier than had been anticipated; the trip took an hour. Once they arrived at Georgetown University Hospital, Jeremy Raden handed Steven over to an orderly while he accompanied Ellie through the intake procedure.

The floor was five times the size of Greyton's Neurology unit. And, walking down the long fluorescent-bathed hallway, lined with endless doors and a multitude of nurses and white-frocked doctors, Steven wondered if Ellie would be lost here.

"In here, sir," the orderly said, reaching the end of the hall and opening a door marked Doctors' Lounge. The orderly pointed out the coffee machine, a sandwich vending machine, and a microwave unit, before leaving Steven alone.

He spent an uneasy hour waiting for word on Ellie. When Raden finally reappeared, it was almost eight. The young doctor's face was hopeful as Steven rose to greet him.

"We've just finished examining Miss Rogers. The surgeon who performed the operation did an excellent job. I thought you should know. And," Raden added with a smile, "if she continues to maintain her stable condition, we'll be able to start the first series of tests tomorrow afternoon."

"When can I see her?"

"Now. But only for a few minutes," Raden cautioned, leading Steven back down the hallway, to the far side. "We're keeping her in our observation unit," he added as they went through a double doorway and into a large central area surrounded by windowed rooms.

Entering Ellie's new room, Steven accepted the now familiar churning of his stomach, caused by the sight of her expressionless face. Her head was still bandaged, but not as heavily. More of her cheeks and all of her chin were now visible.

Her bed was different from the one in Greyton. It was thicker and wider. The low hum of the bed's pneumatic pump was a steady counterpoint to the room's silence. The nurses' station observation window was larger than the one in Greyton.

"We use the air bed to balance the pressure on the skin," Raden explained. "It cuts down on bedsores, and it makes it easier to maneuver the patient into different positions."

Steven went to the bed and trailed his fingertips over Ellie's hand. Her skin was cool. He gazed at her for several minutes before brushing his lips across hers. They were as cool as her hands.

"I'll be back tomorrow," he whispered to her.

Joshua Raden walked with him to the elevator and punched the call button. "I'll watch out for her," Raden said, "but you look out on your feet. I think you could use some sleep."

"Yes, I could," Steven admitted with a wry grin. It had been a long time since he'd gone with as little sleep as he'd gotten these past few days.

Raden handed him a white business card with black printing. "Call whenever you feel the need. My home number is on the back."

"Thank you, Joshua."

Raden smiled warmly. "Thank me when Miss Rogers is out of the coma."

Steven liked the way Raden said when, not if. "You'll let me know what the tests show? The long-term damage?"

"I won't hold anything back once we've made our determination. If Doctor Skolnick's diagnosis is correct, then we'll just have to work from that point forward. If she's lost her memory, there's nothing anyone can do to change that. But once she's out of the coma, she'll need all the help she can get, and probably a hell of a lot more."

"I'll be there," Steven promised.

The cab dropped him off shortly after nine. He stood on the sidewalk, looking up at the renovated townhouse he'd bought eight years before. He'd spent all his free weekends, and a lot of nights restoring the interior of the house to its original elegance.

A sudden sense of despondency overcame him. Within its relentless grip, he understood what he had not yet allowed himself to consider.

With Ellie now in Georgetown University Hospital, and himself standing at the steps of his house, he had to accept the possibility that he may have lost her, or at least the woman she had once been. And the likelihood that she would not know who he was seemed to be growing stronger.

Brushing a strand of hair from his forehead, and trying to cast off his dark demons, he climbed the five stone steps. His legs were like two bars of lead. The ache behind his eyes returned with a vengeance. He fumbled clumsily with his keys, and dropped them.

As he bent to pick up the keys up, someone started a

car across the street. He straightened, holding the keys in his left hand, and saw a car start to pull out from the curb just as another car turned the corner.

In the brief instant that the oncoming headlights washed across the other car's windshield, Steven thought he recognized the driver. The man looked like the FBI inspector who had tried to arrest him in Greyton.

The car pulled away a second later, leaving Steven to wonder if it was Blayne, or if his paranoia was growing.

Shrugging it off as something that his tired mind had dreamed up, Steven extricated the door key and let himself inside. He closed the door, locked it, and breathed a sigh of relief at being home.

Then he turned on the hall light and shrugged out of his coat. The house had a damp and uncomfortable chill which he decided to rectify immediately.

He went into the living room. The thermostat was next to the light switch. He flipped on the lights and peered at the electronic thermostat. The digital readout was set for fifty-five, just as he'd left it.

He lifted the outer casing and reset the temperature to seventy. As he was about to close the cover, he heard a click behind him.

"If you so much as breathe heavy, I'll put a bullet through your goddamn head."

Chapter Nine

"Put your hands on your shoulders. Turn around slowly."

Adrenaline burst into his bloodstream. Fear made his heart pound hard and his breathing shallow.

He turned slowly.

She was sitting on the couch, pointing a black automatic at his midsection. Her face was partially hidden by the shadows cast from the twin lamps set on each side of the couch. From what he could see of her, dark hair framed a strong yet feminine face. He didn't think he'd ever seen her before.

"You're making a mistake," Steven said. He took a step forward.

Her eyes narrowed. The pistol rose, centering on his face. "There's no mistake, Morrisy. Don't move."

Steven stared at her, his muscles knotting with the need for action. The anger of having a gun pointed at him took away his logic. "I don't know who the hell you are, or what you're doing in my house. But I'm going to give you one chance to put the gun down and get out."

"My name is Carla Rogers," she said suddenly.

The name caught him off guard. "Ellie's sister?"

"Very good, Morrisy. You see, I'm here to do to

you what you've done to Ellie."

Glaring at the shadowed face of Carla Rogers, he dropped his hands and took another step toward her. "I don't know what you think I've done to Ellie. But if it's anything other than love her and care for her, you're wrong."

"Don't!" she warned, her voice going shrill.

Her eyes flickered, and her hand tightened on the pistol's grip. But his anger gave him the strength to ignore the pistol. He moved closer.

"I'll kill you if you take another step," she shouted, her voice going high.

"Then kill me. And after you've killed me, you can go out and kill the next person whom you think might have hurt Ellie. But lady, don't threaten me. Either pull the trigger or put the gun down. I'm too tired for all this melodramatic crap."

The gun didn't waver. "You're good, Morrisy. Ellie said you were cool and collected no matter what. Convince me that I shouldn't kill you."

"If you've already made up your mind, I won't be able to convince you of anything. So you just go ahead and do whatever you decide is necessary."

Her eyes widened, and he knew, instinctively, that she wasn't going to pull the trigger. A moment later his instincts were proven right when she lowered the weapon to her lap. "How did you know I wouldn't shoot you?"

"I know Ellie. If you're really Ellie's sister, you wouldn't shoot me. If you aren't her sister, then it's an act and you're not here to kill me either."

Carla's face was expressionless. "And which one is it?"

Steven shrugged. "What do you drink?"

"Scotch or brandy, I don't care. But I do want an answer."

"I don't have an answer yet," Steven said as he went to the bar and picked up a bottle of scotch. "My office has been trying to reach you since yesterday morning," he said without turning to look at her.

"I was in Bermuda, on vacation until this morning. When I found out what happened, I called the hospital and learned Ellie was being transferred to Georgetown."

Steven poured the two drinks and went back to the couch. He gave her a glass. "Then why are you here with a gun instead of at the hospital with your sister?"

Steven followed the motion of her slender hand when she raised the glass to her mouth. He noted that her fingers were long and tapered. She took a drink of the scotch and, while he waited for her to go on, he continued his inspection.

Her skin was lightly tanned, and taut. Her mouth was larger than Ellie's. Her nose was smaller. Her eyes were a similar shade of deep blue. She had a small birthmark on her cheek, an inch below her left ear. Studying her, he thought back to the pictures he'd seen in Ellie's apartment. The woman sitting next to him could be the same one as in the photographs.

"Besides the message your office left on my machine," Carla said after lowering the glass, "there was one from an FBI agent to call him. I did. He told me that the Bureau was investigating Ellie's accident. They believe someone tried to kill her. When I asked the agent who, he wouldn't answer me. Instead, he started asking questions about you."

"So, it was on the basis of some questions from an evasive FBI agent, that you decided to kill me?"

She frowned. "Not quite. First I asked a friend for

a favor—I work at Treasury. They have several investigative branches. When I explained the situation to my friend, he said he'd see what he could do. When he called me back, he told me that all he could find out was that the FBI had you under investigation as their prime suspect."

"So then you came here, intent on shooting me. Why did you change your mind?"

"You tell me."

"I thought I did."

"No, you said I could be one of two possible people: Ellie's sister or some mysterious third party. Which one am I, Morrisy?"

"I'll go with the sister story for now."

"You don't believe me?"

"I don't disbelieve you."

She gazed at him for several seconds before setting the safety on the weapon, lifting it from her lap, and placing it on the cushion next to her. "I guess that will have to do. Now, would you please tell me what's going on?"

Steven held his hands palm up. "I wish I could, but I don't know. When was the last time you saw Ellie?"

Carla frowned. "A couple of months ago. It's funny, I'm the older sister. Six years older. We were never really close, except as kids, but we love each other. We could go for months without seeing each other. An occasional phone call to check in, but that's all."

Steven heard the underlying sadness in her voice, and understood the distance that time puts between people. "Tell me about Ellie," he said in a gentle voice.

She moved her head from side to side, once, and favored him with a strained half smile. "You really are something, Morrisy."

"Steven."

"Steven. You walk into your own apartment and find a gun pointed at you. Then, somehow, you turn everything around and instead of answering questions, you ask them."

"The lawyer in me."

She shook her head quickly. "No, it's not that. All right, I'll tell you about Ellie. She loves puppies and children; and she hates to go to the zoo because the animals are caged up." Carla paused to search Steven's face. "When she was sixteen, she was raped by her high school math teacher and spent six years in therapy.

"But even after that, she stayed one of those idealistic people who never learned that their idealism isn't worth while and nobody really gives a damn. Because she's an idealist, she went to work for Senator Pritman."

Carla took a long drink of the scotch before continuing. "And she's deeply in love with you. I remember talking with her right after you gave her the ring. She said that once the election was over, you would be married."

He thought about their first dates. They had not become lovers immediately; rather, they had dated for almost two months before they'd made love for the first time. What he'd taken for hesitancy and shyness was fear. A physical fear of lovemaking. He felt his anguish for Ellie grow strong again.

"I never knew that. The rape."

"It isn't something one usually speaks of."

"No."

"Now do you believe that I'm Ellie's sister?"

He searched her face, seeking a similarity with Ellie. He wasn't sure there was one. "I never said I didn't. What changed your mind, about killing me?"

She ran a forefinger along her lower lip, thoughtfully. "Because with all her faults, Ellie was one hell of a judge of character. She wouldn't have fallen in love with someone who could kill her. Only I didn't realize it until I met you face to face."

It was her words, and the tone she spoke them in that finally allowed Steven to accept that Carla was who she claimed to be. "Would you mind telling me how you got into my apartment?"

She smiled shyly and pulled a key with a paper tag out of the side pocket of her purse. He recognized his key immediately. "I used this. I was at her apartment, looking for something that might have told me what had really happened to her. I found your keys there."

"Did you notice if her engagement ring was in the apartment?" he asked quickly.

Carla frowned thoughtfully, and then shook her head. "I would have noticed if it was. But she would never take it off."

Steven nodded. "Then whoever tried to kill her, took it."

Carla stared at him for several seconds. "Steven, what's going on?"

Steven shook his head. "I'll be damned if I can figure that out."

"Maybe Ellie found out something she shouldn't have."

"That's the popular theory," he said dryly. "But what could Ellie have learned? She was only the senator's administrative assistant. And Pritman doesn't have any major skeletons in the closet."

"How can you be certain of that? Especially now, with Ellie in the hospital?"

He motioned at the far wall, where dozens of

photographs hung in a random arrangement. These were the photos of his Washington life. Among them were pictures of Ellie alone, he and Ellie, and he and Pritman and Ellie. He pointed to one of the Pritman photographs. "Because I've had him investigated."

Carla's eyes widened again. "*You* had him investigated. Why? Was there something once?"

Steven looked from Carla to the photograph. "A few years ago, when it became obvious that Pritman was looking like a potential candidate, Arnold Savak and I made a decision. If we were going to be Pritman's advisors, we had to be absolutely certain that he was clean. A very reputable security agency handled the investigation. He has nothing important enough in his past to cause him any trouble, politically."

Steven paused. "If Ellie did discover something, it had nothing to do with Pritman's past."

"Okay," Carla said. "Then perhaps it's something Pritman's involved in now. Ellie has access to all the Senator's information. And Pritman's on a lot of committees."

"I still can't see that as a reason."

"Maybe you should put on glasses and take a closer look," she said, her words ringing caustically. In the silence that followed, Carla rose. "And now I'm going to see Ellie."

"They won't let you in at this hour."

She smiled secretively. "I got in here. I'll get in there."

Steven stood and walked Carla to the door. Standing, Carla was about an inch taller than Ellie, and a bit slimmer. "Your friend at Treasury, did he have any ideas?"

"No. But he's looking into it for me."

"If he comes up with anything, will you let me

know?"

Carla stepped through the doorway and turned to him. "Of course I will. And Steven, I am sorry about before."

He smiled. "Don't be. I might have done the same thing."

A half hour later, Steven came out of the bathroom wearing his thick terry robe and toweling dry his hair. As he walked toward the couch, he saw the dark snout of Carla Rogers' gun. It had slipped down between the cushions and she must have forgotten it. He reached for the gun just as the phone rang.

He picked up the telephone on the table next to the couch.

"Steven, it's Arnie. I called the hospital but you'd left already. How did Ellie's transfer go?"

"Fine. There were no problems. How was your flight back?" he asked, belatedly remembering that Savak had flown his private plane from Greyton to Washington and remembering also, his earlier fears about the flight.

"Smooth as glass. No problems, and your car will be delivered to the office tomorrow. I left the keys and the driver's name with Chuck."

"I appreciate everything you've done, Arnie, you know that."

"I know," Savak said easily. "What about Ellie's sister? We still haven't been able to reach her."

"I spoke with her a few minutes ago. She's back and on the way to see Ellie," he said, not wanting to go into their meeting.

"That's great. Will you be in tomorrow, or are you going to the hospital?"

Steven stared at Carla's pistol. It was a Browning nine-millimeter. A very deadly, and very effective weapon. He wondered how Carla would have come into possession of this type of weapon.

"I'll be in tomorrow," he told Savak. "Ellie's scheduled for tests, and there's no sense in my sitting around and worrying."

Steven took a cab to his office. As the driver wound through the early rush hour traffic, Steven found himself looking at the cars around him, searching for a familiar face, Blayne's face. Finally, three blocks short of his destination, he realized that he was allowing himself to give in to the sort of apprehension that could cripple him mentally.

By the time he got out of the cab, he had reconstructed his outlook, and knew that the only way to combat the uncertainties of his present situation, was to go on with his life as if everything were normal. If he didn't go about his typical routine, in his usual manner, then the agents from the Bureau—if they were watching him—would gain extra ammunition for their cannons.

No, he told himself as he entered the building, he had to be the same person he'd always been.

When he reached the Pritman suite of offices, he found that he was the first one in. He went directly to his office, closed the door behind himself, and opened the locked filing cabinet. He took out his attaché case from the bottom drawer, where Savak had left it.

He removed the Entente papers, set them on his desk, and then pressed the privacy button on his phone. When he saw the light go on, he nodded to himself. No one would disturb him until he shut it off. His secretary would see to that.

And then Steven made himself forget about what

had been happening to him, and went to work.

"Make sure that subsections three A and four C are taken out and replaced with what I've just given you," Steven said to his secretary.

"I'll have it for you before lunch," Ruth Benson promised as she closed her steno pad and pushed her glasses back up onto the bridge of her nose. "Don't forget to go over the messages," she added, pointing to a pile of pink slips that had accumulated during his week in Pennsylvania.

"I won't," Steven said. "Ruth, about Ellie—" he began, but was interrupted by the intercom. He picked up the phone receiver and depressed the intercom button. "Morrisy."

"Steven," came the deep baritone of Senator Philip Pritman.

"Good morning, Senator," Steven replied.

Ruth Benson left the office without being asked.

"Glad you're back," Pritman said. "Do you have a few minutes free?"

"I'll be right in," Steven said, hanging up.

Three minutes later he was sitting across from Pritman. The senator's office was modest, smaller in fact than Steven's or Savak's. Pritman liked it that way. It was neat and utilitarian, and fitted the senator's no nonsense bearing.

A sonic humidifier sat on a small table beneath the window, its silent motor sending out a steady mist of vapor. Pritman's sinus condition must be acting up again, Steven thought.

Pritman wore a gray three-piece suit that accentuated his slender build and strong neck. His face was photogenically handsome, and lined with the grooves of responsibility. With his salt and pepper hair combed neatly in place, and his eyes reflecting a somber mein, Senator Philip Pritman conveyed a sense of strength and stability.

"Coffee?" Pritman asked after Steven was settled in the chair.

Steven shook his head. "I've already had a pot this morning."

"I spoke with the head of neurology at Georgetown, a few minutes ago. He assured me that they're doing everything possible for Ellie."

"I know they are," Steven said.

Pritman rubbed his palms together. "Steven, I can't tell you how bad I feel about what happened. Ellie is my right hand. I've made arrangements to visit her this afternoon."

"I appreciate that."

"Steven, don't for a minute think that I didn't want to go to Pennsylvania, when I got news of Ellie's accident. But Arnie and Simon persuaded me that it would be the wrong action for all of us at this point."

While Steven sensed the guilt underlying Pritman's words, he also understood the motives for keeping Pritman in Washington. "They were right, Senator. And in light of what happened in Greyton, your presence would not have been in our best interest."

"You mean that FBI nonsense?" Pritman asked, shaking his head. "That was ridiculous, thinking you would hurt Ellie."

"Someone tried to kill her, Senator," Steven stated, bluntly.

Pritman's expression didn't change. "So Arnie said. But why?"

"I don't know."

"Do you think it has something to do with our proposal?"

"With Entente? No. No one knows about that except for you, Arnie, and myself."

Pritman leaned back in his chair. "I'll be glad when the proposal is out in the open."

"Soon," Steven said.

"Steven, I'll understand if you'd like to take some time off. The proposal can wait a little longer."

He would understand, Steven knew. "Thank you, but no. I think it will be easier to work than to sit around. And now that I've straightened out the Entente problems, as far as legalities are concerned, the rest will be up to you."

"It's good?"

Steven smiled. "Oh, it's better than good, Senator. It will get you into the White House, provided you do your part."

Pritman clasped his hands together, and then rested his chin on them. "I should have taken acting lessons."

"That's not something you need to worry about. You're a natural. What you lack in acting ability, you make up for with honest passion."

Pritman's brow furrowed slightly. "Steven, are you as certain about Entente as Arnold? You've voiced doubts in the past."

Steven stood and walked to the wall of bookshelves. On the center shelf was a photograph of Pritman, with Steven and Savak in the background. It had been taken when Pritman had given his third re-election acceptance speech.

"I like to play devil's advocate. But I'm as sure as I can be, as long as its purposes are as an election tool and a method of arms negotiations. But to put it into effect . . ."

"One day we may have to call on it."

"Yes," Steven said, "should the circumstances warrant it, I'm in full agreement with Arnie as to its use. Senator, if you'd been where Arnie and I were, you'd see that also."

"Arnold's arranged an invitation to that affair for the Chinese delegation. He also worked out a formal introduction with Xzi Tao."

The shock of hearing the name from out of his past jolted him badly. It took Steven a moment to recover his voice and to speak calmly. "So soon?"

"Arnold infers that just being seen talking with Xzi will lend more credence to our plan."

"Be careful of Xzi. He's deceptive."

"Who would have thought a Chinese Intelligence officer would one day be the Ambassador to the United Nations?" Pritman asked. "Hell, who would have thought we'd even have a semblance of normal political relationship with China?"

"Not me," Steven whispered.

Chapter Ten

"What the hell were you thinking about?" Steven demanded, bending over Savak's desk. "Of all the people in the world, you can't let him meet with Xzi."

Savak met Steven's anger with calmness. "I know what I'm doing. Steven, whoever said 'an enemy I know is better than one I don't,' wasn't speaking gibberish. We know Xzi better than anyone else. The man is honorable, in his own way. He'll do whatever is necessary for his country."

"A country diametrically opposed to ours!"

"And to the Soviets as well. Steven, don't stop believing now. We're almost there."

Steven lifted his hands from the desk, his anger easing. "Well at least you'll be there with him."

Savak's lips compressed into a thin line. He double stroked his nose, and then said, "No. It can't be me. It won't work that way."

"Can't? Christ Arnie, this was your idea. You're the tactician behind this enterprise. Pritman needs your sense of timing if he's to meet Xzi."

"It must be you, Steven. Xzi respects you because of what happened. He'll treat you accordingly. If I go with Pritman, it won't have the impact we need."

Steven stepped away from the desk and shook his head adamantly. "I won't go there now, not with Ellie in the hospital."

Savak started to say something, but stopped. Then he nodded. "You're right, Steven. I set this up last week, before Ellie . . . I'm sorry, I wasn't thinking straight. I'm sure Pritman will be able to work it out on his own. He's more than capable. How's the final draft coming?"

Strangely, Steven felt no sense of relief at having escaped the unpalatable task. "I'll have it ready for Pritman tomorrow morning."

"Good. It'll give the senator time to get it down pat for the party meeting."

"I think you're pushing things, letting Pritman and Xzi talk in public," Steven said, unable to let the thought go.

Savak smiled. "I know you do, Steven. And I guess I knew that even when I made the arrangements. But part of the reason we've been successful together is because we compliment each other. You've always been the slow and cautious type, and I've always opted for boldness. The combination works."

Savak paused to lean back in his chair. He gazed up at Steven, his eyes searching Steven's face. "But right this minute, we're involved in a presidential campaign. Slow and cautious doesn't win that race. Slow and cautious merely survives. Besides, Pritman's intelligent. He wouldn't be where he is now if he wasn't."

"It's appearances, not intelligence, that count right now. But you knew that already, didn't you?" Steven asked, his temper flaring with the realization that Savak was pushing him further than he was ready to go.

"Arnie, don't pull a stunt like this again. You came to me thirteen years ago with an abstract concept. You asked me to come to Washington with you and help turn all those things we talked about into reality."

"Steven, I've already apologized."

"No. You apologized because of what happened to Ellie, not for setting this up without talking to me. Damn it Arnie, what we're doing is too dangerous to play games with."

"I'm not playing a game," Savak shot back.

"It sure as hell looks like it to me. Arnie, we're supposed to be a team. Either we work together or I'm gone. And if I'm gone, Entente goes with me and it goes public."

Savak stood defiantly. "You took off for a week! You left specific instructions that you weren't to be disturbed by anyone. When the opportunity to get Pritman into the Embassy party came, I took it!"

"But you won't go yourself."

Steven watched pain replace the defiance in his friend's eyes. "You, more than anyone else, should understand why."

Steven exhaled sharply. The problem was that he did understand. "All right, Arnie. But don't do this again, not without talking to me first."

"Agreed," Savak said. "Oh, I spoke to some people at Justice, about the situation with the FBI. They're going to look into it for me."

Steven nodded. "They'll keep it close?"

"You can count on it. Join me for lunch?"

"I can't. I've got a meeting with Collier, Lerman's legal counsel. He wants to go over the bill Lerman and Pritman are sponsoring for the steel people.

They're introducing it next week and they want to make sure the senator has no problems with the changes that they had made," Steven said as he walked toward the door.

"Which he does. Just remember that we'll need Lerman's backing when the time comes, and I don't want to alienate him because of some minor disagreements with the bill."

"Arnie," Steven said, turning back to Savak and controlling his annoyance at his friend, "the bill will be taken care of exactly the way the senator wants. But he won't go along with those added tariffs that Lerman is trying to tag on, and you know that as well as I do."

"All I'm asking is that you handle the situation tactfully," Savak reiterated.

"Which is what I intend to do," Steven stated as he left Savak's office and returned to his own to review the changes in the steel bill.

Within three minutes of his sitting down at his desk, there was a sharp knock on his door, followed by Simon Clarke's unexpected entrance.

"I hope I'm not disturbing you."

Steven pointed to the chair across from his desk. "What's on your mind?"

Clarke ran a hand through his primly combed hair before saying, "Pennsylvania, the primaries, and the nomination."

Although he should have expected it, Clarke's answer took him by surprise. "And?"

"Steven, you've given us a situation that could be potentially harmful to the senator."

"Simon, every situation is potentially harmful. Even the most innocuous of things can be construed as something dubious by people who want to look at it that way."

"I don't see torture and attempted murder as innocuous. And I don't equate manhandling an FBI agent with the actions of someone who has nothing to be concerned about. Steven, I don't know what happened in Pennsylvania, other than what I've been told, but, I do know what it looks like."

"And what does it look like?" Steven asked, his anger building with the press secretary's thinly veiled insinuation.

"Like very bad press. Steven, we're closing in on our target date. And you damn well know that from the moment Pritman announces his candidacy, the press is going to swarm over us like maggots on a carcass. They'll look into each and every staff member's present life and past history, picking through them for any item that appears newsworthy. They'll look for the dirt too. They always do."

Steven leaned back in his chair and stared at Clarke. Then he leaned forward, clasped his hands together, and rested his elbows on the table. "Simon, do you think I tried to kill Ellie?"

Clarke shifted in his seat. His face remained expressionless. "I certainly hope you didn't. But Steven, whether you did or not isn't the issue. Two members of soon to be presidential hopeful Philip Pritman's staff are involved in a criminal situation. That is news. And Steven, how long do you think we can keep this quiet?"

"Is that all you care about, keeping it quiet?" Steven asked, his voice barely audible.

"In light of what we've been doing for the past several years, what else is there?" Clarke said bluntly.

"Get out Simon, I have work to do. And Simon," Steven added as the press secretary stood, "if the senator feels that I've become a liability to him, I'm quite sure he'll let me know."

The meeting with Congressman Lerman's legal advisor ended just before five.

After straightening out his desk, Steven went to the building's garage. As Savak had promised, his car had been delivered and was waiting for him in his reserved space. He drove to the hospital, and by six, was sitting next to Ellie.

He discerned no change in her. Her eyes were closed. Her chest rose and fell rhythmically. Her color was good, but she was as unmoving as ever.

Behind him, he heard footsteps.

"Mr. Morrisy—Steven?"

Releasing Ellie's hand, Steven turned to Joshua Raden. "Have the results come back yet?"

Raden nodded. His expression was not encouraging. "I'm afraid Doctor Skolnick's diagnosis seems to be correct. But it's still not conclusive. The CAT scan has confirmed the areas of damage, but we still have to determine the full extent of injury to the motor and memory functions.

"I'm also very concerned about the damage to the motor functions. The scan showed that the splinters pushed into the brain didn't just go straight in. It was more of a slicing penetration. With a little luck, the brain itself will sort things out."

"Is that really possible?"

"There have been enough documented cases of regeneration to make me extremely hopeful."

"Can the same thing happen with her memory?"

Raden put his hand on Steven's shoulder. "I doubt it. It's not a matter of the brain being able to shift the work function to a different area, or even to regenerated cells. Memory is a stored commodity. Memory cells are made up of an individual's life experiences. It's not a genetically implanted function. When the memory areas of the brain are destroyed, the information in those cells is lost forever."

Raden paused, shook his head slowly, and said, "I'm sorry, Steven, but there's not more than a ten percent chance that Ellie will retain anything more than poorly fragmented memories."

The finality of Raden's words tore at Steven's heart. He blinked back the emotions that assailed him and, between clenched teeth, said, "She won't remember anything at all, or if she does, it will only be bits and pieces. Is that what you're saying?"

"Pray that her memory is completely gone, or that it's all there. A fragmented memory is the worst kind. Partial glimpses into the past of what once was your life, without having enough of the memory to make even that little portion of the past seem real, would produce horrible psychological torment."

"Without the fragmented memory, will she have a better chance for a normal life?"

Raden glanced away, but not before Steven saw the sadness in his eyes. "What?"

"When thirty years of memories, of life, are wiped away, can there be a normal life?"

Steven poured his third scotch of the evening, and wondered why he wasn't feeling anything. Even his anger at Simon Clarke had abated dramatically in the time since they'd talked. Steven understood the press secretary's motivations, even if he didn't like the man or his methods. But he had known, even when Simon Clarke had been hired, that Clarke had a single-minded drive and ambition, and nothing ever deterred him from his objectives.

Steven rested his head on the back of the couch. The stereo filled the room with soft music. Simon and Garfunkel were singing about being a rock. Steven wished he could become one too.

Over the plaintive lyrics, he heard the doorbell. He set the scotch down on the coffee table and went to the door.

He found Carla Rogers standing on the other side.

"Forget my key?"

She laughed nervously. "Is there any news about what happened to Ellie?"

"Nothing. Come in."

He motioned Carla to the couch, while he went to the bar and made her a drink. Simon and Garfunkel finished their song, and the news came on.

Steven handed Carla her drink and sat down next to her, just as the news announcer's voice took on an ominous tone.

"Late this afternoon, the Pentagon announced that Soviet troops have been moved to the Manchurian border. Political analysts see this as a response to the increased Chinese border troop buildup."

Carla looked at Steven. "It never ends, does it. First one of them goes on maneuvers, than the other stages some sort of a war game. But this time, it seems to be getting out of hand. Do you think one of them will pull back before any real fighting begins?"

Steven studied her eyes for a moment. The dark blue irises almost blended into the black pupils. "Yes, they'll back off. But it will happen again. The two countries are like squabbling siblings. Hopefully, they won't end up like Cain and Abel."

He became aware of the funny expression she was favoring him with. "Is that the Morrisy theory of hostile inter-communistic relations?"

He laughed. It felt strange, almost as if he were betraying Ellie by enjoying himself with Carla. "Common sense mixed with a little knowledge. But who the hell knows anything for sure. I'm not a political analyst."

"Me either," Carla said, her voice changing. "Steven, I've done a lot of thinking since last night, but I'm still not any clearer about what happened to Eleanor. Could it all be a mistake, an accident that everyone is reading too much into? Maybe she really was coming to see you."

He didn't have to think about it. He knew. "No. The lake is northeast of my house. She would have had to be coming from Jersey, not Washington. She didn't know the area very well. It's a summer and weekend getaway place. And . . ."

He stopped, belatedly realizing why Carla had asked the question. "No one told you?" he said, his voice grave.

"Told me what?" she asked, her features turning anxious.

He watched her carefully, trying to judge how she would react. He swallowed hard. "Ellie was tortured."

Her mouth went slack. Steven saw her try to form the words, stop, and take a deep breath. Then her eyes narrowed. "Why?"

"The answer to that is tied into the missing week. Where was she from Monday night until the night she was put into the lake? Everyone is taking it for granted that she left that night to come to see me. That damn note—"

He cut himself off abruptly, seeing the all too

obvious thing he had overlooked. "God damn it! That's what I've been missing! Ellie wouldn't leave a note if she was going away for a week. No, she would never leave without telling Pritman, personally, and making sure he had everything he would need while she was gone."

Carla's brows knitted together, forming a cloud above her eyes. "I'm not following you."

"Whatever happened to Ellie, happened the day I left. She was at work that day. She supposedly went to Pennsylvania that night." Feeling the need for movement, he stood and began to pace. "But she didn't, not of her own will."

He stopped pacing and looked at Carla. "Let's go."

"Where?"

"Ellie's apartment."

They took two cars. Carla drove a Ford Taurus, while Steven used his Bronco.

Ellie's apartment was in a trendy condominium five blocks from American University. The building, an older apartment house, had been renovated and then turned into a condo.

There was no doorman, and Steven used the set of keys that Ellie had given him. They took the elevator to the fifth floor, and went inside the apartment.

Walking through the empty rooms, Steven felt more like a peeping Tom than her fiance. But he set aside his feelings and, working silently with Carla, began a thorough search.

They started in the bedroom. He stared at the picture of himself and Ellie on the mahogany dresser. It had been taken two days after they'd become engaged. She was smiling, holding her hand in front of her so the camera would catch the ring.

She looked so full of life, so happy and content.

He shrugged off the lethargy produced by the picture and went to the closet.

Opening the door, he stepped back and looked at the rack of clothing. On the left, where she always hung them, was her casual clothing. The jeans and tops she preferred to wear when she wasn't working.

He dug into the corner of the closet and came up with her winter boots. "She wasn't coming to see me. Or if she did, it wasn't to stay with me."

"Because she didn't take boots? Maybe she had another pair?"

Steven shook his head. "Boots to go out in the city, yes. But not heavy outdoor boots. She only wore these when we went to Pennsylvania."

He put the boots back where he'd found them, and left the bedroom. Carla followed him to the hall closet.

"Her suitcases are still here," he stated, pointing out the two burgundy leather bags.

Then he went into the kitchen and looked inside the refrigerator. A partially used half gallon of milk was on the top shelf. The date on the carton was the previous Tuesday. He picked it up and sniffed at it.

The sharp and sour jolt filled his nostrils, making him jerk his head back. Behind the milk was a plate holding a chicken breast wrapped in brown paper. Beneath the paper was a pool of congealed blood.

"Ellie had no intention of leaving. She's too fastidious," he said, motioning to the refrigerator. "That chicken breast was Monday night's dinner. And she wouldn't leave milk sitting for a week, either. She'd have given it to one of her neighbors."

Steven continued to look around the kitchen, seeing everything he'd always taken for granted. The little things that marked this place as Ellie's. The flowered paper napkins that she always used were in the center of the small formica table. Her grandmother's tarnished silver salt and pepper shakers were set next to the napkins. A brown and orange kitchen witch hung from the brass knob of a cabinet door.

Ellie's spare keys were hanging on the clear acrylic key rack above the toaster. He took them down and turned to Carla. "Would you get Ellie's mail?"

Carla took the keys and went downstairs. While she was gone, Steven walked through the apartment, trying to ignore the heavy sense of loss that was settling on him. Why did this happen to her? he asked himself again.

He went into the living room, and walked up to the oak wall unit. On the second shelf were a series of pictures. He'd never looked at them closely. Now he did. There was a picture of Ellie and her parents, at her high school graduation. Next to that was the picture of Ellie and Carla that he had remembered the other night. In the photo, their arms were wrapped around each other's waists. He stared at the photograph, and at Carla's upturned face. The picture put to rest any of Steven's lingering suspicions about Carla not being Ellie's sister.

When Carla returned, she was carrying an armfull of mail. They sat down at the dining room table and went through it. Most of the envelopes were bills. There were several sale flyers, and three magazines. At the bottom, Steven found the letter he had mailed to Ellie last Wednesday.

"Nothing," he said in disgust as he fingered the envelope he'd sent. "Tomorrow you should get the mail forwarded. Have it sent to me. I'll make arrangements for her bills to be paid."

Carla's eyes searched his face. "No," Carla said, "I'll take care of that. We have a trust fund that pays for our apartments and little things."

He nodded absently, not questioning her statement. He was just beginning to realize how many things there were that Ellie had never told him about.

Suddenly, once insignificant things were becoming very important to him. He looked around, missing Ellie intensely, and knew that he could no longer wait passively for something to happen. He had to find out why Ellie had been hurt.

He gazed at Carla, studying the planes of her face. "That friend of yours at Treasury—can you arrange a meeting with me?"

Carla moistened her lips with her tongue. "Are you sure you want to do that? You are a suspect."

"Only to the FBI. And Carla, I think you're right. Ellie found out something she wasn't supposed to know."

"Steven . . ."

"It's the only explanation. I don't know what it was, but I'm damn well going to find out."

"Steven, I want to help you," Carla said, her voice low. "What can I do?"

"Just set up the meeting."

Chapter Eleven

Steven was in his office by eight. After returning home from Ellie's apartment, he'd gone straight to bed. But he'd slept fitfully, dreaming of Ellie being tortured by shadows, and of his inability to stop her from being hurt.

His dreams were still weighing down his mind when he sat down at his desk and removed the white plastic lid from the coffee container. He took a sip of coffee, letting the hot drink jog him back to reality, and then looked at the neatly typed papers on his desk.

The Entente proposal was finished. His secretary had left it on the desk before she'd gone home for the night.

Not for the first time did Steven pause to wonder at the enormity of their undertaking. The future of Philip Pritman rested within the pages of Entente. Only Steven, Pritman, and Savak knew what Entente truly meant. Only they foresaw the power it would give the next President.

Steven read the yellow stick-em memo his secretary had attached to the top sheet, asking if this would be the final draft.

He drank more coffee, and went to work. It took him an hour to read the document. When he finished, he marked the memo yes, initialed it, and placed it in the out tray for his secretary to take to Pritman.

Then he started on the next item, a speech he was to deliver to the Washington Bar Association's monthly dinner. The dinner was scheduled for the last Saturday of the month.

He was twenty minutes into the speech when his door opened and his secretary came in. "The special staff meeting starts in five minutes."

Steven smiled at Ruth. "Thank you."

"How is Ellie doing?"

How can she be doing? he wanted to say. She's lying there with her mind torn up. "There's been no change."

"She'll make it," Ruth told him confidently. "She's strong."

Steven stood and tightened his tie. "Ruth, did you notice if Ellie was acting funny last Monday. Did she seem nervous, or upset about anything?"

Ruth shook her head. "She was Ellie. Smiling all the time." Ruth paused. Her large brown eyes grew troubled. Having worked with Ruth for so long, Steven knew her well enough to sense that there was something she wanted to say, but was afraid.

"But . . ."

She straightened her skirt nervously. "Rumor has it that the FBI thinks you—"

He cut her off sharply. His eyes bored into hers. "I don't care what they think. I do care what you think."

"I've been your secretary for six years, I know you didn't do it. I just don't understand how they could even consider that you would do something like that."

"Circumstances," Steven said, paraphrasing Banacek.

"We're all behind you."

Steven stepped out from behind his desk. "I know, and that means a lot to me. Ruth," he said, pausing, "what time did Ellie leave last Monday?"

Steven's secretary's face turned thoughtful. "I left at five-thirty, and Ellie was still here. In fact, she and I were the only ones left. There had been a Foreign Relations committee meeting that afternoon, and everyone was at the Senate Office Building, except for Ellie and myself. Why?"

Steven shrugged. "Just curious."

The conference room was large, twenty by twenty, with a long oval table that sat twelve comfortably. The walls were painted mauve. On the far wall was a television monitor, a tape deck, and a blackboard.

A half dozen people were in attendance. Senator Pritman sat at the head of the table, Press Secretary Simon Clarke was next to him. Roy McGinness, Pritman's domestic policy advisor was in the third seat.

Savak and Steven were across from Clarke and McGinness. Between Steven and Pritman was Linda Commack, the woman who was taking Ellie's place as Pritman's assistant. Linda was young and ambitious and pretty, and all too similar to the thousands of other women looking to move up the political ladder.

Steven nodded politely to McGinness. On a personal level, Steven didn't like the short thin man, but agreed with the others that the obnoxious and opinionated New Englander was the best in the business.

The agenda for today centered around the contingencies for the coming race: The senator's positions on certain bills, and his position on foreign relations.

The meeting started at a fast pace, and did not let up for an hour. They covered the first quarter of their agenda in that hour, but got stuck on the topic of combating the seven declared candidates.

"We can't do anything until you declare," McGinness told Pritman. "We're impotent until then."

"Bullshit," Clarke said sharply. "We're in the best possible position. Those seven are cutting each other to ribbons, and not saying a word about the senator. The fallout has already begun. As of right now we're a hell of a lot better off out of the limelight than in it."

"But every day we wait is time lost from the campaign," McGinness reiterated.

"Simon is right," Savak interrupted, stepping into the role of mediator. "We've all agreed on the time schedule. We re not deviating from it."

"Now is the right time," McGinness said. "If we don't declare soon, we'll lose out in all the early primaries."

Savak tapped the front page of the *Washington Post*. "Not yet. When we declare, it will be at a time that will give us instant momentum. But it's getting close, Roy. A few more of these Sino-Soviet confrontations and it will be time. But we have to wait for the exact moment."

"I fully concur," Pritman said. "Simon has worked out the perfect announcement speech, but the climate has to be ripe."

McGinness frowned. "How much riper can it get. Everyone's scared as hell that China and the Soviets are going to war."

"But they aren't," Steven cut in. "They're sparring, putting up a show of strength. But that's all it is."

"For now," McGinness said. "But it's . . ."

McGinness's words faded from Steven's hearing as he stared at the man. McGinness had messy gray hair. His nose was broad, and his mouth and chin almost concave.

As McGinness made curt argument, Steven found himself wondering if McGinness was the one who tortured Ellie.

As Steven listened to McGinness make his curt argument, he found himself wondering if McGinness was the one who tortured Ellie. Had he tied her up and then used the razor to slice open her skin? Had he poured salt water over the cuts, asking the same question over and over? Had he taken her to the lake, thrown her in, and sent the car hurtling down on her, thinking that she would never be found?

Beads of sweat broke across his forehead. He forced himself to shake off the terrible image and concentrate on what was being said.

". . . I still think we're letting too much time go by. The other candidates are getting all the attention. We need some of that," McGinness finished.

"We'll have all we need. But you'll just have to trust me on that," Savak stated. Then Savak turned to Steven. "How did the meeting with Lerman's counsel go?"

"Just fine," Steven replied, looking at Pritman. "The steel assistance bill is even more important a project to Lerman than we thought at first. Because of that, I was able to get the concessions we wanted. The weak sections have been reworded to give it a more powerful bite. And the tariff add-ons that we caught in the last draft have been dropped. Collier told me that with your backing on the bill, Lerman's been promised enough votes to pass it in the House. He'll owe you big for this one, Senator."

"Which is a part of what we're talking about," Savak interjected at McGinness. "We're not jumping into the arena until we have a solid chance at taking the whole game."

"I think that will be enough on the campaign," Pritman said. "We need to spend some time on real business. Linda, what bills are coming up for votes this week?"

Ellie's stand-in began to read from her notes. She named the three bills that were up for voting, and then fell silent again.

Pritman asked each of his advisors their opinions, and thoughtfully listened to the pros and cons from each.

The meeting went on for another hour, and finally ended at two. As they filed out of the conference room, Steven grabbed Savak's arm and motioned toward Savak's office.

Inside, seated on Savak's couch, Steven said,

"What have you come up with?"

Savak shook his head. "Nothing. It's as if nothing had ever happened to Ellie. I've spoken with my people at the Bureau, and at Justice itself. They won't tell me anything."

"Damn it. As long as the Feds view me as the only suspect, they won't be looking for the real one."

"As soon as Ellie comes out of the coma, she'll clear you. Then they'll have no choice but to look elsewhere."

Steven slapped his thigh. "Arnie, I think if there was any real hope of her being able to remember, Joshua Raden would have told me."

Savak nodded. His eyes went distant. "Wasn't that a coincidence, finding Jeremy's brother living near us after all these years? Steven, how sure is he that Ellie's memory is completely gone?"

"Very sure. The tests have confirmed it."

"I'm sorry, Steven. Maybe I should go to the reception instead of you. Perhaps it's time I faced my past and showed Xzi Tao that he's only a bad memory."

Steven's laugh grated hollowly on his ears. "No, my friend, you've faced your past enough times, it's my turn now."

Savak's intercom buzzed. He picked up the receiver, listened, and turned to Steven. "It's for you."

Steven took the receiver. "Morrisy."

"Steven, it's Carla. You have to come to my apartment. Now."

"What's wrong?"

"My friend is here—the one I told you about."

"On my way," he said after getting her address.

When he hung up, he turned to Savak. "That was Ellie's sister. I have to go."

Concern filled Savak's face. "Has something happened to Ellie?"

"No," Steven assured him quickly. "Carla's arranged a meeting for me with someone from Treasury. Keep your fingers crossed. Maybe we'll finally learn something about this mess."

The drive from his office to Alexandria seemed interminable. It was three-thirty when Steven parked his car in the parking lot next to Carla's tall glass and brick condominium.

Entering the modern lobby, he gave his name to the doorman and went to the elevator.

The ride in the wood-paneled elevator seemed as slow as the car ride from his office. He was brimming with anticipation, and the hope that Carla's friend would be able to help them.

He got out of the elevator on the ninth floor, and walked patiently along the dark carpeted hallway to Carla's door. With each step he felt a sense of anticipation building. Perhaps the time had come for him to learn something that would help him find Ellie's attacker.

A brass plate set beneath a curved knocker read, *Rogers*. Steven knocked twice.

Carla opened the door a few seconds later. She smiled. "That was quick."

Steven followed her into the living room. The room was large, light, and airy. The walls were white, the carpet burgundy. The furniture was gray glove leather and modern. There were large glass sliding doors on the far wall which opened to a balcony.

"Paul," Carla called.

Steven saw a man leaning on the balcony railing. He straightened, turned, and came inside. Carla's friend was about six feet tall, and broad-shouldered. His face was smooth featured and handsome. His eyes were gray-green and hard. He wore a blue Brooks Brothers suit. His black shoes were lace up wing tips. The man, Steven thought, was Government Issue.

"Steven," Carla said as the stranger approached, "I'd like you to meet Paul Grange."

Steven shook the proffered hand. Grange's grip was firm, his palm dry.

"Mr. Grange," Steven said, sizing Grange up. He had seen Grange's type many times before, and knew he was more than just someone at Treasury. "Secret Service?"

Grange shrugged noncommittally. Then his eyes turned hard. "Mr. Morrisy, before we go any further, I want you to understand two things: I've known Ellie Rogers for a very long time; and, the only reason I'm here is because Carla asked me to meet with you.

"When Carla called me, and told me what had happened, I did some checking on the situation with Ellie and you. Everything I've learned tells me you're Ellie's assailant."

Steven checked his rush of anger. He met Grange's hostile stare openly. "Everything *you've* learned is circumstantial. If it wasn't, the FBI wouldn't have backed away from me in Pennsylvania."

"Perhaps they're waiting for something else."

"Mr. Grange, I don't really give a damn what the FBI thinks. I know what I did and what I didn't do. And as far as the FBI is concerned, I've been witness to too many situations where the Bureau, working on what they call inside information, takes one or two facts that seem to fit whatever their puzzle is, and then builds a case thread by thread until they've made it as airtight as possible.

"But the Bureau has no peripheral vision. They put their lasso around the one person they believe is their suspect, and then they wait until they've found what they want. It doesn't matter if circumstance makes their case, not once they've decided who's guilty.

"The problem is," Steven continued, still keeping his gaze locked on Grange," that in too many instances, including the situation I'm involved in, their base facts are wrong. And that's why they're looking at me when they should be looking elsewhere."

A slight flicker crossed Grange's eyes just before he said, "And where should they be looking, and at who?"

"If I had the answer to that question, I wouldn't be here now. I'd be going after him."

"The Bureau believes they're right."

"As I said, I don't really give a damn what lawyers and accountants who like to play with guns believe. I know what the truth is."

"Which is?"

"I didn't try to kill Ellie."

"What would you say if I told you that they might suspect you of espionage?"

Steven couldn't stop himself from laughing. "What the hell kind of information am I accessible to that would make me a spy? I'm the legal advisor to a senator, not a State Department employee."

"Advisor is the key word. You are the *advisor* to a senator who is the head of the Foreign Relations Committee, a member of the Intelligence Committee, and member of the joint Senate-Congressional Watchdog Committee monitoring the NSC. You could be privy to all sorts of information."

"Which I'm not, and which the senator will verify."

"You were also in Military Intelligence. You were a highly trained operative—"

"Lieutenant, not operative," Steven cut in.

Grange ignored the interruption and said, "How easy would it be for an operative to learn things? Especially one as well placed on an important man's staff as you? What real problem would it present for you to get into his private files?"

Steven stepped forward, his hands balled into tight fists. "You son-of-a-bitch. Let me tell you something. I went to Vietnam because I believed what I was told about the war. I went there to help my country, and I'll be damned if I'd do anything to hurt it now."

"Which is another example of what the Bureau has on you," Grange said, studying Steven carefully. "Isn't it true that as a prisoner of war you gave the enemy information? You and Sergeant Charles Latham and Captain Arnold Savak?"

Steven closed his eyes. Finally, after all the years, someone was going to use it. Steven opened his eyes and stared at Grange. "There was no choice in what happened. They used drugs."

Grange nodded. "Two of the men in your squad died; but the three of you—three men from the same town—lived. Why?"

Steven's thoughts turned dark. He fought the bitterness that was growing within him. "Did you read the entire file or just the parts that gave you the most dirt?"

"The entire file."

Grange's answer confirmed Steven's first guess as to who Grange was. It was the only way he could have gotten the files. "Then you know what our mission was, don't you?" Steven asked, unable to keep his voice as firm as he wanted.

"Reconnaissance. Mapping and charting enemy troop movement toward Laos. Its purpose was to get Congressional approval for American troop deployment and bombing of Laos and Cambodia."

Watching Grange's face closely, he said, "Nothing else?"

"No. Should there be?"

There had been no movement of Grange's eyelids, no telltale dilation of his pupils. Grange was not lying. Whatever he had learned from the file, Grange believed it was the truth. Steven felt the darkness within begin to ebb, slightly. "How high is your security clearance?"

"High enough," Grange said.

The simple authority behind Grange's answer

rang true. And it told Steven that something was drastically wrong. "What about the debriefing sessions after we got back?"

"They were there. Each of you admitted giving information. And you were each absolved from charges because drugs were used. You never gave information voluntarily."

"It says we were absolved because of our statements?"

"Yes."

"Didn't those statements tell you anything?"

"What should they have told me?" Grange asked, showing a shade of doubt for the first time since they began their verbal sparring. "They all concurred."

Steven shook his head as a harrowing suspicion began to rise. "What was our mission? What was the information that we gave the enemy?"

"What kind of a game is this? I just told you what your mission was."

Steven moistened his suddenly dry lips with the tip of his tongue. "I take it for granted that you've looked over Savak and Latham's files because of me?"

Grange nodded again.

"And they're all the same?"

"Yes."

Steven realized, belatedly, that he should have expected something like this. "The records have been altered."

Grange's momentary sharp glance to Carla did not go unnoticed by Steven. "In what way?"

"I'm not allowed to tell you that. Were the

records you inspected the Army files or the security clearance reports?"

"Are you saying that the original records contain currently classified material?"

"It was classified when I terminated, and I have every reason to believe it would be classified today," was all that Steven was willing to say. "Which records did you get? My Army jacket or my security clearance report."

"The security clearance reports. As far as the military records, they're the photostats of the files."

Steven breathed easier. "Then maybe they weren't altered. You may not have all the records."

"Oh, I see," Grange said sarcastically.

This time Steven couldn't stop his anger. "You don't see a goddamned thing. You still think I tried to kill Ellie."

"You haven't given me a reason not to."

"I know he didn't try to kill her," Carla said.

Grange looked at her. "Woman's intuition?"

"A sister's knowledge. Paul, he didn't do it."

Grange snorted. "Not good enough. How about it, Morrisy? You want to give me a reason to believe you?"

"Are you married?"

Grange's head arched back. He looked at Steven suspiciously. "Yes."

"Would you kill your wife?"

"Don't be ridiculous."

"I'm not. I'm giving you your reason. I love Ellie. I would never hurt her. It's that simple. You can either believe me or not, that's up to you. And you can also help me if you want, or you can let the

FBI muddle around in their pseudo-intellectual bureaucracy until they've put together enough damning information to put me in Leavenworth for the next century or two, and let the real person behind all of this accomplish whatever it is he's set out to do."

Steven fell silent as he waited for Grange to reflect on his words. Then he saw a subtle shift in the man's eyes. "I don't believe you, but for Carla's sake, I'll give you the benefit of the doubt. But if you didn't try to kill her, who did?"

Steven answered with his own question. "Do I look insane? If I tried to killed her would I be standing here now?"

Grange smiled coldly. "Nobody says a killer or a spy has to be sane. For a traitor who has to protect himself, killing wouldn't be a problem."

"That's just it, Grange, I never turned against my country, even when I had the chance."

Grange pounced on the statement. "Does that mean you were approached by a foreign power?"

"Don't be an ass," Steven said, waving his predictability away. "I need the answer to a few questions."

"That depends on what they are."

"Why does the Bureau think I'm involved in espionage? And why does it center around Ellie?"

Grange looked at Carla. "Please, Paul, what harm can telling Steven do?"

Grange nodded. "It's a ticklish situation. I don't know for certain what the Bureau's reasons are. I have to base my assumption on what they wouldn't tell me, which leads me to believe they're conducting a full scale espionage investigation.

"Hell," he continued, "every agency in Washington has been doing covert investigations for almost two years. Too many secret and highly sensitive matters are getting into Russian hands. You're in a high position, politically, and you're too smart to believe that what's happening with foreign policy matters is the result of an inept administration."

Steven didn't say that that was exactly what he thought. Instead, he said, "But why Ellie? What has she to do with it?"

"I don't know. But she is the senator's assistant. As such, she's been cleared for high level security."

"Of course she has. It's a requirement for the job."

Grange's voice took on a patient tone. "Look at it from my point of view. In all the time the investigations have been going on, she's the first person to have met a mishap. And . . ."

He paused to look at Carla. "I'm sorry Carla, this could go either way. She may have been the leak, and may have decided that what she was doing was wrong. When she told her control she wanted to get out . . . well, that could be another explanation as to why she was taken out."

"Horse shit," Steven snapped.

"It's not unheard of. It's a viable theory, but one I don't want to believe either," Grange added. "Now, it's your turn."

Steven scrutinized the Treasury agent. "All right Grange, in the form of two questions for you to mull over. If what our military jackets say is true, why were all three of us given the Medal of Honor?"

"The escape from the POW camp—"

"A silver star at the most," Steven said disdainfully. "After all, we gave information to the enemy. No," Steven said, his voice going flat, "if you want to learn something about me and about my friends, because you don't want to believe my truth, do it the right way. Get the records, the original ones, including the full debriefings, from Nam and here."

Grange shifted on his feet. His eyes seemed to change as he studied Steven. When he spoke, his voice softened. "I'm not one of the bad guys, Morrisy. I'll admit that I came here knowing that you were the one we're looking for, but after listening to you, I have my doubts. So I'll pull a few strings and see what I can come up with. But in the meantime, I want you to do the same thing at your office. See what you can find out."

"What would I be looking for?"

Grange smiled for the first time. "I'll give you the same answer you gave me, earlier. If I knew, I wouldn't be here, I'd be going after a killer. But Morrisy, if you're fucking with me, I'll destroy you!"

With that, Paul Grange walked out of the apartment.

"Pleasant fellow," Steven commented dryly.

"He usually is. I don't know why he was acting like a tough guy," Carla said, her face registering puzzlement.

"I do. And I don't like it."

Carla put her hand on his arm. Her touch was light. He could feel the warmth of her skin through his clothing. "What did you mean about what wasn't in your military records?"

Steven didn't reply for a moment, his head was still spinning from the encounter with Grange. "The truth about our real mission. Someone altered the records to cover a mistake. A very big mistake."

Steven went to the balcony and stepped outside. He gazed out upon Alexandria, and the Capitol in the distance. The winter sun, low-cast in the west, sent patterns of gold skittering across the glass faces of the distant buildings.

He watched the scene, trying to ease the tension that had corded his muscles and was still churning his stomach. He told himself that he shouldn't be as angry as he was with the outcome of the meeting. After all, it was he who had asked Carla to arrange it.

A short time later, Carla joined him outside. She stood silently next to him, one hand on the railing. Glancing at her, he saw she was troubled.

"What are you doing tomorrow night?" he asked.

"That depends."

"How would you like to go to a diplomatic reception?"

"For any particular purpose?"

"Oh, yes, for a very particular purpose."

Chapter Twelve

"Very well. See if you can penetrate the cover, but carefully. I don't trust the Colombians," Julius Axelrod, Director of the US Secret Service said as he hung up and turned to the man seated across the desk from him.

"Where were we. Morrisy, wasn't it?" he asked Amos Coblehill.

The director of the National Security Agency redistributed his weight on the chair. "Are you sure we're wrong about him?"

Axelrod picked up a single sheet of white twenty-pound bond paper. "According to this report, the risk is within acceptable parameters."

"Which means what?" Coblehill pressed.

"How the hell do I know?" Axelrod growled irritably before checking his temper. "Sorry, this thing's getting me all twisted about."

"No apology necessary. But it worries me, Julius. Asking for those records could be asking for trouble. And not just from the mole."

"It's a chance we'll have to take."

"What makes your man think Morrisy isn't our bird?"

"His actions since they found the woman," Axelrod said, dumping the residue from his meerschaum into a large ashtray. He studied the pipe, running a finger along its side before looking up at his counterpart from NSA.

"Morrisy's actions are those of a man dealing with a severe personal blow. He's suffering a deep loss. He's hurt and angry and wants to know why the woman he loves was almost killed. My man doesn't see it as a front. A deep cover mole wouldn't be pressing for answers. He'd be acting devastated; he wouldn't be forcing issues and voicing doubts that could come back at him in the wrong way. No, a mole would be subtly working to smooth things over and cast suspicion away from him. He'd also have an airtight alibi. One that couldn't be shaken."

"Morrisy's two friends," Coblehill suggested. "They were his alibi. But the plane crash . . ."

"Is still an unknown factor. Whether it was an unfortunate accident or murder will be determined shortly. I've sent one of our people to West Virginia with the FAA inspector. But that's another example of the plausibility factors involved in this case. A mole on our man's level wouldn't take the chance of anything happening to his alibi. He'd have an alibi that was so unshakable we'd end up looking like jackasses just for mentioning his name. And he wouldn't be anywhere near the vicinity of a disposed body, even if it wasn't scheduled to be found for months."

Coblehill nodded. "You're right, of course. I wasn't thinking along those lines. They wouldn't permit that risky a gamble this far into the game."

"Which has always worked to our advantage."

"I'll concede the point, for now, but why the military records?"

"Grange thinks something is in them. Perhaps enough information to point a finger toward the real mole."

"Morrisy will have to be watched carefully, though," Coblehill said.

"Oh, he will be," Axelrod said as he began his pipe-filling ritual. Without looking up from his task, he added, "I'm also concerned about those junior Hooverites. How the hell did they latch onto this? My people had a lot of trouble getting anything out of them. How about you?"

The Director of the National Security Agency held his hands out, palms up. "I couldn't call for obvious reasons. And my assistant had a bitch of a time getting a straight answer from anyone at the Bureau. The best he could come up with is that they've been investigating an espionage ring and have clamped a classified operation lid on it."

"And of course they won't share with any other agency," Axelrod said dryly.

"A national security operation. Their territorial exclusivity. They're acting like we're the CIA."

"I know," Axelrod said. "Earlier, I spoke with an operative who has solid connections in the Bureau. He thinks the Bureau has someone planted on Pritman's staff. He's going to try to run it down."

"Jesus," Coblehill groaned, "if that's true, then everyone's sending in deep cover agents and nobody's telling who or where. For all we know, we may be investigating a Bureau man. I tell you

Julius, this entire operation is becoming ludicrous. Perhaps it's time that we go to the Attorney General and have him order the Bureau to cooperate."

Axelrod shook his head emphatically. "We can't ignore the President's directive. He wants it contained, and that's what we have to do. Bringing the Bureau into it will only put more fingers into the pie. To be candid, I don't think they have any idea of the depth or the sensitivity of our situation. We'll have to keep an eye on them, though. Don't want them popping up where they shouldn't be.

"The files?" Axelrod asked.

"I'll have them sent directly to you. Eyes only."

"Purpose?"

Coblehill blew a stream of air from between compressed lips. "Why the best one possible. Since Pritman is undeclared and not in the race, we set it up to appear that the President of the United States is considering adding Savak and Morrisy to the White House staff, in very sensitive areas. He's asked NSA to run the new security clearances."

"Good," Axelrod agreed. "If Moscow has somehow gotten an ear there, they'll be very pleased."

"What about the other suspects?"

Axelrod depressed the lighter and lifted it to the pipe. He puffed the tobacco into life and, when it was glowing satisfactorily, he put the lighter down. "They're being watched, as is Mr. Morrisy."

After leaving Carla Rogers's apartment, Steven drove to the hospital. As he rode up in the elevator, he found himself questioning his motives for inviting Carla to the reception. But the more he thought about his reason, the harder it was to find an answer.

When the elevator door opened, he set aside his thoughts of Carla, and went directly to Ellie's room. As he reached the observation window, he noticed that the thin curtain was drawn. He leaned against the glass, peered inside, and saw a man standing next to Ellie's bed.

The man's back was to Steven. He was bent over Ellie. He had one hand on her neck, the other was adjusting a dial on her intravenous line.

Something about the way the man was standing seemed wrong. With his sense of alarm growing dangerously strong, Steven rushed to the door, pushed it open and, as he stepped inside, said, "What are you doing?"

The man straightened suddenly and turned. A look of surprised irritation was on his face. "Jesus, Steven, do you always barge into hospital rooms?"

Steven exhaled in relief. His heartbeat slowed. "I think I have enough cause after what's happened to her. What are you doing here?"

Chuck Latham smiled warmly. "Checking up on my patient. Actually," he added, as he walked up to Steven and embraced him, "I think I've been suffering with a bad case of guilty conscience."

Steven's brow furrowed. "Why?"

Latham shrugged, "Because you're my friend. Because I know what you've been going through, and I didn't have enough sense to come to Washington with you and Ellie. I should have been with you for the transfer."

"It went all right," Steven said.

"I wasn't talking about the medical aspects, I was talking about you," he said, tapping his finger over Steven's heart.

"I'm all right, too."

"Are you? I spoke with Joshua Raden. He gave me the results of the tests. Steven . . ."

Steven stepped past Latham and went to Ellie. He looked down at her still form, and felt a wash of sadness spread over him. He swallowed hard. "This isn't right, Chuck."

He felt Latham come up behind him. "I know," Latham said as he put his hand on Steven's shoulder and pressed tightly. When he dropped his hand, he added, "When I got here, I spent an hour with Joshua Raden and the head of Neurology. They have every hope that Ellie will come out of the coma and be able to lead a normal life again."

Ignoring Latham's last comment, Steven reached down and grasped Ellie's hand. Her skin was cool. "Was it strange for you, meeting Jeremy's brother?"

Latham grunted. "It knocked me for a loop. But he seems to be a hell of a doctor. Smart as a whip. Jeremy would have been proud of him."

Steven glanced at Latham. "Why did you really come?"

Latham smiled boyishly. "I wanted to be here for you. You've done the same for me, more times than I can count."

"I really am okay," Steven said, knowing that no matter what Chuck said, his friend wouldn't believe him until he satisfied himself.

"Steven, let's go get some dinner, and then you can invite me to stay at your place tonight. I'm flying back in the morning."

Steven bent over Ellie, and brushed his lips across her forehead. When he was facing Latham again, he said, "Do you want me to call Arnie and have him join us?"

Latham shook his head. "I came here to spend some time with you, not with you and Arnie. I'll see him next trip."

Steven nodded and, with a final glance at Ellie, led Latham out of the room.

Chapter Thirteen

The State Department had chosen the Shoreham for the Chinese Delegation's reception. The elegant ballroom, with its curving dark wood staircase, overflowed with dignitaries. White jacketed and gloved serving people circulated with trays of champagne and hors d'oeuvres, while a seventeen-piece orchestra played classical music on the band-stand.

Every important politician was present, along with all the State Department people who counted. This was not a reception to skip.

Deep within the swarm of high level Washingtonians, Steven and Carla stood together, forming a solitary island amidst the ocean of humanity.

While cordial to all who acknowledged him, Steven held himself back from joining the myriad of conversations. His thoughts, vacillating between Ellie and seeing Xzi Tao again, were introspective. The timing was bad. He did not want to have to face an old ghost with his life in so volatile a state.

"What is it, Steven?" Carla whispered after his silence had drawn on for a long time.

He glanced at her, and saw concern mirrored in her eyes. "I'm sorry, I've a lot on my mind."

"I understand," she said.

Steven took her hand and squeezed it gently before letting go. He believed she did understand. "It's all right. Have I told you that you look stunning tonight?"

In truth, she did, Steven realized. Her formal gown was white silk. It hugged her slim torso before flaring at the hips into a ruffled bottom. It was a simple gown, and very elegant because of its simplicity.

"Thank you. Did you find out anything at the office?" she asked.

Steven shook his head. It had been a normal day at the Pritman offices. Everyone had worked at their usual frenetic pace. He'd spent most of the day going over the Entente proposal with Pritman, showing the senator the points he had refined during his week in Pennsylvania. But he'd learned nothing that might shed some light on what had happened to Ellie. Savak had also spent a good deal of time calling his contacts. No one, it appeared, seemed to know anything.

"According to my secretary, Ellie was her normal self all day last Monday. Which means, that whatever she found, it was after everyone left, and—" He cut himself off when he saw Pritman leave the group of senators he had been talking with, and start toward the side of the ballroom.

He followed the senator, bringing Carla with him as he had all evening. He had explained, earlier, that he wanted to keep Pritman within hearing distance. Carla had not questioned him.

When Pritman stopped to chat with a senator

from California, Steven said to Carla, "We'll talk about Ellie later."

"Of course," Carla said as a tall and heavyset man angled toward them.

"Steven, this is a pleasant surprise," the man said, coming to a halt in front of Steven, and cutting Pritman off from view. "I had expected Arnie."

Steven took the offered hand and smiled. "Jack, it's been a while. Arnie was tied up," Steven lied smoothly as he turned toward Carla. "Carla Rogers, meet Jack Metzger. Jack's with State."

"Miss Rogers," Metzger said, shaking Carla's hand. "It's a pleasure." To Steven, Metzger said, "I'd like to get together with you and Arnie, soon."

Steven didn't miss the open message. Metzger wanted to be on the winning team, and he had already decided who that would be.

"I'll arrange it," Steven replied.

"Miss Rogers," Metzger said, according Carla a bob of his head before fading into the crowd.

Steven checked on Pritman, who was still talking with the Californian. "What was that about?" Carla asked.

"Jack's a career man with the State department. He wants to make sure his career will continue to climb."

Carla appeared puzzled. "How can you do that for him?"

"Not me, Pritman. Metzger's looking toward the next election. If Pritman is nominated, and wins, Metzger wants to be visible to us."

"I see," Carla said, nodding.

A moment later the crowded room seemed to ripple. The thunder of a hundred conversations ended abruptly when upper doors of the Grand Ballroom opened.

The Chinese Delegation had arrived.

Steven tensed as the delegation came down the curving staircase. Waiting to greet the Ambassador on the main floor, the Vice President, the Secretary of State, and the American Ambassador to the U.N. along with their wives had formed a formal reception line.

Steven spotted Xzi Tao the minute his foot touched the top step. The years were stripped away in an instant as he watched the tall Chinese dignitary descend the staircase and be greeted by the Vice President.

Steven bit his lower lip as his internal tension mounted.

"Steven," Carla said, tugging lightly on the sleeve of his tuxedo.

Steven shook off his sudden paralysis and looked at her. She had a linen handkerchief in her hand, and raised it to his lips. She wiped quickly, coming away with a scarlet stain of blood.

Steven wiped his tongue across his lip, and felt the sting from where he'd unconsciously bitten down.

"What is it?"

"Nothing. I'm fine," Steven said as the last of the Chinese delegation filed past the reception line.

"Morrisy," came a low, almost guttural voice. Steven turned to find Harry Canter coming toward him. Canter, a political columnist for the *Washing-*

ton Post, was a short bald man with a barrel chest and big, hamhock-like hands.

"I can't tell you how sorry I was to hear about Ellie's accident. How is she?" Unfeigned worry carried in his voice.

"It's too soon to tell," Steven said, uncomfortably.

"Is it true, about her memory?"

"We don't know yet."

"If there's anything I can do, please call me. I like Ellie. She's one of those rarities in Washington, a nice person."

"Thank you," Steven said, and then introduced Canter to Carla, to whom he again offered his regrets, and his help.

Then Steven saw Pritman nod to him and start toward Xzi Tao. Steven's stomach churned. It was time.

"Harry, would you look after Carla for me?" Steven asked the columnist.

The newsman followed the direction of Steven's gaze. "On baby-sitting duty tonight?"

Without replying, Steven went after the senator. He caught Pritman just before the senator reached the Chinese delegation. "No specifics, Senator. Pleasantries and a hint of a future meeting that could be of immense benefit to both our countries is what we're after."

Pritman favored Steven with a patient and forbearing look. "I've been contending with dignitaries long enough to have learned how to say one thing and mean another. But don't worry, Steven, I shan't try to play at international diplomacy until I have the authority to do so, and," Pritman added with a quick smile, "I shall remember that a Chinese name is surname first."

They stopped a polite distance away from the State Department Chief of Protocol and Xzi to wait for the Chinese Ambassador to finish speaking with the British Ambassador. While they waited, the churning in Steven's stomach worsened.

Xzi seemed not to have aged at all, except for a slight graying at his temples. His face was smooth and unlined. His eyes were bright and intelligent. He had maintained the slender physique that Steven remembered, and his carriage was as proud now as it had been in Vietnam.

A few moments later, the British Ambassador bowed formally and stepped back. The Chief of Protocol motioned Pritman and Steven forward, and said, "Ambassador Xzi, may I introduce Senator Philip Pritman and his aide, Steven Morrisy."

The Chinese aide translated rapidly. Xzi bowed politely to Pritman and spoke in Chinese.

"It is my great pleasure to meet you, Senator," said his aide, translating the greeting into precise English.

"And mine to meet you, Ambassador," Pritman replied, shaking Xzi's hand.

Steven, staring at Xzi, wondered why he was using an interpreter. Xzi spoke English with a perfect upper class British accent.

The man from State stepped out of hearing as soon as the introductions had been performed. When they were as alone as they could be in the huge crowd, Steven saw Xzi glance at him. He did not miss the hint of humor submerged in the

Chinese Ambassador's eyes.

And then Pritman, in opposition to his earlier diplomatic words to Steven said, "I was under the impression that you spoke English quite well."

Xzi's aide stiffened and stepped forward. Xzi froze the aide with a sharp glare before saying, "At times I find it convenient not to understand another's language, Senator. Something we were taught by our neighbors."

Pritman nodded. "Yes, the Soviets do enjoy playing those games."

"All in the name of diplomacy," Xzi said. "And Mr. Morrisy. I have heard much about you and your endeavors in Washington."

Steven, expecting something like this from Xzi, kept his features stoic and worked hard to speak in a smooth and level voice. "I didn't realize I rated a dossier."

Xzi laughed. "A habit of mine is to know the people with whom I must eventually deal. If I am not mistaken," he added to the senator, "my country shall be dealing with you in the coming years."

"I've indicated nothing to warrant that assumption," Pritman said softly.

"It is our political analysts who see you in our future."

"If that does happen, I hope it will be of benefit to both our nations, and to assure the security and sovereignty of our countries."

"That would be my wish as well."

"I am encouraged to hear that."

Xzi suddenly switched to Chinese. His interpreter said: "Nations of greatness should consider all options. To rule out anything is to be foolish in the use of power and intellect."

Without missing a beat, Pritman said, "I fully concur, Ambassador. I hope the remainder of your stay will be enjoyable, and I look forward to meeting you again."

"I too look forward to such an event, Senator Pritman." After his aide translated the last, Xzi gave another polite bow, turned to Steven, and spoke rapidly in Chinese.

"It was a pleasure meeting you, Mr. Morrisy."

Steven did not reply; he bowed formally and turned away. Behind him, Steven found the reason for Xzi's reversion to his native Mandarin. The Secretary of the Treasury and the White House Chief of Staff were waiting for their audience.

Away from the group, Pritman said, "He seems nice enough. Well educated. The file Arnold gave me was very good."

It should be, Steven thought, Savak and he had put most of the information into it. And Steven was sure that Savak had somehow gotten the rest from the CIA data bank. But he'd never told Steven exactly how.

Suddenly, the tension drained from his body. He had succeeded in keeping a calm front throughout their talk with Xzi. He felt he should be proud of himself, but the acrid taste in his mouth brought on by his roiling stomach told him he had a long way to go before he would be able to talk or even look at Xzi without pain.

When Steven and Pritman reached Carla, Harry Canter was still with her.

"When will you announce?" Canter asked, pouncing like the true predator he was.

Pritman studied the columnist for a moment. "You sound very sure that I will."

"Senator, I've been in this town for thirty-eight years. I think I can be sure about you. I'd just like to know when?"

"Harry," Steven cut in, but Pritman stopped him with a gentle hand on his shoulder.

"Harry, if I decide to run, you'll be among the first to know."

Canter laughed. "Along with the rest of the media."

Pritman shrugged. "How do you feel about it?"

"About what, Senator?"

"My running, if I decide to?"

"Good," Canter said. "I'd like to see you in a hard race for a change."

"And why is that?"

"To see what you're really made of Senator."

"If I throw my hat into the ring, Mr. Canter, I'll make no promises at all."

"That's a novel approach, but somewhat naive."

"Perhaps, but there is one thing I'll damn well try to do—stop the world from eating itself up."

"And how would you do that?" Canter asked quickly.

Pritman smiled broadly. "If I enter the race for my party's nomination, and if I am nominated, you'll be among—"

"—The first to know. Very good, Senator. Very good indeed. Steven, Miss Rogers."

Alone again, Pritman looked at Steven. "I think

I'd best make the rounds and go. I want to get some sleep tonight. Big day tomorrow."

"Good idea, Senator. By the way, the items you want to question on the Scott-Wellborn bill are in my memo. Pay particular attention to sections eighteen and twenty. I don't think they can hold up under constitutional scrutiny. Get the committee to accept your changes and the bill will work."

"I'll make sure they agree. Miss Rogers, if there is anything at all that I can do for Eleanor, call me. Steven, please give Miss Rogers my private numbers."

"Thank you, Senator," Carla said.

"Don't thank me. Eleanor has been my right hand. No, hell, she's been half my brain these last two years. I need her back."

When the senator was gone, Carla turned to Steven, her expression one of surprise. "That wasn't an act. He really meant that, didn't he?"

"That's what I've been trying to tell you. Pritman didn't harm Ellie. He adores her."

"I—"

Before Carla could go on, Steven's beeper went off. He silenced it immediately. "Do you mind if we leave?"

"Not at all," she said.

While Carla retrieved her wrap from the coat check room, Steven went to the bank of phones, dialed his service, and learned that the call was from Savak with an urgent call back request.

He jabbed sharply at the buttons on the phone. Carla reached him just as Savak answered. "Couldn't you give me a chance to leave before reporting in?"

"It's not that," Savak said, his voice coarse. "Steven . . ."

At the strained sound of his friend's voice, Steven's hand tightened around the receiver. "What Arnie? Is it Ellie?"

"Not Ellie. I . . ." Savak paused again, and Steven heard him take a deep breath. In the momentary silence, Steven's nerves began to shriek.

Finally, Savak spoke again. "Banacek's been trying to reach you. The FAA has made its initial determination. They found the remains of explosives and a detonator in the wreckage of Londrigan's plane. Steven, this whole thing is getting crazier. Londrigan and Lomack were murdered."

Chapter Fourteen

The only illumination on the dark road came from the headlights of the black Oldsmobile sedan. They were twenty miles outside of Washington, heading nowhere. Steven was behind the wheel of the Senate staff car that protocol required he use for tonight's affair.

"You couldn't have done anything about it," Carla said, repeating what she'd told him shortly after he'd explained about Londrigan's sabotaged plane.

Rationally, Steven understood that he was blameless; but the more he thought about the deaths of his friends, the more certain he was that they had been killed for only one reason: to destroy his alibi.

"Someone's weaving a hell of a trap around me," he stated as anger cleared the cobwebs from his mind. "First they tortured and then tried to kill Ellie. But they didn't do it right. Then Londrigan and Lomack were murdered because they would have been able to prove I was with them that night."

"You don't know that," Carla cut in sharply.

"Yes, I do! You heard what Grange said about how it's all leading to me. No, they'll make their case now." Steven hit the brakes hard, U turned the car, and headed back toward Washington.

"Where are we going?"

"I want to see Ellie."

He felt her eyes searching his shadowed face and sensed the question she wanted to ask. Instead of explaining, Steven took his wallet from the inside pocket of his tuxedo and handed it to Carla. "Joshua Raden's card is in there, please get it out."

While Carla hunted for the doctor's card, Steven picked up the cellular phone and dialed the operator. When she came on, he asked to be connected to the sheriff's office in Greyton.

Suddenly Steven thought about his house in Pennsylvania, and how it had been searched. Then he remembered thinking he had seen Blayne waiting for him in front of his house the other night.

He looked in the rear view mirror, giving in to his growing paranoia. Seeing nothing but blackness behind him helped him to hold back this unwanted onslaught of anxiety.

A half a minute later, when Banacek's voice came over the speaker, Steven said, "It's Morrisy. What happened?"

Oddly enough, with Banacek's easygoing voice drumming in his ear, Steven felt himself grow calm. "The FAA people found C-3 plastique residue. The control cables and engine parts had been rigged. The radio was tampered with, also. That's why Sam never radioed a distress call.

"The local police chief said that FBI Inspector

Blayne showed up requesting information and spouting his national security bullshit. Morrisy, what the hell are you involved in?"

"You still feel the same way about me that you did?"

"You didn't hurt her, if that's what you mean."

"That's what I mean. Sheriff, I don't have an answer for you, but I'm starting to get one hell of an idea. Thank you."

"Morrisy, I'll have to let the prosecutor know about this."

"I understand, Sheriff. I'll keep in touch," he pressed the disconnect button and handed the phone back to Carla. "Call Raden."

She dialed the number and gave Steven the phone. The doctor answered sleepily on the fourth ring.

"Joshua, it's Steven Morrisy. I'm on my way to the hospital. Call the floor and let them know to admit us."

"What is it?" Raden asked, his voice sounding fully alert.

"I need to see her. It's important."

"All right. I'll meet you there myself and take you through."

"It's not necessary."

"Yes it is. It's midnight Steven. The hospital frowns on unauthorized visitors."

Raden was waiting for them in front of the main entrance. After Steven parked the car at the curb, he and Carla joined the young doctor.

"Thanks for coming, Joshua," Steven said.

Raden waved off Steven's words and led them past the security guard and into the hospital. They walked to the elevators, and rode up silently.

When they reached the door to Ellie's room, Steven turned to Raden and Carla. "I'd like to be alone with her for a few minutes."

Inside, alone with Ellie, he went to the side of the bed and gazed down at her. He took her hand between both of his and tried to warm her cool and unresponsive skin. He looked at her face, wanting only to see her eyes open and alert.

His throat constricted. He swallowed several times before he was able to speak. "They say you can't hear me, Ellie, but I think you can. You know I love you, and that I want to be with you. But I don't know if that will be possible any more. Ellie, this may be the last time I can come here. There are people who say it was I who tried to kill you, but we know better."

He paused, moistened his dry lips, and said, "I've done a lot of thinking about what's happened to you, and to me. And I also know that as long as the authorities think I tried to kill you, they won't look for any other alternatives. So it's going up to be up to me to find out who did this to us. It's the only way I can help us. I know now that they won't let you live. I should have seen that from the beginning, but I didn't make the connection until tonight, when I found out that Sam and Larry had been murdered.

"Ellie, they were killed because they would have been able to clear me of trying to kill you. And whoever's done this to you can't take the chance that you might recover and remember. Since I'm the only suspect, it falls on me to stop him from doing it again. I won't be back until I do. It's the only way I can protect you."

He drew her hand to his mouth, and kissed the soft flesh. Suddenly, her hand tightened around his. He looked at her face. Her eyes were open. Her mouth was moving.

His heart pounded. He turned to the observation window. "Get in here. Get in here now!" he shouted.

He turned back to her, "Ellie, what is it?"

Her eyes were still open. Her hand was tight on his. Her lips were moving, but her voice was barely audible. He bent closer, straining intensely, but the words he was hoping to hear were only incoherent mumbling sounds.

Raden, Carla, and several nurses rushed in.

"She's coming out of it. Damn it, Joshua look," Steven ordered.

Raden didn't look at Ellie; he looked at the monitors and the readout from the EEG. After studying the patterns for several seconds, he came over to Steven. Very gently, Raden peeled Ellie's fingers from Steven's. While Raden was loosening Ellie's second finger, her muscles went limp and her hand dropped lifelessly back on the bed.

Raden probed Ellie's eyes with a thin stainless steel flashlight. "It was an involuntary muscle reaction. It's not unusual in cases like this," he added as he straightened and faced Steven.

"But her eyes," Steven stated, pointing to her

open eyes. "And she spoke, Joshua. Damn it man, she spoke to me."

Raden shook his head slowly. "All her vital signs are the same, except for the initial EEG burst when her muscles spasmed. She's still in the coma. I'm sorry, Steven."

Staring into Raden's compassionate eyes, Steven saw the truth. He took a long and shaky breath. "It's all right," he said to Joshua before turning to Carla. "Do you want to stay longer?"

"No more," Carla whispered. Her face was chalky, her lips were stretched into a tight line. But it was the plaintive quality of her voice which told Steven that Carla was even more shaken than he.

He put his arm protectively around her, and drew her close. "Let's go."

Without releasing her, he started to the elevator. Raden walked on Carla's other side. Steven pressed the call button, and turned to Raden.

"Will you hire a private duty nurse. Someone who will be with her twenty-four hours. I don't want her left alone again, not for one second. Joshua, whoever tried to kill her will try again if she regains consciousness."

Raden gazed at him for a moment, making Steven wonder if the young doctor thought he'd gone around the bend. "It will have to be two nurses," Raden said at last.

"I'll send you the money to pay the nurses. Joshua," he began, but stopped as a new thought slipped through the chaos of his mind, "before his last mission, did your brother write home? Did he tell you anything about what he was doing?"

Raden blinked several times. "He always wrote. And when he did, the letters were all marked over, large blocks were censored out. He explained it once, saying that if anything was missing, it was because the army didn't want the enemy to gain information. But yes, there was a letter, it came almost a year after he was captured."

"A year?"

"It was mailed from the States. Did you know he was going to be a writer?" Steven shook his head. "He was. Before he went into combat, he would write down his feelings. He put it all on paper: The reason he was going out, what his mission was. And then he would give it to his buddy in case he didn't make it back. They had an agreement. No real mail out of Nam. Only when they got home."

"Do you still have it?"

Raden nodded. "At home."

"I'd like to see the letter."

"Why not," Raden said as the elevator door opened.

They started in, but stopped when the duty nurse called Raden's name. All three turned at the same time.

"A security guard just called up. There's a problem with Mr. Morrisy's car," the nurse said, her eyes darting nervously toward Steven.

"What kind of a problem?" Steven asked.

"He said two FBI agents are searching it."

* * *

Paul Grange walked down the long hallway to the director's office. In his right hand were two manila files. The first was the FAA report; the second was Morrisy's army records which had been delivered that afternoon.

He held back a yawn as he entered the director's empty outer office and went straight to the inner door. He knocked once.

"Come."

Grange entered the office and went to the desk. Julius Axelrod looked up from his paperwork and motioned for Grange to sit on the chair next to the desk. "Long night, eh?"

Sitting, Grange placed the manila files on his lap and said, "Yes sir, a very long night."

"Have you come to any conclusions?"

Grange's face was pensive. He tapped the files with his index finger. "The service jackets you were able to pull for me, back up my initial feeling about Morrisy. The C-3 they found in the plane in West Virginia confirms it. There's no doubt that the military records dealing with that mission in seventy-one were altered. I'd sure as hell like to know what really happened to Morrisy and the others."

"You couldn't find anything?"

Grange shook his head sharply. "It's exactly what Morrisy said. It's not what's in the files that counts, it's what's been taken out. But I have some leads, and there was definite CIA involvement. But it'll take a while. We'll have to bring in some of the general staff officers who were part of Command Saigon at the time—if we can."

Axelrod filled the bowl of his pipe, tamped it, and lighted the tobacco. "We can, and we will. Put it in a report, my eyes only, and I'll make a determination on how best to proceed. I'll need it by nine."

"Sir, when I spoke to Tom in West Virginia, he told me the same two FBI agents were there as well—Blayne and Grodin. They know the plane was rigged."

Axelrod frowned. "We couldn't stop them."

"If they arrest Morrisy, they'll jeopardize our entire operation."

"I'm well aware of that. But the problem is more complex than that. By killing the two men, the mole has now thoroughly locked in Morrisy as the only suspect."

Pausing, his face thoughtful, Axelrod stared down at his pipe. "There's got to be a way to turn this around. Something that we can do to turn things our way."

"There is one thing," Grange stated. "I could recruit Morrisy. He's already agreed to nose around the senator's offices. And he did go through the special CIA training when he was in Military Intelligence. He'd be a natural to sniff out the mole. His incentive is personal, and once he knows what's going on, he'll be more than willing to cooperate."

Axelrod puffed studiously on the pipe. No trace of approval or disapproval showed on his face. "No good. We'd have to step between the Bureau and Morrisy to do that. And if we have this figured right, then the mole would know something was wrong as soon as we took that action. Paul, even though you think Morrisy is a white hat, you could be wrong."

Grange exhaled with annoyance. "We could run him cold, use him to draw the mole out."

"Iffy."

"It may be our only option," Grange said, holding the director's gaze with his own. "As I see it, the frame around Morrisy was set quickly because Ellie Rogers didn't die. The longer the investigation goes on, the more time the mole has to tighten the frame. But to frame Morrisy effectively, the mole's active participation is needed. He wants Morrisy to take the blame, so he's got to orchestrate more incriminating situations for Morrisy. By getting Morrisy to run, the mole will have to come out into the open.

"And in order to make Morrisy look guilty, the mole has only limited options. The first would be to find Morrisy and report him to the Bureau. The second would be to put Morrisy down and if he takes that option, it would have to be made to look like an accident, suicide, or have him somehow put down by the Bureau so that they would take the credit and the mole would stay clear."

Grange paused, his hands working absently on the files. "The third alternative would be to have his Soviet contacts take Morrisy and then put out the propaganda that Morrisy went back to Russia. That would serve the same purpose as killing him and would be more preferable than having Morrisy in the Bureau's hands where they run the risk of having the whole thing blow up in their faces.

"However, and what is of prime importance," Grange continued, "is that we run the operation, and not have to play catch-up with the mole. And Morrisy is smart. Once he figures out what's going on, he'll go into the cold alone. If he does that, the mole will have a shot at him before we can protect him."

Axelrod nodded ponderously. With Grange's assessment of the situation matching his own, the choice was gone. "How will you put him on the run?"

"I plan on meeting with him tomorrow to see if he'll tell me what happened in Nam. After that, I'll tell him that I learned the Bureau is going to arrest him. I'll send him to a safe house and have word leaked to a couple of people on Pritman's staff."

"Which house?"

"Hagarstown."

"Let me think on it, Paul. I'll let you know in the morning."

Grange stood. He left the files on Axelrod's desk. "Sir, I don't want to lose this one. And I don't want to see Morrisy take the fall either."

Chapter Fifteen

Steven, with Carla and Raden standing close behind him, looked out the lobby window. He saw Blayne and Grodin, the two agents from Pennsylvania. Their search was apparently over, for they were hovering next to the car, waiting for Steven.

Their presence followed a logical sequence of events, Steven knew, a sequence that started with Ellie's disappearance, and ended with the discovery of the sabotage of the airplane in West Virginia. Yet he found it hard to accept that the two men had come to arrest him.

"Do they really expect you to just walk out to them and let them arrest you?" Carla asked.

Steven felt a strange calmness settle over him. He had made a promise to Ellie, minutes before, and he would not break that promise.

"I'm a lawyer," he said, answering Carla's question, "not a 'desperate fugitive.' They most likely believe that I think I can outmaneuver them legally, as Savak and I did in Greyton." Steven turned to Raden. "Joshua, can you have the guard go upstairs and stay with Ellie until the private nurse comes?"

Raden went to the uniformed security guard and

said something in a low voice. The guard spoke into his radio, and then went to the elevator.

"All set," Raden said when he came back. He'll stay in Ellie's room until he gets relieved."

Steven gazed at Raden for several seconds. "Thank you, Joshua. Now I want you to get your car, and then wait for me on the next block."

"Maybe I should stay," Raden offered, glancing at the two men who waited for Steven.

"Bad idea. I don't want you involved. I need you to help Ellie. Carla, go with him," Steven said. Then, without giving Carla a chance to speak, Steven strode to the door and went outside.

Blayne and Grodin stiffened as soon as they saw him. Steven kept a straight face, nodded to the agents, and started forward.

Halfway to the car, he heard the sound of high heels coming up behind him. She hadn't listened to him. She was involving herself anyway.

Stopping several feet away from the agents, Steven drew himself tall. When he spoke, he put just the right degree of outrage and anger into his voice. "I hope you have a warrant this time, Blayne. A real one!"

Blayne smiled broadly. "Your makeshift alibi is dead, Morrisy, just like the two men you killed. You work quickly, don't you? Who did you hire to rig the plane?"

"Without a warrant, you had no right to search my car."

"Probable cause, Morrisy."

"Bullshit. Get the hell out of our way, we're leaving."

"Only with us," Blayne stated before looking at Carla. "Miss, I'd suggest that you find another way home."

"Who are you?" Carla asked, feigning ignorance.

Blayne withdrew his wallet and showed her his identification. "FBI."

Carla looked from the agents' identification to their faces. "I . . . I don't understand," she stammered.

"It's simple, Miss," Grodin said. "Your friend here is a murderer. I'd think you'd want to put as much space between him and you as possible, and quickly."

Carla looked at him, her face blank. "You're mistaken. Steven isn't a . . . a murderer."

"Tell that to his girlfriend," Grodin said.

Steven took Carla's elbow and squeezed it hard. He turned to her and said. "Call Arnie Savak. Tell him what's happening."

Carla stared up at him. He stood still as her eyes searched his face. He sensed that she was afraid for him, and wanted to help him somehow.

"I don't want to leave you alone," she said, finally. She held her evening bag in her right hand and nervously tapped it against her left palm.

"I'll be fine."

Carla sighed loudly, and then nodded. "I'll be right back."

As she turned, Blayne started forward. "Don't try what you did the other day," he warned Steven.

Shadowing Blayne, Grodin drew his gun. "He won't."

Carla was a half dozen feet away, walking backward, and watching the scene unfurl.

"Put your hands behind your back. Turn slowly," Blayne ordered, taking his cuffs from his belt clip.

When the two agents edged forward, Steven accurately read the anxiety on Blayne's face, a reminder of their scene in Banacek's office. Steven's exhale was filled with capitulation. He dropped his shoulders and turned as Blayne had instructed.

Steven's pulse raced. He knew he had only one chance to break free.

He felt the sweat begin to pop out across his brow. And then, the instant he felt the metal of the handcuff touch his skin, time ceased to exist.

Steven curled his fingers around the cuff, spun, and pulled Blayne forward and off balance. The agent's face registered shock, and then anger. Behind Steven, Grodin shouted a warning.

Steven ignored Grodin, counting on the fact that Grodin wouldn't shoot as long as Blayne might be hit. With his free hand, Steven gripped Blayne's wrist, twisted hard, and spun him around. Then he yanked up on the wrist, hammerlocking the arm.

Blayne bit off a sharp yelp of pain.

As he started to turn Blayne to face Grodin, Steven heard a woman's loud cry. Then he saw Carla racing forward, screaming wildly at Grodin. When the agent's attention wavered between Steven and Carla, she lunged at him and slammed her purse into Grodin's face.

The agent gave a strangled groan, and sank to his knees. His service piece fell from his hand as he tried to staunch the blood spurting from his nose. Carla was there instantly, kicking his pistol from his side.

A second later Carla had Grodin's pistol in her hand. She stepped back, just out of his reach, and aimed the weapon at his head.

"Don't be stupid," Blayne pleaded.

Steven tightened his grip further, cutting off Blayne's air. Blayne fought, kicking his legs back, trying to knock Steven down. Steven countered by lifting Blayne up and putting more pressure on the hammerlock.

"Morrisy," he gasped, "you're making it worse."

Steven laughed. "What's worse than being charged with three murders and espionage?"

"Morri—"

Steven's anger peaked. Using a technique from Nam, Steven pulled back hard and cut off Blayne's air supply. Twenty seconds later the inspector's body went limp. Steven released Blayne, bent quickly, and pressed two fingers to the base of Blayne's neck.

When Steven stood, he turned to Carla. "He's out."

Steven picked up Blayne's handcuffs from the sidewalk and put one end on Blayne's wrist. He removed Blayne's revolver, straightened, and looked at Grodin. The younger agent was still on his knees. The only thing that had changed was that he held a handkerchief to his nose.

"Get over here."

Grodin stood. "You can't get away with this."

"I already have."

When Grodin reached Steven, Steven backed

away slightly. "Put the cuff on your right wrist."

Grodin shook his head. "Morrisy—"

"Do it!" Steven shouted, aware that they were standing in front of a hospital. "Now!"

Grodin knelt next to Blayne. He put on the cuff and locked it, never once taking his eyes from Steven.

"Give me your cuffs and keys. Then give me Blayne's keys." Again, Grodin followed Steven's orders.

"Pick him up," Steven ordered. When Grodin held Blayne, Steven motioned him to his car. "Back seat."

Carla opened the door, and Grodin manuevered himself and Blayne in.

"Cover them," Steven told Carla as he went to the driver's side and got in. After he found the ignition key and started the engine, he turned and pointed the pistol at Grodin. "Carla, get in."

When Carla was in the passenger seat, and again covering the agents, Steven drove to the rearmost area of the parking lot and parked in the darkest spot.

He shut off the ignition, motioned Carla out, and stared hard at Grodin. "You tell Blayne that he's wrong about me. Tell him that you've both been sniffing at scents that were put under your noses."

"What the hell are you talking about?" Grodin asked.

"Just make sure you tell him to check out whoever is giving him the information about me. And then both of you should try using your heads for a change. You might even learn something. Give me your left arm."

When Grodin hesitated, Steven reached back and grabbed his wrist. Bending it over the seat back so the agent couldn't fight, he snapped the second set of cuffs on Grodin. Then he hooked Grodin to the steering wheel.

"What the hell are you doing? You can't—"

Steven smiled, reached back with his right hand, and found the nerve endings at the base of Grodin's neck. He pressed hard, once. Grodin slumped forward.

Standing, Steven said, "They'll be out for at least an hour, maybe more." He went around to the passenger side and leaned in. With two hard chops of the pistol, he smashed the radio. Next, he went to the trunk, opened it, and tossed Blayne's pistol in. After wiping Carla's fingerprints from the pistol, he placed it next to Blayne's, and then threw the car and cuff keys into the trunk before slamming it closed.

"Let's move," he said, taking Carla's hand and running back to the staff car. Steven sped out of the hospital's curved drive, and turned the corner.

Raden was parked there, sitting on the fender of his car. When Raden saw Steven, there was obvious relief on the doctor's features.

Steven went over to the young doctor after telling Carla to wait for him. "I need a favor," Steven said. "But you're free to say no."

Raden glanced from Steven to where Carla sat in the car. "Ask."

"I want to see Jeremy's last letter, but I can't

involve you any more. Not after what just happened."

Raden hopped down from the fender. "I've been involved since I got the paperwork on Ellie. Follow me to my house."

"No. I'll call you later, when I'm some place safe."

"All right. I'll bring the letter when I hear from you. Steven," Raden said in a strained voice. "I don't know what's going on, but if there's some way I can help . . ."

"There is," Steven said. "You never saw me after I left Ellie's room."

Raden nodded. "I'll be waiting for your call."

In the car once again, with his heart slowing and the reality of what he'd done sinking in, he turned to Carla. "Thank you. That was fast thinking."

He sat still under her silent scrutiny, until she said, "I couldn't let them take you. What are we going to do now?"

"I'm going home to pack a bag and make a couple of phone calls. You're going home to call your friend Grange and have him square you with the Feds."

"They don't know who I am."

"They will."

Steven was acutely aware that he was racing against the clock. Although he told Carla that the agents would be out for an hour, there were other factors involved. Someone might have seen the confrontation and reported it to the police, or either agent might have awakened sooner than the hour Steven had predicted. And even if the men were undisturbed for the full hour, he was well aware that he'd already used up a half hour of his escape time meeting with Raden and getting home.

But the time had not been wasted. During the drive to his townhouse, he'd fallen back on the old habit he'd learned in Nam. He began to plan objectives for the hours and the days ahead. His first objective was to simply disappear. The second objective was harder—to formulate his hunt for the killer.

When he reached his townhouse, he left Carla in the car with instructions that if she saw anyone coming, cops or FBI, she was to leave and not look back.

He entered cautiously, checking to make sure that no one was there. When he was certain that he was alone, he shut down the thermostats, and took a suitcase out of the hall closet.

He checked his watch. Time was going too fast. He went into the bedroom and quickly and methodically threw clothing into his suitcase. Next, he took off his tuxedo and put on jeans and a pullover shirt.

Then he went to the closet and pushed aside the clothing until he found a pair of Ellie's jeans and a sweater. He packed them into the suitcase for Carla.

Whether Carla knew it or not, the Bureau would be sending out a bulletin about him and Carla. Their last description would be used—that of a woman wearing a white formal gown and a man in a black tuxedo. Neither of them could afford to be seen in their formal wear.

Steven shut the suitcase and took it into the living room. He left the case in the hallway, and went into the den. He saw that the phone machine was blinking.

He rewound the tape and played it back. There was a message from Paul Grange, asking Steven to call him. Grange left two numbers which Steven wrote down.

He put the numbers in his shirt pocket, and went to the wall safe set inside the bookshelves. He opened the safe and removed an envelope. The envelope contained his emergency money—twenty hundred dollar bills.

He put the money in his pocket, went to the phone, and dialed Arnie Savak.

While the phone buzzed in his ear, he glanced outside. He saw Carla, silhouetted in the car window. She was bent forward. He thought he saw her bring the car phone to her ear.

Just as Steven was about to give up on Savak, his friend answered. Speaking rapidly, Steven filled him in on the night's events, finishing with, "Arnie, I have to hide for a while."

"I understand," Savak said, his voice tense. "I'll start making calls. I'll try to get this taken care of, but I don't think it will be as easy as in Greyton. I don't know what the FBI thinks they have on you, but we've got to find out exactly what it is, so that we can get it taken care of. Call me when you're safe."

There were a hundred things he wanted to say to his friend, but none of them reached his lips. "Arnie, thank you."

"Get moving!"

Steven hung up, took a final look at his home, and started out. He stopped at the hall closet and pulled out his leather jacket. Outside, he tossed the suitcase into the back seat and got behind the wheel. He started the car, put it into drive, and pulled away. Then he slammed on the brakes.

"What?" Carla asked.

"We can't use this car. The FBI knows the vehicle, and Carla, I'm sure the phone is bugged. How else could Blayne have known I'd be at the hospital? Damn it!" he shouted, hitting the steering wheel with the heel of his hand. "I used the phone in the house. It's probably tapped as well."

He thought back to his talk with Savak, and realized he'd given no clue as to his destination. "We'll have to switch cars. We can use my Bronco. When I pull it out of the garage, put this one inside."

Minutes later they were in the Bronco and heading for the highway. "Did you call Grange from the car phone?" Steven asked as he turned the corner and headed for the Beltway.

Carla looked at him sharply. "Yes. He wasn't in." Steven nodded. "I saw you from the window."

"I left a message," she said a moment later. "I told him that you were in trouble. I said we'd try to call him later."

"Nothing else?"

"No."

"Okay. The Feds won't be able to make anything of that."

"Where are we going?" Carla asked when Steven pulled onto the beltway and headed toward Maryland.

"A motel," he said. An hour had passed since leaving Blayne and Grodin in the car. He had to act as if the alarm was out.

They decided on the Red Top motel just outside of College Park. The nondescript motel catered to businessmen and college students. It was as safe as they would get. During the ride there, Carla had gone into the back of the Bronco and changed into Ellie's jeans and sweater.

"My shoes," she said as Steven rolled to a stop.

"It's late," he replied, looking down at her formal satin high heels. "The clerk won't notice." He handed her a hundred dollar bill.

She was gone for five minutes. When she got back in, she smiled and said, "We have a back room. Drive around the rear. It's the second room, first floor."

They parked in front of their door and went inside. The room was decorated in motel modern. There were two double beds, a small desk, and a chained television all set atop a gold wall-to-wall carpet. The placard on the fake walnut veneer TV told them that HBO was free of charge and on channel three. A framed landscape print hung between the two beds. The bathroom was large and utilitarian.

Steven closed the door and turned to Carla. "Call a cab."

She looked at him from over her shoulder. Her jaw jutted stubbornly forward. "Why would I do that?"

"I want you safe."

She turned, standing arms akimbo. "Steven, my sister loves you and trusts you. And there's someone out there who tried to kill her, and is trying to frame you for it. I owe it to Ellie to stay with you until we find out who."

Steven shook his head. "Carla, all I'm doing is dragging you deeper into something you may never be able to get out of."

"I came willingly, didn't I? Besides, don't you think that what happened at the hospital shows you that you need me?"

"I would have handled Grodin."

"Maybe so, but we'll never know. Why don't you give the macho act a rest and say thank you."

He gave up the argument and smiled. "Thank you."

"You're welcome. What's our next step?" she asked, her eyes brightening.

Watching her, Steven realized that even though he'd asked her to get out of this, he was glad she'd stayed. He wanted her help. "Joshua Raden and his brother's letter."

Carla's brows joined ends. How will that help us?"

"It depends on what Jeremy wrote about the last mission. If it's what I think it is, it may help Grange to believe me."

Steven called Raden, who answered on the first ring. Without identifying himself, he gave the motel's name, address, and the room number. Raden told him a half hour.

"There's some vending machines in the office. I'll get us coffee," Carla said.

When she left, Steven turned on the television and laid down on the bed. He put his hands behind his head, and watched the all news cable station.

For the last hour and a half, he had been running on adrenaline, planning his next move without thinking back to the reason for the arrest attempt.

Why was the Bureau so damn sure he was the one? Was it because of the plane? Or was there more to it?

He thought back to his first meeting with Grange. Was the Secret Service man's explanation about classified information being leaked to the Russians accurate? It didn't make any more sense now than it had when Grange first told him.

No one in Pritman's office had access to the high echelon secrets that Grange had spoken of. It had to be something else.

Before he could think of an answer, he found himself watching the TV and seeing the reception for the Chinese Ambassador. The newscaster was speaking in voice-over as the camera panned across the room. Steven watched Pritman talking with the senator from California. Then Steven saw Xzi Tao enter the grand ballroom and shake the Vice President's hand.

"That's spooky," Carla said when she came back. She knelt on the side of the bed, and handed

Steven a cup of coffee.

The video tape ended and the newscaster began to editorialize about the possibilities brought out by the Chinese Summit that would be taking place over the next few weeks.

Steven went over and shut the TV off. He took a sip of coffee and grimaced at the bitter taste.

"I know," Carla said, apologetically, "but it was all they had."

"It's fine." He looked at his watch, and then out the window.

"It's only been fifteen minutes," Carla said.

Steven nodded. "I've been trying to figure out what Grange said, about the espionage. It doesn't make sense."

"None of it makes sense," Carla said. "Not the espionage, not Ellie's being hurt, and not your being blamed for it."

Steven felt a surge of warmth for Carla. "You're really something. Five days ago you were lying in the sun in Bermuda. Now you're hiding out in a motel in Maryland, defending the man accused of the attempted murder of your sister."

Carla shrugged her shoulders.

"We'll find out who did it," Steven said in a low voice.

Carla's eyes changed. Something dark formed within their recesses as she said, "I know we will."

Arnold Savak impatiently paced the bounds of his living room, a white and gray portable phone glued to his ear. On the seventh ring, Simon

Clarke picked up the phone.

The senator's press secretary sounded sluggish and irritated when he answered.

Without preamble, Savak said, "I want you to have a series of statements ready for Pritman. All of them will be about Steven and Ellie and their present situation. All of the statements will, in one form or another, say that Pritman is sticking by Steven."

"What happened?" Clarke asked, concern replacing the anger of seconds before.

"Steven had another tangle with the FBI. Simon, make the statements good. They must be convincing."

"Arnie, what the hell is going on. You know we can't afford something like this."

"I know that. But we can't take the chance that all of this is a setup to discredit Pritman. If it is an opposition ploy, and we don't react positively, we'll blow the nomination before we got our shot at it. Simon, I'm going to try and keep this contained, but if I can't . . ."

"I don't like the way this is escalating," Clarke said. "Maybe it's time we cut Stev—"

"I don't want to hear it. Just get those statements done," Savak ordered before hanging up.

Savak tried another number, but was informed that the person he was calling had left for home a half hour before. Savak paced again, his muscles demanding exercise, as he waited the ten minutes he deemed necessary before calling again.

When the ten minutes were up, he dialed the number. As he waited for the call to be answered, he pictured the house where the phone was ringing. It was a large white clapboard colonial, set on an acre of well manicured grass, in a very expensive section of Alexandria. The house was owned by the Assistant Director of the Federal Bureau of Investigation.

When the phone was answered, Savak said, "Tim, it's Arnie Savak. I need your help."

"I was expecting your call," Timothy Courtney said in a guarded voice. "But you're wasting your time. Arnie, your friend stepped way over the line tonight. I can't help you any more, not after what Morrisy did to Blayne and Grodin."

Savak stared at a painting on his living room wall. His eyes narrowed. "You owe me, Courtney. No ifs, ands or buts. You came to me two years ago and asked for my help and for Philip Pritman's help. You got it, and you also got your promotion. Now I'm asking for your help."

"Arnie, there's nothing I can do," Courtney said, "Morrisy assaulted two agents. A federal warrant was signed by Judge Crawford, not more than a half hour ago. The entire Bureau is on alert. I can't stop his arrest this time."

Savak began to pace again. "But you can keep it contained within the Bureau. You can make sure that the arrest orders read not to shoot."

Savak heard the man's deep sigh. "I won't make you any promises, but I'll see what I can do."

"No. You'll damn well do it. Because, Timothy, if you don't, when you wake up tomorrow morning, the only future you'll have left in Washington will be in planning how to pack up your house and family and move back to Pocatello."

"Are you threatening me?" Courtney demanded, his voice rising sharply.

"No," Savak replied in a half whisper, "I'm just stating a fact. I need your help. You're my friend, Tim. And Steven is my friend. I don't turn my back on my friends, and I expect the same thing in return."

There was a pause in which Savak heard the Assistant Director breathing unevenly. Finally, Courtney said, "I'll see what I can do. But Arnie, no matter what you think you can do to me, if this is some sort of cover-up to protect Pritman, I won't be a part of it."

"This isn't for Pritman. He has nothing to do with this. It's for Steven."

After hanging up the phone, Savak began to pace again. A few minutes later, his doorbell rang. Wondering who would be calling on him, he answered the bell.

When he opened the door, he not only knew who, but why. A hastily dressed Simon Clarke was standing there, behind him were Roy McGinness and the rest of Philip Pritman's top advisors and staff.

They marched inside and, when they were all standing in the living room, Simon Clarke said, "We're going to talk about this situation, now."

Chapter Sixteen

Exactly thirty minutes after hanging up on Joshua Raden, headlights blossomed in the room's window.

The lights went out. A car door closed. Steven peered from behind the window's curtain. "It's Joshua," he told Carla, who went to the door and opened it.

The young neurologist was wearing the same clothing he'd been in earlier. Under his arm was a small metal letter box. He put the box on the desk and took off his jacket.

"Did you have any problems after we left you?"

Raden shook his head. "I went home and waited for your call. No one else called or came by."

"Good," Steven said, relieved that the Feds hadn't connected Raden to him.

"I'll make the arrangements to get Ellie two private duty nurses, first thing in the morning. But in the meantime, I called the head of security and had the guard cleared to stay with Ellie until the end of his eight-to-four shift. At four, another guard will replace him. That guard will stay in the room until the first private duty nurse starts her shift."

"Thank you, Joshua," Steven said. "It means a lot to me."

"Steven, I brought all of Jeremy's letters," Raden

said, pointing to the metal box.

Steven went to the desk, sat, and opened the lid. He took out the letters. Without putting them in any order, he began to read.

Before he'd finished the first censored paragraph, he was transported in time and distance to the days of the war. As he read, he visualized everything Raden had written. The presence of the two people in the room were forgotten. All there was, was the Vietnam—The Nam, The War.

Steven read for almost an hour before he finished all the letters. At the end, he separated Raden's last letter, written the night before they'd left on their mission.

Rubbing his eyelids, Steven exhaled softly before facing Carla and Raden. "Your brother saw the fallacy from the very beginning. Christ almighty, why didn't he say something to us."

"It was only a guess," Joshua said.

"A prophetic one. If Jeremy had lived, he would have been a hell of a writer."

"Would one of you like to tell me what you're talking about?" Carla asked.

Steven moistened his dry lips. The emotions brought out by the letters were still thick in his head and voice. "The mission in Nam when we were captured. Joshua's brother was with us."

Carla blinked. She looked from Steven to Joshua Raden and back. "Then you knew each other before this?"

"No, it was coincidence. We met on the helicopter that took your sister from Greyton Memorial to Georgetown. I was on duty when we got word that

Ellie was being transferred here, and was being accompanied by a Steven Morrisy of Senator Pritman's staff. I recognized Steven's name immediately. And, because important names, like Senator Pritman, command big attention at the hospital, I was able to wrangle a spot on the transfer team."

"I understand," she said with a single bob of her head. "But what about the mission?"

"In a funny sort of a way, it parallels with what's happening to Ellie and to myself," Steven said softly. "The mission, like the frame being engineered against me, was very different from what it was made to appear."

"How?" Carla asked, her eyes wide with interest.

"Not now," Steven said abruptly. He picked up the last letter Jeremy had written in Vietnam, and looked at it. "Joshua, may I keep this letter? I'll do my best to get it back for you."

"Of course. If it will help you."

"I believe it will. Thank you Joshua, for everything. Take care of Ellie."

Frowning, Raden cocked his head to the side. "You sound like you won't be back."

Steven took a moment before answering. He glanced at Carla, and then looked down at the letter before saying, "I don't know if I will be back. But I'm going to try like hell. Just make sure that Ellie is never alone. Not for a minute."

"Steven," Carla said, "if you really think Ellie's in danger, I can have Paul arrange for protection. He'll do it for me, and for Ellie."

Steven wondered just how close she and Paul Grange really were. And exactly what their relationship was. "Are you sure?"

"He'll do it for me," she repeated.

"A private duty nurse is still a good idea," Raden said. "I planned on putting Ellie into coma recovery therapy next week. We'll need a trained nurse for that. It's a laborious procedure, done on a continual basis throughout the day."

Steven put his hand on Raden's shoulder and exerted a light and friendly pressure. "Joshua, the FBI will question you, eventually. You must maintain that you had no knowledge of what happened at the hospital."

"I know what to do," Raden said. "You just make sure you take care of yourself. Ellie will need you when she comes out of the coma. Don't forget that, Steven."

"You'd better go," Steven said. "Even a doctor needs sleep. I'll be in touch when I can."

He walked Raden to the door. When the doctor was gone, Steven felt as if a piece of him had left with Raden. Then he told Carla about Grange's message.

"We should call him, now," she said.

"Not yet. I need to talk with Arnie and see if he's had any luck with the Bureau."

"Do you think that's wise?" Carla asked. "They may have his phone tapped too."

Steven picked up the phone and dialed Savak's house. "It's a chance I'll have to take. But I doubt they've tapped his phone."

"Where are you?" Savak asked after Steven said hello.

"It's best if you don't know. Have you come up

with anything?"

"Too much," Savak said. Steven tensed at the tone of Savak's voice.

"What's wrong?"

"A Federal judge has signed a warrant for your arrest."

Steven had already accepted that the warrant would be issued. "Can't something be done?"

"I've spent the last few hours trying. I've called in every favor owed me, but no one will touch this. I was able to pull one string, though. What happened tonight will be contained within the Bureau. There won't be any further police bulletins, and whatever might have gone out already, if anything, will be followed up with a rescinding memo. No one will know about the warrant, except for the Bureau agents."

Steven felt a little of his apprehension ease. "That will help."

"Steven, I—" Savak began, but his voice broke suddenly.

Steven's nerves went tense again. His knuckles turned ashen as he gripped the phone tighter. He made himself ignore the feeling of unease, and waited silently for Savak to continue.

"I'm sorry," Savak said at last, "this isn't easy for me. I . . . Damn it, Steven!"

Steven sat heavily in the chair. He was aware of Carla watching him. Her mouth was taut with concern. He was sure of what would come next. He and Savak had touched on it in Pennsylvania.

Swallowing hard, Steven closed his eyes and said, "I'm not going to help you this time, Arnie, spell it out."

"The West Coast meeting is set for the end of next week. In nine or ten days, Pritman will be on the front page of every newspaper in the country. It's what you and I have worked so damn hard for. Steven, are you willing to let it all go down the tubes?"

Steven held his silence. He wasn't sure what he wanted at this very moment. But he was getting angrier at his friend than he wanted to be.

"Steven, no matter what, I promise that I'll find a way out of what's happened. But you've got to work with us. If this gets out, and Pritman's connected to it, then it will all be for nothing."

Steven wiped his hand across his eyes. He blinked hard. "Say it, Arnie. I want to know exactly what *they* want from me."

"A letter of resignation dated the Friday before you left for Pennsylvania."

Like Jeremy Raden's prophetic letter from Nam, Steven's forecast of his future had come true as well. The taste of copper flooded the back of his mouth. He turned to Carla, who was still intently watching him. "All right, Arnie."

"Steven, they felt that there was no choice left. I tried to make them see what was happening, but . . . You do understand what I'm saying, don't you?"

Steven closed his eyes, squeezing off the visions of defeat and loss that were massing against him. If his friends, as well as the people he'd worked beside for almost thirteen years, didn't believe him, then who would? Yet the governing rule of political aspiration was that in order to stop something from tainting a candidate, that candidate had to be distanced and protected from the problem at all costs. Steven was one of the costs.

"Oh yes, Arnie, I understand perfectly," Steven said in a tight voice. "But I'd like to know who made the decision."

"The whole group. It was a . . . a majority decision. Pritman doesn't know yet. Since the meeting, I've given this a lot of thought. I believe in you, and in us. If you want, I'll drop off the staff. We can work together to find out who's behind this mess."

Steven moistened his lips. Savak's offer was tempting, but rash. Pritman could navigate the campaign trail without one of them, but not without both, especially the tactician and architect of the Pritman organization.

"No, Arnie," he said in a low voice. "You have to stay with him."

"I'm going to find a way to help us, Steven. I promise I won't stop until I do. But you'll have to keep in contact with me."

Steven laughed. "I'm running. I may not be able to."

"Call me at the office, once a day. Vary the times. Use my private number. If there are any changes I'll let you know."

Steven hung up abruptly, unwilling to say more to Arnie. Intellectually, he knew it had had to happen. Politics is not bound by friendship, and Pritman had no choice but to disenfranchise himself from Steven and his troubles. But it hurt like hell.

Savak's offer had helped to ease the hurt, but it wasn't enough to make up for the lack of faith and trust from the others.

"What was it?" Carla asked.

Steven twisted the kinks out of his neck, stalling long enough to get his thoughts under control. "I've been dumped. I'm no longer part of Pritman's staff. In fact," he said, smiling sardonically, "I haven't been employed since the Friday before Ellie was hurt."

Carla's eyes deepened with disbelief. "I'm sorry Steven. I . . . But they can't do that now, not after last night. People saw you at the reception. You were videotaped with Pritman."

"That means nothing. A strong denial citing the Vietnam Stress Syndrome, and someone's omission of having my name taken off the guest list. When I showed up at the reception and forced the issue, Pritman didn't want to embarrass me in front of everyone so he let me play my usual role."

"But I was there. I can back you up with the truth."

"To what point?," Steven asked, shaking his head. "Besides, it's already been done." He paused, flashed a smile he didn't feel, and said, "What Grange said the other night—about the leak originating from Pritman's office. Do you believe him?"

Carla hesitated. She glanced down. Her hands were entwined. She released them and looked back at him. "I've known Paul for a long time. He wouldn't have said it if it wasn't true."

"You have no doubts about him at all."

She met his eyes openly. "I'd trust Paul Grange with my life."

Steven searched her face. "Are you lovers?"

Carla sat on the edge of the bed. "Paul and I went

to school together. I've known him a long time. He's a good man, Steven. You can trust him."

Seeing that Carla had pointedly avoided answering the question, Steven didn't press the issue. Rather, he said, "It's not just your life I'll be trusting him with, it's my life as well. But Carla, no matter what Grange thinks, there's no way that one of Pritman's top level people is a Soviet spy.

"And as far as Pritman himself, he's the most straight-forward politician I've ever known. Oh, he knows how to wheel and deal, and how to make political arrangements. He has to, because that's his job. But he's never made those easy accommodations that can come back to haunt him later."

"You're telling me that he's an honest man."

"As honest as a politician can be, yes. And that is what's wrong with Grange's theory, unless . . ."

"Unless what?"

Steven shook his head. "I'm starting to see conspiracies."

"What kind?"

"The kind that get very big people into very deep water."

"How big?"

"The very biggest. The President is in political trouble. His administration is in a mess. The way each of his foreign policy maneuvers is countered as soon as he makes them, is getting him farther and farther behind in the public's image. It also lends credence to a theory of security leaks. If a circumstantial case can be made to show that someone outside of his staff was giving foreign powers our secret policy decisions before they were acted on, it would exonerate the President in the public's eye.

"And, if our thinking is right, Philip Pritman has the best chance of knocking the President out of the box. What," he continued, not taking his eyes from her, "if the White House is pointing the finger at Pritman to make it appear that someone on his staff is sabotaging American foreign policy? Wouldn't that derail Pritman's campaign before it began and, wouldn't it just about assure the President of re-election?"

"They wouldn't do that," Carla said, her voice edged with outrage. "And Paul Grange wouldn't be a part of it."

Steven's laugh was bitter. "Grange wouldn't even know. And of course they would, if they had the chance. There are plenty of precedents. You're old enough to remember what happened to Eagleton during the elections. You don't think a reporter dug up that tidbit on his own, do you? No, it was hand fed to him, with lots of love from the other side.

"Carla, dirt and scandal are becoming a mainstay of the election process. The public sits and watches and when the innuendos and implication pile up, they watch to see who can climb out of the muck and stay in the race.

"Think about it!" His words became staccato. "The smallest hint that someone on Pritman's staff has given secrets to our enemies will discredit the senator. The public won't think about the good things he's done for them, all they'll remember was that he'd exercised poor judgement by hiring a spy. He wouldn't even get the nomination, and that would be a shame."

"I can't accept the idea that the President would do that," Carla reiterated.

"The President may not even know. Someone on his staff could be behind it. And that's only one possibility."

Carla hugged herself. "I hope it's the wrong one," she whispered, "And you still haven't answered my question. What are you going to do?"

Steven hadn't answered the question because, until that very moment, he hadn't known. Then, looking at Carla, he made his decision. "Trust you."

Steven took Grange's number from his pocket, and called the Secret Service man. "It's Morrisy," he said when Grange answered. "You left a message."

"Where the hell are you?" Grange asked abruptly. "Are you on a safe line?"

"I believe so."

"You'd fucking better be," Grange shouted. "Are you out of your mind? Assaulting two FBI agents?"

"They didn't give me a choice."

"What the hell are you trying to do, Morrisy? They aren't going to let you get away, you know that don't you?"

"They'll have to catch me, and that won't be easy."

"This isn't Nam, Morrisy. You don't have any jungles to hide in. You need help!"

"Carla was with me. You'll have to get her uninvolved with the Bureau. Can you do that?"

"I figured she was the woman with you. I checked with a source at the Bureau. They haven't identified her—yet. They won't now."

"Do you still think I tried to kill Ellie? That I'm some sort of a spy?"

Steven caught the hesitation in Grange's reply. "I've been looking into that matter you suggested."

"And?"

"I need to discuss it with you in person. And as soon as it can be arranged."

"Where?"

"I'm sticking my neck out for you, Morrisy, so you're going to have go along with me on this. Are you sure no one knows where you are?"

"One person, but I trust him implicitly."

"From your office?"

"No."

"Carla is with you."

It was a statement that Steven didn't bother to refute. "If she is?"

"There's an old farm outside of Hagarstown. My uncle's. Carla knows where it is. She's been there. But don't take any main highways. Use country roads once you're out of Washington. Wait until rush hour before you leave. Get lost in the traffic, and then take your time. Don't reach the location until noon. I need the time to work things out."

"Grange, can you arrange protection for Ellie?"

"How much safer can she be than in the hospital."

That's what Steven had thought until tonight. "I don't think she's safe at all. Whoever tried to kill her, killed my friends because they could alibi me. Ellie was supposed to die. She's still alive, so she's still a target. And even though everyone thinks she's permanently lost her memory, the person who put her in the lake can't take the one chance in a million that she might remember what happened. Do you follow what I'm telling you?"

"I think I do. I'll have it taken care of. And Morrisy, for what it's worth, I do have strong doubts about the validity of the Bureau's charges. May I speak with Carla?"

Steven handed Carla the phone.

"Paul, I think Steven is right about Ellie," she said while looking at Steven. A moment later she smiled, and gave Steven a thumbs up sign.

"Yes, we're fine," he heard her say as he stood and went into the bathroom.

When he came out, Carla was off the phone. "Did he tell you about Hagarstown?"

Carla nodded. "I know the farm. We'll be safe there. It's out-of-the-way. Are you going to give him Raden's letter?"

"I don't know what I'll do, yet. That will depend on Grange."

Chapter Seventeen

Julius Axelrod hung up the phone and relit his pipe. He looked around the office, wondering when he would get a chance to go home again. He thought that it wouldn't be for quite a while.

And, to add to his problems, Morrisy had been forced into the cold before he and Grange had been able to set their own plan into motion.

Axelrod's anger at the Bureau's meddling sent his blood pressure rising dangerously. The damn idiots at the Bureau never know when to stop. They looked upon themselves as the country's watchdog, and trusted no one but themselves.

He breathed deeply, exercising a firm control over his emotions, and told himself that this was not the first time, nor would it be the last that the FBI would interfere with a security agency operation, knowingly or unknowingly.

After setting the dark thoughts of the Bureau aside, Axelrod leaned forward and pressed a memory button on the phone. Rapid paced electronic tones filled the air as the connection was made. Four rings later, Amos Coblehill answered the call.

"Morrisy is on the run, without control. The Bureau's men made a grab for him at the hospital," Axelrod reported matter-of-factly to the director of the

National Security Agency.

"Is he covered now?" Amos Coblehill asked. Coblehill's voice, booming over the speaker phone, sounded as tired as Axelrod felt.

"To a good enough degree. Grange was able to talk him into going to a safe house. Once he's there, we'll leak word in tomorrow's NSC session. Pritman will be briefed on it. Then, if everything goes according to schedule, we'll be able to contain and conclude the situation."

"I'll inform the President," Amos Coblehill said.

Axelrod drew on his pipe, and exhaled fully before adding, "But Morrisy is at risk until he meets Grange, tomorrow. The Bureau's move put him into the open, and no one knows where he is. He wouldn't tell Grange."

Steven woke just before seven. Looking across the chasm created by the two beds, he saw Carla sleeping peacefully. He decided to give her a few extra minutes, and went into the bathroom. He shaved with the disposable razor the motel supplied, took a quick shower, and dressed.

When he came out, Carla was sitting up, wiping at the inside corners of her eyes. She wore one of his tee shirts. Her breasts were outlined beneath the thin fabric. Her hair was disheveled.

"Is there time for me to shower?"

Steven nodded somberly. Carla got out of the bed and walked to the bathroom. Watching her, Steven found himself thinking that if this was another time and place, his feelings toward this very desirable woman would be different. And if there was no Ellie.

But there was an Ellie, and he loved her. When the bathroom door closed, Steven turned on the TV and dressed to a network morning show.

When the news came on, he watched, feeling relief that there was only a brief mention of the Chinese reception, and nothing about himself.

He shut off the television, went to the desk, and reread Jeremy Raden's letter. He pictured Jeremy Raden, as he had been when Steven had first met him, and wished that he had known the man for longer than the three weeks they had been together.

Then he took out a sheet of motel stationery and began his letter of resignation. Even though he knew it had to be done, the right words were difficult to find. He went through five sheets of paper before he finally reduced what he had to say to a simple paragraph of resignation for personal reasons.

He signed the letter, folded it, and put it into an envelope. After addressing it, he slipped the envelope into his inside jacket pocket.

"All set," Carla said, coming out of the bathroom.

"Hungry?"

She nodded. "Can we chance it?"

"We'll get something in the coffee shop. To go," he added when he saw her expression of worry.

They drove the Bronco to the front, and parked in the only available space. As they entered the lobby, Steven bought a stamp from the desk, put it on the envelope, then dropped his letter into the mailbox. The coffee shop was crowded, and although he felt uneasy, they waited patiently until they were able to order.

When they finally emerged from the motel's main entrance, with coffee and rolls in a brown paper bag, Steven looked around. The sun was up and glowing.

The day promised to be mild. He checked everywhere, trying to spot Blayne or Grodin, or anyone that might appear to be an FBI agent, but he saw no one suspicious.

There were a half dozen men in suits, who were either heading to the lobby, or going to their cars. A couple in their sixties was just getting out of a twelve-year-old Cadillac. A bus stopped abreast from them. Three women in maid's uniforms lumbered onto the sidewalk and started toward the hotel.

Steven guided Carla toward the car. Halfway to the Bronco, he heard the discordant sound of a horn being blasted. Glancing over his shoulder, he saw a car swerve sharply, its tires squealing as it barely missed a silver Ford that was crossing the center line.

Steven saw that the driver of the Ford was fighting the wheel. The man's face was drawn, his eyes wide.

The silver car was thirty feet away from them when it veered toward the motel and reached the curb. The sharp explosion of a blowout echoed. The driver continued to fight the out of control vehicle. The car swerved again, and was heading straight at Steven and Carla.

Steven stood still, his muscles tense, waiting to see what direction the car would take next. And for the instant that he was rooted to the spot, he thought he saw the man staring directly at him. Steven shoved Carla away and dove after her, falling half on the ground, and half across Carla's legs. He heard the whoosh of the car's tires close by his ear, and felt the backwash of air as the car narrowly missed them. Before Steven could turn, the car side-swiped a parked car, and bounced off without slowing.

Lying on the ground and holding Carla close to him,

Steven was transfixed by the horror of the scene. The car continued onward, hitting a man head on, sending him spinning over the top of the car.

It continued onward, its speed unabated, mowing down everyone in its path. Finally, it jumped the high curb of the motel's entrance and rammed into the plate glass window of the lobby before its came to a stop.

Screams of panic and cries of pain filled the air. On the highway, traffic came to a halt. Steven pushed himself to his feet. He checked to make sure Carla was unhurt, and then ran into the mass of confusion.

To his left, Steven heard a man groaning in pain. He paused, turning just as one of the maids reached the injured man. The man's face was covered in blood. His arm was bent at a place where there was no elbow. Ten feet farther on, another man lay silent in a pool of blood.

Steven looked at the vehicle that had caused this destruction. The car door opened. The driver stumbled out and sank to the ground next to the car. Steven watched the driver. The man was pale, his eyes wide and frightened. The motel desk clerk burst through the door and ran to the man.

The driver was staring out at the people. His face was rigid with shock. "I . . . The car just took off. I didn't even touch the gas. It just took off. And then the tire blew out. I couldn't stop. I couldn't . . ."

Steven turned from the helpless reaction of the man, and saw the older couple. The man was kneeling amidst broken glass. He was clutching the broken body of his wife, and rocking back and forth.

Bile flooded Steven's mouth. He started toward the old man when Carla yanked on his arm. "Steven. No."

Somewhere off to his left, a woman shouted for

someone to call an ambulance.

He jerked his arm free from Carla's grasp, but she grabbed it again and tugged urgently. "We have to get out of here."

He shook his head, unable to take his gaze from the horror of the scene. "We can't leave them . . . Jesus, Carla, that could have been us."

Carla put her hand on his cheek to force him to look at her, and to break the morbid grip the accident had on him. Her face was pale, her eyes wide and pleading. "We can't help them, Steven. We can only get hurt ourselves. Think about Ellie! Think about us! Steven, the FBI is looking for you. There's going to be press here. If we're here, and we get arrested, the press will pick it up. Then, you'll be the lever that starts the scandal you think the President is rigging. We have to get out of here."

Her words formed the catalyst that broke through his reluctance to leave. Reaching deep inside himself, he turned away. "Let's go."

They got into the car and drove quickly away. He felt sick to his stomach. As the motel faded behind them, the accident played over and over in his mind. He heard the muted thuds of bodies being hit, and the harrowing cries of the driver's victims.

"That could have been us," he whispered.

Carla put her hand on his forearm and pressed gently. "But it wasn't. Steven, for both our sakes, let it go. We have other things to worry about."

He was taken back by her apparent callousness; yet, he knew that she was not speaking out of insensitivity, but rather with concern for Steven. "You don't get it. What I meant was that *should* have been us. Carla, the accident was wrong."

From the corner of his eye, he saw her head snap toward him. "Wrong? How?"

"It was out of sequence. Carla, the driver was trying to kill me—kill us."

"Steven, you're on the run. Everything seems to be directed at you. It was an accident."

"Was it? Think about what happened. What was the first thing you saw?"

"The car weaved into the wrong lane."

"And then it jumped the curb."

"No," she said, "there was a blowout. Then it jumped the curb."

"That's the way you would naturally remember it, because that's the way it should have happened. That would be the logical sequence of events. But the blowout came just after the car jumped the curb and was already in the motel drive, headed toward us."

"No, it . . ." He saw her eyes go out of focus. "Oh my God, you're right. But Steven, how . . . No one knew where we were."

"Grange could have had my call traced."

Carla shook her head emphatically. "To what purpose? You've already agreed to meet him at some out-of-the-way place? And even if he does think you're the mole, why would he want you dead? No, he'd want to question you."

He had no argument for that.

"What about Joshua Raden?" Carla asked. "No matter what he said about wanting to meet you, doesn't it seem just a shade too coincidental that Joshua Raden has come into your life at just this time?"

Steven bit off an immediate denial, and thought about it. "No, it wasn't Joshua," Steven stated, intuition, not full knowledge, giving him his certainty.

"Someone had to have followed us."

"Or followed Raden. Steven, pull over," Carla said suddenly, pointing to a public phone on the corner. "I want to call Paul. He'll be able to find out if what happened at the motel was an accident or not."

Knowing that Carla was right, Steven stopped at the curb. He stayed behind the wheel while she went to the phone. As he watched her put a quarter in the slot and dial Grange's number, he fought down the turbulence in his stomach. He was unscathed, but once again, innocent people had been hurt and killed. And, he was sure, it was because of him.

Then, within the rising wash of nausea that gripped him, a new realization burst free. Until the attack with the car—if it was an attack and not paranoia—whoever was behind his troubles had been trying to frame him. But something vital had changed. Now they wanted him dead. Why?

Carla finished her call and returned to the car before he could take the thought further. "He wasn't there, but I left word about the accident."

"Weren't they curious?" he asked.

"To say the least. I told them to give Paul the message. And to do it immediately. You'd be surprised what putting outraged authority into your voice can accomplish."

"No, I wouldn't," Steven said, shifting the Bronco into gear and slipping into the steady stream of rush hour traffic. "We're not going to Hagarstown. At least not until I'm positive that we're not being followed."

At the next red light, Steven swerved into the oncoming lane and made a quick left turn. He drove a block, turned left, and left again. When he got back onto the main street, he headed toward the Beltway.

Forty minutes and three direction changes later, they crossed the bridge into Alexandria. He left the highway at the first exit. "Your pistol. The one you had at my place. Where is it?"

"In my apartment," Carla said without hesitation.

"I want it—just in case." Steven said as he drove toward Carla's apartment. He continued to drive erratically, making random turns and always looking in the rear view mirror to see if anyone was following.

When he was secure that they were in the clear, he drove to Carla's apartment building. As he approached Carla's street, she said, "Go to the next block. We can go in the back way."

Steven followed her instructions and parked diagonally across from the building's rear entrance. They stayed in the car, scanning the area to see if the Feds were anywhere around.

"It seems clear," he said.

Once safely inside, they took the service elevator to her floor. The hallway was empty and quiet as they went into Carla's apartment. "I'll be right back," she said, leaving him in the living room.

She came back with the nine-millimeter Browning. He took it, saying, "I want you to stay here. Grange is clearing you with the Bureau. I don't want you in any more danger."

"It's too late for that," she said. "And if you're right about it not being an accident, then the driver was after us, not just you, Steven, but *us*."

"Grange will set up protection for you," he said, watching the stubbornness grow on her face.

"I'm not going to argue with you Steven. I am going with you."

Steven saw his defeat in the determined set of her

face. He cupped her chin in his hand and said, "I had to try one more time."

"No, you didn't," she replied, her voice going strangely husky. Her eyes went cloudy, and she stepped back from his touch. "Let me pack a bag and change my clothing. Ellie's clothes aren't quite my size."

While she was in the bedroom, and absently holding the Browning in his right hand, Steven looked around the apartment. On his first visit, he had not been interested in the apartment, only in Paul Grange.

He studied the paintings above the sectional. They were abstracts, crisp and sharp with a multitude of colors that flowed together nicely. He was familiar with the artist, and the recent fame the man had been gaining.

The furniture was all glove leather, soft, and expensive. The coffee table was marble, the carpet Berber wool. He walked to the far wall in the open dining room. On it were pictures of the Rogers family. Most of the pictures were duplicates of the ones in Ellie's living room. Several were different. He paused to study one of the Rogers family pictures and then glanced at the photograph next to it.

The photo, framed in black and covered with glass, was a picture of Carla with Paul Grange. They were both a good ten years younger. Their arms were about each other's waists, and they wore identical college sweatshirts.

Steven was still staring at the younger versions of Carla and Grange, again wondering about her relationship with Grange, when Carla came up behind him. "I want to try and call Paul again."

"No," Steven said, turning to her. Grange was a member of an intelligence organization and would expect Steven to keep on the move, to avoid anything traceable, and to make sure he didn't lead anyone to their meeting place.

"Steven, I think it's important to speak with him."

"The only thing that's important is for us to get out of here before someone sees us. We'll speak with Grange when we see him," Steven said, popping out the magazine of the Browning and checking the clip. It was filled with nine-millimeter parabellums. He loaded the clip into the pistol, slapping the butt solidly with his palm.

The hard jolt of metal against his skin made him think of how often he'd performed the same movements in Nam. Then he thumbed on the safety, slipped the automatic into his belt, and adjusted his jacket so it concealed the weapon.

"If we make it there."

Chapter Eighteen

It took them five hours of driving to reach Hagarstown, three hours longer than if Steven had driven directly there. To make absolutely certain that they weren't being followed, Steven took a misleading and circuitous route from the Washington area to Culpepper, Virginia, across Virginia, and finally back into Maryland, near Hagarstown.

Throughout the long serpentine ride, Carla kept watch to see if there were any familiar cars behind them. Not once during the drive had the same vehicle been behind them for more than a ten mile stretch.

During the drive, Steven tried to sort out his thoughts. So much had happened in the past few days that the events all seemed to have blended together into one huge and bubbling cauldron.

He turned on the radio, found a classical station, and let the music ease some of his tension. And, as he drove, he watched Carla, who faithfully kept track of all the traffic behind them as well as any cars that passed.

When they reached the outskirts of Hagarstown, Steven followed Carla's instructions to bypass the city and go deeper into the mountains. There, they passed several sprawling farms, set peacefully amidst the rolling hills, before reaching the cutoff for Grange's farm.

When Steven turned onto a well maintained single

lane road, he immediately noticed that Grange's uncle's farm was very different than the others that they'd passed. A high chain link fence separated the property from the road. A thick line of spruce pines prevented any view of the property or the buildings. No hunting and no trespassing signs were posted every fifty feet along the high fence.

"He likes his privacy," Steven commented.

Carla laughed. "It's not a working farm. It's more like a retreat. If the fence and signs weren't up, the hunters would be all over the place."

After driving another quarter of a mile, they reached the main entrance to the farm, an open wrought iron gate attached to two square brick pillars. There was an old fashioned gate house set five feet back from the gate. It appeared empty.

Steven drove through the open gate. Two hundred yards later, when the main buildings came into view, Steven saw the reason for the fence and the posting.

The main house, painted beige with brown trim and shutters, was a large and formal Victorian. It was at least a century old. There were two smaller residences set behind and off to the side of the main house. Fifty feet farther down the drive was a barn of classic structure. As he drove closer, he saw that the barn had been converted into a garage with three lift style doors.

Steven's eyes were never still. He searched everywhere, looking for something out of place, something that didn't feel right.

He stopped the Bronco in front of the house and the door opened and Grange appeared. A second man followed. He wore a dark suit. There was a plastic earpiece in his left ear. A coiled clear wire ran into his suit jacket collar. He carried a thirty-eight in his right hand

and a walkie-talkie in his left.

"Where the hell have you two been?" Grange asked, opening Carla's door and motioning her out. "Let's get inside, Morrisy."

The second man stood five feet from them. He was not looking at Steven or Carla as they got out of the car; he watched the road behind them. Steven opened the back door and took out the two bags before following Grange and Carla toward the house.

When Grange passed the other agent, he nodded his head toward the car. "Put it away."

The agent went to the Bronco and started it just as Steven entered the house.

"Just leave them there," Grange said, nodding at the bags. Steven put them down and went into the living room with Grange and Carla.

The inside of the house was as perfectly maintained as the exterior. The floors were highly polished parquet, covered with oriental area rugs. All the moldings and trim were of dark stained wood. The furniture was antique, and the fabric of the curtains was coordinated with that of the furniture.

Belatedly, the chain link fence, the converted barn, and the farm itself clicked together in Steven's mind. A sudden flash of anger turned quickly into a feeling of acceptance. He laughed, and said, "Your *uncle* has good taste and a lot of money. Uncle *Sam,* isn't it?"

Grange's reply was a pursing of his lips and an arm motion toward the couch. "Do you want a drink? Some food?"

"We had some lunch about an hour ago," Carla said, sitting next to Steven.

"I'll take a scotch," Steven said, still looking around. "I imagine this is one of those infamous safe houses we've all read about, and pay a portion of our taxes for."

"Yes," Grange said after making Steven his drink. "What happened at the motel?"

Steven held the glass of scotch, but did not drink it. Letting himself fall back on his perfect memory, he went accurately over every aspect of the accident, from the first moment he heard the discordant sound of the loud revving engine. He finished with a detailed description of the trip to the farm.

Grange stared at Steven, his expression that of wonder. "You have a remarkable memory."

"It's not something I asked for," Steven said, shrugging. "Did you find out anything about the accident?"

Grange glanced at Carla. "After you left the message for me, I had the accident checked out. It wasn't." He looked at Steven. "You were right. It appears to be a sanction."

"A what?"

"A sanction. A hit. A contracted killing. What happened to you has professional sanction written all over it. Someone is trying to kill you."

"I've already worked that out myself," Steven said, trying to ignore the morbid effect of Grange's confirming words. "But what I can't figure out is why."

"Nor can I. But all the evidence points to it. When we checked the driver's name and license number, we learned that the name belongs to a man who's been dead for five years. The license was Californian, and phony.

"Because it was an out-of-state license, and a rented car, I doubt that the police would have gone to any great lengths to check the driver out, especially if you had been the accident victim. With the Federal warrant on you, the FBI would have been able to take jurisdiction from the local police, told them to forget the whole thing, and say a silent thank you to your killer."

The all too casual way in which Grange reeled off the facts of what might have been, turned Steven cold inside. "The police aren't supposed to be involved. Only the Bureau," Steven said, recalling Arnie Savak's promise.

"Oh, I know," Grange said with a half smile. "What happened was that the Bureau sent out a bulletin, and then rescinded it an hour and a half later. And when we get the time, you can tell me just how you worked out that little trick. But getting back to the accident, if you had been killed, the Bureau boys would have known immediately.

"However, that's history now. When we checked further on the driver, we came up with some very interesting items," Grange said, pausing to change position in the chair. "Following routine procedure, a policeman accompanied the ambulance to the hospital. While the driver was waiting for X-rays, the policeman took his statement. The last time the cop saw him was when the driver was taken into X-ray. The attendants left him alone in the room for a few minutes, and he slipped out and disappeared.

"There's an all points bulletin out on him now. Two people died at the motel, nine more were injured. Three of the nine injured are in critical condition and are not expected to live."

Grange ran his fingers through his hair. "Our next step was to have department technicians check out the car. It was a rental, and there were no fingerprints. But they did find a device hooked up to the throttle to make it appear that the throttle jammed. The blowout was induced by a small amount of explosive in the wheel rim."

Steven took a short sip of the scotch. "So you believe me now?"

"Oh, yes," Grange said in an intense whisper. "We have several of these types of accidents in our files. What happened this morning fits one particular pattern to a 'T'."

Grange paused. He stared at Steven for several seconds before saying, "There's a Soviet operative, known to us as Anton. This man's theater of operation is the Americas—North and South. Anton is a terrorism specialist whom the Soviets use to recruit, train, and finance subversive groups. He has two main specialties, depending on whether the sanction is for propaganda purposes or a quiet hit: Car bombs that explode spectacularly; and, the use of automobiles to make a hit look like an accident.

"But what I still don't understand, and what doesn't fit in with everything else, is why you were sanctioned," Grange admitted. "From the outset, everything pointed to you as a spy and a killer. All the real mole had to do was to sit back and wait for the noose to tighten around you. Then, without any apparent reason, the mole changed his plans and tried to kill you."

"It doesn't make any more sense to me than it does to you," Steven ventured. "Last night I was being arrested by the FBI; this morning a Soviet agent tries to kill me." Steven stopped as the recurring vision of the accident came back.

"There's always a reason," Grange said. "Did something happen from the time you started running until the accident?"

Steven shook away the mental after-images of that morning, and looked at Carla, who shrugged. "Nothing." Steven said, still working over everything Grange had told him. "Let's forget this morning for now. Last night, when I went to my place to change, you'd already left a message. When we spoke, you inferred that you had learned some things that changed your mind about me. What?"

"Your army records."

"What did you find in them?"

Grange leaned back in the wing chair and smiled. "Just what you said I would. Nothing where there should be something. Your files were a duplicate of the original security check. But in going over the originals, I found obvious changes. Obvious at least to me."

"Then you still have nothing."

Grange ignored his remark. "So then I went into the medical records from the debriefing. Either they missed those, or they figured no one would bother with them since there was only a brief mention in your jacket, and they exonerated you." Grange's voice dropped, his eyes brightened.

Steven remained silent, trying to hold back the sense of anticipation that was rising with each word Grange spoke. "At first, the psychiatrist's initial comments matched with all the information. But as his report went on, he expressed the belief that you were lying about what had happened in the prison camp. So he ordered the use of drugs. That was why you had that second battery of tests—if you've ever wondered about it. The shrink was trying to find out how you could produce a drug block. The tests failed.

"Because of that failure, the doctor concluded that under the influences of a powerful mind drug, you had a natural subconscious ability to misdirect the understanding of a question."

Steven continued to sit still beneath Grange's hard and probing stare. "Which means what?" Steven asked, neither agreeing or disagreeing.

"It means that when you returned to Saigon, you lied about what happened at the prison camp. It means that you never broke when you were a prisoner of war, did you? You were the only one who didn't tell them what your mission was."

Steven's hand trembled. The scotch rippled in the glass. He put the drink down, stood, and walked to the window. He stared out at the peaceful hills, wishing that some of its serenity could reach him. Grange was fast and smart, and Steven knew that the Secret Service man would see through anything less than the truth.

"No, I couldn't break. If I had, I would have given them more than just our mission orders," Steven said before he turned to face them. Carla was staring at him. Her eyes were wide, her lips compressed. Grange was leaning forward, his expression eager.

"What would you have given them?" he asked.

Steven took out Jeremy Raden's letter. "The truth."

He unfolded the letter slowly. "This was written by Sergeant Jeremy Raden the night before we left on the mission. I'm going to read it to both of you."

" 'Dear Mom,

If you read this letter, then I never made it home. Today I was assigned a mission. Its code name is WEREWOLF. This is a bad one, Mom. They're sending us to hell, and I don't know if we'll make it back.' "

Steven's head started to spin. He closed his eyes under the impact of having inadvertently hit a dangerous memory trigger, a trigger he'd been stringently avoiding for so long. But, as he stared at Grange and Carla, all the years of effort he had put into his struggle to keep the war buried within him, were wiped away by Raden's prophetic phrase.

He shook his head, fighting the memories, and knowing that he couldn't just read Raden's letter to them, not yet, not until they knew more.

"Steven, what's wrong?" Carla asked.

He opened his eyes and saw her face was a mask of apprehension. Then he looked at Grange, and saw the question in the man's eyes.

Steven folded the letter closed. "Before I read Raden's letter, I'm going to tell you what happened in Vietnam, in nineteen seventy-one. I think it may be the only way that Raden's letter will make sense to you."

Steven went back to the couch, sat, and took a long pull of the scotch. While the woody tasting liquor worked its way into his stomach, he mentally prepared himself to accept all the pain that would accompany his return to the past.

And, even before he uttered his first words, the barriers he had so diligently erected when he'd returned from Nam fell against the force of his perfect memory. The very things he had refused to remember, for more years than he wanted to admit, returned with a clarity that brought the past back to life.

He cleared his throat, and said, "I was with Military Intelligence, stationed in Saigon . . ."

Chapter Nineteen

Steven was at his desk, working over the latest reports from the field intelligence units when his phone rang. He picked up the receiver without taking his eyes from the handwritten report of NVA infiltration movements in the south. "Morrisy."

"Lieutenant, Colonel Botlin would like to see you in his office. ASAP."

"On my way," Steven said. He put down the report, gathered the other papers he'd been studying, and put them in the steel filing cabinet next to his desk. He locked the cabinet, straightened his uniform, and left to find out what the Assistant Adjutant of Military Intelligence wanted.

He was certain it would be nothing good. It never was. The last time he had been called into Botlin's office, he had been told that the information gathering networks in Cambodia and Laos had been compromised and that he and a dozen other MI logistics officers were to work out a new network setup and have it on his desk in seventy-two hours.

He hoped this would not be a similar disaster.

He entered Botlin's outer office and walked up to the corporal at the room's only desk. "Lieutenant Morrisy to see Colonel Botlin."

"In there," drawled the blond, crater faced soldier,

directing him with a bored flexing of his right thumb. Steven went to the door, knocked, and opened it. When he stepped inside, he froze.

Sitting at the long conference table was Arnie Savak. Their eyes met, and Savak was out of his chair in an instant. Steven, wondering if he was seeing a ghost, started toward him. They closed the distance quickly, and embraced warmly. They both spoke at the same time, fell silent, and gestured for the other to talk.

"You first," Steven said.

"Christ, you're the last person I expected to see. What the hell is this all about?"

Steven took in the tired planes of his friend's face, and the new wrinkles around his eyes. "Damned if I know. I just got a call to report here."

Savak smiled, shook his head. "Jesus, this is great. How long has it been?"

"Two, two and a half years. Too long."

They were still holding each other when five foot-nine inch, crew cut and jut-jawed Colonel Ted Botlin entered. Botlin, known to his underlings in Military Intelligence as the "Box", was partial to straight line military policy, and believed that patriotism meant that whatever the army said was right, so long as we won. He was also known as a man who got his assignments accomplished no matter what the risk or odds.

Steven released Savak and turned to face Botlin.

"I take it you two have known each other for a long time. 'Cause I can't think of any other reason for two men to be hugging each other when there's no shrapnel a-flying."

"We grew up together," Savak said, laughing.

"Well, gentleman, I don't mean to put a damper on

your reunion, but we have business to discuss."

"Yes, sir," they said simultaneously.

The colonel motioned to the side bar and its contents. "Pour yourselves a drink. Make mine bourbon . . . straight up."

While Savak fixed the drinks, the colonel seated himself at the head of the table beneath a large topographical map of Vietnam, Cambodia, and Laos.

Steven sat near the center of the table. After handing out the drinks, Savak took the seat next to Steven. When the colonel raised his glass in a silent toast, his West Point ring facing them, Steven and Savak followed suit.

The colonel regarded them silently for so long before speaking that all of Steven's warning senses came flaring to life.

"The two of you have been chosen for a very special mission. It is strictly voluntary," Botlin said, his ice blue eyes giving nothing away.

The colonel fingered his Academy ring. "All I'm permitted to say until you accept the assignment, is that this mission might possibly enable us to change the currents of this damn war and allow us to regain some of our pride. It may even show the people back home that we aren't the bad guys. It will be more hazardous than anything either of you have been involved in before."

Savak laughed. "I don't think so."

Botlin thrust his box chin forward, riveting Savak with the stare of a full bird colonel. He spoke through clenched teeth, his words coming in a sharp and precise cadence. "You can bet your ass it will be, Captain. I know all about what happened to you in the delta. And I can tell you this will be even harder. But this mission, if successfully completed, has the potential to become the most pivotal component of the war."

Steven stole a glance at Savak. Savak was already looking at him. As if reading each other's minds, they shrugged simultaneously.

"As curious as it might seem you—matching two friends from back home, and from different divisions—you've been chosen for this mission because of your individual talents. Morrisy, you have one of the keenest analytical minds in Saigon. Your ability to pick out the faults in strategy and correct them has proven to be close to infallible. Your covert field experience is more than adequate, and your field competence ranks very high.

"And you, Captain," Botlin said, locking eyes with Savak, "You rank up there with the best of our young military tacticians. If you weren't, you'd never have gotten your command out of the delta. We need the combination of both your talents for this mission, gentlemen," Botlin finished.

Although the colonel's words were straightforward, Steven couldn't shake the suspicion that all wasn't quite right. "May I speak freely, sir?"

A curt nod was Botlin's go ahead.

"We've all heard about these end-the-war missions. None seem to have worked so far. I thought we were de-escalating. Isn't that the reason for the bombing moratorium?"

Botlin's eyes hardened. "You're damns right the past missions haven't come off as planned. For a lot of reasons, including a lot of our own stupidity. And the de-escalation wasn't exactly our idea. You're both aware of what's happening back home. Our country is being divided by people who have no conception as to why we're in Southeast Asia, or what we're trying to do here. A lot of pressure is being put on the administration. But gentlemen, it's all one-sided. The slants are still killing our people, more and more everyday. If we don't pull this off . . ."

Steven found himself understanding what the man was trying to say. The effects of the 68 Tet offensive and the ever increasing dissention at home and in the ranks was crippling their every move. Yet, Steven still held hope that somehow they would be able to pull things together and come out of Southeast Asia with their heads held high.

"Will this mission really help?" Savak asked, "or is it another of those bullshit games the brass likes to play to justify their need to keep the war going?"

Botlin met Savak's biting challenge with an unusual calm for a staff officer. He held Savak's hawkeyed stare openly as he said, "No bullshit. This one's for real. And the reason the two of you were chosen for this was because we found that by your working together, there was a seventy-eight percent chance of success. With the right backup."

"Which is?" Steven asked before Savak could.

"You two will form the nucleus of a five man team. The rest of the team will consist of two special forces men and a ranger scout. This scout has spent the last ten months in and out of the target area. This is something the General Staff has been working on for six months. It will save lives. You have my word on that."

Steven contemplated the colonel's impassioned promise, and felt his suspicions lessen. He made up his mind abruptly. "All right Colonel, I'm in."

"Oh, shit. Me too," Savak added.

Botlin straightened in his chair. His features softened.

"I'd hoped that would be your answer. All right, gentlemen, to put it into a nutshell, you will be the advance scouting team for what will become the largest single combined assault of the war. Your team will be dropped into Laos, near the Vietnamese border. Your objective is to cross back into Nam and chart the course of the invasion."

"Why?" Savak asked, his voice again guarded. "What the hell is wrong with aerial photographs?"

The colonel picked up several photographs from the table and disdainfully tossed them to Savak. "What do those tell you?"

Savak glanced at the black and white photos before passing them to Steven. "That there's a lot of trees."

"The thickest fucking jungle you've ever seen, gentlemen. And we have to know what in the hell's under that leaf cover. We can't drop defoliant. Might as well send a cable to Hanoi with our plans."

Steven glanced up from the recon photos. "Exactly where are we going in?"

Standing, Botlin went to the large map on the wall. "You'll be dropped here," he said, pointing to a spot in Laos a few miles inland from the border. And then you'll go here," he added, moving his finger into the Vietnam bottleneck.

Steven felt his insides turn to ice. He cursed himself for following his emotions. His inner warnings had been right, and he'd been a fool to ignore them. His mouth was dry and he had to work up saliva in order to speak normally. "That's North Vietnam."

"I know what it is. Your team will have two weeks from the date you're dropped to get the mapping and charting done, and to return to the extraction point in

Laos. You'll be working in conjunction with a CIA team that's been in Laos for nine months. Gentlemen, we need that information, desperately. Without it, I don't think we've got one chance in a thousand to get out of this hell we're stuck in."

"When do we go?" Savak asked.

"Tomorrow. But now, gentlemen, I'd like you to meet the rest of your team." Botlin leaned forward and jabbed the button on the intercom. "Send them in."

The door that Steven had entered through opened. A Green Beret corporal and sergeant came in first. The two men were tall and muscular and, like all the Special Forces men Steven had seen, they carried themselves with an air of confidence that was purely physical. The two Green Berets were followed by another sergeant in a Ranger uniform.

Steven took one look at the scout's face, and he knew that the army's high command had sprung the last trap.

Next to him, Savak whispered, "Son-of-a-bitch."

Still, Steven couldn't speak. All he was capable of doing, was to stare at Ranger Scout Chuck Latham.

Steven squatted beneath the cover of a huge tree. Savak was next to him, his index finger hovering above the map, charting the course he wanted Steven to mark out.

Using an indelible pen, Steven plotted the morning's findings, and the best route through the rain forest. Then he folded the map and put it with the others. He looked at his watch. "Two days and ten hours and we're out of here."

Savak grunted in agreement. "The first thing I want

when we get back is a hot shower followed by a long soak in an even hotter bath. About two hours worth for starters. Then I want to get drunk and laid. In either order. And dry boots. I don't think I can remember what my feet feel like when they're dry."

The insects had feasted on his blood. He'd swallowed as much dirt as he had food. And, although they'd passed any number of streams and ponds, they weren't able to chance bathing. If soap residue was spotted, someone would start looking for the source. They couldn't piss or take a crap without finding a spot that wouldn't show evidence of their presence.

The team was far enough inside North Vietnam to not have to worry about heavy NVA patrols, since most North Vietnamese troop movement took place on the main routes into the South. However, there was enough enemy movement in the area to keep them on full alert. There were only a few scattered villages in the mountainous jungles, which the five men gave a wide berth. But Steven knew that one mistake was all that would be necessary for them to be discovered. So far they hadn't made a mistake.

By the second day of the mission, the day they'd crossed the Laotian border into North Vietnam, Steven knew that the two Special Forces men, Corporal Tom Cole and Sergeant Jeremy Raden, were the best jungle soldiers he'd ever come across. It had been their ability to make the team fade into oblivion whenever an enemy patrol was near that had kept them from being discovered.

Latham was the equal to the Green Berets in his ability to move undetected through the jungles. He had been the advance scout for this very mission; and he had been in the area a half dozen times on single man recon.

It was the high cover routes through the dense foliage that they were interested in. Their assignment was to chart the passages that would allow the large scale troop movement necessary to launch a double flank pincer invasion.

To date, they'd accomplished everything they'd set out to do. Now, Steven thought, all they had to do was to get their information out. In the back of his mind—as he was sure it was in everyone's—rested the words of Colonel Botlin's final briefing:

"The reason why all of you, and not just Captain Savak and Lieutenant Morrisy, have been given the complete details of this mission is so that if only one of you survives, that man will be able to complete the mission and bring back the map case and its contents.

"Under no circumstance is the enemy to learn why you are in their territory. You have orders not to be captured. Therefore, each of you has been issued new uniforms. The buttons contain a fast-acting poison. All you have to do is rip one off, bite it in half, and put it under your tongue. And gentlemen, I guarantee you that using the poison is a preferable alternative to what Charlie will do to you."

Along with the uniform Steven had been issued, had been a special canvas and plastic map case. Sewn into its flap was a small black container. The container was a magnesium and acid fail-safe device should the mission go sour. If spotted by the enemy—and if he or Savak judged escape to be impossible—Steven would pull a wire embedded in the tube. When the device was activated, the acid would ignite the magnesium. The map bag itself had been impregnated with a flammable substance that the magnesium would set off.

In fifty seconds, the maps and notes would burn past recognition. If Steven was lucky enough not to be captured, after the maps had been destroyed, and he made it back to the extraction site, he would recreate every note and route.

Squatting in the jungles, with mosquitos buzzing around his face, and snakes and centipedes crawling over his feet, Steven understood that it was his total recall abilities and not the abilities Botlin had listed at their first meeting, which was the true reason for his presence on the mission.

"Time to go," Latham said, materializing from behind a tree. His round face was marked with black and green strips of camouflage make-up, as was everyone's.

Steven slipped the strap of the map case over his head and stood. When Savak rose, the three friends started forward in single file. Latham always took the point. They kept at least ten feet distance from Latham, and six between themselves. The two Green Berets were on the flanks. They travelled east, moving stealthily, always searching for pratfalls in the routes of the coming invasion.

An hour before sunset, they made camp in an unusually dense copse of trees. Moss hung thickly from the old and thick branches, cutting off the last of the daylight and giving the ground a false and eerie dusk.

The Special Forces men and Latham spent a half hour securing the perimeters of the camp and setting up their special network of baffled alarms, while Steven and Savak wrote out the notes about the four miles they had just covered.

They ate at sundown, in two shifts. Their food was a

mixture of cold rations and whatever roots and vegetables they found growing wild. They had not lit a fire since leaving Laos; they would not until they returned to the extraction point.

During their meal, Sergeant Raden and Corporal Cole briefed Steven about what they had seen out on the flanks, and their feelings about the route they'd been over that day. Steven noted their extra information, and added it to his own.

After their meal, the team went about their regular duties. The Green Berets took up their guard posts. Steven and Latham and Savak remained in the camp.

"We're going to make it," Latham said after burying the remains of their meal and squatting on his haunches near Savak and Steven.

"Of course we are, we never lose," Savak promised, smiling confidently as he spread out the supplies. The inventory of their supplies was a nightly ritual that Steven and Savak had taken on.

"We're getting low on solids," Savak stated, gesturing to the dried rations. "I don't know if there will be enough rations for us to make it back."

Steven shook his head. "We'll manage, even if—"

"Quiet." Latham's hoarse whisper abruptly cutting him off as the rattling sound of branches hitting together whispered through the air.

Steven froze, listening intently to the jungle. He heard nothing. Then, slowly, he realized just how much nothing he was hearing.

The silence was almost total. No birds called in the day's end. No insects chirped their welcome of the night. There was only the shallow sound of his breathing. The faint cracking of a branch breaking from a tree and striking the jungle floor reached them as a spooky echo.

Latham had his rifle set. Savak was unholstering his forty-five. Steven did the same while sweeping his gaze along the boles of the thick trees.

"That was one of the perimeter warnings," Latham said, his voice barely audible.

They held still for another ten seconds. Nothing happened. There was no sound.

"Raden. Cole," Latham called loudly.

The two Special Forces men gave no reply.

A sharp burst of adrenaline was released into Steven's blood. His heart began to pound like a jackhammer, and his breathing shortened. His senses expanded, heightening his hearing and sight.

Moving quickly, he took off the map bag and hooked his finger into the metal pull ring of the magnesium tube. "Ready," he told Savak and Latham.

Hearing a low thump from behind, Steven spun. He saw the round tube of a Soviet made grenade rolling toward him. An instant later, a noxious cloud of smoke steamed out from its end.

"Do it, Steven." Savak ordered as he began to fire short bursts into the trees.

Latham joined Savak in laying down a barrage of covering fire for Steven.

Steven pulled the ring and tossed the map bag from him. Three more grenades landed near him, spewing up thick belches of gray smoke. The acid did its job. The magnesium flared clean and white amid the thickening fog. Eighteen seconds later the impregnated map bag burst into flames.

"Where are they?" Steven shouted, searching wildly for the hidden enemy as he executed a slow three-sixty from his crouch. He held his modified forty-five in an extended double handed grip, the fumes from the grenades choking and blinding him.

Before he could complete the circle, the world tilted sideways. An instant later the jungle floor rushed up to meet his face.

Steven woke slowly, his head throbbing and feeling twice its normal size. It was dark. The only light came from a full moon. His tongue was thick and his mind slow.

He looked around. The other four men were with him. He tried to sit up. A wave of cramps kept him down. The foul smell of mildew and rot permeated his every breath. He felt clammy.

"Easy," said Cole, the Special Forces corporal.

Steven drew in a deep breath that sent an unexpected wave of pain oscillating through his chest. When the pain eased, he sat up slowly. They were in a bamboo hut, maybe fifteen by fifteen. Moonlight sifted through the double layer of heavy wire mesh that barred the narrow window opening.

And then he realized why he felt clammy. He was naked. So was Cole. He glanced at the others: Savak and Latham and Raden were still out. The moonlight cast an eerie pall over their naked bodies.

A terrifying sense of dread spread through him. Despair grew with lightening speed. He stood shakily, and found that his legs were not quite ready to hold him. Using the side of the hut for support, Steven went to the mesh wired windows.

He looked out. To his right were the shadowed outlines of several low slung hut-like buildings. The darkness prevented him from seeing how many buildings there were.

Craning his neck, Steven pressed his cheek to the thick strands of wire to get a better view. Off to his left was a similar series of flat roofed and small wooden buildings.

Set in the center of the two wing-like rows of bamboo dormitories, was a larger two story structure. Light seeped through shaded windows on both levels. Steven looked across from where he stood. In direct line of sight, fifty feet away, was a guard tower.

Steven had seen similar layouts before, from choppers and from recon photos. They were in an NVA prison camp. Turning from the window, he looked around the hut, searching desperately for what he knew was not there.

A strange sense of mental numbness overcame him. He sank onto the damp floor and looked at Cole. "God help us," he whispered hoarsely. "They took our clothing. They've got the pills. We have no way out."

Chapter Twenty

On the morning of their third day in the prison camp, shortly after their morning meal of cold rice had been thrust at them, the sky turned malevolent. Dark clouds billowed angrily. The air became damp. The humidity was so thick it made breathing hard inside the bamboo hut.

The hut's two windows, covered with a double layer of heavy metal mesh, allowed only a small amount of stagnant air to stir. The dirt floor was always damp, the sleeping mats filthy and lice-infested. Sores and lesions had already started forming on everyone's bodies.

Looking out the window, Steven thought that their imprisonment would never have been, had their uniforms—their means of dying quickly and painlessly—not been taken from them while they lay unconscious.

The first night had been the worst. Each of them, as they'd woken from the gas, had gone through the same reactions of hopelessness that Steven had.

They'd kept awake as long as they had been able to, but the effects of the gas had stayed with them, and they'd slept on and off.

Shortly after daybreak of their first day, they'd been given rancid rice, a tub of brackish water, and coarsely woven pajamas.

No one spoke to them the rest of the day. They were given no other food. The five men took turns at the window, learning as much as they could about the prison camp, and seeing the impossibility of their situation. The only thing of value that they had learned on the first day, was that the low slung building on the far side of the prison compound housed other Americans.

Raden and Cole, downcast and angry at their failure to have detected the ambush, were totally uncommunicative. They blamed themselves for the capture of the team, and nothing that the other three could say was able to break their mood.

The second full day was a repeat of the first. And by the end of the second day, each of them had begun to question why they were being isolated from the other American prisoners.

But on the third day, a half hour after they had finished the cold rice, Steven saw the camp commander, accompanied by a small contingent of guards, heading toward their hut. He drew back from the window and signalled the others. The five men stood together in a tight group.

The captain opened the door and entered. He was of average height for a Vietnamese, about five-four. His uniform was wrinkled, but his leather was shined. His face was heavily pocked. His lips were thin and drawn back. His teeth were stained brown.

Behind the captain were four uniformed guards carrying Russian made AK-47s. The captain strode to the middle of the floor. Two guards stayed at the door. The other two guards stopped on his flanks. "I am Captain Lin Tam Ho, commandant of Qua Doc prison camp. You call me Captain Lin."

He paused to give the five men a shark's smile. A shiver ran along Steven's back at the malignant hatred contained within the man's expression.

"Spread out against wall," he ordered.

The five prisoners followed Lin's orders, and pressed their backs to the wall. Slowly, without speaking, Lin inspected each of the men in turn. When he was finished, Lin pointed to Tom Cole. The two guards at his sides moved forward. They separated Cole from the others, using their rifles to push Latham and Raden back.

Dodging beneath one rifle, Jeremy Raden kicked up and out with his left foot. He caught the guard in the solar plexus. The man fell backward, writhing in pain. Then Raden launched himself at the second guard, the hard and calloused edge of his palm slicing toward the guard's neck. But before Raden's hand could reach its target, the captain reversed his pistol, leaned forward, and swung. He hit Raden at the base of his skull, stunning him long enough for one of the door guards to race forward and slam the stock of his assault rifle against Raden's temple.

Then Captain Lin stepped over Raden, bent, and put his automatic to the sergeant's head. He cocked the pistol, paused, and looked at the other prisoners. He smiled at their expressions of horror.

Slowly, Lin drew the weapon away from Raden's head. "His turn next."

Lin backed away and motioned to his men. They grabbed Cole's arms and dragged him out. Steven went to his knees next to Raden. The sergeant was unconscious. Fortunately, the skin on his scalp was unbroken.

Latham, Steven, and Savak crowded the window. As they watched, Captain Lin showed them what they would all eventually be facing.

They tied Cole to a set of crossed bamboo beams, twenty feet from the hut, and began to question him. Lin started his interrogation by asking simple things. Cole refused to speak. After ten minutes of unanswered questions, Lin picked up a long, half inch thick branch to whip Cole's abdomen. With every lash stroke that Lin applied, Cole strained against his bindings. He never cried out.

In the beginning, Steven and the others called out to Cole, to let him know that he wasn't alone. But as the minutes passed, and the torture continued on unabated, their shouts slowed, and stopped.

Steven watched Lin, surprised that the captain had taken it upon himself to torture Cole personally. Most NVA officers were of a higher class than their troops, and did not engage in torture. But as Lin carried on the beating, understanding filled Steven's mind. Lin, Steven realized, was an outright sadist.

Then, after an hour of methodically whipping Cole, Lin tossed the whip to the ground and went to a small square wooden table. He picked up a highly polished mahogany case. His movements turned reverent, and Steven could only wonder what the North Vietnamese captain was going to do.

Before Lin opened the case, it began to rain. Not hard torrents, as Steven had expected, but a drizzle. Lin opened it and withdrew something white. A moment later he flicked his wrist, and a shining steel blade snapped outward.

Staring at the object in Lin's hand, Steven's bowels twisted sharply. Lin stepped toward Cole, his shark's grin firmly in place as he held the pearl-handled straight razor before Cole's eyes.

With the grin of a madman, Colonel Lin Tam Ho began to carve an intricate pattern of cuts on Cole's chest, arms, abdomen and neck.

Each excruciatingly slow slice of the razor cut through skin and muscle and nerve endings. And, at the end of each razor slice, another question was asked.

With every cruel and sadistic cut, Steven and Savak and Latham shouted their hatred at Captain Lin until Raden made them stop.

"You're giving in to them. This is exactly what Lin wants you to do," the Green Beret sergeant said. "They take every word you say, every shout and every plea as a sign of weakness. We have to show them our strength by keeping a unity among ourselves. None of us will speak except to each other. It has to be that way."

Steven immediately perceived the wisdom of Raden's reasoning. Savak and Latham were no slower on the uptake. They remained silent as the grisly scene continued.

Whenever Cole passed out from the pain, he was revived with alternating buckets of salt water and tepid fresh water until not even those could rouse him from his pained stupor.

Cole was strong; despite all of Lin's tactics, the Green Beret corporal lasted four days. He was left on the bamboo structure at night, and was given no food or water.

Cole didn't break: Cole died of dehydration and blood loss, on the fifth day.

Lin left the dead corporal hanging on the cross for two more days. He also left the four remaining men alone, so that their fears would grow as they watched their companion's lifeless body.

But during the two days that they watched Cole's body being desecrated by guards urinating on him during the days, and by the night time feedings of rats and larger rodents, the resolve of the four Americans grew stronger, along with the knowledge that they had fallen into an even worse situation than they'd first thought.

Steven kept a constant vigil on Cole's body, burning the memory of what had been done into his mind. When he wasn't watching Cole, he was talking with Latham and Savak and Raden. They would work out a plan of escape, mentally follow it through, and then look for any loopholes. But despite the optimism of their plans, Steven knew that escape was tactically impossible at this stage.

And when they weren't talking about escape, or what had happened to Cole, they talked about home, and about their families and friends. Raden spoke about his brother, his wife, and his mother. Latham about his family, and Savak about his shattered dreams of entering the diplomatic corps.

Steven didn't talk about home or family; rather, he chose the responsibility of guiding the other men by keeping them occupied, and their thoughts as far from what was happening as possible.

Three days after Cole's death, their isolation ended

with the hut door exploding inward. Lin entered with the seven guards. Four of the soldiers rushed forward, their weapons at the ready, and pinned each of the Americans to the wall.

Lin stepped to the center of the hut and pointed at Raden. Two of the remaining guards went forward, took Raden's arms, and hustled the sergeant out of the hut. The other guards backed away slowly, keeping the weapons trained on the remaining three men.

Outside, the Vietnamese dragged Raden to the cross, and made him stand still while Lin used American prisoners from the other side of the compound to cut what remained of Cole from the cross and take him to a burial ditch. When Cole's carcass was gone, Raden was tied to the crossed bamboo posts.

Lin worked on the Green Beret sergeant for five hours the first day. Steven made himself watch. Latham and Savak were at his sides. Lin did not use the long wooden whip, nor did he use the pearl handled razor; he used a narrow leather strap, whipping and beating Raden across his stomach. By the time he was finished, Raden's abdomen was criss-crossed with high red welts and jagged skin tears. He left him hanging there, unconscious.

Raden's second day of torture began with a guard emptying a bucket of salt water on Raden's stomach. Then they scrubbed off the dried blood with rough cloth and crude soap.

Through it all, Raden kept his silence, staring stolidly at Lin.

Steven watched Lin's preparations. As the captain reverently opened the gleaming wood case that held his razor, Steven's stomach went queazy. He doubted he'd be able to keep down what little rice he'd eaten.

"Today you tell about mission," the captain said, unfolding the straight razor. "Today you talk."

Raden didn't move or speak, he simply stared at Lin.

Lin went to work. He alternated slow and painful slices across Raden's abdomen and chest with taunts at Raden's stupidity, offers of leniency, and finally rewards for telling Lin about the Americans' mission.

Twenty minutes after Lin started, Raden passed out. "Thank God," Steven said.

"We've got to do something," Savak pleaded. "We've got to help him."

Latham stared at Savak. "How the hell are we going to do anything?"

"Break out. Get Raden and run."

"We wouldn't make it ten feet." Steven spoke unemotionally, presenting them with a simple fact. He pointed to the watch tower across from their hut. The tower was manned twenty-four hours a day. The fixed fifty-millimeter machine guns were always aimed at their hut.

"At least we'd save ourselves from that," Latham said, nodding toward the window.

Steven gripped Latham's shoulders, painfully digging his fingers into Latham's muscles and forcing Latham to meet his eyes. "They know we were in the North for a reason. They want to know what it was. Arnie, if we try it, they'll go for our legs and knees, but they won't let us kill ourselves."

"Now!" they heard Lin shout. Steven turned just as a bucket of salt water was thrown on Raden.

Raden woke, writhing. Lin bent over him. "No more play. You give me answers or die!" Lin flashed the razor in the air, waving it over Raden's stomach.

Moving the blade quickly, he slashed Raden from hip to armpit. A stream of blood gushed over the edges of the separated skin. Steven saw that Raden had been biting on his lower lip. Blood trickled down his chin, mingling with the three-week growth of beard.

"Ah, so brave you are," Lin said loudly, nodding toward his two assistants. The man with the salt water started to raise it. Lin stopped him with a preemptive gesture.

"Perhaps your throat. You like that? You want to die here, far from family? Your mother never know what happen to you. She never know you alive or dead. You want that?"

Lin reached into his pocket and withdrew something. He smiled at Raden, and held the object up for Raden to see. It was a photograph.

"Your family. A happy family, yes? Your mother and father. This your brother? Your wife or sister this one?" he asked.

Raden looked from the photo to Lin. His eyes were flat. "Go fuck yourself."

The captain smiled, pushed the razor against Raden's throat, and drew it from side to side. A thin red line of blood formed an obscene grin.

Steven lost his food violently.

Captain Lin laughed. "A scratch. The next be deeper. But you save self, Raden. End silence!"

Steven watched Raden work his mouth and try to spit. But the man was dehydrated, the attempt useless.

"You force me to do this." Lin shouted, again pressing the razor to Raden's neck. He moved it a fraction of an inch at a time. Raden's skin parted like stretched nylon against a scissor. "Talk! Talk to me and you see family again."

Blood poured from beneath the blade. Steven's knuckles were white. He couldn't catch his breath. Latham was white-faced.

Raden said nothing as the razor crept along. Steven saw the tendons on the sides of the sergeant's neck bulge outward.

The razor reached the carotid artery, and hovered. All Lin had to do was push forward a quarter inch and he could end Raden's life.

Raden's eyes flicked toward the prison hut. Steven felt them lock with his. An arc of knowledge passed between he and Raden like a blue spark of static electricity.

Suddenly Steven knew.

"No!" Steven screamed, grabbing onto the mesh wire of the window and shaking it with all his strength as his cry turned into an elongated howl of pain and fury.

Raden rammed his head forward and then twisted it to the side.

Blood spurted in thick belches, splattering Lin's face and uniform. As his life blood drained from his body, Sergeant Jeremy Raden stared at Lin.

They took Savak the next day.

Lin was taking no chances that the three remaining prisoners would revolt. Lin and five guards burst into the hut before the morning meal. Four of the guards beat Steven and Latham to the floor while Lin and another guard grabbed Savak and rushed him out.

As soon as the door was closed and locked, Steven and Latham ran to the window, ignoring the pain from the blows. They watched Savak being tied to the same bamboo cross that Cole and Raden had died on.

Lin paced back and forth impatiently while Savak was spread-eagled onto the bamboo beams. His wrists and ankles were tied to the wood with wire that bit into flesh at the slightest movement.

Lin held his pearl handled straight razor in his right hand. Lin's two assistants stood attentively by. One held a bucket of salt water; the other held plain water and a rag dripping with ammonia—the prison camp version of smelling salts.

When Lin was satisfied with Savak's positioning, he began.

The Vietnamese captain didn't bother to ask any questions, or even use the branch whip or leather strap. He went right to work with the razor. Within minutes, Savak's abdomen and chest were slick with blood from the slashes Captain Lin had engraved so freely upon him.

Then the captain leaned over Savak, and spoke in broken English. "This only the beginning. You talk. I stop. Much better for you, yes?"

Savak shook his head.

"Foolish Captain Savak. Why you bother? Pain end now. We care for you, treat you with respect of officer. All you do is tell what mission was."

Savak glared stonily at his interrogator.

With a smile, Lin positioned the razor just below Savak's left nipple. Slowly, in order to induce the maximum amount of pain, Lin drew the razor down and across Savak's abdomen, ending at the right hip.

The low guttural sound emanating from between Savak's caked lips sent shivers along Steven's back and churned his stomach with revulsion. He wanted to close his eyes, to shut out and deny what was happening, but he could no more leave Savak alone than he had Cole or Raden.

Lin stepped back. He motioned to the guards to continue with the ritual. The man holding the bucket of salt water emptied it over Savak's stomach. Savak's body arched away from the wood. The wire holding his ankles and forearms bit into his skin, slicing deeper into his flesh and drawing fresh blood.

"What your mission? Why you here?" Lin shouted, his mouth an inch from Savak's ear.

Groggy, Savak lifted his head. His eyes were pain-glazed yet defiant. "No."

The captain spat at Savak and went back to work with the razor.

Latham fell to his knees and threw up. When he was able to stand again, he grabbed Steven's wrist in a death grip. "He's going to kill Arnie. Steven, how much more of this can we take? That madman's already killed two of us."

"It doesn't matter," Steven said, his voice dull and listless as he watched the captain open a new gash across Savak's stomach. Bile rose into his mouth. He swallowed. The bile burned the back of his throat, triggering a retching response. He didn't give in, he kept swallowing.

He looked at his friend, at the dirt on his face and the vomit on his chin. "We can't tell them, Chuck. God damn them!" he shouted, unaware that he was crying. "Why did they take our clothing?"

The guard threw another bucket of salt water on Savak. This time Savak screamed.

Steven closed his eyes. He bit hard on his lower lip, letting the pain wash away his friend's cries.

He opened his eyes just as the second guard dumped the bucket of fresh water on Savak's face. The captain leaned forward and slapped him twice. Savak groaned.

"What was mission?" the captain screamed, moving the razor in a zig-zag motion down Savak's chest and stomach.

Above Savak's moaning cry, Steven heard the distant drone of a large helicopter. The sound increased steadily, and even Captain Lin had to look over his shoulder.

Within moments, the camouflaged belly of a large helicopter broke above the tree tops. Steven recognized the symbol of the People's Republic on its belly.

Soon the walls of their prison hut began to vibrate.

Outside, all activity stopped while everyone waited for the copter to land. When it settled to the ground, a hundred feet from the hut, the rear door opened, disgorging three uniformed men.

The man in the lead carried a medical bag. The two soldiers behind him hauled a varying assortment of cases. Steven stared at the officer when he passed the hut. The newcomer's uniform was Chinese, not

Vietnamese. His rank was colonel.

Reaching Lin, the Chinese officer spewed out a burst of Vietnamese. The captain stiffened, threw a sharp salute, and replied while gesturing at Savak with the bloody razor.

Steven was able to make out most of their shouted talk. The colonel was censuring Captain Lin for acting like a barbaric fool. Didn't he comprehend how valuable these men are? The officer asked acerbically. Was Lin trying to sabotage the People's war efforts or was he just stupid?

Lin defended himself by citing his orders to break the captives immediately. The newcomer spat a slanderous epitaph about Lin's ancestry before ordering Savak to be taken to the prison camp infirmary, which was situated in the two story headquarters building.

Steven squinted in an effort to make out the smaller insignias on the colonel's uniform. When he did, the shock he felt was as much physical as mental. He stumbled back, sat heavily on the damp dirt floor, and slowly lowered his head between his hands.

"What's wrong?" Latham asked, his voice riding the edge of panic as he crawled closer to Steven.

Steven swallowed hard. He couldn't look at Latham. He stared at his shaking hands. "God can't even help us now, Chuck, they've sent a Chinese intelligence specialist."

Latham stared at Steven's confusion. "Chinese? But I thought the Soviets . . ."

Steven took several deep breaths. When he had himself under a semblance of control, he looked at Latham. "Since Ho Chi Minh's death, the new regime has been accepting more outside help. Who they call on for help depends on their needs at the moment. Jesus, Chuck, the Chinese wrote the book on interrogation."

"Arnie won't break!" Latham swore.

The tight set of Latham's mouth, so at odds with the fear burning in his friend's eyes, made Steven want to agree. But his experience told him that he had to prepare Latham for what would be coming. "You've heard the rumors, everyone in the field has. They aren't rumors, Chuck. I've debriefed enough men to know they're true. Arnie will break. So will you, and so will I. And it won't be our fault."

"We'll work it out. We'll fight it!" Latham protested. Steven stared at Latham, understanding that his friend could not accept the truth. So instead of telling him more, Steven put his arm around his friend's shoulders, drew him close, and held him tight. "You're right Chuck, we'll fight it."

On the heel of Steven's words, the door to their prison hut was flung open. Captain Lin and his five guards entered. "Up!" Lin ordered.

When Steven and Latham got to their feet, Lin motioned to his men. They broke up into two sets of twos. The fifth covered them with his rifle.

"You go with them," Lin said.

"Where?" Steven asked.

Glaring at Steven, Lin swung his hand upward. Lin's open palm caught Steven on his cheek, rocking him backward. "You no speak unless permission given! Move!" he commanded as the two guards took his arms.

"Fight them, Steven! Don't give in!" Latham cried.

The guard to Latham's left rammed his rifle stock into Latham's stomach, doubling him over. Working in unison, the two guards dragged Latham out.

Lin motioned to the guards holding Steven. They took him out and marched him to a hut three away from the one he and Latham had been in since arriving at the camp.

The guards stopped at the door of this new prison hut. They pushed Steven hard, knocking him off balance and propelling him into the hut. He landed on his hands and knees. Turning, he rose just as they closed the door.

He looked around. The hut was empty. Three bed mats were rolled in a corner. Slowly, the understanding came. The Chinese colonel was nobody's fool. He had done what Lin should have done from the beginning. Separate them. Leave them alone and let them fall prey to their fears.

And when those fears began to leech at their minds, he would break them.

Chapter Twenty-one

Nothing happened for the next forty-eight hours. Food was brought once a day. The area between Steven's hut and Latham's remained empty.

For forty-eight hours, all Steven could do was think. He spent all his waking hours going over the details of their mission. He backtracked, using the perfection of his photographic memory to replay every word that had been said. Still, he couldn't quite put it together.

On the morning of the third day, he awakened abruptly. He was bathed in sweat. His heart was pounding heavily, and his breathing was shallow. He'd been dreaming about the final minutes of Jeremy Raden's torture and death.

Steven remembered the terrible instant when his eyes had met Raden's, and he'd known what the sergeant was going to do.

He focused on that precise moment, and the answer came to him with a harrowing flash of insight.

From behind, he heard voices. He ran to the window and saw three guards open Latham's door and go in. When they reappeared, two of the guards held Latham between them. The third walked behind Latham, keeping his rifle pointed on Latham's back.

They marched him to the central building, where they had been keeping Savak since cutting him down from the bamboo poles.

"It's okay, Chuck," Steven whispered, tears tracking down his cheeks. "You can tell them Chuck, it's okay."

Steven slumped to the floor, still chanting his litany. He knew Latham would talk, as he was sure had Savak.

And so would he. Steven knew that with complete certainty. Part of his work in Saigon had been spent debriefing escaped prisoners. For five months, he'd heard the horror stories of what went on in the POW camps. Steven knew that he would be powerless to stop himself from talking under the mix of drugs and pain.

He looked around his cage, desperately seeking a way out. He spotted a cracked strand of bamboo on the door. He scrambled to it, dug his nails into the crack, and began working to loosen the wide splinter. It took him a half hour to get the piece bent far enough back to work free. He broke three nails at the quick, but did not feel the pain.

When he finally held the slim and jagged shard of bamboo in his right hand, he moved to the center of the hut. He sat cross-legged, his head bowed and his eyes closed.

He cried then, for Savak and Latham, and for Cole and Raden. He took off his shirt, wadded the end, and stuffed it in his mouth so even if he cried out, no sound would pass the walls.

Then he began to saw at the skin on the inside of his wrist.

The pain was intense, made even more agonizing by its reason. But each time he faltered, he brought up the image of Jeremy Raden turning his neck across the razor. He didn't know how long it took for the dull wood finally to cut deep enough, but there came a point when the pain faded, and his mind and body went numb.

He looked down at the scarlet stream pumping from his left wrist. He had cut deep enough. He spat out the wadded material stood shakily, and went to the window. He stared at the building Latham had been brought to. He watched until his vision blurred, then turned away and slid his back down the wall. When he was seated on the dirt floor, he transferred the bamboo sliver to his left hand. His fingers had no sensation. He couldn't feel the wood.

Carefully, he brought the sliver of bamboo to his right wrist. He pressed down, trying to cut his skin, but the wood slipped from his lifeless fingers.

He stared at the bloodied bamboo for several seconds before realizing that it didn't matter. The blood was still coming fast from his left wrist. He rested his head against the wall and closed his eyes.

"Soon," he whispered. And because he so fully understood the necessity for Raden's death, and for his own, Steven gave himself up to the only salvation he could believe in.

Thankfully, there was no more pain. It was a

good sign. Pain was part of life, not death; peace was part of death.

And with that thought, the darkness swallowed him.

Steven woke sluggishly, feeling a tight pressure on his chest. He opened his eyes to the sight of a thatched bamboo ceiling. A light fixture with an incandescent bulb dangled snake-like three feet above him.

Disoriented, he tried to sit up. He felt pressure across his chest. He fought it, but couldn't move. He looked down along his chest. There were two leather straps pinioning him to the bed. He raised his left hand as far as he could and saw the bandage.

He closed his eyes. Self-loathing at his failure to die came swiftly and bitterly.

Then he heard a husky whisper as someone called his name. He opened his eyes and turned his head toward the sound. Savak was strapped into the bed next to him.

Savak's face was strained. Dark half-moon shadows accented red-rimmed and haunted eyes. Savak's thin lips were pale and bloodless. A muscle pulsed on the surface of Savak's cheek.

"What happened?" Steven asked after absorbing the despair filling Savak's eyes.

"They found you before you lost too much blood. They did a straight transfusion from Chuck to you. The dogtags gave them the information. We're in the infirmary."

"Where's Chuck?"

"Back under."

Steven stared at him, confused. "Back under? Under what?"

Savak looked away. He swallowed several times. Steven watched Savak's Adam's apple bob. "We've been getting drugged. Truth serums. Pentothal. I don't know what else. Jesus, Steven, Chuck and I talked. That's why the brass gave us those pills. They weren't afraid of us breaking under torture; they knew we couldn't hold out against drugs . . ."

Savak paused for a moment. His eyes turned distant. His tongue wiped across his lips. "How did they find out about us, Steven? How?"

Steven held Savak's pleading gaze and, hurting with the knowledge that the truth could not be spoken aloud, he said, "There has to be a spy in MI headquarters."

"But if they already knew what the mission was, what the hell purpose does interrogating us serve?"

He had to find the plausibility. He closed his eyes, exhaled. "I don't think they know the specifics of the mission, just that we were sent out with orders not to be taken alive."

Savak nodded. "Maybe that's why they sent Xzi Tao. Steven, he's . . . he broke me, and he broke Latham. But Steven, for some reason, he doesn't act as if he believes the information he's gotten from us. I think that's good."

Steven started to speak, but stopped himself and looked around warily. It was doubtful that the infirmary was bugged, but he couldn't take any chances. "He got the information from his own drugs."

"Maybe he doesn't trust them. I've been through it twice. Chuck's with him now. You'll go next."

Savak's statement rattled him, sending his thoughts back to his suicide attempt. "I can't let them get anything from me, Arnie. I can't."

"You won't. Not willingly."

Not willingly. The two words laid on the surface of his mind. He played with them, using them to work out some sort of a solution. But as the minutes passed, and no ideas came, Steven turned back to his friend.

"Tell me what you told them."

Speaking in a reluctantly dull voice, and keeping his face averted from Steven, Savak went over the details of his interrogation. He had no idea of what he'd said when he was under the control of the drugs, but Xzi had recorded everything, and had played it back to him at the end of each session. "The bastard doesn't miss a trick."

Savak continued talking for a half hour, going over all his replies. When he finally fell silent, Steven saw that his friend was pale and trembling.

"You didn't give them the information voluntarily, Arnie. Don't keep blaming yourself."

Savak turned to Steven. A tear squeezed out of the corner of his eye. When he spoke again, his voice cracked with hopelessness and abhorrence. "It doesn't matter whether or not I volunteered anything. If Botlin goes ahead with the invasion, I'll be responsible for killing thousands of men. God almighty, Steven, I don't know if I can live with that."

"They won't go ahead with their plans. They

can't. Not without our information."

Savak smiled sardonically. "No? Do you really think we're the only team they sent out?"

Steven blinked. He knew the answer; but, he doubted if Savak would believe him. "Why would they send out more than one?"

His haunted eyes fastened on Steven, staring at him as if Savak was seeing through him. "I don't think we were the only team that was sent out. But Jesus, Steven, I pray we are. Because if we're not . . ."

Two guards came the next day and took Steven to a small room on the second floor of the central building. They pushed him into a metal chair in the middle of the room, tied his ankles to the chair legs, and then secured his wrists together behind the chair back. The chair faced away from the door.

Then the guards left him alone.

He looked around. Like the infirmary, a naked bulb hung from wires in the ceiling. But unlike the infirmary, the walls were padded. No outside light penetrated the room. There was a table across from him with several hypodermic needles, a small medical bag, and a large reel to reel tape recorder. Against another wall was the only other piece of furniture—a metal cot with a thin worn mat on top of a webwork of springs.

He shivered.

The door opened behind him. He made himself sit still as the footfalls came closer. A moment later the Chinese colonel stood before him. The man was tall for an Oriental, about five-eleven. His face was oval, with a wide nose and a small mouth. Steven saw intelligence in the man's face, rather than the raw savagery of his Vietnamese captors.

"It was foolish for you to try to kill yourself, Lieutenant. Heroic, perhaps, but a waste of effort in light of the circumstances," Xzi said in a precise British accent.

Caught off guard, Steven said nothing. He held himself rigid, fighting as much against his own fears and tension as he was his interrogator's surprisingly melodic voice.

Xzi Tao studied him for another minute. "I am going to give you an injection. You will feel some dizziness at first, and then you will feel normal. But you won't be normal, Lieutenant Morrisy. I can assure you of that.

"I will ask you questions," Xzi continued smoothly, "and you will answer them. It will be over soon, and you will not be ashamed, for there is nothing that you can do to prevent yourself from giving me the information. Your superior officers know you have no way to stop yourself from talking or they would not have given you those suicide tablets, would they?"

When Steven maintained his silence, Xzi Tao went to the table and picked up a syringe. He reached into the black medical bag and withdrew a vial of clear liquid. He turned back to Steven, and made an elaborate show of filling the needle.

Xzi walked slowly toward him. The Chinese colonel's mouth was tightly set. When he reached Steven, he lifted the loose sleeve of the prison pajama. Every muscle in Steven's body tensed. His eyes were riveted to the clear liquid in the syringe.

The needle moved to Steven's skin. Steven looked up at the instant Xzi plunged the needle into his arm, and found the colonel's black eyes were carefully watching him.

Steven didn't blink or give any outward sign with the sting of the needle's entrance, or the force of the drug as the syringe was emptied into his muscles. Nor did he so much as blink at the second sting, when Xzi pulled the needle free.

The dizziness that Xzi had promised came less than a minute later. Soon, his mind was floating pleasantly. He felt above himself, out of himself. It was as if he was an observer, and not a participant in the situation.

"Who are you?" Xzi asked.

"Lieutenant Steven Morrisy. United States Army. Serial Number RA555669476," he heard his disembodied self answer.

"Where were you born?" Xzi asked, his smile becoming friendly as he moved closer to Steven.

"Greyton, Pennsylvania."

"What unit are you attached to?"

"Military Intelligence, Saigon."

"And your mission?"

"Reconnaissance."

"Reconnaissance for what purpose?"

Steven closed his eyes and willed the world to steady. When he opened his eyes again, and as he stared at Xzi, he brought up Jeremy Raden's image at the instant of the sergeant's death. Then Steven took a deep breath. "Purpose?"

"Yes," Xzi said, leaning forward expectantly.

"Purpose," Steven replied sluggishly. "P-u-r-p-o-s-e. Noun. Two syllables. Accent on break following p-u-r. Result or goal that is desired. Object or reason for which something is made or exists. A determination in striving toward a specific goal. Act or re . . ."

Steven's head pulsated. It hurt just to open his eyes. His mouth was dry and cottony. His tongue was swollen. He tried to build up saliva, and failed. He sat up, fighting the enormous pain.

The room spun. His stomach spasmed. He spotted the shit pot in the corner and threw himself toward it. He stayed bent over the pot until the heaving stopped. Then he dragged himself back to the cot.

He found a bowl of water on the floor next to the cot, and drank it greedily. His stomach cramped. He clenched his teeth and waited for the spasm to ease.

Then he began to breathe easier. Looking around, he realized that he was still in the interrogation room. He saw the tape recorder on the table, but the reels of tape were gone. The medical bag and the syringes were nowhere in sight.

Was it finished? Had he been left in the room to regain consciousness? He wondered if it was still day, or if night had come.

Then his head began to pound again. He leaned forward, cradling his forehead on his palms. *What did I tell him?*

Steven didn't know how much time had passed when he felt a hand shaking him. He opened his eyes, and found Xzi bending over him.

"How are you feeling, Lieutenant?" The Chinese colonel asked, his face showing an affected concern.

He fought down his anger and his hatred, knowing that any show of emotion would be a mistake. "You tell me," he said in his calmest voice

Xzi smiled. "Dry."

"Very good."

Xzi's smile widened. "You are proving to be an interesting subject, Lieutenant. Please, come to the chair."

When Xzi started to turn, Steven quickly judged the distance between himself and Xzi. He bent his knees in preparation to rise. But, just before he lunged at Xzi, he saw a shape materialize from out of the shadows. The shape turned into a Vietnamese guard with a pistol.

Steven exhaled slowly, forgetting his hasty plan to jump Xzi and run.

"Excellent, Lieutenant. You are a fast learner," Xzi said as he completely turned his back to Steven.

Steven stood silently. A wave of vertigo tried to sweep him back to the cot. He clenched his fists and spread his feet to brace himself while he waited for the dizzying weakness to pass.

"You see," Xzi said, looking Steven directly in the eyes, "you do not have the strength nor the mobility to complete the attack. Now, Lieutenant,"

Xzi went on, his voice taking on a sharp edge, "sit in the chair!"

Steven went to the chair. The guard moved behind him, pulled his wrists back, and tied them with more force than necessary. Steven grimaced against the pain, and bit his lower lip to stop himself from crying out.

He watched Xzi put a reel of magnetic tape into the recorder, thread it, and prepared the next injection.

I must not tell him anything, Steven said to himself. He kept on repeating the phrase, over and over.

When Xzi was satisfied with the dosage, he lowered his arm and, holding the syringe before him, walked back to Steven.

"Yesterday I used Pentothal on you. Today I will try something else. And Lieutenant, no more spelling lessons," Xzi added as he plunged the needle into Steven's thigh.

Steven looked down just as Xzi injected the drug into his thigh.

The dizziness came quicker this time.

Steven finished the bowl of rice, set it on the floor, and leaned back. He hadn't been hungry, but he'd forced himself to eat, knowing that the weaker he became, the easier the drugs worked.

There had been no day or night since they'd brought him to the interrogation room; he'd lost track of the number of times Xzi had drugged him. There had been at least five sessions, perhaps more.

That in itself was important. It told him he had not yet broken. Steven wondered how Savak and Latham were doing. Better than he, he prayed.

Steven stood, groaning with the effort. After his last interrogation, he'd woken to discover his ankles had been shackled. His skin was raw, small amounts of caked blood rimmed the metal cuffs. Ignoring the pain, he stretched, went to the corner, and relieved himself.

He was on his way back to the cot when the door opened. Steven saw daylight behind Xzi and the guard.

"Sit on the chair, Lieutenant," Xzi said.

Steven did, knowing that the ritual was to begin again. While Xzi put his black bag on the table, the guard went behind Steven and secured his wrists.

Once again, Steven watched Xzi put a reel of tape into the recorder, and then fill a syringe with whatever drug he had decided on for this session.

Xzi turned on the machine before turning back to Steven. Then he smiled. "Today, Lieutenant, you will tell me what I want to hear."

Steven stared stonily at him.

"Listen to the tape, Lieutenant," he said just as Arnie Savak's voice rose from the speaker. Steven stiffened, fighting back the anguish he felt when he heard the lifeless tone of his friend's voice.

He kept his face emotionless as he heard Savak first, and then Chuck Latham give all the details of their failed mission. Twenty-five minutes later, Xzi shut the machine off.

"As you see, Lieutenant, I haven't been lying to you. Your comrades have told all they know. Why don't you do the same. I assure you that it will make life more bearable."

Steven held Xzi's gaze, and remained silent.

Xzi scrutinized Steven carefully. The colonel's mouth was drawn into a bloodless gash. A muscle above Xzi's left eye twitched. "Lieutenant, the extended use of these drugs will damage your mind and body. They will change you. They may even kill you. I appeal to your intellect. Tell me what I must hear. When you do, all of this will end."

Steven favored his inquisitor with a smile.

Xzi's weary sigh was long and sibilant. "You sadden me greatly, Lieutenant," the Chinese officer said before putting a new reel into the recorder and turning it on.

"Lieutenant," came Xzi's recorded voice. "What was the mission code named WEREWOLF?"

Steven fought to keep himself calm when he heard his own voice say, "Werewolf." But when he heard himself speak next, he could barely hold back the elation that followed his learning that he had not given up anything to Xzi.

"W-E-R-E-W-O-L-F," the voice—his voice—coming from the recorder said. "Noun. Two syllables. From European folk lore. A human being who has the power to turn himself into a wolf. Old English from WER—Man and WULF—Wolf."

Xzi shut the recorder off and then approached Steven. He held the needle out. A growing teardrop of clear serum leaked from its tip.

Steven watched the liquid with fascination. Its clarity and pureness made him wonder why it should be so dangerous.

"I want you to understand something right now,

Lieutenant. If you recite any more dictionary definitions, you will no longer be able to distinguish between man and beast!"

With that, Xzi drove the needle into Steven's upper arm.

The guard gestured impatiently with his rifle.

Steven stood, his muscles protesting the movement. He was sore and in pain. He'd had a bad reaction during his last interrogation session. He didn't know exactly what went wrong, but the results had been violent.

When he'd come to, he'd been in the infirmary. He hadn't been able to open his left eye. Radiating lances of pain had shot from his ribs with his every breath. He tried to sit up, but felt hands on him, pushing him gently back. With his good eye, he saw an American bending over him. The man was gaunt, with sunken cheeks and sallow unhealthy skin.

"Wha—", he tried to say, but could only manage half the word.

"Easy Lieutenant," the man had said, keeping his hand on Steven's shoulder. "I'm Baker, a medic. I've been here for a year. You had a seizure during the last interrogation. They brought me in to care for you."

Steven had stared at the man. "My friends, are they—"

Baker shook his head. "We haven't seen them. They're being kept away from us."

Steven had tried to focus on the man, but his vision was blurred. "How . . . How many of you are here?"

"Almost forty Americans."

"Forty. Jesus . . ."

"Easy, Lieutenant, just stay down and rest," Baker had advised as he gave him a sip of water. A moment later, Steven fell back into unconsciousness.

Steven walked ahead of a guard as he was taken from the infirmary. He could only take small steps. Although the shackles were gone, they had served their purpose well. His ankles burned with agony at every step he took.

Outside, Steven drew in a deep breath. He felt the warmth of the sun, and looked up at the clear blue sky. It felt good.

He glanced over his shoulder, toward the segregated huts. As he wondered how his friends were, the guard gave Steven a sharp jab with his rifle.

"I'm going, asshole," he said, favoring the guard with a smile.

The guard brought him to the central building. It took him a full minute to negotiate the ten steps leading up to the door. Once inside, he found Xzi sitting behind a desk.

"Leave us," Xzi ordered the guard in Vietnamese. "Sit," he said to Steven in the same language.

Steven stood still.

Xzi smiled. "Please, Lieutenant, one of the few things I did learn from you was that you understand this country's language," he said again in Vietnamese.

When Steven refused to acknowledge Xzi, the

colonel sighed, and smiled. "You would have made a wonderful Oriental," he said in English. "Very well, Lieutenant, please sit down."

Steven did not allow himself anything at the small victory, if it was a victory.

After Steven was seated, Xzi lifted a porcelain tea pot and poured two cups of tea. He pushed one toward Steven. "It's not Vietnamese."

Steven shook his head.

"Lieutenant, this is to be only a friendly chat. Have some tea," he says, pushing the cup closer to him.

"What's in it?" Steven said at last.

Xzi Tao laughed, his head bobbing in amusement. "Nothing Lieutenant. But if it will ease your mind," he said, switching his cup for Steven's.

"I'll take the first one."

Again Xzi Tao laughed. "What do you Americans call it? A double cross? I assure you, Lieutenant, there are no drugs in either tea cup."

Steven picked up the porcelain cup, sipped some of the thin tea, and let the warmth ease the soreness in his throat. "Why am I here?"

"To talk."

"About what?"

Xzi put his cup down and stood. He walked to the window and looked out for a moment before turning back to Steven. "You and myself. Vietnam and America. You're an enigma to me, Lieutenant."

"So?" Steven asked, not sure of what Xzi was up to.

"Why will you not accept the truth of what your

own people have done to you?"

"I'm sorry Captain Xzi, but I cannot participate in this conversation."

Xzi favored him with an understanding look. "Strangely enough, I too am sorry. But Lieutenant, the time for your bravery is at an end. I have given you all the proof you need that we know everything about your mission. It is all the evidence any rational person could want, yet you refuse to accept it. Why?"

Steven stared past Xzi, and out the small window. He concentrated on the trees in the distance, and cleared his head of all thoughts of the mission.

"Cooperate with me, Lieutenant, and I will make sure that the remainder of your imprisonment will be endurable."

Steven drew his eyes from the trees, and looked down at his tea cup. It would be so easy to give in, to play the game and tell Xzi the story of their mission, using the same words as Savak and Latham. But he couldn't do it, not after having beaten the drugs. "By the rules of the Geneva—"

"No!" Xzi snapped, the gentleness of seconds ago gone. The colonel's eyes were hard and flat. His voice turned coarse. "For you, and for all the criminals participating in the illegal military action in Vietnam, there is no Geneva Convention. No war has been declared, Lieutenant. Surely you are aware of that."

"I have no such knowledge. As a member of the United States Army, I am protected by the rules of the Geneva Convention, governing the treatment of prisoners of war—"

"Stop!" Xzi commanded, his eyes narrowing into two dark slits. "You are not a prisoner of war, Lieutenant. You and Savak and Latham have *not* been listed as such. To your government, you are missing-in-action. No one knows your fate."

"I do," Steven said softly.

"Do you really, Lieutenant?" Xzi asked in a low, soft voice. "I wonder about you. I wonder why you persist in maintaining your charade. I wonder why you refuse to acknowledge what your own people have done to you. And, while I think on those questions you bring to my mind, I want you to ponder this: Your stay in this camp will be long and arduous, possibly even fatal for yourself and your friends, unless you come forward and speak truthfully with me."

Xzi stopped speaking. He stared hard at Steven, challenging him with a silent gaze for almost a minute. Then, finally, he said, "You may leave."

"It's over?" Steven asked, incredulously.

"For now."

Chapter Twenty-two

After leaving Xzi's tea party, Steven had been put back into his solitary hut. An hour later, a helicopter had come for Xzi. Steven didn't see Xzi Tao, or anyone else except for his guard, during the next two weeks.

The loneliness was the worst part of it. He was thirty feet away from Savak, and fifty feet from Latham, but he couldn't speak to them. Whenever he or the others called out, a guard would walk up to the mesh window and jab a rifle butt at them.

For the long hours of each day, Steven would stand at the window and stare at his friends' huts. He would see them watching him or each other. But even silent, he was able to draw comfort that they were alive and close by.

By the third day following Xzi's departure, Steven had formed a daily routine. After awakening, he would clean himself as best he could, using a part of the small ration of water allowed him for drinking. Then he would eat the cold rice, chewing it slowly to make it last as long as possible.

Following his meager breakfast, he would exercise quietly. Situps, pushups, knee bends, and squats comprised his hour-long routine. After finishing his physical routine, Steven went to the window and watched Savak's and Latham's huts.

Whenever one of his friends saw him, they would wave and give thumbs up sign. Their small and shared gestures were enough to help him make it through the day.

While he stood at the window, watching the workings of the prison camp, and thinking about escape, he tried to puzzle out how he had kept from breaking under Xzi's drugs.

The second meal of the day, and the last, came a half hour before darkness. The food was the same as the morning meal—rice. But at night, sometimes, there was meat in it. Steven thought that the meat was either monkey, rat, or snake. But he didn't dwell on the origins of the meat; he ate it. He had already lost twenty pounds. Any more weight loss would be muscle, a commodity he could ill afford to lose.

Following dinner, he would return to the window to watch his friends while he continued to think and plan. Then, with the full descent of night, he would watch the nighttime workings of the prison camp.

The only variations he allowed in his daily routine was in his sleeping times. He would go to sleep at different hours, and wake at different times, all to study the nighttime routines of the camp's duty guards.

And while he thought and planned his eventual escape, he studied the layout of the prison camp with greater and greater intensity. Because of the denseness of the jungle around them, the Vietnamese had used the natural contours of the land. The camp itself was kidney-shaped. The huts that contained the other American and South Vietnamese prisoners were at the south end of the compound. Steven's hut, and the huts that housed Savak and Latham were on the north end. Steven guessed that before their capture, these huts were used for supplies.

The central building had been constructed in the narrowest part of the camp, and permitted Steven only a small clear area to see the south end. But it also served to cut off a good deal of the view from the south into the north end of the camp.

If they got the opportunity to escape, Steven knew that they would have to use the narrow center area to their advantage.

Steven's solitary routine lasted for fifteen days, and ended with Xzi Tao's return. An hour after the Chinese intelligence officer's helicopter landed, Steven was sitting across from Xzi Tao. On Xzi's desk were two hand-enameled and steaming cups of tea.

Pushing one of the cups toward Steven, Xzi said, "I have given you ample enough time to think about our last meeting. Have you done so?"

Steven picked up the tea, cupping it between his palms, and sipped the hot and soothing beverage. "Yes."

"And?"

"I have not changed my mind."

"You realize, of course, that you may be condemning your friends to death, do you not? By speaking truthfully, you and Savak and Latham can spend the duration of the Peoples' revolution in comfort. I promise you this, Lieutenant. At the first opportunity, I will guarantee all of you an early release."

Reading Xzi's face, Steven sensed that Tao was speaking honestly. It was the man's eyes, and the set of his mouth that told Steven the colonel was not offering false succor, but a real promise that Steven was certain Xzi would maintain.

Still, Steven shook his head. "I can't, Colonel Xzi. I am an officer in the United States Army, and have sworn never to willingly cooperate with my enemy."

Xzi didn't speak immediately; he drank from his cup, lowered it, and exhaled. "Why do you feel the need to spend the rest of your internment like a caged animal?"

"While I am here, and with or without bars, there will always be a cage around me."

"You will die as so many of your people have, from disease, from malnutrition, and hard labor. Please Lieutenant, spare yourself this indignity. Spare your two friends as well."

Steven swallowed. He shook his head no.

Xzi sat back and regarded Steven through lowered eyelids. "If you will not do this for yourself and your friends, consider the folly of your being sent here. Is it not humiliating to know that your lives are being spent for nothing? Your own people have failed you, yet you insist on maintaining your false faith. You are a courageous man,

Lieutenant, and I feel deep sympathy for you. You may leave now," he ordered abruptly.

Steven stood as the door opened and the guard returned. He followed the guard out, slowly negotiating the steps down. But instead of taking him back to his hut, the guard brought him to the one that he and the others had woken in on their first night of captivity.

He found Savak and Latham inside. Steven embraced them warmly. He gazed at them fondly, for several long seconds before saying, "Xzi's leaving soon."

Savak turned away. "He's got everything he wants," he said, his voice filled with self-loathing.

Steven shook his head hard. "No, not everything. There's still a chance to save it."

"What chance. There's not a hell of a lot we can do from here," Latham said.

Steven smiled. He reached over and took their hands in his. "Exactly."

Xzi didn't leave as quickly as Steven had expected; instead, and for every day Xzi remained at the prison camp, at exactly nine in the morning, Steven was brought to Xzi.

A fresh pot of tea was always on the table. Tidbits of food were on a porcelain platter. Steven always took the tea. He never ate the food.

After Xzi's formalities with the tea and food, they would talk. Sometimes Xzi would question Steven about the mission; but for the most part, he would talk about the history of China, of Vietnam, and of America.

Laced within these talks were oblique references to military movements that were currently being run by the American command. When Xzi spoke of these manuevers, he frequently drew from his vast store of historical knowledge and used parallels from World War II to explain to Steven the futility of the American side of the fighting.

As these meetings continued, Steven was almost seduced into thinking that he was sitting with an old friend. But each time he felt his resistance falter, he made himself understand the ploy that Xzi was utilizing to weaken his determination.

At the end of each morning's session, Steven was returned to the prison hut. As soon as the guard left, he would go over every word of his talk with Savak and Latham. After Steven finished his report, they would spend the rest of the day planning their escape.

But on the eighteenth day after Xzi's return, the morning came and went, and Steven was not brought to Xzi. He paced the confines of the hut, wondering why. He had seen no unusual activity. Nothing had changed in the area, or in the prison camp routine.

Finally, just after the sun reached its zenith, Steven was summoned to the colonel. Although he was on the alert for anything unusual, he sensed nothing untoward at the beginning of their meeting.

Before their tea, Xzi opened a magnificent mahogany case and took out a small white bone handled knife in a hand-painted leather scabbard. It was Oriental in design, and Xzi looked at it fondly. "I received this yesterday. It was a present from my wife, for my birthday."

"It is magnificent," Steven said as Xzi put the knife back into the mahogany case and poured their tea.

After finishing the first cup of tea, Xzi poured a second, and then leaned back in his chair. He steepled his hands, rested his chin on his outstretched fingertips, and stared at Steven for so long that all of Steven's senses came alert.

"Lieutenant," Xzi said at last, "this will be our last talk together. I leave today. I will not be back."

Taken aback by the finality of Xzi's words, he remained silent for several seconds before saying, "I'll miss our little chats."

A half smile formed on Xzi's face. "Perhaps we could continue them, away from here and in comfort. Talk to me, Lieutenant. If you tell me about the mission, I will take you and your friends out of here, today."

Steven swallowed hard. "No."

"I do not understand why you persist in playing this idiotic role, Lieutenant Morrisy. Cooperate, and I will see to it that you and your friends fare well. At the proper time, I will make sure that the three of you are sent home. You have the word of a Chinese officer."

Steven took a long drink, before setting it down and saying, "We'll take care of ourselves."

"I find it ironic," Xzi continued, ignoring Steven's remark, "that your high command chose you for this mission. Ironic and stupid. Your two friends have given all the information they possess. But not you. I've heard of cases of natural resistance to the drugs, but have never come across one personally."

"There's always a first time."

"But you have missed my point. The totality of your resistance has forced me to ask myself why, whether in a drugged or normal state of mind, you will not admit to the purpose of your mission or corroborate what your friends have told me. I keep mulling over the possibilities. I continually ask myself what the harm would be?"

"Maybe it's just the way I'm made," Steven offered.

"No, Lieutenant, it is not the way you are made," Xzi said, his voice turning solemn. "But it is the way you have made yourself. So," Xzi continued, "I must ask you one final time. What was your mission?"

Steven put down his cup. "I'm sorry Captain, by the rules of the Geneva—"

"No more," Xzi Tao said.

Steven peered at him strangely. He believed Xzi this time. "This really is the last time, isn't it?" Steven asked. "No more drugs, no more questions?"

"Lieutenant, you are the enemy, but you are still a man. I will not degrade you any further."

Steven was oddly touched by Xzi's words, and for the first time, volunteered something about himself. "If it helps, I can't tell you why you failed with me."

Xzi Tao smiled. It was an open smile, almost a friendly smile. "But I can. You have a . . ." he paused, searching for the word. "The sort of memory that allows you to recall all events in complete detail, yes?"

"Photographic."

"Yes. Well, you closed off the portion of your mind that concerns your mission, and made yourself misdirect my questions to an area you could answer."

"I didn't know that was possible."

"Anything is possible, Lieutenant. In this instance, what you have done—and what could not be foreseen by your people—has given me the proof of what the reality is that underlies your mission. Most people would believe that by your refusal to admit what the others have, that it confirms the others' statements. But in this instance, it becomes just the opposite. Lieutenant, you know and I know that you were supposed to break under our interrogation."

Xzi paused in his dialogue to finish his tea. When the cup was empty, and he set it down, he gazed into Steven's eyes. "Do not blame yourself; rather, the fault lies with those in your high command. They have not learned how to fight us, and they will never learn."

Steven shook his head slowly, not so much in disbelief as in wonder at the workings of the Chinaman's mind. "They aren't that stupid," Steven said.

Xzi smiled. "Aren't they? But that is no longer the point. What becomes important for you, now, is that I leave today. Once I am gone, you and your friends will be back under Captain Lin's control.

"Lin will put you in with the other Americans, for now. He will work you without mercy. But I do not think that will be the worst of it. The Soviets will come too, within a week, to question you and Savak and Latham. They will want to verify what I have already reported. They, too, will be merciless."

"I will remember that," Steven said, puzzled as to why Xzi was telling him about the Russians without once again offering him an alternative.

And then Xzi Tao stood. "I sent the guard away. I wanted no other ears to hear our conversation. I will get the guard now," he said, going to the door.

Steven watched Xzi disappear through the door. Xzi had never left him alone before. Then he looked at the knife on Xzi's desk—Xzi's birthday present. Should he take the chance? Behind him, he heard Xzi's voice. Reacting instinctively, Steven reached across the desk, pulled the knife from the case and slipped it into his waistband.

"Lieutenant," Xzi Tao called from the doorway.

Steven stood, turned, and walked toward Xzi and the waiting guard. When he was three feet from Xzi, the colonel offered Steven a formal bow.

"Good-bye Lieutenant Morrisy. I truly hope you survive this camp, and will one day see your home again."

* * *

"You're sure he's going for good?" Savak asked, after Steven had buried Xzi's knife in the corner of the hut, and the three friends sat together, speaking in low voices.

Steven nodded. "He's leaving today. He also warned me that we can expect to go through the whole damn thing again in about a week, when the Soviets get here."

Latham looked at the spot where Steven had buried the knife. "I'll kill myself first."

Steven's smile was hard. "You won't have to. We won't be here. Xzi also told me that Lin is planning to move us to the other compound."

Savak looked from Latham to Steven. "Which means what?"

"That once we're in with the other prisoners, we're finished," Steven stated in a tone that barred any argument. "I've watched the camp routine for a month. I've charted out all the watch shifts, day and night. Lin keeps a dozen men on guard duty over the regular prison huts. He keeps them fresh by changing the shift every three hours. There's no way to take them by surprise."

"Then we have to do it on the way there," Latham said, seeing what Steven was leading up to.

"We'll never make it," Savak said. "Unless . . ."

Steven smiled. "Exactly. And I think that's just what Lin will do. He likes using fear tactics. He'll come in for us during the night."

"What about the fifties in the tower?" Latham asked.

Savak looked out the window, and at the two

guards manning the tower's fifty-millimeter machine guns. "Somehow, we'll have to find a way to do it without their seeing us."

"Chuck, if we can get out, can you get us back to Laos?" Steven asked.

This time it was Latham's turn to smile. "Just get us out. I'll get us home."

Xzi's copter landed late in the afternoon, just after the other prisoners had been brought back in from the paddies.

Steven had spent every minute since leaving Xzi, waiting for the guards to burst into the hut, looking for the knife. But as the afternoon wore on, and they were left alone, Steven began to believe that Xzi had packed away the knife's case without having looked inside.

As he watched the proceedings for Xzi's departure, he did so with mixed feelings. Steven knew that as soon as the copter took off, they would be at Lin's mercy. Two of them had already died by the Vietnamese captain's hands; the possibility that they would all die was strong.

"Shit! They're coming this way," Savak called. Steven left the window he was using, and joined Savak and Latham.

Xzi Tao and Captain Lin, with two NVA soldiers carrying Xzi's belongings, and two more following behind, came down the steps of the central building. When they reached the ground, Xzi spoke to two of the soldiers, and pointed toward the copter.

The men carrying Xzi's bags started off toward the copter while Xzi and Lin, with their guards, moved toward the prison hut. Once again, Steven felt dread build. Had Xzi been playing with him again? Had the man let Steven believe he'd gotten away with stealing the knife?

Steven looked at the spot where the knife was buried. No sign of it showed. Should he get the knife? Should they try their escape now? No, he told himself, they had to brave it out.

Moments later the door opened. Xzi Tao and Captain Lin came inside. Lin positioned himself against the wall, next to the door, while Xzi Tao walked up to the three men.

"All of you," Xzi said, "performed your duty to your country in a manner that you can be proud of. I would ask no more from my own men. When the fighting ends, and you return home, you will have no need to be ashamed of whatever happened here."

Xzi returned his gaze to Steven. "Lieutenant Morrisy, I wish you to have these." He pulled something from his pocket and offered it to Steven. "Too many people, on both sides, will be mourned without any final knowledge."

Looking at what was in Xzi's hand, Steven's throat constricted. Slowly, he lifted Cole and Raden's dogtags from Xzi's palm.

Curling his fingers around the dogtags, and pressing the metal into his hand, Steven looked quizzically at Xzi. But Xzi said nothing; he simply turned and walked out of the hut.

Steven was suddenly lightheaded. Xzi had not

realized his knife was missing. They had a chance now.

He called them together and, accepting input from each, began to refine his escape plan.

It was almost midnight, halfway through the second guard shift, when Steven heard footfalls approaching. "Time," he whispered.

They lay unmoving, listening intently to the approaching steps.

"Four of them, maybe five," Latham said, calling on his training as a scout.

The three friends had gone over the details of their escape, looking for anything that might trip them up. The only unknown was the number of men Lin would use to transfer them to the other side of the compound.

The known factors were all accounted for: The guard shifts, the number of guards at any given post, and the distances between guards.

There was only one location that suited their plans. It was a spot close to the central building, in the narrowest area, where the view from both the northern guard tower and the southern guard post would be cut off.

Steven touched his left arm. Using his fingertips, he traced the outline of the knife he had hidden beneath his shirt sleeve. The knife was tied to his forearm, handle down. He forced himself to leave the knife alone, and keep his arms at his sides.

As the approaching soldiers' footsteps grew

louder, Steven felt his nerves begin to hum.

Suddenly, the room came alive with strong beams of light. "Up. Up." Lin screamed, kicking Steven and the others.

The three men floundered, as if they'd been caught by surprise. Lin and the guards laughed and pushed them to their feet. Steven and Latham cowered away from the soldiers, holding their hands over their eyes to ward off the powerful hand-held flashlights.

One of the guards grabbed his shirt and pulled him forward. Steven let himself go, and was flung to his knees, near the door.

"Move!" Lin shouted, kicking Savak in the back of his thighs.

They struggled to their feet while letting themselves be manhandled out of the hut.

Then, as they stood outside, the guards in the tower turned on the spotlight and pinioned them within it.

"Now you join others. Now you learn what it like to be prisoner," Lin said, sneering obscenely at them. "Move!" he ordered, nodding to the guards who prodded them with their rifle barrels.

Steven glanced around quickly. There were only four men—Lin and three soldiers. The guard behind him jabbed him again. Steven started forward, Savak and Latham flanked him.

As they crossed the compound, the light from the tower tracking them carefully, Steven's palms turned moist. He continually rubbed them against his thighs.

When they were twenty feet from the central

building, and entering the narrowest part of the compound, the tower's searchlight no longer reached them. Ahead of them was the central building. Behind that was another gun tower, its searchlight on and waiting for the small group to step within its circle of illumination.

Steven lifted his hand to his mouth and coughed.

Suddenly, Savak stumbled.

Steven half turned to Savak, his hands outstretched. Before he could complete the movement, the guard watching him swung the butt of his rifle into the pit of his stomach.

With a strangled groan, Steven sank to his knees and clutched his stomach.

"Up!" Lin snapped, angling toward him even as Steven's guard reversed his rifle and aimed it at Steven.

"Leave him alone, you bastards!" Latham shouted, taking a step toward Steven.

In the fraction of an instant that the three guards and Lin looked at Latham, Steven moved. He slipped the knife from the scabbard and lunged at his guard. He caught the man in the throat, severing his carotid artery and opening his windpipe with a single stroke.

Within the frozen seconds of time that Steven moved, and before the guard hit the ground, Steven heard a sharp snap from his left, followed by a strangled moan to his right as Savak and Latham took out their men.

Without hesitating, Steven whirled, and lunged at the spot where he had last seen Lin. The captain was just bringing his pistol to bear when Steven reached him. Lin's eyes widened, but he was too late. Steven's free hand clamped over Lin's wrist, preventing him from moving the pistol.

In the same motion, Steven struck with the knife, pushing it hilt deep into the captain's stomach, and then ripping up. Lin stiffened. His eyes widened in astonishment, and the pistol fell from his hand.

Steven released the man, and Lin fell to the ground, dead.

Steven turned again, his knife at the ready, and found Savak and Latham silently stripping the weapons from the dead guards.

Steven picked up Lin's pistol just as the alarmed shouts of the guards on the south end of the camp began to echo.

"Let's go," Savak ordered.

The three took off in unison, disappearing into the thickness of the Southeast Asian jungle.

Chapter Twenty-three

The telephone rang. Its shrill, urgent call severed the past's trenchant grip on Steven's mind. One moment he was back in Vietnam, and the next, he was watching Paul Grange answer the telephone in the living room of a farm in the Maryland mountains.

The timely interruption gave Steven the chance to clear the pain-riddled sharpness of his memories, and the opportunity to stabilize himself in the present. He looked down at his hands, and saw that he'd been holding Jeremy Raden's letter throughout his hour-long discourse.

"Sorry," Grange said, after hanging up. "Please go on."

Steven put Jeremy Raden's letter down next to him. "Tao was right about why I didn't break under the drugs. And he was partly right about the reason for the mission's failure. But it's not the whole reason," Steven said, his eyes locking on Grange's.

Carla, not Grange, spoke next. "I feel like I'm missing something important. How could your not breaking under drugs turn your mission into a failure?"

Steven studied her face for a long moment. "If

I'd broken immediately, or even after two or three sessions, and backed up Savak and Latham's information, our information might have been accepted. But my resistance was absolutely total."

The puzzlement on Carla's face deepened. "I still don't understand why that caused the mission to fail?"

He handed her Jeremy Raden's letter. "Read it."

He watched her closely while she read the letter, and saw her face register surprise. When she finished, she looked at Steven with dawning comprehension. Then she passed the letter to Grange.

As the Secret Service agent read the letter, his eyebrows shot up in surprise. A moment later Grange frowned. But it wasn't until several seconds after Grange finished reading, that he looked at Steven.

"Raden caught it first," Steven said with a nod. "He had a sharp mind—very creative. It was Raden's years in the Nam, and his rank, which enabled him to see through MI's plan. Our having been gassed rather than shot, and our uniforms being taken away so we couldn't get to our suicide pills should have been confirmation of that. I didn't want to believe it—not at first. Yet it was so damned logical. The brass was digging into their tried and true barrel of tactics, and utilizing the strategies that had always worked in conventional warfare to outmaneuver an enemy who was defeating them! Misinformation. Misdirected intelligence made to look faultless and true, complete with invasion plans, ship routes imbed landing sights."

Nodding, Steven said, "We were sent into the north, to reconnoiter the jungles for the best possible invasion routes for an attack that would catch the Cong by surprise and defeat them. That was our mission. We believed in it completely, because we wanted to. But that was also the major difference between Nam and World War Two. In World War II, they made the *enemy* spies believe. In Nam they tried to use us to make the enemy believe."

"But Sergeant Jeremy Raden didn't believe it," Grange said as he leaned forward and extended Raden's letter to Steven.

Steven looked down at the letter. "No, he didn't believe it. Raden saw through the hoax because the brass wanted him to know all the details of the mission. As he says in the letter, corporals and sergeants are never privy to that kind of information, no matter what the mission is. He smelled the skunk before anyone knew there was one. That was why, when I figured it out, I believed I had no other choice but to try and kill myself."

Laughing bitterly, Steven drew up his left sleeve and showed them the ragged scar tissue.

"But if Raden died, and you didn't break, how could they have found out?" Carla persisted.

Steven took several shallow breaths, fighting

down the harsh recall of his memories. "I didn't break because of the way my mind is set up. And Xzi refused to accept the information he'd extracted from the others. He told me that unless I talked, he could not believe any of it. And, when I refused to corroborate. He began to suspect.

"What happened when you escaped?" Carla asked, leaning forward eagerly.

Steven glanced at Grange. "Was that in the files?"

"According to the files," Grange said, "after you took out your guards and Lin, and went into the jungle, you didn't head for safety; rather, you waited until a patrol was sent out after you, and then the three of you went back to the camp, took out the guards in the south tower, and then killed or captured the rest of the NVA troops. You waited in ambush until the patrol returned, and you took them out as well."

Pausing, Grange turned to Carla. "In all, they freed forty American and South Vietnamese prisoners. Then, with Latham leading the way, and Steven and Savak controlling the large party, they worked their way from the North Vietnamese bottleneck into Laos.

"When they reached the original extraction site, it was deserted. They travelled on foot from Laos into Cambodia, and then into South Vietnam. It took them almost two weeks to reach American troops. They came home soon after that. Is that accurate, or were there some other deletions in the records?" Grange asked, turning back to Steven.

"Up to a point, except for the going home part," Steven agreed. "While we were running, I told Savak and Latham about what had happened. I couldn't have before, because of the ongoing interrogations. They didn't want to believe me, but in the end they had no other choice.

"When we reached safety, and as soon as our arrival had been reported to Saigon, Latham and Savak and myself were separated from the others and flown back to Saigon. They didn't even give us enough time to take a bath.

"We got to Saigon on the day after Christmas, December twenty-sixth, nineteen seventy-one. We were brought directly to Colonel Botlin. We told him that our mission had failed."

Steven looked from Grange to Carla. "After welcoming us back with a smile and a handshake, and without letting us get in another word, Botlin told us, quite confidently, that our mission had in fact been successful. I took it upon myself to tell him the truth. 'No, sir, it failed. They didn't buy our story.'

"Then the colonel, after expressing his deepest sympathies for our travails, told us that we were wrong. In fact, he admitted, our capture had been intended all along. He spoke to us as if what we had been through had been nothing more than a police lock-up back home.

"Botlin went on to confirm that the information we had given up, had been exactly what was intended of the mission. Then he tried to assure us that we would have been freed very soon, for the assault would indeed be taking place. But not in the way we had understood.

"Savak asked him when the assault was to start. Botlin had smiled, looked at his watch, and said, 'In a few minutes, the first bombs will fall on Hanoi.' "

"Dear God," Carla gasped, the brightness gone from her eyes.

Steven fixed her with a hard stare. "There is no God in the army, only superior officers, jackasses, and grunts," he said angrily. "I can't even begin to describe to you, the loathing I felt for Botlin and the others like him. Botlin was immune to our feelings as he explained to us how aerial reconnaissance had shown extensive troop movement near the border, indicating how totally our false information had been accepted. He went on to say that the reason we three had been chosen for the mission was because we'd grown up together and had always worked well as a team.

"Apparently the computers in Intelligence had come up with our names. Then the shrinks and computer experts went over our personal histories with a fine tooth comb. Their pre-mission evaluation indicated that we would not break under physical torture because we would not want the other two to see any weakness. And our resistance would add more validity to what the interrogation under drugs would finally reveal."

"That sounds about right for the time," Grange said tersely.

"For any time, Grange," Steven corrected. "When we told him it was a trap, he wouldn't listen. He went on to say that in part, this massing of troops violated agreements drawn up before '68, it gave the Americans the ability to bomb Hanoi into oblivion, as well as the troops on the border. While the bombing went on, a pincer attack would be effected, cutting off the NVA in South Vietnam from their supply lines in the north. Once that was accomplished, the NVA would be broken and destroyed.

"I don't know whether you can imagine the desperation of our arguments with Botlin. We tried to explain, over and over and over, that the mission had failed—not the mission we were told about, but the mission that they had programmed us to bring about."

"What happened then?" Carla asked, her eyes probing his, her upper teeth worrying at her lower lip.

Steven picked up his glass of scotch and stared at the amber liquid. "Eight hours later, Command Saigon learned we were right. They panicked. They couldn't just call off the bombing, so they kept it up for five days, going along with what they originally intended; but the assault mobilization was cancelled at the last instant.

"Savak, Latham, and myself were shipped home that night. We were debriefed for ten days, and informed that a top secret classification had been put on WEREWOLF. We were ordered to forget about everything that had happened."

"But the Medals of Honor?"

Steven looked at Carla, his face stoic. "On the surface, it was for the escape and liberation of the prisoners that we led out of the prison camp. In reality, the medals were as much a balm to salve guilty consciences, as they were a bribe to keep us quiet. I guess the record alterations were to make sure that even if we said something, it would be disproved."

"And the rest is history," Grange said solemnly. "The bombing of Hanoi put the last nails into the coffin of the war."

"And ironically," Steven added, "Xzi used our own history to turn the plan around and make what Botlin hoped to be his Normandy, into his defeat by making Botlin and the high command believe that their plan had worked."

Carla stared at him. Her eyes were distant, as if she were someplace else. Then she bobbed her head, once, and said, "Now I understand why you were so edgy at last night's reception. Ambassador Xzi . . . Colonel Xzi . . . Seeing him again must have been very hard."

Had it been hard to face the man who had shown him that those things he had believed in were lies? "Oh yes," he whispered.

"Morrisy," Grange began, "we need to—"

Steven turned to Grange, cutting him off with a firm wave of his hand. "Whatever you need can wait," he said, holding Grange's surprised look.

He had told his story and, for the first time in a over dozen years, opened his mind to the pain of the past. Now the time had come to learn if he had made a mistake about Grange, and to find out if he was here and free, or if he had merely exchanged the FBI for the Secret Service.

He rubbed his side, and felt the hard lump beneath his jacket. "Before I go any further, with anything, there are certain things I need to know." When Grange nodded, Steven put the scotch down. "How many men do you have here, besides yourself?"

"There are two men outside. Two more are in hidden watch posts at the entrance. There are four additional teams, in cars, posted in strategic spots along the highway," Grange answered.

Steven's muscles tensed with anticipation. He picked up Raden's letter and very carefully folded it. Then he shifted, resting his right arm on the back of the couch, his fingertips grazing Carla's shoulder. "Have you found out why they tried to kill Ellie?"

He caught Grange's quick glance at Carla, before the agent said, "I've gone over it a hundred times. I've put myself in your fiancée's position, and all I can come up with is that Ellie must have either learned who the mole was, or she'd found something incriminating enough to have eventually led to the mole's uncovering."

"That's your professional opinion?" Steven asked, looking down at Raden's letter as if he'd forgotten he was holding it. He looked back at

Grange and casually put the letter into his shirt pocket. Then he dropped his hand to his lap.

"Yes," Grange said, obviously puzzled, "it's my professional opinion."

Moving suddenly, Steven pulled Carla's pistol from his waistband. At the same time, he grabbed Carla's hair and yanked her to him. Before she or Grange could react, he pressed the barrel to the underside of her chin.

"Is that your *professional* opinion as well?" he asked, his voice cracking.

Twisting her neck, Carla stared at him. Her eyes were level with his. He saw no fear in their blue depths. "I asked you a question," he said, jabbing the metal roughly into the soft skin on the underside of her chin.

From the corner of his eye, Steven saw Grange reach for his weapon. "Don't even think it. Just keep your hands on your lap."

"Morrisy . . . Steven—"

"Shut up, Grange," he snapped. Then he focused his attention on Carla. "You're a good actress, Carla. You had me convinced. But I know better now. Who are you?"

"Put the gun down, and I'll tell you."

Her voice held the same sharp tone of strength that she had used earlier, when the car had missed them. "Grange," he said, "I want you to take out your weapon and set it on the floor. Use your left hand. Two fingers only on the barrel."

Grange complied without argument. When his pistol was on the floor, Steven said, "Carla, I'm going to let go of you. Don't make any sudden moves."

He released her and stood abruptly. He backed up several feet. "Sit next to her," he told Grange, motioning with Carla's Browning.

When Grange was on the couch next to Carla, he said, "Morrisy, we're not your enemy, we're your friends. I know you're not involved in what's been happening."

Steven laughed at him. "But I am. I'm very involved."

"I meant as the enemy."

"The Enemy? Grange, I don't know who the hell the enemy is. I never have," Steven said in a low voice. "And I'm starting not to give a damn. What I do know, is that the woman I love is laying in a hospital. She may never know who she is or who I am; two lifelong friends are dead; the FBI thinks I'm a spy and a murderer; and, earlier this morning—according to you—a Soviet terrorist hit man tried to kill me, along with a woman who claims to be my fiancée's sister.

"And the more that these things happen, the more I feel like I'm stuck in the middle of a Hitchcock movie, as confused as the audience. So until Carla answers my question, you are *the enemy.*"

After a glance at Grange, Carla folded her hands on her lap. Looking directly at Steven, she began to speak. Her face was calm, and her eyes were clear. "My name is Carla Statler. I'm an agent of the United States Secret Service, Department of the Treasury. Paul Grange is my control supervisor. My team's assignment is to find the mole who is leaking foreign policy decisions before they can be implemented. We've been working on this assignment for the past nineteen months."

She paused, took a deep breath, and then said, "My personal assignment in this case is as backup for the deep cover main operative in Senator Pritman's office . . . Eleanor Rogers."

Chapter Twenty-four

Steven felt the world go askew. Of every explanation he'd considered for Carla's presence and role, what he'd been told had taken him completely by surprise. He fought a short and intense inner battle which mixed disbelief with incredulity.

Then he burst into laughter. He stared at the two Secret Service agents, shaking his head and trying not to lose what little of his sanity still remained. "You almost got me. Jesus Christ, you people are good. You really do have your parts worked out to perfection. But Ellie a secret service agent? No! If Ellie was an agent I would have known."

"She was planning to tell you after the elections," Carla said.

"Oh, yes, absolutely!" he said, his voice laden with sarcasm. "And with Ellie in the hospital, you can tell me whatever suits your fancy, because she may never be able to tell me the truth."

"It's the truth!" Grange snapped irritably, his voice echoing in the house.

Steven couldn't stop his sneer. "Prove it."

Grange's exhale was filled with impatience. He jabbed a finger toward the end table, and the phone sitting there. "301-555-8101. Ask for the director. The identification code for the day is Blue Three Silver."

"Director of what?"

"Call the number, Steven," Carla said.

He looked from one to the other, trying to see through their facades. Something about the two of them, he wasn't sure what, told him to try.

He picked up the receiver and laid it on the table. Then he dialed the number with his left hand. All the while, the pistol in his right hand remained pointed at both agents. When he finished dialing, and heard the connections being made, he picked up the receiver.

The call was answered on the second ring. A woman said, "Line one priority."

"The director."

"Identification."

"Blue Three Silver."

The line went dead instantly. Several seconds later it came on again. "Axelrod."

Steven had no doubt that it was Julius Axelrod on the other end of the phone. He had seen the director several times at governmental functions, and had heard the man's distinct voice enough times to be able to remember it.

"This is Morrisy. One question. Who is Eleanor Rogers?" He heard the director of the Secret Service draw in a breath. "Is Paul Grange there?"

"Yes," Morrisy said. "I want an answer."

"Eleanor Rogers works for me, Mr. Morrisy."

Steven hung up, flipped on the safety, and lowered the pistol to his side.

"No more games. I want to know what's going on, and I want to know now. Start with Ellie."

Grange and Carla launched into a detailed synopsis, giving Steven a complete background scenario of the case. He listened without interruption, digesting each piece of information and filing it away in a specific corner of his mind. When they finished, he knew they had told him the truth. Eleanor Rogers, the woman he loved, was a Secret Service Agent.

Had it all been an act? Had she let him fall in love with her just for the sake of her investigation? Was he that easy? He felt disgust for himself growing strong.

"Was our engagement part of her cover?" he asked in a deadly level voice.

"Oh, Steven, no," Carla said, raising her hand toward him and taking a half step forward. She stopped suddenly when he tensed, and said, "Just before you gave Ellie the ring, we talked. She knew you were in love with her. And she was in love with you. It was a very difficult situation for her."

"Especially if I was the mole."

"Ellie had no doubt about you at all," Grange interjected smoothly. "She tried to convince me, but she couldn't. However, being engaged to you assured her of having access to you at all times, so we agreed to let her go ahead. It also helped to solidify her cover."

"You agreed to let her go ahead," Steven said, his thickening voice the precursor of a growing rage.

"That's right," Grange said with no hint of apology. "And it wasn't an easy decision to make. I was faced with two bad choices: Either pull Ellie off the case because of her involvement with you; or leave a possibly compromised agent in place. My decision was based on her ability to handle her job, and to handle you."

"In other words, you couldn't pull her because you couldn't replace her," Steven said dryly.

"Not quite. If we were absolutely certain you were the mole, we wouldn't have needed Ellie on the case any longer."

"You have a way with words."

"Morrisy, try to understand that there's more to this than you know about. The focus of the operation wasn't aimed solely at Pritman. We have other operatives working on other suspects, including an operative inside the upper echelon staff of the White House. She's being phased out now."

Steven was caught short by Grange's admission. "Why the White House?"

"Because the President asked for it," Grange stated. "And the White House staff has been cleared."

"Which is why we know that what's happening isn't something that the President or his aides have set up to discredit Pritman," Carla added.

"How can you be that certain? You work for the man."

"No," Carla said in a low and fervid voice. "We work for Julius Axelrod."

"Six weeks ago," Grange cut in, "in an effort to pin down the mole, we set up a program of false information. That information was given to three separate committees. Each committee was given a similar but slightly different version of a new foreign policy initiative. One committee was made up of White House staff. The second committee was a senatorial committee, and the third was a house committee. In each of those groups were people of whom we had reasonable suspicions. Three weeks after the meetings, the information found its way to the Soviets. Any guess as to which group?"

"Pritman's," Steven whispered.

"Yes," Grange said.

"He's not a mole and he's not leaking information."

"I hope not," Grange said.

"And that's the entire story?"

"Up to this morning's murder attempt."

"I see," Steven said, thoughtfully. Then he sat straighter, and glared at Grange. "Now, I have a few more questions that I want straight answers to. I know now how the FBI knew I was at the hospital. But what I don't know is how this man you call Anton knew I was at the motel. And why, all of a sudden, do they want me dead?"

Grange's face went taut. He glanced at Carla, and then back to Steven. "What do you mean, you know how the FBI knew you'd be at the hospital?"

"They tapped the car phone."

Grange seemed to think about it for a moment. "Tapping a cellular is easy. They get a direct link to the transmission relay. But that's not the answer you're looking for."

Steven nodded. "No. It's just an answer. Like why Carla helped me with those feds. A joint operation to make me believe in her, right Carla?"

"Wrong," she said.

He ignored her, and spoke to Grange. "But what about the attack this morning?"

Steven saw Grange staring at a spot beyond him. Then the agent closed his eyes. "Because I'm stupid," Grange said, opening his eyes and reaching into his jacket.

With the movement, Steven lifted his pistol. His heart pounded hard again, and his finger tightened on the trigger. "Don't!"

"Would you stop acting like we're your enemy and put the damned gun down! We're on your side." Grange withdrew a radio transmitter from his jacket. He pressed the call button. "Jamison. Sweep Morrisy's car."

"It's not the staff car we had last night, it's my own car," Steven said.

"It doesn't matter. If you were bugged, it would be on all the vehicles you use. And you're partially right about Carla. After Ellie was taken out, Carla's job was to keep an eye on you and to see if she could find out something about the mole.

"But we aren't working with the Bureau," Grange added quickly. "In fact, we still don't know why they're involved in this at all."

Grange's name crackled out of the radio. He pressed the button. "What?"

"We've got a positive read. Witt found the transmitter." Grange exhaled sharply. "Pull it," he said to the agent. "Now you have your answer. The transmitter was how they knew where you were."

A moment later a second voice came over the radio. "Paul, we've got another problem. The steering assembly and brake lines are rigged with C-3. There are more packets on the gas tank."

A cold chill passed along Steven's body. He glanced at Carla and saw that her eyes had dilated.

"Detonator?" Grange asked.

"Not yet. I'm looking."

"Get rid of the transmitter," Grange ordered again.

The radio came alive again. "Paul, I can't pull the transmitter, it's wired to the explosives. The detonator is a remote, but all the charges are rigged with backup fail-safes. And there's a hell of a lot more charges than I thought. If this car goes, it's going to take a lot of things with it."

"Get up here," Grange ordered.

While he was listening to the exchange, a cog clicked suddenly into place. He felt the blood drain from his face. Placing the pistol on the table, Steven walked to the window. The cooling ball of the sun was in its final descent, casting a dull orange-yellow glow over the mountains.

Steven tried to draw some comfort from the peaceful scene, but could not ease the tension rampant within him. "I know why," he said.

"Why what?"

"The change of plans—why they want me dead instead of being handed to the FBI on a platter." He turned to Grange. "The protection you arranged for Ellie. Is it good?"

"She's one of us, Steven. The protection is the best."

"She's going to need it." Steven walked across the room, stopping before Carla. "Do you remember what happened the other night, in the hospital?"

"A lot of things happened," Carla said, puzzled.

"One very specific thing happened. Ellie opened her eyes. She grabbed my hand and spoke. She mumbled gibberish, but if someone heard about it . . ."

". . . They might think that she told you something, especially after you roughed up the FBI men and started to run," Carla finished for him, her eyes reflecting the full understanding of his thoughts.

"Which is why the mole is trying to kill me now. He thinks that Ellie told me who he was."

"Or he can't take the chance that she may have given you some sort of a clue," Grange added as the other two agents came into the living room.

"How bad is it, Witt?" Grange asked the shorter of the two.

The agent Steven had seen when he'd first arrived said, "Real nasty, and very professional."

Grange's expression wasn't one of defeat. He introduced Witt and Jamison to Steven, and then said, "There's a way to turn this around. It's a slim chance, but we don't have much choice. We're going to move the car. If the car is followed, we'll spring our own trap, away from here. But if the car isn't being tailed, we'll have to assume the sanction will come at the farm because the position has been marked."

Grange paced as he drew out his plan. Steven followed it carefully, listening while Grange detailed every contingency. The supervising agent decided on using the state park to plant the car. Jamison, in an agency car, would stay a mile ahead of Witt, in the Bronco. Two other agents would trail Witt and Jamison at a five-minute interval, to see if Steven's Bronco was followed. There would be no contact between Witt and Jamison, and the other two agents.

When Grange was finished, and had given everyone their orders, he turned to Steven. "I'm sending you to another safe house."

"Why? If he's looking for me, I should be here."

"It won't be the mole who's coming after you.

It will be Anton, or someone like him."

"I want to stay."

Grange went up to Steven, put his hand on his shoulder, and pressed gently. "I know you do. And the best way for you to help is by doing what I ask. You'll be the bait, Morrisy, but we'll be in control."

Steven looked past the surface of Grange's eyes before he nodded his acceptance of the agent's plan.

For the next ten minutes, Steven sat quietly on the couch, watching Grange efficiently set about his plan. When he was finished, and had dispatched the vehicles, he reported everything to Axelrod. Only then did he sit down again.

"When did you realize Carla wasn't Ellie's sister?"

Steven glanced at Carla. She was regarding him with a curious stare. "There were a lot of little things that made me become suspicious. But I wasn't sure until we got here."

"Suspicious of what?" Carla asked.

"Last night, when you took Grodin out. I thought it was a brave but stupid thing to do. I didn't see the whole thing, but I do remember how you took his gun from him, and covered him. Your stance was that of someone who has handled weapons before, and not casually or for sport. And there was the matter of that," he added, pointing to the nine-millimeter Browning on the table.

"The night when I came home and you were

there. Your pistol had slipped between the cushions, and you'd left it behind. I wondered why you would have a weapon like that. But it didn't fully register, and when everything got hectic, I forgot about it.

"And this morning, when the car tried to kill us . . ." He paused, looked at Grange, and then back to Carla. "My first reaction was to help the people. Your first reaction was to get away."

"Steven you don't under—"

Cutting her off, he waved away her protest. "It's all right, because I understand now what I didn't then. It wasn't that you didn't want to help them, it was that you had to protect me."

"And that's what tipped you off?" Grange asked.

"No, that's what started to make me think about Carla. When I finished telling you about Nam, and we got into the whys and wherefore, she said, 'It must have been difficult knowing that he had penetrated the mission's cover.' "

Steven looked at Carla. "No one uses terminology like that, unless it's their job."

Witt drove Steven's Bronco west on the narrow two-lane highway. Jamison was a mile ahead, in one of the agency cars. They had been on the road for fifteen minutes and were in communication by walkie-talkie, using a frequency that would not affect the bomb's detonator. Witt had seen no other vehicles for the last five minutes, and was beginning to feel the tension of driving a bomb. He thumbed the transmitter, and said, "Jamie, where the hell is the turn off?"

"Another mile or two. There's a state park direction sign."

Four minutes later, Jamison reported the turn off. When Witt reached it, and the sign that said the park was eleven miles farther down a narrow and tree lined road, he breathed a sigh of relief. Turning onto the narrow road, Witt drove for two miles without seeing any oncoming headlights.

Just as he was beginning to think that Grange's crazy plan would work, headlights flared in his rear view mirror. His knuckles turned white on the steering wheel of the rolling bomb. "We've got company," he radioed to Jamison.

"Make out who?"

"Too far back," he said as he slowed the Bronco. "I'm going to pull over and let him pass."

"Wait," Jamison ordered. "Let me flip around. Keep coming until you see my headlights, then, pull over."

A minute and a half later, Witt saw the oncoming headlights flash and then go off. He pulled off the road and waited for the car behind him to pass.

When the car was almost upon Witt, it slowed and stopped. Witt had his service piece out, and was lifting it when the passenger of the other car rolled down his window and said, "You okay? Do you need some help?"

"I'm fine," Witt said, "just taking a rest."

The driver smiled, waved at him, and started off. Witt, ignoring the cold and clammy skein of perspiration that had broken out over his body, picked up the radio and said, "False alarm."

"Roger that," Jamison said. "Let's get the hell out of—"

His words were cut off by the eruption of a fireball in the spot where the Bronco had been. The night lit up. Jamison saw pieces of the vehicle fly skyward before he was forced to turn away.

When his vision cleared, he started his car and drove forward. He stopped across from the burning remains, got out, and went toward the wreckage. The flames were too intense. From twenty feet away, the heat seared his face. He closed his eyes, and shook his head, realizing that there would be nothing left of Witt.

Finally, he turned and walked back to his car. He stopped at the door, drew his service revolver, and looked around.

"Where are you," he whispered, thinking about the other two agents who had been keeping pace behind them. He raised the walkie-talkie and thumbed the transmit button. He called out one code, and then another. There was no answer. He tried again. Nothing. Instinctively, he knew that the backup agents had been taken out.

In the distance, headlights blossomed. The sound of a car's engine was loud. Tires protesting against the road, screamed into the night.

Jamison sidestepped into the road and dropped to one knee. He set himself in a double-handed firing position, as the car bore down on him. He waited for the car to come closer and, aiming above and to the left of the driver's headlight, he fired.

He got three rounds off before the car plowed head on into him.

"Everything's settled," Grange announced, returning to the room after a twenty-minute absence. "I've spoken with the director. He's sending out a second team. You'll be going to the new safe house as soon as Witt and Jamison get back."

"Where?"

"Virginia. Witt and Jamison will drive you to an airstrip on the other side of Hagarstown. The director is having a plane dispatched to pick you up there," Grange said, sitting down across from Steven.

Steven was still adjusting to the revelations about Ellie. He no longer doubted the truth of Carla's disclosure, he only doubted his own ability to understand why Ellie had not trusted him enough to tell him who she was.

He also realized, with the clearness of perfect hindsight, that if Ellie had told him, he wouldn't be where he was, and she wouldn't be in the hospital.

"Who are the prime suspects?" he asked, pushing aside his thoughts to study Grange. He sensed a reluctance in the supervising agent, but was not certain about what.

"There are several people under investigation: Pritman, yourself, Arnold Savak, and Simon Clarke."

Thinking about Savak and Pritman, Steven shook his head. "It isn't Arnie or the senator. And I just don't envision Simon Clarke as a suspect. His ambition doesn't run along those lines."

"I'm sorry, Steven, it has to be one of them. And Simon Clarke, according to Ellie's reports, does have access to the senator's papers, if not the meetings themselves."

"What makes you so goddamn sure?" he asked, aware that the fire in him was no longer as strong as he wanted it to be. If Ellie was a spy, he rationalized, why couldn't one of the others be as well.

"Those men, and you, were the only ones privy to all the information that was leaked to the other side."

"I don't see it. I think you're wrong."

"About what?" Carla asked as she came in from the kitchen with a tray of sandwiches.

"Who the mole is," Grange said, taking a tuna sandwich.

Steven chose a turkey sandwich, and took one of the three cups of black coffee on the tray.

They ate the light meal silently, each wrapped in their own thoughts as they waited for Witt and Jamison to return. When Grange finished his sandwich, he looked at his watch. "They should be back soon."

Steven drank some coffee. "Earlier, you said I'd be the bait. I'm curious about that."

"We'd worked it out yesterday," Grange said. "We were going to make you a runner, to draw out the mole. But the FBI did that for us."

"How were you going to do that?" he asked softly.

Grange laughed at Steven's expression. "Nothing sinister. A controlled run that would draw the mole after you. We were going to bring you here, and then bait the trap."

"Not quite last night's scenario."

"Actually the FBI helped us for a change. The mole knows it was the Bureau who sent you on the run, which keeps us out of the picture, at least for now. Unless Witt and Jamison have screwed it up," he added, again looking at his watch.

On cue, his radio came to life. "Our car's coming back," said a voice Steven hadn't yet heard. He guessed it was one of the mobile teams out on the road.

Grange stood a few seconds before a buzzer sounded in the drawing room. "Front gate warning. Infra-red," Grange explained. Seconds later a wash of headlights panned across the window. Ghostly shapes fluttered along the ceiling until the lights passed.

Grange went to the window. "It took them long

enough. Time for you to get out of here," he added.

They went into the hallway, where Steven and Carla put on their coats.

A car door closed. A moment later footsteps echoed up the outside steps. "Time," Grange said. Steven and Carla picked up their bags.

Steven turned and started forward.

Grange opened the door.

And the night exploded in a staccato burst of gunfire.

Chapter Twenty-five

The barrage of bullets lifted Grange, tossing him backward like a rag doll. He landed in a heap against the wall.

Steven reacted to the gunfire by flinging his suitcase at the figures framed in the doorway. As they dodged the bag, he dove at the door.

Crashing into the heavy wood with his shoulder, Steven slammed it shut, and threw the latch home.

Still moving quickly, he went over to Grange, grabbed the agent under his shoulder, and dragged him out of the line of fire. Behind him was the sound of bodies pounding against the door.

He released Grange, pulled the agent's pistol from his shoulder holster, and faced the door. Carla was next to him, aiming her automatic.

There was another hard crash. The door frame shook. Plaster dust rained down from upper edges of the frame. "It won't hold much longer," he told Carla. "On my mark, fire on the center of the door."

Steven tensed, waiting. His finger was tight on the trigger, his sights chest high on the door. The blood pounded in his temples. He counted the seconds in his head. At six the crash came.

"Now!" he said, pulling the trigger twice. Carla fired five times.

A surprised cry of pain reached them. Steven waited. When nothing happened, he looked downs at Grange. The agent was alive. A jagged groove ran from his temple into his hairline. His hair was already matted with dark blood. Steven tore open Grange's shirt and studied the other wounds. One round had hit him in the shoulder. Two wounds were grazes across Grange's ribs. A fourth bullet had punctured the girdle of muscle low on his right side. More blood ran from where a bullet had entered Grange's left thigh.

"He's alive," he told Carla. "But there's nothing we can do for him right now."

He glanced at Carla. She was pale, her eyes were fixed on the door. Then he heard footsteps in the front. He lifted the pistol, but Carla fired first, letting go a three-burst volley.

Steven spotted Grange's radio in the hallway. It had been crushed by the agent's weight. "No help coming," he told Carla, nodding toward the radio. "We'll have to do it ourselves. Keep firing through the door," he directed as he started toward the back.

"Where are you going?" Carla whispered while she reloaded.

"To protect our backs." He got to his feet before she could argue, and started for the kitchen.

Carla fired at the door. This time there was answering fire. Steven heard a bullet pierce the door and give a dull thud as it buried itself into the plaster wall.

He stepped into the kitchen heard someone at the back door. Flattening himself against the wall, he side-stepped toward the door. He held the pistol in a two-handed grip. He was five feet from the door, when it opened and a figure dressed in black entered stealthily.

Steven held his breath, waiting until the man was abreast of him. "Don't move," he ordered. The man turned, leading with his weapon.

Steven fired twice and dove to the floor. The man staggered back. The machine pistol arched upward. A deafening burst of parabellums stitched across the ceiling.

And then the man fell to the floor.

Steven bent over him. He was dead. Two of Steven's bullets had ripped his throat open. Blood poured to the floor. Steven didn't think about the violence. He couldn't let himself, not yet.

Kneeling, he tore the machine pistol from the dead man's hand, and did a quick body search. He found two magazines and a pocket full of money. There was no wallet.

Steven stared at the man's face, looking into his death-glazed eyes, and willed himself to remember if or when he'd seen him before. He found no familiarity in the man's coarse features, no sense of recognition.

Steven left him on the floor. He shut off the overhead light, closed and locked the back door, and then rammed the high placed brass bolt home. Before returning to Carla and Grange, he hooked a ladder-back chair under the doorknob.

His mind was running at full speed as he tried to work up a plan of action, without knowing how many the enemy was. All he knew with any certainty was that his body was pumped up, and his senses were shrieking for action.

He found Carla kneeling next to Grange, just where he had left them. Her attention was on the bullet-riddled door.

He studied Carla quickly. Her face was flushed. While her breathing was slightly uneven, her hands were steady and her eyes showed no uncontrolled fear. "Our visitor brought us a present," he told her, handing Carla the machine pistol and magazines. "Get me Grange's spare clip."

After putting the fresh clip in Grange's Beretta, Steven cocked it, and knelt next to Carla. "Count a slow thirty and then start firing out the window," he said, pointing to the sitting room.

Carla shook her head. "We have to stay here. Help is coming."

"Is it?" Steven asked pointedly, not anywhere as sure as Carla that help was on its way. Nor, did he plan to wait and see. "Do what I said," he ordered her.

Without giving her a chance to protest again, he raced into the kitchen, stepped over the dead man, and pulled the chair free from the door. He closed his eyes to help adjust to the dark night, counted to three, and opened the door.

Outside, the cold night air danced across

Steven's skin, raising goose bumps over his body. He opened his eyes and was able to make out the moonlit landscape. Moving cautiously, he worked his way around the house. He never lost track of the count.

At the count of twenty-five, he reached the front corner. Stopping, he pressed his back to the house and peered around. Steven spotted the second man instantly. He was crouched behind the rear fender of the car. The man's right arm hung limp.

At thirty, Carla fired a short burst through the sitting room window. Her bullets danced over the car's body, raising sparks. The man returned fire. Bolts of lightning spat from his machine pistol. Steven broke cover and ran into the drive. And then, amidst the bedlam of nine-millimeter gunfire, headlights cut the darkness, pinioning both Steven and the assassin.

The assassin spun when the headlights hit him. His useless arm windmilling as he fought to bring his weapon to bear.

Steven threw himself sideways, rolling beneath the first burst of fire. The bullets ripped up dirt to his left. He stopped rolling, sighted on the man, and squeezed the trigger.

The man spun away from the car and fell heavily, his legs spasming.

Steven pushed off the ground, and warily approached his attacker. The man lay still. Steven kicked the bulky weapon from his lifeless hand. The headlights came closer, fully illuminating the man. Steven recognized the dead man's slavic features immediately. He was the driver of the car at the motel.

Anton.

"I'm coming in," Steven shouted to Carla as the approaching car screeched, came to a halt and its doors opened.

The front door to the house opened when he reached the top step. Carla stared at him in question. "He's dead," he said simply. "How's Grange?"

"Not good."

The heavy pounding of running feet reached the stairs. Carla looked over his shoulder. Steven saw anger flash across her face. "Where the hell have you been?"

The first man shook his head. "We thought they were Witt and Jamison. They were driving Jamison's car."

Ignoring them, Steven went inside and knelt next to Grange. He saw the supervisor's eyes were open. Pain tightened his features. "I think you'll make it," Steven said with a half smile he didn't feel.

"I know," Grange said weakly. "Carla, report in." When Carla went to the living room phone, Grange said, "Did you recognize them?"

Steven nodded. "Only the one out front. He was the one who tried to kill us this morning. Short dark hair. Heavy features, ruddy complexion."

Grange smiled and winced for his trouble. "Anton. Good. You're a hell of a soldier, Morrisy.

You took out the mole's back-up. Now the mole's only got himself. You've got to play the game. It's up to you to pull him from cover."

Steven gazed at the injured agent. He felt respect growing within him as Grange, wounded and in obvious pain, kept up his role to the hilt. But Steven had reached his limit in this fruitless game. "No, Grange, I'm not playing it your way any more. This time we'll do it the right way."

Grange shook his head forcefully. "You've been out of it for too long. You were good then, Morrisy, but this isn't Nam."

"Fuck you, Grange. And fuck all the rest of you shadow players. It's my blood the mole wants. And I'll get him by my rules."

Grange stared at Steven for a long moment before he finally nodded his head. "You may be right—this time."

Carla returned then, saying, "They're dispatching full cleanup crew and a copter. We'll get you to a hospital soon."

"Get him out of here, now," he told Carla and two of the other agents.

Carla shook her head. "No more. We almost blew it tonight. I don't want Steven used as bait."

"We have to," Grange said.

"No."

"Grange is right," Steven said, his voice low and matter-of-fact. "It's the only way. But I'm going alone. Your mole knows your procedures. He wants me, but he won't come after me unless he's certain he can reach me. It won't work if anyone else is with me."

Carla looked at him, her expression anxious. "You're not trained for this."

Steven couldn't stop the smile from coming as Grange said, "Carla, Morrisy may be even better trained than you."

She looked from Grange to Steven. "You're a long time away from Vietnam."

Steven considered her words, and thought about his method of keeping the past locked inside his mind. "No, I'm not," he said swallowing hard. "I've been there every day of my life."

"I'm going with you," Carla stated. "The mole thinks I'm Ellie's sister. Report procedure?" she asked Grange before Steven could speak.

Grange coughed, groaned, and held his side. Steven saw the blood begin to run again. "Use Priority One only," he instructed. "Morrisy, what happened to Ellie was because she discovered who the mole is. And it was someone in Pritman's office. You've got that trick memory, use it. Figure out why he wants you to take the blame. You're the key, Morrisy."

It was almost midnight when, after a predominately silent ride, they checked into a downtown motel in Pittsburgh. Steven registered as Mr. and Mrs. Theodore Adams, paying for one night, and using some of the cash he'd taken from the dead man in the kitchen.

Their room was modest, with flower-patterned

wallpaper on a beige background that matched the carpeting, a king size bed, and an easy chair recliner. The traditional television was chained to the wall. There was a small desk in front of the window.

Steven put their bags on the aluminum stand at the foot of the bed and turned to Carla. "I think we can relax for now."

Carla nodded and started toward the bathroom. But when she was next to him, her steps faltered. Steven saw the tears in her eyes.

Rather than speak, he took her in his arms and held her close. The sobs came then, body-wracking spasms that shook her uncontrollably. Steven knew that the cause of the tears, as well as her silence on the long drive, was a delayed reaction to the fight at the safe house.

When her crying lessened, he eased her onto the bed and sat next to her. He held her as he spoke. "When I first met Grange, I had the feeling that you and he—" he stopped and smiled at her. "I once asked if you were lovers. You are, aren't you?"

Carla shook her head. A smile etched with memories graced her lips. "A long time ago. Not now, not for years. But seeing him shot. Seeing him lying there, bleeding and helpless. God, it was horrible."

"I know. But he'll be fine."

"Until the next time," she said, turning to stare at him.

"You're both in a dangerous profession."

Carla looked away. "Maybe I picked the wrong one. Look at me, I'm a wreck."

"You're no different from anyone else. Everyone reacts differently to them, but everyone does react. Some fall to pieces during the fight, others, like yourself, react afterward, when it's safe to fall apart. It's a sign of a strength, not weakness."

"Oh, right, I'm brave," she said sarcastically, lifting her hands to show him how badly they were shaking.

Steven knew that to keep pushing it now would only make things worse. He had to find a different subject.

"Did you meet Grange at the agency?"

"No. We were in college together. I told you that already, didn't I?"

Steven nodded. "When you first told me about Grange."

"Right. Well, the agency recruited us at the same time. We both seemed to have an aptitude for the work."

"And Ellie?"

Carla smiled softly, her voice lightened. "She joined about five years after me. She was a computer expert, codes and stuff. The agency primarily used her in the organized crime division."

"I still have trouble accepting her as a secret service agent."

"She was a damned good one too. And she loved you Steven. She was going to resign."

The thought of Ellie's future weighed heavily on him. "Now she'll have no choice."

"Not necessarily. We look after our own. We have to. We're the forgotten agency. All anyone thinks we do is bodyguard politicians. But we're much more."

"So I'm learning."

"We work with Treasury on drug and counterfeiting operations. We handle territorial espionage operations as well. And we're autonomous." Carla yawned, surprise registered in her eyes. "I don't believe how tired I am."

"It's been a long day," Steven stated.

"Too long," Carla agreed. "I'm going to take a shower."

"Want me to order from room service?"

Carla shook her head quickly. "No. We don't want any more people than necessary to see us."

She was right. He chastised himself for not having thought of the same thing. "Take your shower."

Carla came out fifteen minutes later, with a towel wrapped around her head, and wearing a short terry bathrobe she'd taken from her apartment.

"How are you feeling now?"

Carla smiled. "Fine . . . Steven, thank you."

He waved away her thanks. "Get some sleep."

"In a little while. I'll watch some TV first."

After Carla turned it on, and the screen came to life with Liza Minelli fighting with Dudley Moore, she went to the bed and lay down.

Steven took his shower. When he came out, Carla was asleep. She was breathing gently, the lines of tension that had been on her face were gone.

He covered her, and felt a new emotion form. It was admiration, and pity. She had chosen a hard life.

Steven went to the small desk, sat, and stared out the window. And Ellie? Was she like Carla? He didn't know what Ellie was like any longer. She wasn't the same woman she had been a week ago. At least not in his mind.

Then he made himself focus his thoughts. Savak. He was supposed to call Arnie. Should he take the risk? What if Savak's phone was tapped? It was a chance he would have to take, Steven decided. He needed to talk with his friend.

He picked up the phone and dialed Savak's apartment. At the sound of his friend's voice, he relaxed a little.

"Yes, I'm fine," he replied to Savak's first question.

"The feds have been in the office all day. But so far, the investigation is being contained in the Bureau."

"Someone's trying to kill me, Arnie. They tried this morning, and again tonight."

There was silence for several seconds. "Are you sure?" Savak asked.

Steven thought about the people Anton had mowed down with the car. Then he thought about Grange. "Oh, yeah, I'm sure."

"Who, Steven?"

"We don't know."

"We?"

"Carla and I," he said.

"You've got Ellie's sister with you. Are you crazy?" Savak half shouted.

Steven wanted to explain to Savak who Carla was, as well as the actual events of the past day, but decided not to risk it in case Savak's phone was tapped. "What was I supposed to do? She was with me last night, when Blayne tried to arrest me. She helped me to get away."

"Then you really didn't have a choice. Look," Savak added quickly, "I need time to get things straightened out. Jesus, I've spent most of the day going from one judge to another, and then fighting through the chain of command at Justice. Steven, I'm up against a double-edged sword. I'm trying to get them to back off of you and, at the same time, keep Pritman's name clear of this whole situation. But until I get this worked out, you've got to stay in hiding. We can't take the chance that what's happening will become public knowledge."

"I know, for Pritman's sake," he said, trying to keep the rancor from his voice. He paused, debating whether to warn Arnie about what he had learned. He realized there was no choice. "Arnie, keep an eye out. There's a spy in the office. A Soviet mole."

Steven heard his friend's breathing change. When Savak spoke, and his voice was tainted with sadness. "Don't do this to me, Steven. Please, don't start the conspiracy shit again."

"It's fact, Arnie. There's a spy on our staff."

"That's not possible. Steven, we know everyone on the staff."

"Take my word for it."

"Goddamn it, Steven." Savak exploded. "Don't fuck me around. If there is a spy, I have to know who it is. It will help me get you out of this."

"I don't know who, yet. If I knew, I would be there, not here. But I will find out. And there's something else," he added quickly. "You've got to concentrate on the Entente proposal. Get Pritman to move up the schedule. He's got to make the committee understand just how strong a position we'll have for the elections. After he meets with them, get him to announce. It has to be done before any of this breaks."

"It's scheduled for next Friday."

Steven had a feeling that he wouldn't be able to hold out until then. "Move it up."

"What if he needs you for the proposal, to fix things, to help him."

Steven closed his eyes for a moment. Then he leaned over the table and stared down at a *Nightlife In Pittsburgh* magazine with a smiling blonde on the cover. Steven knew that Arnie's plea wasn't for Pritman. It was for Arnie, it was for their friendship. "It's finished Arnie. There's nothing else I can do with it. It's ready, and it's good. And Arnie, I did what everyone asked, I mailed out my resignation this morning."

There was a long pause before Savak spoke again, his voice thick. "I— Take care of yourself, please. And call me whenever you need. And

Steven, I'm going to get you out of this mess. I promise."

Not this time, Steven thought, the only person who would get him out of this was himself. "Good-bye, Arnie."

He hung up and looked back at Carla. She hadn't changed position. He wondered how Grange was doing. Then he remembered Grange's words about his being the key.

"How?" he asked himself aloud.

Why didn't Ellie trust me? He put himself in Ellie's position, and then the answer came. She couldn't tell me because she was afraid that the mole might have been someone close to me.

He thought back to the day when he'd given her the ring, and he replayed her promise that they would be married. Strangely, he found that his memory was a reaffirmation that she did love him, and that she would have told him about herself.

Why was she left in Lake Pompton? The area she was found in was very deep, and that particular area of the lake was rarely used during the winter. That could be one reason it was chosen. And because of the underground spring that kept the ice thinner there, it would be easier to put a car through it.

Yes, he told himself, it was the perfect place to dispose of a body without being seen. It might never have been found if the car hadn't gotten hung up on the roots. But because she wasn't in the car, her body would have eventually been found.

If the mole's plans had gone as intended, he would have been the prime suspect when Ellie's body was found in the spring. He remembered telling Banacek that Ellie's attacker had made a mistake in not leaving Ellie in the car. But he had been wrong. It hadn't been a mistake: It had been part of the plan from the very beginning. The mistake had been in not making sure the car had gone under the water.

And the method of torture was one he was familiar with—one that could easily be attributed to his past. The method of her torture was the final proof.

Suddenly, his perception of the reasoning behind Ellie's tragedy was changed. Nothing about Ellie's intended death had been the spur-of-the-moment happening that he had first thought. He was now absolutely positive that Ellie's involvement was only because she had been caught by the mole. The accident, and the frame-up of Steven, had been carefully planned during the week that Ellie had been missing. Only the fact that Ellie had been found alive had changed the long range effect of the plan. But, once the frame-up had been set into motion, there had been no reason to alter it.

However, and in complete opposition to the elaborate staging of Ellie's death, the murder of Londrigan and Lomack was a spur of-the-moment plan. The two men would have proven that Steven had not tried to kill Ellie. That was the reason that they had been taken out.

Still, the single most important question lingered. What had Ellie discovered that had almost cost her her life? And by whom?

She had been tortured. No one would have taken the chance of moving her at that point. It would be too risky. A small traffic violation and it was over.

Where had she been?

When the answer came, he knew he was right. He must have been in Greyton. She must have been there all along.

Steven picked up the phone and called Banacek. As soon as the sheriff came on the line, he identified himself and said, "We may be able to find out who tried to kill Ellie. I need the names of all the owners of the vacation homes at Lake Pompton. Can you do that for me?"

"Why bother?" Banacek asked, his voice cold. "It's over Morrisy. You screwed it up. We're finished with games. We found it."

"Found what?" Steven asked, stunned by Banacek's change in attitude.

"The ring. Just where you left it. It's always the little things that get you in the long run. Goddamn you, Morrisy, I believed in you!"

Steven's mind raced. He knew this was just another piece of the frame, but he had to make Banacek accept that too. "Where did you find it, Sheriff?"

"You tell me."

Steven closed his eyes. He pictured his mother,

and then Helene Latham. "On the window sill over the kitchen sink."

"At last we get some truth. She must have taken it off to wash the dishes. You never gave her a chance to put it back on."

"You're forgetting something, Sheriff. She didn't take her ring off—she couldn't. Remember those gouges on her knuckle? The ring was too small. It was taken off, forcefully, and put on the window sill to tighten the noose around my neck."

"But you knew where it would be."

"What does your wife do before she does the dishes?"

"She—"

Steven cut him off. "Just work that idea over in your mind before you ask for extradition on me. And call those two FBI agents. My house was searched when I was at the hospital. It had to be them: Ask them about the ring. And Sheriff, get me that land list."

Banacek's voice was no longer distant, but Steven still sensed the sheriff's doubt. "Where can I reach you?"

"You can't, I'll reach you. I'll also have someone call you tomorrow to back up what I've told you."

"And who will that be?"

"Ellie's sister," he said, and hung up.

He leaned back, and he felt his energy drain. He looked at his watch. It was two o'clock. He could no longer deny his need for sleep. He went over to the bed and lay down next to Carla.

He was almost asleep when the elusive tendril

of what he had been searching for came out. His eyes snapped open. He stared at the pattern of shadows on the ceiling and had his answer.

He felt stupid, betrayed by his own inability to have seen the obvious. And it was all too obvious to him, now.

He was the key, as Grange had said. But he was far more. Ellie was coincidental. What had happened to her had no real bearing on him. Ellie was a fortunate event for the mole, and the mole had used her to his advantage.

He no longer had any doubt that the mole was either someone in Pritman's office, or someone close to one of the people there. If Ellie hadn't discovered the mole, if there had been no Secret Service investigation, Steven would still be in danger.

That was why Ellie had been put into Lake Pompton. And as he had thought, Ellie was supposed to have been discovered in the spring. That, Steven realized, was the most important factor. The frame-up wasn't about what was happening today, or what had happened yesterday, or even what would happen tomorrow. It had to do with the spring.

What exactly was supposed to happen in the spring, and why did the mole want him out of the picture then?

Chapter Twenty-six

In the private dining room, three floors above Amos Coblehill's office, Julius Axelrod pushed aside his half-eaten breakfast. His appetite had been declining steadily for months, exactly as the doctors had predicted. But while his health was out of his hands, Steven Morrisy's fate wasn't—not yet.

Axelrod had reached the hospital just before the helicopter had brought Grange in. And as Grange was being prepped for surgery, Axelrod had listened to the man's report.

The director had stayed at the hospital until Grange had come out of surgery and had personally received the surgeon's report. The bullet Grange had taken in the side had passed though without damaging any organs; all but one of the other wounds had been relatively minor. The one bullet that had done the most serious damage, had entered Grange's thigh, hit the bone, and had been deflected downward into the knee.

The knee had been shattered and would have to

be completely rebuilt. Paul Grange would never again have the full use of his left leg. His career as a field operative was over.

Axelrod rubbed a tired hand across his eyes. He looked at his counterpart in the NSA, and picked up from where he'd left off a few minutes ago. "Grange will be on limited duty for several months after he leaves the hospital."

"At least he'll be leaving the hospital," Coblehill said. "Too bad about his knee, though."

"Yes," Axelrod agreed. "Perhaps it's timely. Grange's potential is far and above that of a field agent."

Coblehill motioned the lone steward for more coffee. "Are you still of the opinion that Grange's most propitious use of the situation was in letting Morrisy and Statler run, even in light of what happened to the other four men?"

"Absolutely," Axelrod replied. "Amos, it wasn't the mole who took out Witt and Jamison and their back-ups, it was Anton. And just in case you missed the irony of it all, remember that it was Morrisy, not our people, who took out Anton and his colleague. And that, with luck, leaves our mole without any back-up."

Axelrod paused when the steward refilled their coffee cups. When the man walked out of earshot, he continued. "But, whoever our mole is, he has a thorough working knowledge of our security apparatus and operations. Grange was witness to that last night. I must assume that by our allowing Morrisy to control the scenario, we have a damn good chance of pulling the mole into the open. Morrisy's way will be spontaneous, without any set pattern."

"Where are they now?" Coblehill asked.

"In the Lexon Motel, in Pittsburgh. We have a five-man spotting team on them."

Steven and Carla were up, dressed, and had ordered breakfast by seven. Steven had chosen a rear table that afforded a view of everyone coming into the motel's coffee shop. Although he felt uneasy at being out in public, he had to find out if anyone had made them yet.

"I guess I was wrong," Carla said, putting her coffee cup down.

"About?"

"You. You haven't forgotten much since Vietnam. There hasn't been a person coming in here that you missed."

"Natural caution," Steven said easily. "I want to see the faces. Just in case we see them again, later."

Carla took another sip of coffee. As she lowered the cup, she asked, "What did you do in Nam?"

"Desk work for the most part—screening intelligence reports. Occasionally I went into the field."

"As an operative?"

Steven mulled over the question. "I was trained as a full field agent. I went through the regular Military Intelligence training, and then some special CIA schools."

Carla's head bobbed once. "That's what Paul meant last night, about your training."

Steven shrugged without elaborating.

"What made you go into law?"

"Jack Rittenban. He lived two houses from me," he said as the waitress arrived with their food. When she left, he spread marmalade on his toast, took a bite and swallowed. "He was a funny man, tall and gawky. His clothing always hung loosely on him, and he used to stoop over to talk to most people. But he was a warm and kind man. We walked our dogs together, in the evenings. He would tell me what it was like to be a lawyer, and how important it was to be able to help people."

Steven smiled at the warm memories of his youth. Jack Rittenban had been, in many ways, Steven's surrogate father. In high school and during the summers, Steven had worked in Mr. Rittenban's office. He had even done a little clerking for him, in his senior year.

Steven shook his head, glanced around the restaurant, and then took another bite of toast. "When we got home, after Nam, things were hard. It was a bad time for everyone who had been over there. And I needed to do something that I could still believe in. I could believe in law, the way Jack Rittenban practiced it."

"Did Savak and Latham feel that way too?" she asked, scooping out a grapefruit section.

"We all felt dirty. I remember the first time we met, after our discharges. It was in Greyton. We went to a local joint and did our best to get drunk."

"Was that when you and Savak decided to get involved in politics?"

"No," Steven said, breaking the yoke of an egg with the toast. He studied the broken yoke for a moment before looking up at Carla. "Politics came later. But Arnie went back to school for his masters' degree in political science. He wanted—still wants—to change the way we were trained to think about war, as well as the way we deal with other countries."

"I'm surprised that Latham didn't join you two as well."

"Only because you don't know him. Chuck was never a political person. After Nam he became even less of one. He loathed what had happened there, and here as well. He couldn't understand how the people at home could be so callous to the ones who'd fought in Southeast Asia. I'm not sure he'd ever thought about becoming a doctor until after Nam.

"But within months of coming home, Chuck decided to go into medicine. He graduated college, and went on to medical school."

Carla finished her grapefruit, and buttered a slice of toast. She raised the triangle of bread to her mouth, but lowered it untouched. "Could Savak be the mole?"

Steven thought about last night's breakthrough, and about one of his two closest friends. "I don't think being a traitor is in Arnie's character."

"But you said he'd felt betrayed by us. Maybe—"

"Betrayed by the army brass, not by his country. Carla, Arnie Savak has devoted the last sixteen years of his life to developing policies that will keep our country out of wars—any wars."

"Which still doesn't tell me that Savak isn't the mole," Carla countered. "Giving information to the Soviets, helping them to become more powerful than us, while crippling our own efforts, can accomplish the same thing."

Steven shook his head. "The odds that it's Savak are astronomical. Arnie Savak's hate of the Soviets and the Chinese is so deeply personal and so passionate that only someone who has been through what he has, could come close to comprehending. Carla, he gave up information once, and he has never forgiven himself for it."

"But he was supposed to talk."

Steven gazed at her, wondering if he could make her understand with words. "That doesn't make any difference. He didn't know that was the intention of the mission. To Arnie, his giving up of information to the enemy, whether under drugs or torture, was a sign of failure. He believed that he wasn't strong enough to resist."

Carla finally ate some of her toast. "And Simon Clarke?"

Steven shrugged. "Clarke may have access to Pritman's papers, but he doesn't have the background or the training. We did some checking on him before we hired him. He was never in the service. Clarke went straight from college to a national magazine. He spent five years there before joining us."

"Well, if neither Savak or Clarke are suspects, where do we go from here?" Carla asked.

Steven leaned back in the chair. His eyes swept over the occupants of the coffee shop. "I'm not sure yet. But I need you to make a call," he said telling her about his phone conversation with Banacek.

"All right," Carla agreed without voicing the disapproval of last night's phone call that Steven saw was so apparent in her eyes.

After finishing their breakfast, Steven escorted Carla to the pay phone in the lobby. She called Banacek and, holding the receiver away from her ear so Steven could listen, gave the sheriff the same story Steven had.

"I know he didn't try to kill my sister," she finished.

"That's very accepting of you," Banacek's down-home drawl made Steven smile. "But he could be pulling the wool over your eyes."

"He's not," Carla stated. "But if it will help, I have a phone number for you to call that will help clarify things." She gave him the number, said good-bye, and immediately dialed the Priority One number at the agency.

Reacting quickly, Steven put his hand over the receiver. "What are you doing?"

"I have to let them know about Banacek."

"Carefully," Steven warned.

Carla nodded and drew the phone away from him. When the call was answered, she spoke with her new control supervisor about Banacek. But when Steven heard the man on the other end ask where they were, he took the receiver from her and hung up.

She gave him an amused smile. "That wasn't necessary."

"Yes it was," he stated. "Not because you would say anything, but because I wanted to give them a message. I want them to understand who's running this now."

Outside, while Steven guided Carla toward the car, he kept remembering the morning before at the motel in Washington. He listened intently for any out-of-sync sounds, relaxing only when they were driving out of the motel parking lot.

When they reached the outskirts of Pittsburgh, Steven took a highway paralleling the Pennsylvania Turnpike. He drove cautiously, always checking the rear view mirror. An hour later, Steven found what he was looking for: Two cars that kept changing positions every few miles.

"Your people are driving a blue Chevrolet and a silver Dodge," Steven told Carla. "I'm going to lose them."

Carla touched his arm lightly. "If they're ours," she warned. "Pull into the next gas station."

Startled because he hadn't been thinking along the same line as Carla, Steven didn't argue. They found a Shell station three miles down the road. The blue car was the closest, about a hundred yards back. Without signalling, Steven pulled into the station. The blue car drove past without slowing. The driver and his passenger didn't turn their heads.

Watching Carla's face, he saw the recognition of the car's inhabitants in her eyes.

"They're ours," Carla said as they both looked for the silver car.

But the silver car never passed the gas station.

At the full service island, Steven shut off the ignition. "I had really hoped that Grange understood," Steven said, disappointed at the agency's blatant stupidity.

Carla shook her head adamantly. "It's part of the original plan. Paul didn't set this up. He's out of it. The agency is just following normal operation procedure."

"Damn it Carla, that's the point! Whoever is behind this knows your *normal operating procedures* as well as you do: He knows all your moves and he anticipates them. And he probably knows your people as well. Do you understand what I'm saying?" he asked, staring hard at her.

"That's impossible, Steven."

He took her hand and squeezed it gently. All the while he stared into her eyes. "Impossible? Carla, we're in a gas station in Pennsylvania, not in the safe house in Maryland. Why?"

Drawing her hand from his, she turned away. "Steven—"

He cupped her chin, and turning her face back to his. "You have to make a choice, Carla," he said, his voice low and flat. "You either believe in me or you go back to the agency. But if you stay it's because you're working with me, not for them."

As he waited for her decision, he saw the conflict rampant on her features. Finally, she moistened her lips and said, "with you."

When the attendant came over to the car, Steven signalled for a fill up. After paying for the gas, he pulled back onto the highway. A minute later, he spotted the silver car in the rear view. The blue car came out of a junction a quarter mile farther down.

Steven played with them for a half hour, making sure to keep them both in sight, while Carla worked with the map.

"There's a small town coming up. Right after it is a road that goes into the mountains. It may be a good spot to lose them."

"We'll find out."

Carla's words proved accurate. Two-thirds of a mile onto the twisting and winding road, Steven knew the road was perfect for their plan. When he was on a straight stretch near the crest of the mountain, he slowed to a crawl. Once he had both cars in the rear view mirror, he speeded up. He went into a long climbing curve and looked for a side road. He found one just before the crest.

Turning sharply into the single lane road, when the cars were out of view, Steven drove off the road and U-turned behind a clump of trees. A half minute later the blue car sped by. The silver car was almost on its bumper.

"Now," Carla said.

Steven shook his head. "Wait."

Two minutes later, the cars went by again, heading back toward the town. Steven pulled back onto the main road, and continued on in the direction he had been going originally.

He saw Carla smile. But a moment later, her mouth had turned pensive. "That was too easy."

This time he smiled. "I know. We were supposed to spot them and lose them."

She turned to stare at him. "I don't think they have any idea of how good you are."

"Is the car bugged?"

"It's an agency car. Standard issue is a driver activated transmitter with a twenty-five mile range. It has remote capabilities."

"Procedure?"

"They'll keep back five to ten miles so there will be no slip ups. Figure a fifteen-minute difference."

"Time enough."

At the bottom of the hill, they drove into a small village. Steven pulled into the general store's parking lot, and went to the phone booth. With his back to Carla, he made his call, and returned to the car.

"Where to now?" Carla asked as he pulled onto the road.

"We're going back to Pittsburgh."

"Pittsburgh. Why?" Carla asked.

"To confuse them," he said before asking Carla to look at the map and find a route to Pittsburgh that kept him off the turnpike, and off the road they had taken out of the city. He had no desire to be involved in turnpike traffic where he would be unable to keep track of who was or was not following him.

While Steven drove, his mind revolved around Grange's cautioning words about his being the key to the puzzle. With each passing mile, Steven played with different angles of his past. But each time he sought a path toward understanding, he would find himself thinking about the prison camp.

The thoughts scared him. If what was happening was a part of that time, then despite his belief in Savak, Arnie might be the mole.

The possibility shook him badly, taking away the certainty of his belief in his friend. Steven knew himself well enough to understand that the doubt he had just raised would fester and grow in his mind until he was able to regain the assurance of his friend's innocence.

Steven also realized, with an even deeper shock, that he did have the means to find out if Savak was the one. He felt beads of perspiration break across his forehead at the thought. His hands tightened on the steering wheel. Could he do it? Steven exhaled sharply. He had no choice.

Carla turned to him at the sound. "What?"

Steven shook his head. "Nothing. Just thinking."

She went to back watching the passenger side view mirror.

Twenty miles outside of Pittsburgh, he saw Carla stiffen, and take a quick look over her shoulder. "There's a brown car, two behind us, I've seen it a few times on the trip."

Feeling his nerves tighten, Steven glanced in the rear view mirror. He spotted the car, riding a couple of car lengths in back of the car behind them. Steven slowed to forty. The two cars maintained their speed and passed him a few moments later.

Steven kept his speed steady, and within five minutes the brown car had opened a half mile lead. "I think we're okay," he said, relaxing slightly.

They reached the outskirts of Pittsburgh at noon, without spotting the brown car again. Steven drove downtown, and parked across the street from the motel they'd stayed at last night.

"There's a car reserved in your name," he told Carla, pointing to the rental car agency. "Pick me up in front of the motel."

She left the car without a word and, when she entered the rental agency, Steven drove across the street and parked near the rear of the motel. At the motel's lobby desk, he changed a ten into silver and went to the bank of phones.

He stared at the telephone for several seconds before picking up the receiver. Again, sweat broke out across his forehead. He almost hung up, stopped himself, and called Washington information. He got the number, dialed, and then deposited the amount of money the operator asked for.

When the phone was answered, he spoke quickly and urgently. He was put on hold for almost a full minute, until the man he'd asked for came on the line. Steven spoke softly but urgently, without letting the man speak.

A half minute later, Steven hung up and returned to the front desk where he asked for a room. He registered, using his real name, and paid for two nights. He took both keys, put them in his pocket, and went outside to the car.

He took out his bag and Carla's from the trunk and, as he was closing the trunk, he saw the brown car pull into the parking lot.

Steven froze, and then realized he might give himself away if the driver was indeed following him. Forcing himself to move casually, he closed the trunk, picked up the suitcases, and went back into the lobby.

As soon as the door closed behind him, and he saw the car's driver get out and start toward the lobby, Steven walked quickly across the lobby and out the front door. He found Carla sitting behind the wheel of a nondescript burgundy Chevy Corsica. He got into the passenger seat.

"Which way?" Carla asked, her eyebrows raised in question.

Steven pointed west. "We'll stop for some lunch on the highway," he said as he glanced at the motel entrance and saw the man framed in the glass doors. The instant their eyes met, two simultaneous events occurred: Carla pulled away from the curb and the man spun and raced back toward the rear entrance.

Watching the side mirror, Steven waited for the brown car to appear. He spotted it four blocks later.

"We've got company."

"Who?" Carla asked, her eyes flicking to him.

"The brown car you made earlier. He pulled into

the motel right after me. He's behind us now."

"My people wouldn't be—"

"No," Steven agreed with a half smile, "they wouldn't be that stupid."

"The mole?"

Steven shook his head. "I've never seen that man before. Maybe one of his men. We'll find out soon enough," he added as he took out Carla's nine-millimeter and checked the magazine.

"How do you want to do it?" she asked, her voice edged with tension.

Again, Steven smiled. "The first fast food place you see will do fine." Then he explained what he intended to do.

They found what Steven was looking for at the base of the highway. Signalling well in advance of the place, Carla turned into the drive-through lane. She followed the lane to the rear of the building, turned, and drove up to the pedestal menu and ordering stand.

As a faceless adolescent voice asked for their order, Steven told Carla to order, and opened the door. "Pay, and then go back to the street. Wait for me on the next corner."

"Steven, be—"

He didn't wait to hear what she was going to say. Rather, he ran to the edge of the building, flattened himself against the wall, and looked out. He saw the car at the curb. The driver was watching the exit lane for the drive-through.

Moving quickly, Steven blended in with several people walking toward the side door. At the door, he got behind two other people who were carrying take-out.

As he neared the sidewalk, and the brown car, his pulse speeded up. He was conscious of the weight of the pistol in his belt. He saw the man look around. Steven tensed, hunching down behind the man he was following. The driver didn't spot him.

Then Steven saw Carla driving slowly toward the street. The instant the driver's eyes marked Carla, Steven split from the people in front of him, and headed toward the brown car. He had the pistol concealed with his jacket.

When Steven was three feet from the car, the driver leaned forward. Steven saw him reach for the shift lever; but, the man's hand stopped before it touched the lever, and Steven knew that the driver had seen that Carla was alone.

The man started to turn, and Steven lunged at the car. Praying that the passenger door was unlocked, he grasped the handle and pulled. The door opened and Steven slid into the passenger seat.

He pressed the nine-millimeter into the driver's side. "Keep your hands on the wheel, and don't even think about moving."

The driver stared at Steven, his pupils dilated. "Please," he said, "I don't have much money. I—"

"Shut up," Steven snapped. "Who are you. Why are you following us?"

"I'm not fol—"

Steven jabbed the barrel of the Browning into

the driver's side. The man grunted, and cried, "Wait."

"Who are you?" Steven asked the ruddy-skinned man.

The man's brown eyes narrowed a fraction of a second before he started to turn. His right hand came away from the steering wheel.

Anticipating the man's move, Steven blocked the swing with his forearm, raised his pistol, and chopped once on the driver's temple. The man slumped forward.

"Damn it," Steven muttered. He leaned toward the man and did a quick search. He found a Browning, just like the one he was carrying, in a quick draw shoulder rig. He pulled the man's ID case from his inside jacket pocket. Next to the photo was a gilded eagle symbol he recognized instantly.

"What the hell is happening?" he asked as he dropped the ID on the seat, got out of the car, and ran to where Carla waited.

"Go!" he ordered, pointing to the highway ramp.

As she speeded up, Steven leaned back in the seat, and closed his eyes.

"What happened?" Carla asked, her voice laden with anxiety.

Steven looked at her. "Our tail was a man called Jacob Lowenger. He's CIA. Get off and make a U turn," Steven said suddenly.

Carla exited at the next ramp, went underneath an overpass, and got back on. As she entered the flow of the highway, he saw her glance at the large overhead signpost.

"Washington?" she asked.

"I have a meeting set for tonight."

Chapter Twenty-seven

Steven drove along M Street, passing the closed shops and open pubs lining the main district of Georgetown. Three blocks later, at exactly ten fifty-five, he pulled into an outdoor public lot that served a self-contained mini-mall. He drove to the center of the last row and backed in against the abutment. He did not shut off the engine.

Behind them flowed the Potomac River. In front of them was an empty parking lot and a row of darkened stores. The parking lot was lit by old fashioned street lamps that cast more shadow than light. Steven had chosen this spot because the stores were closed at this time; and, on cold winter nights it was far enough away from the bustling mainstream of Georgetown's night life to keep most people from parking there.

"Now we wait," he told Carla after sweeping the lot to make sure there was no movement. On the ride from Pittsburgh to Washington, Steven had explained parts of his plan to Carla.

"Steven, it's not too late to get out of here," she said, looking around nervously. "Coming back to Washington was crazy. The whole idea was to get you to draw the mole after us, not have you going to him."

"It's necessary," Steven reiterated without going into detail. Although his instincts told him he could trust Carla, he hadn't wanted to tell her exactly what he was doing.

"Steven," she whispered, putting her hand over his on the seat, "I—"

She stopped speaking when a black Mercedes entered the parking lot. Behind it came a second black Mercedes. This one was a limousine. The two cars drove slowly past them, and parked twenty feet away. A few seconds later, three men emerged from the limousine, two others came out of the lead car. They conferred briefly before one of the group broke away and walked to the abutment bounding the Potomac. The man stopped in a spot where the light from the lamp posts was weakest.

Steven scanned the parking lot one final time. When he was satisfied that they were alone, he opened the car door and said, "Cover me. But no matter what happens, don't leave the car."

"Be careful," Carla cautioned as she cocked her weapon.

Steven got out and took a deep breath of the cold night air. He exhaled a cloud of white vapor, squared his shoulders, and walked to the waiting man. A hundred feet behind the man, the cruising lights from a tour boat bobbed peacefully along. Although it was winter, Washington still catered to its tourists.

Stopping three feet from him, Steven bowed from the waist. The Ambassador of the People's Republic of China did the same.

Without further amenities, Steven said, "I am going to ask you a question. The only answer I want is the truth. Without it, both our countries may perish."

"Please, Lieutenant Morrisy, I have come as you asked," Xzi Tao said. "There is no need for melodrama."

"I wish it was only melodrama, Ambassador, but it isn't. Someone is trying to kill me. They've already tried to kill the woman I love. And they've succeeded in killing two of my friends. I am wanted as a spy, traitor, and murderer by the Federal Bureau of Investigation."

Steven saw a flicker of emotion cross Xzi's features. "Your woman, she is safe? She is well?"

"She is in a coma, Ambassador. She may never be well."

He stood still under Xzi's intense scrutiny. "They have called you a traitor?"

Steven nodded once.

"How may I help you?"

Steven looked over Xzi's shoulder, at the distant lights of the boat. From across the Potomac came the faint sound of another boat engine being started up. It was a busy winter night on the Potomac.

Steven's mouth went dry. His mind stumbled under the realization that he was about to ask the man who had been his enemy, the man who had been his inquisitor, and his jailor, for help. He dug his nails hard into his palms to remind himself why he was here. "The other night, at the reception, you hinted that you believed Senator Pritman would be our next President. You based that on your country's political analysts' opinions, did you not?"

"Yes," Xzi agreed. "Unless something of . . . of great bad fortune happens to the senator, we see him as your next President."

"Great bad fortune?"

"You Americans have a way of canonizing your high officials' public and private aspects. But when they show that in the privacy of their own lives, they are mortal, you cannot forgive them."

"A scandal, you mean?" Steven asked, realizing the Xzi was unsure of the proper English word.

"Yes," Xzi said, thoughtfully. "A scandal."

Steven smiled lightly. "Did you turn either Latham or Savak? Are they working for you?" Steven asked suddenly.

Xzi blinked, and then he laughed good naturedly. "You learned interrogation techniques well, Lieutenant."

"I had a good teacher."

Again Xzi nodded, the glint of humor returning briefly to his eyes. "If I had turned them, what point would it serve to tell you, other than to expose them?"

"Because I know how you feel about your country. And I can tell you with complete confidence, that if you don't want China destroyed, you will answer me truthfully."

Xzi's eyes turned intense. "How would such an unthinkable event be possible?"

"What would happen if the United States and China signed a mutual protection and retaliation pact? What would happen if the United States and China joined together to prevent the Soviets from any further world aggression?"

Xzi's eyes became hooded. "If such an event was even remotely thought possible, the Soviets would have no choice but to attack China before such an agreement could be reached."

"If they learned of it beforehand, but as an already presented fact, I think not."

"It would be untenable; the amount of secrecy involved would be impossible to achieve."

Steven grunted. "Not at all. In closed meetings with the proper committees, the President could have the treaty worked out and ready. I believe the same thing would be done on your end with far more ease. Looking across the border to the Soviets, a similar treaty could be quickly accomplished in the Politburo.

"Ambassador, you have the Russians mobilizing along your borders. The analysts see it as a long siege, perhaps lasting until after our elections. Why this unusual flare in hostilities? It seems more than a coincidence that Soviet-Chinese relations are breaking down at this time, so close to our elections. Unless, of course, the Soviets and the Chinese each independently believe that with a change in administration such a treaty is within reach either to themselves, or to the other, and believe themselves to be acting from a position of strength, or of fear."

Xzi started to speak, hesitated, and then said, "You believe that this . . . No, such a thing is impossible."

Ignoring the cold wind that had picked up its pace and was now whipping over them, Steven asked, "Can you be certain? Ambassador, please, return to your embassy tonight and consider what I've said. Look back over the past two years. I know you, Xzi Tao, well enough to be sure that when you do, you will reach the only conclusion possible. Then you must find out if such a thing as I described is actually taking place."

Xzi looked out over the dark water, his eyes following yet another boat that had come into view from their right, a large cabin cruiser. He clasped his hands behind his back, and spoke without looking at Steven. "There have been rumors," he said, his voice so low Steven had to strain to catch the words. "They were discounted because of the far-reaching consequences. No, Lieutenant, I did not turn either of them," Xzi said, facing Steven again.

Steven had no reservations about believing him. He smiled uneasily. "It's funny, but between us there has always been truth, even in the face of the lie that brought us together."

"I will call Beijing tonight. Where will I be able to reach you, if this madness you propound proves correct?"

"You won't. Do you know who Julius Axelrod is?"

Xzi's eyes glinted with genuine humor. "As well as I

know who heads our own internal security forces. Lieutenant, what kind of danger are you in?"

"I'm not important. What's happening to our countries is."

Xzi nodded solemnly. "I would not consider those words from any one else. Nor would I have ever thought that we would meet again. But perhaps I should have expected it, for you are a resourceful man."

"When I have to be."

"And as such, you should have found a way to return my birthday present." Before Steven could recover from his surprise, Xzi said, "Call me tomorrow, if you can. I will have an answer about your theory."

"I will try," Steven said.

They bowed formally to each other before Xzi started away. He stopped after two steps and, without turning back to Steven, said, "When I learned of your escape from the prison camp, I was pleased."

"You knew that they wouldn't believe me when I told them that their plans had failed, didn't you?"

Without answering, Xzi Tao started walking again. Watching him, Steven's emotions became mixed. He wanted to believe that his doubts about Savak were unfounded. And although Xzi had helped to ease some of his concern, Steven acknowledged that there were still other possibilities which had to be looked into.

When Xzi was a dozen feet from him, and as Steven started away from the abutment, he heard the low-throated sound of a boat's engine close behind him.

Glancing over his shoulder, Steven froze in mid-stride. The large cabin cruiser that had been moving toward them, was almost abreast of him. On the flying bridge was the dark silhouette of a man holding a rifle.

Steven spun, shouted to Xzi, and raced after him as the thunder of semi-automatic gunfire shattered the night. Bullets stitched a path ahead of him, tearing up the pavement leading toward the ambassador. Just as he came within reach of Xzi, one of the ricochetting bullets skipped up from the pavement and hit Xzi in the arm.

Five feet from Xzi, Steven catapulted himself into the air. He caught the ambassador by the shoulders, and hauled him to the ground. When they landed, Steven covered Xzi's body with his own.

Two of Xzi's guards charged forward, firing at the boat. The other two raced to the lead car. Carla was out of the rental car and running toward Steven and Xzi when the familiar coarse and grunting thud of a grenade launcher came from the boat.

Steven half raised himself above Xzi. "Down!" he shouted to Carla.

Carla obeyed instantly, diving to the pavement. Xzi's two guards did the same, throwing themselves onto the black surface of the parking lot and covering their heads with their arms.

A heartbeat later, the black Mercedes nearest them blew apart. Flames leaped upward and outward, hurtling metal and glass and gasoline over the parking lot. The second car, so close to the first, was bathed in flames, the high octane fuel from the first car covering it like napalm.

And as the flames from the two cars turned the night into day, Steven saw the disbelief mirrored Xzi's face. He stood, helping the ambassador up at the same time.

Carla had already reached her feet, and was running toward Steven and Xzi when, suddenly, the gas tank of the second car exploded.

Everyone was thrown from their feet. Steven, lifted and twisting above the macadam like a rag doll, felt something rip into his cheek. Then he was on the ground, rolling beneath a second rain of flaming metal and glass.

He covered his head with his arms and hands, as the bullet-like debris peppered his back. Something heavy and burning hot hit him just below his left shoulder. He bit off a scream as the pain spread over him. He rolled, trying to dislodge the burning debris.

Carla was on him instantly, smothering his burning clothing with her own jacket, and bringing him back to the present. He fought to his feet and ripped off his coat and shirt.

When he stood with his chest bared to the cold night, the burning eased slightly. Carla went behind him. He heard her breath catch. But instead of speaking, she picked up his shirt, tore some of the material free. She wadded it into a lump and extended it to him. "Your cheek," she said.

Steven took the makeshift bandage and pressed it to his cheek. He winced at the first touch. The pain was bearable, but he knew it would get worse very soon.

Xzi had gained his feet and joined them. He held his arm. Blood seeped through the fabric of his coat, and over his fingers, but his face was expressive with concern for Steven. "You must go before anyone arrives."

"Your men?" Steven said, ignoring his wounds while looking toward the burning car that Xzi's two guards had gone to.

Xzi shook his head. "Go before the authorities come. You have no choice. Lieutenant," Xzi added, "I will do what I can."

He gazed at Xzi for a fraction of a second longer before turning toward the car.

Each step became a shockwave of pain that radiated along his back. When he finally reached the car, he motioned Carla to drive. He sat heavily in the passenger seat, a wave of nausea catching him unprepared. Without realizing it, he leaned back. Pain raced along his back. He cried out. Then he bit down hard on his lower lip.

"Move," he ordered Carla.

"Where?"

"Just get the hell out of here," he snapped, turning to look at Xzi, who was standing with his men, watching Steven and Carla.

Carla sped out of the lot and onto M Street. She drove several blocks and then, as the sounds of sirens reached them, turned off the main street and pulled to the curb.

"Steven, your back," she said, leaning toward him and lightly touching his bare shoulder.

"I'm fine," he said through the pain.

"No you aren't. Those wounds have to be treated. You've got a bad burn. And your face . . ."

He pressed the bandage against his cheek, but felt nothing. It had gone numb. He pulled down the sun visor, turned on the overhead light, and looked in the mirror.

Lowering the blood-soaked bandage, he exposed a jagged three-inch slice on his cheek. He guessed that a piece of glass had hit him a glancing blow. The blood was coagulating. Most of the bleeding had stopped. He thought the cheek might need stitches.

"I can't take the chance of calling anyone."

"What about Joshua Raden?"

"No. Carla, everyone I come in contact with is being hurt or killed. I won't expose anyone else. Find an all-night drug store."

As they drove, his anger and frustration mixed with the increasing physical pain. All he could see were the red flames of the car, and the pattern of bullets on the pavement. "How?" he shouted, his voice thick with futility. "How the hell did he know?"

He turned his head to look at Carla, who drove ashen-faced and silent. "How?" he repeated.

She shook her head but said nothing.

"Every move I make. Everything I do, I'm one step behind him. What do I have to do?"

"Steven," Carla said, reaching across to take his hand. "I think we should go in. Let the agency handle this. Too many people have been killed."

Steven yanked his hand from hers, wincing at the surge of pain in his back. "And let him win? No. Pull over!"

Following his orders, she rolled to a stop at the curb. He bent, ignoring another ripping of pain, and reached across Carla to open her door. "Go," he ordered angrily.

Her lips narrowed. Her face turned red. She slammed the door shut. "Not without you," she said, hitting the gas.

A half hour later, on US 1, in Greenbelt, Maryland, Carla found a Giant supermarket with a large drug department. Leaving Steven in the car, she went inside and bought burn ointment, aspirins, and bandages.

Steven watched her enter the store, wondering if somehow Carla could have reported in. That could explain what had happened at the parking lot. But she hadn't been out of his sight since they'd left Pittsburgh. Except for two gas station bathroom visits, and she couldn't have called anyone then.

Then who?

He remembered the man in the brown car. The CIA could have found out where he was going. All they'd have had to do was to trace his call from the motel phone.

But why would the CIA want to kill him, and Xzi Tao? No, he was still missing something important.

He tried to focus on the problem, and to ignore the worsening pain in his back. But soon, his thoughts blurred and he leaned forward to rest his head on the dash and wait for Carla's return.

The next thing he was aware of, was Carla, back in the car and leaning anxiously over him. After making sure he was conscious, she got back on US 1.

From that point on, time became insignificant to Steven. The pain kept growing, and he was fuzzing in and out of consciousness. Without warning, Carla swung into the entrance to a Holiday Inn.

"No," Steven said, speaking through pain-clenched teeth.

She pulled to a stop under the concrete awning and turned to him. "Ever since Paul Grange was wounded, you've been giving me orders. This time we're doing it my way!"

Staring defiantly at him, she shut off the ignition and pulled the keys free. "This won't take long."

Steven, groggy and gripped with pain, was unable to stop her.

Carla returned quickly, and drove around the side of the building. She parked near the side center entrance and said, "Stay put. I'll bring the bags to the room first, and then I'll come back for you."

He passed out again, awakening only when Carla tried to maneuver him out of the car. He helped her as best he could, leaning against the car.

Thankfully, their room was on the first floor. Once inside, she guided him to the bed and helped him to lie face down.

"Easy," she whispered when his muscles spasmed in pain. She went to the door, locked it, and emptied the contents of the supermarket bag on the bed.

"How bad?" he asked.

"I've seen better," she replied. "There are pieces of shirt stuck in your skin. I . . . I have to get them out. Please, Steven, let me call Joshua!"

"Do it yourself, or leave it alone. They'll be watching him."

"It's going to hurt."

Steven nodded. "Just get it over with."

Carla rummaged through her purse and came up with eyebrow tweezers. Swallowing hard, she poured alcohol over the metal and went to work.

The first touch brought incredible pain. His body arched. He bit down on the pillow and fought the pain.

She worked on him for fifteen-minutes. He accepted the pain as best he could, using the pillow to muffle the groans he could not hold back. Then through his fog of pain, he heard her warn him that there was a small piece of metal imbedded beneath the last piece of fabric.

He felt the tweezer grasp it and tug tentatively. There was a pause, and then she pulled. A bolt of pain ripped through him turning everything red and white.

"It's out," she said. "I . . . I have to put antiseptic on it. Steven . . ." she said as she began. It was the last thing he heard before the pain turned into fiery agony and he passed out.

Amos Coblehill studied the notes he had made on the yellow legal pad. The Director of the National Security Agency had been at his desk all night—for the second night in a row.

He poured more black coffee from the thermos into his cup, and then added a splash of brandy from the bottle on the tray. He took a long drink, set the cup down, and once again reviewed the events that had led up to this moment.

Yesterday afternoon, according to the reports from the field, Morrisy had ditched the team that had been following him. Morrisy's move had been anticipated and expected. The emergency transmitter had been activated, and the surveillance team had kept a fifteen minute spread between themselves and Morrisy, all the way back to Pittsburgh.

When the team had reached Pittsburgh, they'd found the parked car at the motel. They'd checked with the desk and learned that Morrisy had taken a room for two nights. Morrisy had used his own name.

It was Coblehill's assessment that Morrisy had done this to see if the mole was onto him.

Shortly after the new field control supervisor had arrived in Pittsburgh, he'd discovered that none of the agents had seen Morrisy or Statler since they'd found the car. He had further found out that Morrisy and Statler had not made any calls from the room, nor had they ordered any room service.

By six that evening, Grange's replacement had decided it was time to make sure about Morrisy.

He went to the room. When there was no answer to his knock, the supervisor and his team went in. It was empty, the beds had never been used. He'd called in on Priority One.

After Axelrod had issued a code two alert—a check on all car rental agencies, the airport, buses, and taxis—the director had called Coblehill. Coblehill was still awaiting the results of the alert query.

Coblehill took another generous drink of the brandy laced coffee. He'd had bad feelings about this operation from the outset. And with each day the mole went free, more and more problems arose.

The retired general found himself thinking about the attack on the Chinese ambassador, earlier that night. It was as if he didn't have enough problems to face already. Murphy's law, he decided.

With a little luck, the newspapers would report what they were told, which was that while the Chinese diplomat had been having dinner in Georgetown, his driver had been parked a few blocks away, and had been smoking in the car. Apparently, there had been a gas leak.

It was thin, he knew, but it was the best they'd been able to come up with. And because it was so obvious, it just might work. Besides, Xzi Tao had refused to comment at all, except to say that someone attacked them from the Potomac and he expected a full scale investigation to be conducted.

Before his thoughts could darken further, his phone rang. He glanced at the phone board. His private line was blinking. He depressed the speaker button. "Coblehill."

"Amos," came Julius Axelrod's voice. "We found out how they got away. They rented a car, and not under Morrisy's name. It was Statler who signed the papers."

"But—"

"Exactly," Axelrod says. "Our people never expected the car to be rented by one of us. They figured that if Morrisy wanted another car, she would set it up so he would have to rent it."

"Could he have forced her?"

"No. She knew what she was doing. She's well trained and must have assumed we'd check for both of them, not just Morrisy. Why else would she have put the Priority One telephone number on the rental papers?"

"What now?"

"They've been out of contact for eighteen hours. Time's running out. We have no choice but to find out how the hell the Bureau got into this. We need to know who their contact is, why they've kept us in the dark, and then we've got to sift through every last bit of their information."

"There's only one way to do that," Coblehill said with obvious resignation.

"I know that, Amos," Axelrod replied.

Coblehill shut off the phone, sighed expressively, and

then dialed a special number known only to a half dozen people in the world. When the call was answered, he said, "I'm sorry to disturb you at this hour, Mr. President, but . . ."

Chapter Twenty-eight

Opening his eyes slowly, Steven saw fractured rays of sun slanting through the small opening between the barely meeting drapes. He started to turn, but pain stopped the movement. And then he remembered.

Very carefully, he shifted his body on the bed so that his legs came off first. He slid from the bed to a kneeling position, and using the mattress for leverage, stood.

There was pain with every movement, but not as intense as it had been last night. He looked around. The motel room was empty. Where was she? As he started forward, he saw a note stuck on the mirror. *Went to the store. 7:00 a.m.*

He checked his watch. It was five to eight. He walked gingerly to the bathroom, used the toilet, and then looked in the mirror. There was a bandage on his cheek. She must have done that after he'd passed out.

Peeling back the corner of the gauze, he gazed at the plaster tape Carla had used to butterfly the jagged cut together. It was a professional looking job and, with a little luck, the scar wouldn't be too bad.

He washed what he could of his face, and rinsed his mouth with cold water. No sooner had he shut the faucet off than he heard the door open and close.

He turned cautiously. Carla was standing in the room, holding two bags. One was small and white, the other larger and brown.

"What?"

"Codeine and antibiotics," she said, holding up the smaller bag first. When she lifted the larger one, she added, "Coffee and rolls."

He held back a surge of anger. By going out, she had put them into danger. "I asked you not to call anyone."

"You need medication for the burns. I called Joshua. Steven," she quickly continued before he could interrupt, "he was on duty last night. He arranged with another doctor to call in the prescriptions. It's all right."

"And Ellie?" he asked, knowing that Joshua would have sent some word.

She shook her head. Her eyes did not quite meet his. "No change. But there are two agency people with her at all times."

Steven exhaled softly. Too much time was passing, and Ellie was not recovering from the coma. That wasn't good. He shook away the thought and concentrated on his own problems. "We can't take the chance that Joshua's phone was tapped, or that someone was watching him. We'll have to get out of here."

"I covered myself," Carla stated. "I called Joshua from a pay phone, and gave him a number to call. He called me back from a pay phone in the hospital lounge. We're all right, for a while. But we will leave soon. I also turned the car in and got another. In case they made the first one."

He felt himself relax. She had made the right move. He went over to one of the chairs, sat on the edge of the cushion, and thought about last night. "How could he have known about the meeting? It doesn't make any sense."

Carla didn't answer. She put the brown bag on the table and removed two covered styrofoam cups of coffee and two wrapped rolls. Then she opened the other bag and took out an amber prescription bottle with a white twist cap. She got a glass of water from the bathroom, and brought it to him with two codeine tablets and an antibiotic.

He took the antibiotic, but said, "Not yet," to the codeine.

They ate the light breakfast in silence and, when they finished, Steven stood. His wounds and the confinement of the motel room made him feel vulnerable. "I want to get out of here."

Carla nodded. "After I change the dressings."

It took her a quarter of an hour to put on the fresh bandages. When she was finished, she insisted that Steven take the pain killers. He didn't argue this time.

While Carla put their things together, Steven went to the dresser and picked up the phone.

"What are you doing?" Carla asked, alarmed.

"I have to make a call." He dialed information, got the number of the FBI, and called. An operator answered, and he asked for Inspector Blayne.

The operator informed him that Blayne was not in. Steven asked to be transferred to the supervisor on duty.

A sharp edged voice came on the line, identifying himself as Conklin. "I need to speak with Inspector Blayne," Steven said.

"Inspector Blayne is not in. May I take a message?"

"Can you get me through to him?" Steven asked.

"He's in the field. Who—"

Steven cut him off. "This is Steven Morrisy. Will

that help me get through?"

There was a hesitant pause, and then, "Give me a number. I'll have Blayne get back to you."

Steven exhaled in annoyance. "Don't be an ass, Conklin. Give Blayne this message. Tell him that his source is corrupt. Tell him to find out why."

"And he's supposed to believe you?"

"I really don't give a damn if he does or not—that's his problem. But he and all of you are being played like puppets. I'm not the one you're looking for. Tell Blayne it's either his source, or someone who's feeding his source."

"Morrisy—"

Steven hung up abruptly and turned to Carla. "Let's go."

"They may not have had enough time to trace the call."

"Yes they did. The minute I gave him my name, he activated a computer trace. If he doesn't have this number already, he will within the next few minutes."

When they were on US 1 four and a half minutes later, Steven said, "The one good thing about last night was that I learned that the mole is definitely not Chinese."

Carla shook her head. "Of course not. I told you the mole is Russian."

Steven smiled. He felt a tugging in his cheek. "No, it only appears that way. You, your agency, and everyone else looking for the mole is working under a false premise. Someone who has an intimate knowledge of the workings of our intelligence community is making it appear that a Soviet mole is leaking secrets. He's not an agent of a foreign power."

"How can you be so certain?" she asked, stopping for a red light and turning to him.

"Because there's no other explanation for what's

happening—at least not in my mind. Why didn't you leave last night, when I asked you to?" he asked, abruptly changing the subject.

"I couldn't," she whispered.

He smiled. "Semper fi?"

Her mouth tightened; she stared directly into his eyes. "No, you. I . . . I care for you Steven."

Caught by surprise, he could only stare at her. He wanted to say something, to tell her that it couldn't be, but he sensed she knew that already.

He nodded, and she started off. A half block later, he pointed to the Beltway.

"Where are we going?"

"To Greyton."

The sun had set three hours before Steven and Carla passed the Greyton line. The air outside was freezing. Gusts of wind tossed random snowflakes against the windshield. For most of the trip, Steven had given himself over to seeking out an answer by backtracking through his mind. The only answers he came up with, were too outrageous even to consider.

He had to start considering any possibility, he told himself as they passed into the more populous outlying area of Greyton. Time was running out. It was Monday evening. A week had passed since Ellie had been taken out of the frozen lake.

A half mile before downtown Greyton, Steven instructed Carla to turn onto Edmond Street. Banacek's house was the third on the left.

When Carla shut off the ignition and looked at Steven, he accurately read the fatigue that had settled onto her face. "Are you ready for this?"

"Do we have a choice?"

"No," he admitted.

Leaving the car, they went up to the front door. Steven felt the pain beginning again, and knew the effects of the codeine were wearing off. He'd take more after they left Banacek.

Banacek opened the door before Steven could knock. He stood in the doorway, his barrel chest expanding the uniform shirt to its maximum.

"Good evening, Sheriff," Steven said. "This is Carla Statler."

Banacek looked Carla over from head to foot. "I thought it was Rogers," he said, stepping back to let them enter.

"No, it's Statler," she told him, her voice weary. She opened her purse and extracted a slim leather case which she held up for Banacek's inspection.

He looked at the identification. "Sure has been a lot of federal tin around here lately. Why don't we talk in the kitchen."

Banacek led them into the large and cheerfully decorated room. Steven and Carla sat on uncushioned spindle-back chairs at a highly varnished pine table while Banacek poured three cups of coffee.

Once the sheriff joined them, he said, "I called that number you gave me. Spoke with the director. He asked me to go along with you for now. But I'd sure like you to bring me up to date on what the hell you've gotten yourself into."

Steven matched Banacek's somber expression. "I'll tell you what I can," he said, and detailed most of the events of the past week, culminating with last night's attack on Xzi Tao and himself.

When Steven finished, Banacek lit a Camel filter and took a deep drag. "If Miss Rogers was Secret Service, why in the hell was the FBI involved in this?"

"We're not sure," Carla said. "Our guess is that the

person we're looking for is using the Bureau as a smoke screen. And because of the delicacy of our operation, we couldn't and still can't let them know about Ellie, or us."

"Do you think Blayne will believe the message you left for him?" Banacek asked Steven.

Steven shrugged. "Realistically, no. But I can always hope. Sheriff, where's Ellie's ring?"

"At my office."

"What about the home owner listings?"

Banacek studied Steven's face for a moment. "To be frank, I didn't know when you would show, or even if you would, and I wasn't so sure that I was going to bother. But I'll have something for you by tomorrow, late morning. They buried Londrigan and Lomack yesterday," he added suddenly.

Steven stared at a small picture on the wall behind Banacek. "I hope no one else will be hurt."

"So do I."

"We'll be going now," Steven said, standing. "We'll be at my house."

"Do you think that's wise?"

Steven shrugged. "It's as good a place as any," he said leading Carla out.

Just before ten o'clock, Carla turned the car onto Steven's long single lane drive. Steven's nerves were on edge. Although he'd put up a front of bravado with Banacek, he had not been all that sure if he was ahead of the mole or not.

And as Carla drove slowly with the bright lights on, Steven took the nine-millimeter from beneath the seat and studied the snow-covered drive illuminated by the headlights.

He felt a small measure of relief when he saw no tracks in the snow that had fallen sometime during the week. He also knew that the absence of tracks wasn't proof that there were no visitors. Tracks could be covered.

Carla stopped at the garage door and looked at him. He took out a set of keys and nodded. They left the car together, both of them armed.

After opening the door, they searched the house cautiously, making sure there were no unexpected surprises. Following their search, Steven drew all the shades and curtains, in an effort to keep the house looking unoccupied. He knew that there would be tell-tale signs of occupancy, but he did his best anyway.

Then they brought in their bags and the groceries they'd picked up after leaving Banacek. He'd taken a pain killer at the store, and the pain had receded to bearable limits.

Finally, when everything was taken care of, and the car was parked inside the garage, Carla looked around the living room. "It suits you," she said.

"Tired?" Steven asked.

She shook her head. "I could do with some more coffee."

Steven turned the boiler on and reset the thermostat while Carla made the coffee. She brought the pot into the living room, poured the coffee, and set the glass carafe on the table.

Then she walked to the fireplace, and looked at the photographs on the mantel. Steven followed her every move, waiting patiently until she returned to the couch and sat near him.

"Now," Carla said, turning her upper torso to him.

"Now what?" he asked, already knowing the answer.

"You asked me to be patient and trust you. I think I've been both. Now, I want to know what you've got in mind. And why you're so damned certain we're wrong about the mole."

Steven glanced at the desk where he'd been working when he'd gotten Savak's phone call last Monday. Had it only been a week since they'd found Ellie? So much had happened that Steven found it hard to believe. And it was all tied into what had brought him here in the first place.

"You're right," he said. "It is time. But you'll have to bear with me."

"Yes. I'm all ears."

Steven looked across the room, to the photo of Ellie and himself. "In order to understand why your mole is after me, I'll have to go back to when I started in politics. I'd been in private practice for two years. I was working with the local people and about as happy as I thought I could ever be.

"Then Arnie Savak came home one weekend to visit. He reminded me of all our talks, when we were in the POW camp in Nam." Steven paused, turned, and met Carla's eyes. "When we were in the hut together, those last few weeks, we used to spend hours trying to figure out how, if we ran America, we could stop war and bring some form of peaceful stability to the world."

"Fantasy politics," Carla said.

"Call it what you want, but we came up with a theory that would work—under optimum circumstances.

"Until Savak came to me that day, I'd never really thought about it after leaving Nam. But that weekend he brought it up, and told me he was working on it. He outlined everything, including the man who he felt could pull it together—Philip Pritman. We spent three days talking and arguing and remembering. Before Arnie left, I agreed to join the senator's team."

Steven drank some of his coffee. "It was the best decision I'd made in years. I love Washington, and I love the ability I have to help get things done. Between Savak and myself, we were able to guide the senator toward the very things we'd been striving for."

Carla leaned forward eagerly. "Entente."

She said the word almost like a invocation. Steven nodded without feeling any surprise that Carla knew. "I imagine Ellie gave the agency as full a report as she could."

"Which wasn't much. Something to do with parallel pacification treaties."

"We kept it close," Steven admitted. "It was just Savak and Pritman and myself. Simon Clarke knows some of it, but not the real scope or the basis behind the proposal."

"What is Entente?"

Steven moistened his lips. He had been keeping the secret for so long that talking about it to Carla felt like betraying a trust. Then he realized how paranoid and foolish his thinking had become over the last few years. "Entente is an extremely complicated method of turning adversaries into allies by making a political aggressor into a defender."

Carla shook her head. "Which is just a reworking of political doctrines that have been with us for ages."

"Yes and no. Entente has always been with us, but this time we've evolved it far from its roots and mistakes of the past."

Carla scratched at her chin. "Okay, let's say that I see where you're leading, but if the countries signing the protection agreement are diametrically opposed politically . . ."

"It wouldn't make any difference."

"You're talking about China and Russia," Carla stated.

"Or any communist country for that matter. Communism is a political entity, just like democracy. And like a democracy, communism is run by politicians. The basic difference is that in a free democratic society, people are given choices. In a communistic society, they are dictated to in the name of the people. But the people who do the dictating are not necessarily in agreement with what another communist country might consider as their true political goals."

"Such as the Soviet and Chinese governments."

"Yes. Two countries that have similar governmental ideologies, yet have very different political goals. The Soviets want communism to be the only political belief of the world, with themselves at the governmental helm, of course. I believe, as do many theorists, that the Chinese want to control their country, and guide other Asian nations, but do not necessarily want to spread their rule over other continents. So, in our vision of Entente, we would align a free democracy with a communist country at odds with another communist country, and theoretically have the ability to avert war on two fronts."

"But can it be done?" Carla asked.

"If used properly, Entente can be the lever that will ease the tensions of world aggression. I won't say it's not an extremely dangerous lever. But the way Savak and I have engineered the proposal, it's intended as a means to make arms control viable.

"And it's a hell of a Presidential platform to boot," he added. "There would be no promises, just a willingness to meet with one's enemies and to show strength by agreeing to certain things."

"The public won't go for it. They'll look on it as a sign of weakness," Carla argued.

Steven stood and walked slowly to the fireplace, following the same path Carla had taken moments before. He looked at the mementoes of his life, an ever-so-accurate trail of what had brought him to this point. He stared at the picture of the football team, and at the teenage faces of Lomack and Londrigan. He felt a heavy sadness for their deaths.

He turned back to Carla. "Actually, it's so damned feasible a proposal that someone is killing people and trying to sabotage it before it gets out. Carla, I think that the Soviets are getting information about Entente and are afraid it will be used against them. The same thing is happening with the Chinese, which is most likely why they're mobilizing along their borders.

"Someone has learned of the Entente proposal and is using it to create worldwide hostilities so that such a proposal could never take place."

"That may well be true. But there's another scenario that fits," Carla said in a low voice.

Steven studied her, wondering if she had picked up the same thing he had. "And that is?"

"The opposite of your theory about the President, or someone on his staff, trying to set you up, so that he could keep Pritman from getting the nomination. Steven, what if the classified information being leaked to the Soviets—foreign policy decisions as well as your Entente proposal—is nothing more than a ploy to make the President look incompetent and assure Pritman the election?"

Holding her gaze, he felt his respect for her increase.

"The only weakness in the theory is that Pritman hasn't announced."

"It's a given, Steven. It has been for two years."

"But there's much more involved," he said. "Even the attempt on Ellie's life wasn't what it appeared to be. It was another case of misinformation."

When she remained silent after his unexpected revelation, Steven knew that the time had come to explain everything. "Carla, the attempt to kill Ellie was only a by-product of what's happening. The blame for her would-be death was set up to be directed at me from the start. You see, I'm the person your mole wants out of the way. Ellie just had the bad luck to discover him at the wrong time, and she became the method of getting rid of me."

"Why?" Carla asked, her eyes clouded.

"That's still the unknown aspect."

"Then how are we going to learn who's behind everything?"

"Possibly from the land listings I asked Banacek to get for me. It's a long shot, but Ellie had to be kept somewhere while she was being questioned and tortured. I think it was here. When we get the names of the property owners from Banacek, we'll see if there are any familiar names. If not, we call the owners to see if their property was rented two weeks ago."

He started back to the couch, but froze in midstride. With everything that had happened, he'd forgotten about his phone call to Savak their first night on the run. "Damn it," he half shouted, "I've got to stop Pritman from going to the meeting."

"What meeting?"

"I called Savak and had him push up Pritman's meeting with the party brass. I told Savak to have Pritman explain the Entente proposal."

Angry at himself for not having thought it through before calling Savak, Steven went to the phone and dialed his friend's home number. He hoped he was wrong, prayed he was wrong about the unsettling doubts he felt about Savak. He tried to find an alternative to making the call, but knew there was none. His only link to Pritman was Savak. He had to trust his friend one more time.

When Savak answered, Steven said, "Arnie, get the Entente papers out of the senator's safe. Don't let him bring Entente into the meeting."

"What the hell are you talking about?"

"I can't explain it, not yet. Just do it, Arnie."

"Steven, you're not making sense."

"We can't use Entente yet!" Steven half shouted.

"The hell we can't! That's why we created it. Steven, I did what you wanted. I brought the meeting forward after you told me to make sure Pritman got in and made his announcement. Pritman is in California now. He's speaking tonight at the Press Club dinner. I made arrangements for the party people to be there as well. He meets with them tomorrow evening, and he'll announce his candidacy the following morning. He has the proposal with him."

Steven pressed the inside corners of his eyes with his thumb and index finger. "Arnie, get to Pritman—cancel the meeting."

"I can't. It's too late."

"Goddamn it Arnie, don't argue with me! On our friendship, on everything we've been through, you must stop it."

There was a moment's silence, and then Savak's voice came out of the receiver sounding doubtful. "What's wrong with it?"

"The only thing that could be—Russia and China know about it!"

"There's no way for that to have happened," Savak said patiently.

Steven took a calming breath. He had to find a way to make his friend believe him. "It's a fact. Why do you think Ellie almost died? It was because she found out that someone on our staff is leaking the information—to both sides. I'm the next victim. And then you, Arnie, because you're the only other person who knows how to make Entente work."

"My God, Steven, think about what you're saying. Think about the way it sounds. No one but you, myself, and Pritman know everything about Entente. And you can't seriously think Pritman would—"

"I don't know who it is, but I will. I came back to find out who. Get Pritman to cancel. And either get those papers into a safe, or destroy them."

Steven felt Savak's hesitation as if it were something physical. He wanted to scream at his friend, but held himself back. Finally, Savak said, "I'm scheduled on a morning flight to the coast. I'll stop Pritman from bringing up Entente. But Steven, if you're wrong, it may cost us the election."

"I'm not wrong. I wish I was. Stop Pritman." Then, just as he was about to hang up the phone, he thought about his car, and the way it had been bugged.

"One more thing, Arnie. When you had my Bronco driven to Washington. Who drove it?"

"You mean the person's name?"

"Exactly."

"I haven't the faintest idea," Savak said, obviously puzzled at the tangent Steven had taken. "I called a service and made the arrangements for them to pick up the car at Greyton Memorial. I left the keys with Chuck."

"I see," Steven said. "Thank you Arnie, and please, do what I've asked," he reiterated before hanging up.

"Will he do it?" Carla asked from behind.

Steven turned. "I think he'll have to. If what I believe is true, there's no other choice. But he has to believe me first."

"How's the pain?" she asked, crossing the room

toward him.

"It's there."

"I have to change the dressing again. And then I think you should get some sleep."

Steven nodded. "We'll sleep in shifts. We can't take the chance of being caught by surprise."

Her brow furrowed. "No one followed us."

"As far as we were able to determine, no one followed us yesterday either. And no one knew we were going to see Xzi Tao," he reminded her. "I've been thinking about it all day, and I keep coming back to the same thought. Whoever wants me dead has studied me. So we'll have to take it for granted that when he can't find me, he'll come looking for me here."

"Maybe . . ."

"No," Steven said, looking deep into Carla's eyes, "I'm counting on it."

Chapter Twenty-nine

The sound of rain brought Steven from sleep to consciousness. He turned his head and looked out the window. The sun was out, the sky clear and blue. Then he realized it was the shower. Carla had relieved him on watch, at four. He'd taken two pills and fallen into a deep sleep. He was a little groggy from the codeine, and decided not to take any more. He needed to be completely in control from this point on.

He sat up. The pain had diminished a little, but he was stiff. His back was healing too, and the pressure of the bandages against his skin was easing. He swung his legs off the bed just as Carla came in. She was wearing his bathrobe.

"Hi," she said with a smile. "I was coming to wake you before I got into the shower. How do you feel?"

"Better. What time is it?"

"Eleven. You were sleeping so soundly that I thought it best if you got a little time. Coffee's ready and Banacek hasn't called."

She spun out of the room. Steven stood and put on a pair of sweat pants. He went to the kitchen and poured a cup of coffee.

Ten minutes later, just as the shower went off, the phone rang. Steven stared at it suspiciously. He flashed back to the last time he'd had that same sense of apprehension.

Steven picked up the phone but did not speak. "It's Banacek. I just talked to Irv Coleman. He'll have the list ready after lunch."

"Thank you, Sheriff. I'll be there at one."

"No," Banacek said. "I think it would be better if I picked up the list and brought it out to you."

"Why?" he asked, his sense of warning coming out strong.

"Seems your friend Blayne ran out of patience. I got an FBI advisory bulletin this morning. It says you're armed and dangerous. They want you, Morrisy, any way they can get you."

"Thank you, sheriff," Steven said. "I'll wait for you."

Steven hung up and looked out the kitchen window. He was sure that his letter of resignation had been received at the office. He was also certain that Simon Clarke would be breathing easier.

Obviously, Blayne hadn't paid any attention to the message he'd left. He could only pray that this would end before the media picked up on it.

"Banacek?" Carla asked.

Steven glanced over his shoulder. Carla was standing in the doorway, her hair wet and tousled, lending a new softness to her features. The robe clung to her damp body.

"Yes, it was Banacek. We'll have the listing around one."

At a quarter after one, and after Carla changed his bandages, the phone rang. It was Banacek.

"Morrisy, there's been a bad accident out on the Brynman Pike. I'm on my way there now. I don't think I'll be back before two or three. I'm sorry, but you'll have to go into town. I've already called Irv Coleman to let him know."

"I'll handle it."

"You be extra careful. I haven't seen any federal people around, but you can't always tell. Come into town the back way and use the side entrance to Irv's office. He knows you're coming. And Morrisy, I want to know if you come up with anything."

"You will," Steven said. After hanging up, he explained the situation to Carla.

"I can go for you," she said.

He shook his head hard. "They'll be looking for you too. No, we'll go together."

Ignoring her continuing protests, Steven led the way to the car. He followed Banacek's advice and, using the back streets leading to City Hall, they made the drive in fifteen minutes. Steven didn't see anyone tailing them.

But before leaving the car, Steven double-checked the streets and the scant few people walking on them. Seeing nothing out of the ordinary, he and Carla left the car and went to the side door of City Hall.

Steven knocked twice. The city clerk unlocked the door, and motioned them in. Irving Coleman was a wizened old man with a fringe of white hair surrounding a speckled pate. The pince-nez resting securely on the bridge of his nose, accented pale cheeks and bloodless lips and an inherent attitude of propriety.

Coleman was sixty-two, according to all the records, yet he looked closer to seventy-two, which Steven knew he was. But as Banacek had said a week ago, Greyton looked after its own; and Irv Coleman had always been part of Greyton. Steven had dealt with Coleman many times in the past, when he'd had his private practice.

"Mr. Morrisy," Coleman said, nodding his head but staring pointedly at Carla.

"Mr. Coleman," Steven replied without introducing Carla. "You have something for me?"

Coleman handed Steven a large manila envelope. "Sheriff said to give these to you. Mighty irregular, this whole business."

"Thank you," Steven said, taking Carla's arm and guiding her back outside and to the car.

When he got behind the wheel, he tapped the envelope on it thoughtfully. He was gripped by an irrational fear. Then he made himself face the possibility that a friend of his was trying to kill him.

No, it was more than that. Whoever this person was he was trying to do more than just kill Steven, he was trying to kill Steven's dream. Steven would not permit that to happen.

From the corner of his eye, he saw Carla alertly watching the sidewalk and the streets around them. He took a deep breath and opened the envelope. There were five sheets of green bar computer paper. He slid them out and looked at the title above the list of names, addresses, date of purchase, and property descriptions read: ZONE 3407 POMPTON ESTATES.

Steven went slowly down the list. He found what he was looking for on the third page. A gut-wrenching sensation of disgust made him shudder. He held his emotions in check while he went through the rest of the list.

Then he returned to the familiar name and stared at the address. Eleven Deer Walk Lane. He closed his eyes, but could not shake the name that was now imbedded in his head.

He thought back to the beginning, and remembered the phone call. Then he pictured Ellie's hospital room in Georgetown, and the large man who had been standing over her, doing something with the intravenous line.

"Who is it?" Carla asked.

Steven didn't look at her; he handed her the list. A moment later, she said, "Chuck Latham? That doesn't add up."

Steven started the car and pulled away from the curb. "I know it doesn't, but he's the only one on the list who's connected to me."

Steven U-turned and drove the ten blocks to Greyton Memorial Hospital. Leaving Carla in the car to keep watch, he went to the front desk and asked for Latham. The receptionist told him that the doctor had taken a long weekend off, and wasn't scheduled for duty until late that afternoon.

He called Latham's house from the hospital. There was no answer. He went back outside and stared at the rental car. Carla was sitting in the passenger seat, watching him.

Steven looked around. He'd grown up here, spent most of his life here, but now everything had become strange and alien. There had to be an explanation. Chuck Latham was not a killer.

Or was he?

Steven drove home in silence. Whenever the pain in his head would become too much, he leaned back in the seat and used the physical pain of his burn to relieve his emotional anguish. While he drove, he worked the facts over and over in his head. Just because Latham owned a vacation house on Lake Pompton didn't mean he was responsible for what was happening. The resort area was popular. A lot of people invested in property and rented it out every summer. Finally, Steven made himself stop rationalizing. He knew it was a pointless exercise. What he had to do was find out, one way or another, if Chuck Latham was involved.

He pulled to a stop in front of his house, and stared at the front door. Cursing himself for not leaving something to tell him if someone was there now, or had been there, Steven shut off the ignition.

"Get your pistol out," he said to Carla. She eyed him silently, and drew her weapon from her purse. "Just in case," he added as he pulled the Browning from his belt.

They went to the door together. He tested it, and found it locked. He didn't unlock it; rather, he motioned Carla to go around one side of the house, while he went around to the other. He walked slowly, searching the ground, bushes, and exterior of the house. When he and Carla met up in the back, neither had found any footprints, and none of the windows appeared to have been jimmied.

They returned to the front. He unlocked the door and slipped quickly in. He held the weapon outstretched. The room was empty. With Carla acting as back-up, he searched the rest of the house before he felt safe enough to lower the weapon and put its safety on.

"What now?" Carla asked, taking off her coat.

"We find out if Chuck rents out the lake house, and if he does, if it has been rented lately." Steven went to his desk and took out the phone book. He rifled through it, until he found what he wanted.

Pointing to the listing, he said, "Joanne Freeland is the largest real estate agent in Greyton. She handles most of the rental properties. Give her a call. Ask about renting Chuck's property."

"Steven," Carla said as she picked up the receiver, "Latham has been your friend all your life. Why didn't you know about this house?"

Steven shrugged. "He never mentioned it to me. He bought it three years ago," he added after checking the date of purchase.

Carla glanced at the date, and then dialed the number. Steven began to pace, his thoughts bogged down in the years of friendship he and Latham had shared. He tried to picture Chuck in the role of his and Ellie's executioner, and failed.

Something inside of him told him that it wasn't possible. Yet, in the past week too many things that had happened, that were just as impossible. He turned when he heard Carla hang up the phone. "What did she say?"

Carla moistened her lips, hesitating. "It's an income property. But the house is only available for rental from May through September. No exceptions."

"I want to see the house."

Carla looked out at the clear sky. "I think we should wait. We've been very visible today. It makes sense to wait until dark."

He shook his head impatiently. "If it's a seasonal rental, there won't be any electricity. We need the daylight. It's almost three now. We've only got an hour and a half of real light left."

"I . . ." She stopped herself and, instead, said, "All right, but do you think you could turn on the heat in here so it'll be livable when we get back?"

He'd been so wrapped up in his thoughts that he hadn't noticed how cold the inside of the house had become in their absence. Nodding, he went to the thermostat and saw that it was set at seventy. But when he looked at the temperature reading it showed only fifty-three.

"The boiler must have gone out," he muttered. "I'll be right back." Steven went through the kitchen and into the utility room. He checked the water heater. It was cold. He knelt to peer at the pilot on the boiler. It was out, as he'd thought.

Returning to the kitchen, Steven got a wooden match from the box on the shelf above the stove. He started back into the utility room, but stopped when he passed the stove.

He looked at the stove, and then at the floor. There was a scratch on the floor near the left front corner of the stove. Then he remembered that Banacek had been at the house, searching it. He'd found the ring on the window sill.

He went back into the utility room and, kneeling on the floor, he turned on the gas and pressed his nose to the boiler.

When he was satisfied that there was no leak, he moved the lever to pilot. Then he pushed the red button in and lit the match. He held it in the opening for the required thirty seconds. When he released the button, the pilot flame stayed on.

He turned the switch full on, waited until he heard the flame start, and went back to the living room.

"All set," he said as he reset the temperature on the thermostat.

Carla slipped into her coat and picked up her purse and the manila envelope.

"It'll warm up in a few minutes," he told Carla as he put on his coat and started toward the front door. "We can g—" He cut himself off at the sound of a low pop. The hairs on the back of his neck stood out stiffly.

Reacting to what he instinctively knew would happen, Steven grabbed Carla and shoved her toward the front door. Just as he opened the door, the house exploded around them.

A gust of hot air slammed into them. He caught Carla around the waist, pulling her against him before the force of the blast tore him from his feet and sent them both tumbling out of the house.

They crashed down the steps of the porch, and out onto the ground. Carla landed on top of him, driving his back agonizingly into the frozen ground.

And then there was another explosion, louder this time. He rolled instinctively, turning them away from the blast. He held Carla close, keeping her face buried against his chest and shielding her from the blast. Parts of his house were being blown everywhere: A piece of two by four hit him a glancing blow in the back of the head.

Pain raced over him and through him, but he continued to hold Carla until the hail of debris ended. When he released her, they both scrambled to their feet.

"Are you all right?" he asked, looking her over from head to toe.

"I'm fine," she said, staring wide-eyed over his shoulder. Steven turned and saw his house being consumed by a behemoth of flame.

He stared silently. The flames roared high, consuming everything in their path. The home he had built after returning from Nam was being devoured by the burning fury.

Steven's physical pain faded into oblivion as this newest catastrophe held him in its grasp. He thought of Ellie, and of his friends Lomack and Londrigan, and even of the secret service agent, Paul Grange.

Anger came then. A rage so coldly intense that he was able to turn away from the hell that was consuming his home, and start away. Behind him, Carla followed. He felt her hand on his arm, but shook it off.

He skirted the burning house, and went a hundred feet beyond it, to a wooden storage shed partially hidden by overgrown evergreen bushes. The door was locked with a padlock. He reached above the door, and searched inside the wood joining were he'd hidden the key. He found it and opened the lock.

"Steven, please." Carla called. "We have to get out of here."

"We will," he said, entering the shed.

The inside of the shed was cramped with a tractor lawn mower, and the supplies necessary to take care of his property. At the rear of the shed were shelves. He went to those, and took down a green metal box from the highest shelf.

He brought the old ammunition box outside, set it on the ground, and opened it. He extracted a plastic bag, and unsealed it. A flood of memories hit him. He ignored them and withdrew a canvas bundle. Opening the bundle, he revealed an oil-filmed Colt forty-five automatic. It had been his back-up sidearm from Nam. He hadn't turned it in, because a friend had done him a favor and issued it to him under a different name.

Then he pulled out three clips wrapped in another canvas towel. Still without saying anything, he wiped the gun down and checked the clips. Then he took out a box of full jacket forty-five shells, and loaded one clip. Still squatting on his heels, he slammed the clip home, pivoted, raised the pistol and fired twice.

The loud and crisp explosion combined with the

sharp recoil told him the pistol was in as good a shape as it had been the day he'd put it in the shed and set about forgetting that he owned it.

Using the small terrycloth towel he'd kept on the bottom of the metal box, he wiped the remaining oil from the pistol and loaded the two spare clips. As he worked, he looked back at what had been his home, and began to channel his hatred and rage until he was under full control.

When he was finished with the pistol, he reached back inside the ammo box. There was only one object left in it. Slowly, he withdrew Xzi Tao's bone handled knife.

He looked at the instrument that had been his salvation so many years ago. The handle was cold and smooth. The leather of the scabbard was cracked; the hand-painted ornamentation was brittle and flaking. He put the knife back into the box.

And then he stood.

"Steven," Carla whispered. He turned, and saw her eyes were fear-widened.

"We can go now," he said. Slipping the forty-five into the waistband of his pants, he returned the box to the shed, and locked the door.

In the car, Steven started the engine but did not pull away. He turned to Carla. "Did you call in?"

Her eyes went from shocked disbelief to anger. "When could I have called in? I've been with you all the damn time."

He read the truth in her stormy eyes. "I'm sorry. I had to ask." Shifting in the seat, he handed Carla her Browning and hit the accelerator.

"How did he know where we were?" Carla asked.

Steven stared straight ahead as he drove. He exhaled sharply as one of the remaining elusive threads came to him. It had been there all along. He should gave seen it before, and had almost killed himself and Carla.

"Predictability," he said through tightly clamped teeth. "Everything I've done has been predictable, from my reactions about Ellie, to going to see Xzi Tao, and even to coming here. I told you that I thought he found me because he'd studied me. But I may be wrong. If it was Chuck Latham, he already knows the way I think and, apparently, even knows what I'll do in most situations."

Reaching the main road, Steven floored the accelerator.

"How did you know there was a bomb?" Carla asked.

Steven's laugh was harsh. "It was a neat set-up. I imagine it was plastique, the same stuff he used to kill Lomack and Londrigan. He used the mercury switch in the thermostat as the timer. As soon as I turned the boiler back on, it activated the thermostat. Once the house warmed up, the mercury switch would have leveled off and ignited the bomb. When that happened, we would have been blown apart with the house."

"But it happened right away."

"Only because I reset the switch manually. By doing so, I'd leveled the mercury vial, instead of waiting for the heat to do it."

Carla said nothing for a moment. "Who is it?"

The cut-off for the lake came up quickly. Braking hard, Steven veered onto the lake road. "I don't know. It could be Chuck," he said, accepting the hurt of having to admit the possibility aloud.

After another half hour of swift and silent driving, they reached Lake Pompton. Steven slowed by the wide curve of the lake's tip, and pointed to the spot where Ellie had been found.

The only remaining evidence of the attempted killing was in the thinner coating of snow on the ice near the shore and the marks on the trees. Carla shivered and hugged herself.

Steven continued on into the resort community. It was eerily quiet. The sun had almost reached the peaks of the western mountains. Soon, the area would take on the unsettling false and early dusk that marked the end of a short winter day.

The fifth street in the community was Deer Walk Lane. The houses were set a comfortable distance apart. Latham's property was the fourth house on the lane. It looked as deserted as the rest of the houses.

Steven pulled into the curved drive of the house across the street. He parked behind a neatly planted group of tall evergreens that lined its drive.

He shut the engine off and leaned his head against the headrest. His pulse was speeding, his mouth was dry. He didn't want to go across the street because he already knew what he would find.

"Steven?" Carla asked, her voice low.

"I'm all right."

"I can go alone, if you want."

He smiled, reached across, and took her hand. "I have to see for myself. Do you have your weapon?"

Nodding, she withdrew her hand from his, opened her purse, and took out the nine-millimeter Browning.

The pistol was smaller than his forty-five, but every bit as deadly. "Let's go," he said.

He opened the car door, stood, and stared across the street at Chuck Latham's rental house. His feet felt like lead as he crossed the street and prepared himself to discover if the person trying to kill him was one of his two closest friends.

"I'm scheduled on a morning flight to the coast. I'll stop Pritman from bringing up Entente. But Steven, if you're wrong, it may cost us the election."

Julius Axelrod shut off a cassette player, popped out the cassette, and turned to Amos Coblehill who was sitting in one of the two leather chairs across from him. "I think that takes care of our doubts about Pritman. It clears Savak as well."

"That conversation between Savak and Morrisy took place hours ago. Why did it take so long to get it?" Coblehill asked, a frown of annoyance making his face stark.

"It's an unmonitored tap on Savak's home phone. The tapes are picked up once a day, around noon. The conversation came late in the tape. Amos, we can't let Pritman attend that meeting. The President will have to authorize the move."

"He has no choice. Not with that tape. He'll see that. When it's over and we've sorted it all out, he'll have a private meeting with Pritman, and explain everything."

"What about Morrisy? Have you located him?"

Axelrod shook his head. "I sent a team to his townhouse. He wasn't there."

"Pennsylvania?"

"On their way, by helicopter," Axelrod said. "They should be in Greyton in an hour."

"I still find it hard to believe that Xzi Tao called you and volunteered the information."

"Not so hard after hearing what Grange had to say about Xzi and Morrisy in Nam. But we need the name of the Bureau's informant. That has to be our man."

Coblehill nodded. "The director went into a God-damn fury when we met. And it wasn't a put-on. Julius, he didn't have any idea of what was happening on that investigation."

"Christ," Coblehill exploded. "He's the director of the Bureau, not someone taking orders under a need-to-know screen. And that means that only Blayne knows who the informant is."

Coblehill looked at his watch. "The director should have called by now." With a shake of his head, he picked up the phone from the table set between the two chairs, and dialed the Bureau's director. He spoke his name, and then fell silent, staring directly at Axelrod. Forty seconds later, he hung up.

"Blayne is three hours overdue to report in. They don't know where he is. Blayne's supervisor told the director that the information on the mole came from the CIA."

"The CIA?" Axelrod said, his eyes hardening.

"That's what he said. There's more," Coblehill added when Axelrod shook his head. "The director called them. Langley is denying any knowledge of the investigation or the cooperation between the Company and Blayne."

Standing slowly, Axelrod walked over to the corner window and looked at the stately buildings across Pennsylvania Avenue. "Amos, we can't afford to wait any longer. We must call Langley and find out what the hell they're up to now."

"Of course," Coblehill said, his voice telling Axelrod of his reluctance to pull rank on his counterpart at the CIA. He picked up the phone again, and dialed the number. Seconds later, he was speaking to the man with the answers.

Axelrod continued to stare out the window until the head of the NSA hung up the phone. When he turned back, he saw Coblehill's face had gone dark with anger.

"God help us," Coblehill said. "We must make sure those papers are confiscated from Pritman, no matter what the price is that we might end up paying."

"You know, then?"

Coblehill stood and walked to Axelrod's desk. He fingered the loosely piled papers on the center of the desk until he found the list of suspects. He pointed to a name a third of the way down the list.

Axelrod walked back to his desk and looked at the name Coblehill's thick finger hovered above. He shook his head in disbelief, and then said, "Let's notify our teams. They'll have to move fast."

Chapter Thirty

Steven looked around cautiously. The resort community was deathly quiet. The only sound came from the wind blowing through the trees. Not even a winter bird seemed to be present.

Glancing over his shoulder, he saw that the leading edge of the sun was almost touching the mountain tops. He estimated that there was no more than a half hour of daylight left.

It would be enough.

He motioned to Carla and started across the street. The snow crunched beneath their shoes. On Latham's narrow drive, the snow was deeper than the street, and muffled their steps.

Steven paused to take in the house. It was a two-story, nondescript vinyl sided house. It was a mirror image of all the other homes in the area.

Chuck Latham's house was set in the center of a quarter acre lot. It had an idyllic, peaceful appearance and seemed well suited as the perfect place to spend summer week-ends, go fishing, and barbecue. He prayed it would continue to look the same from the inside.

At the stoop to the front door, Steven turned to Carla and signalled her to keep watch while he made a quick circle around the house. He found nothing that showed the house had been recently occupied. The new snow had obliterated any footprints that might have been left behind by Ellie and her torturer.

Returning to the front, he shook his head to Carla, and motioned her forward. He tried the front door. It was locked. "We'll have to try a window," he said.

"No. There's only one lock." Opening her purse, she withdrew a small leather case and slid out two thin metal wire tools. Thirty seconds later, the lock clicked and Carla pushed the door open.

Steven entered first, his Colt outstretched before him. Carla followed, holding her weapon in a two-handed extension.

It was dark in the house. Pitch dark. Steven pressed himself to the wall and searched for a light switch. He found a switch on the wall and turned it. An overhead fixture flared into life.

That answered one of his questions: The electricity had not been shut off for the winter, or it had been turned on recently.

After adjusting to the light, Steven understood why it had been so dark inside. The windows had been covered with heavy canvas drop cloths and sealed with silver duct tape. The job had been expertly done. Steven was sure that no light could be seen from the outside.

He felt a burning begin in the pit of his stomach. The black-out coverings told him that his nightmare had come true. "Goddamn you," he whispered.

Without saying anything else, Steven and Carla went through the first floor. There was nothing in the living room, but the family room yielded an ashtray overflowing with unfiltered cigarette butts.

In the kitchen, they found a plastic bag filled with garbage. The sink was clean, as was the stove.

Carla bent over the garbage bag, and peered through the clear plastic. "They used paper plates and plastic utensils."

Steven noted Carla's use of the word they, not he. It made sense. If Chuck Latham was involved, he would have had to have help in watching Ellie while he kept on with what passed for his real life.

"Upstairs," Steven said.

They checked the master bedroom first. It was empty, and showed no signs of having been occupied lately. The large bed was unmade. Just a mattress sitting on a box spring and frame.

The second bedroom was empty as well, but it wasn't as clean as the first. Another ash tray, filled to overflowing, was on the small night stand next to the bed. A burned down butt was next to it, a half inch scar leading to the filter tip marred the wood of the table.

Because of the cigarettes, Steven had to reevaluate his original thought. There had been at least two people here, beside Chuck. The hope grew that maybe his friend wasn't involved: Chuck didn't smoke.

Steven backed out of the room, and started toward the last bedroom. Carla came out of the hallway bathroom. "Shaving residue and cigarette butts were all I found," she said. "There were two types of cigarettes, filter and plain."

"I know," Steven said as he put his hand on the brass door knob of the third bedroom. The burning in his stomach grew worse. He ignored it, and the sudden dryness in his mouth. If there was anything, it would be in there, he thought, staring at the closed door.

He turned the knob and pushed the door open, knowing that as things stood, it made no difference whether or not he left his fingerprints on the metal. The room was pitch black. He reached in, felt along the wall for the light switch and, when his fingers touched it, turned it on. Carla's sharply drawn breath echoed loudly in his ears.

Across the room was a vision out of his past. He closed his eyes and clamped his teeth shut. A wave of nausea swept through him. His stomach cramped. Swallowing hard, he opened his eyes again.

Leaning against the far wall was a sight that had haunted him for far too many years: Two wooden beams, constructed in the shape of an X. But he had been wrong about one thing, it wasn't exactly out of his past. This present day horror had been made from two-by-fours instead of bamboo.

He stared at the crossed beams for a second longer before he walked slowly toward it. Memories of the prison camp in Nam danced madly in his head. Pictures of Raden and Cole and Savak tied to the wood, their blood seeping to the ground, rose vividly in his mind's eye. And then, as he passed a high dresser, he caught the reflection of metal out of the corner of his eye.

Stopping, he stared at the dresser. In the center of the high piece of furniture, resting on the flat glass top, was a highly polished pearl-handled straight razor. It was open, the blade of the razor extended. Spots of dried blood, like rust, coated the sharp edge of the razor.

He reached for the razor, but stopped himself and continued on to the cross. The nightmare trip through the room seemed to take an eternity before he was finally standing in front of the wooden cross.

He examined the wood carefully, and saw notches cut into it from where Ellie's wrists had been tied. He looked down and saw blotches of dried blood on the floor.

It was Ellie's blood. He knew that as surely as he knew his own flame. This was where she'd been kept for the week. This was where she'd been tortured for the week. This was where they'd tried to open her mind, and steal what was in it.

They had failed, and had run out of time, so they'd decided to kill her. But they had failed in that as well; because of their need to frame Steven, they had inadvertently done what they'd set out to do in the first place, steal her mind.

He took a deep and rattling breath, and back stepped from the cross. He stopped when he was at the foot of the bed. He looked at the stripped bed, and saw bloodstains in its center. Then he saw something small and gold on the floor near the foot of the bed.

He knelt and looked at a small gold stud earring. It was Ellie's. When he leaned forward to pick it up, he saw a dark shape under the bed.

The sickening sensation of learning the truth worsened when Steven pulled Ellie's black shoulder bag from under the bed. He stared at it, his mind darkening.

Inside was Ellie's wallet, along with a small packet of tissues, her house keys, a compact, and a tube of lipstick.

Feeling eyes on his back, he stood and turned. Carla was standing above him. Her gaze went from the black purse to him. "Ellie's?"

"Yes," he said, dropping the purse on the floor. "Let's go."

Minutes later they were in the car and heading out of Pompton Estates. Steven stared straight ahead. His pulse seemed to have stopped. His only emotion was a rage so deep that it had replaced every other force in his life. With his awesome rage came the clarity of hindsight. He no longer had any doubts as to who the mole was. He knew.

"The bastard had us all fooled," he whispered, more to himself than to Carla.

"Who, Steven? Who is it?"

"Chuck Latham."

Carla shook her head. "No, you haven't thought it through. It doesn't make any sense. Latham isn't in Washington, and he's not on Pritman's staff."

Steven braked the car suddenly, and pulled onto the shoulder of the road. He turned to her, his eyes raking her face. "He doesn't have to be. Chuck is my doctor. He's Arnie's as well. We see him all the time. Once a year we spend three days in the hospital for a very special physical that he does for us. When we were in Nam, all of us, at one time or another, were in defoliant sprayed areas. It's become a matter of habit to have carcinomac testing done. Any time during those three days, he could get the information from us by injecting us while we're sleeping."

"But you wouldn't give him that. You don't crack under drugs."

"It's not that simple," he said. "I don't talk when I'm aware of my enemy—when I'm being interrogated. Chuck Latham is my friend; I trust him. Under drugs, I'd have no compulsion to hide anything from him. It all makes sense when you put it in the proper perspective.

"You see," Steven continued, his anger abetting enough to allow him to speak calmly, "Chuck is in Washington at least once a month. He goes to seminars for his specialty. He usually stays either with me, or with Savak, which would give him plenty of opportunities to gain information. Jesus, he spent the night with me last week. He said he came to Washington because he was worried about Ellie, and about me."

Steven shook his head. "I'll have to call Banacek and find out if he told Latham that I'd asked for the land listings. Maybe that will explain Chuck's long weekend."

"If the sheriff did tell him, that would explain how he knew you were here, and why he blew up your house."

"Exactly," Steven agreed as he pulled out onto the road again. And then he found the thing he had been looking for, the seemingly pointless little clue to the mole's identity.

"Where are we going now?" Carla asked.

Steven felt his lips stretching in a death mask of a grin. "To Latham's house. Damn," he said, striking the wheel with an open palm. "I was so stupid not to have seen it before."

"Seen what?"

"The first crack in Latham's story. The one thing of significance I should have realized from the minute I'd talked to Chuck last Monday morning."

He paused and stared at the road. "When he called me, to tell me that Ellie was in the hospital in Greyton, he said he'd tried to call me in Washington. Why?"

Steven glanced at Carla and saw her shrug. "Because he thought you were there."

"Exactly. But if he hadn't had anything to do with what happened to Ellie, and he had just seen her in the emergency room, as he'd said, why wouldn't he have called me at the house in Greyton before trying me in Washington? Carla, Ellie would never be in Greyton without me. She'd have no reason, and Chuck knows that."

"Then how?" she asked.

He paused for a second before the answer came. "He must have called during the week. Then he'd have known that I was away, and that I'd left instructions that anyone calling me be told I was out of town on business. Chuck must have figured it for a lucky break.

"And when I got to the hospital that morning, Chuck asked me if Ellie and I had been fighting that night. If he'd really thought that, why did he call me in Washington, and then Arnie? No, the phone call was Chuck's first real mistake. He compounded the error with his questions at the hospital. But I made some mistakes too."

Steven paused for a breath. He exhaled sadly. "In the hospital, that morning, he must have realized the mistake. Before I could ask him why he'd called me in Washington, instead of trying me here in Greyton, he'd told me that when he recognized Ellie, he had panicked and called Washington. And I believed him."

This time Carla had no choice but to agree. "Which is why we couldn't figure out who the mole was. We were so sure he was in Washington, on someone's staff."

"He didn't have to be. He got all the information he needed without any risk."

"But why?" Carla asked. "And what was he using the information for?"

"That's what we're going to find out," Steven said as he speeded up.

"They weren't in the house," said the voice booming out from the speaker phone.

Julius Axelrod glanced at Amos Coblehill before saying, "And where are they?"

"We don't know, sir. I'm with Sheriff Banacek now. The only things he's certain about, is that at between one-thirty and two p.m., Morrisy and agent Statler met with the county clerk and picked up a land listing for Lake Pompton Estates. Then, around three p.m., Steven Morrisy's house exploded. We're getting a duplicate land listing made up now."

"Find them," Axelrod said, his voice low. "We're running out of time."

"Yes, sir," the Secret Service field supervisor said before disconnecting.

"Do you think they will?" Amos Coblehill wondered aloud.

"They'd better. And they'd better get everyone else who is involved as well. Between the confiscation of his papers, and his forced and escorted exit from his hotel, Senator Pritman is kicking up quite a fuss. If this doesn't go down the right way, the mole will have succeeded in accomplishing at least one of his objectives—the toppling of the current administration."

Amos Coblehill almost smiled, but the situation didn't warrant even that little amount of humor. "Well, there's one thing that we'll most certainly gain from this."

"Oh?" Axelrod asked, his eyebrows rising as he puffed on his meerschaum.

"We'll definitely learn what kind of a man Pritman is, and how well he can handle crisis situations. A hell of a warm-up test for the Presidency, isn't it?"

"When he is due to arrive?"

"In the hour," Coblehill said. "And then we're all scheduled to meet with the President at six."

"Hopefully, this will be resolved by then."

"It has to be," the man in charge of the National Security Agency said.

Steven finished his phone call and returned to the car. After sliding behind the steering wheel and driving off, he said, "Latham hasn't reported in at the hospital, and there's no answer at his house. We may be too late. He might have gone already."

"Where?" Carla asked. "If you're right, and he's doing this because of a deep rooted psychopathic disturbance, he has no place to run. He can't go to the Soviets, and he certainly can't go to the Chinese."

"There are hundreds of places for him to go," Steven stated. "Carla, there's an entire network of vets who will watch out for him, take care of him, and hide him because of who he was in Nam.

"The people in this . . . underground, I guess you would call it, are the men and the women who still have not been absorbed back into the mainstream of society. They're the outcasts and the misfits who don't trust the people they fought for."

Carla turned from him and looked out the windshield. "It's been so many years since the end of the war. Dear God, Steven, how can they still feel that way?"

Steven laughed bitterly. "Because our fellow countrymen made them feel that way when we came home."

"It's so unfair," Carla said as she looked at him.

"Tell me about it," he said before turning onto Chuck Latham's block. He pulled the car to a stop in front of Latham's red brick colonial and shut the ignition off. The sun had set completely. The darkness of the winter night had settled firmly over Greyton.

"It looks deserted," he commented, seeing nothing in the driveway. The front door was closed. The house was dark.

They left the car without a word. Steven led the way to the front door, where he drew the forty-five and cocked it. Carla pulled out her Beretta.

Steven tried the doorknob. The door was unlocked. He pushed it gently. It swung free, stopping only when it hit the wall behind it. A heavy spurt of adrenaline kicked into his bloodstream. His senses turned acute. He stepped inside, his pistol at the ready. Carla was behind him. He could hear her shallow breathing.

He stood still, extending his senses, listening. There was nothing. The house was quiet, eerily quiet. He sniffed the air. It was stale. There was a slight off scent of old garbage.

Using what little light was cast through the windows from the street lamp, Steven began to search the first floor.

The entire first level was deserted. Everything was in its proper place. There were no signs of disorder.

When he finished, he leaned close to Carla's ear and whispered, "Upstairs."

When she nodded, he started up the center staircase. He was conscious of everything: The sound of Carla's breathing mixing with his own; and even the low noise their feet made on the uncarpeted steps.

Steven paused on the upper landing. It was darker in the hallway, but he was still able to differentiate things in the shadows.

He knew the layout of the house intimately. He had been there enough times. The master bedroom suite was to the right. It was made up of three rooms: The bedroom, a large bathroom, and a sitting room between the other two rooms.

To the left were three more bedrooms. One had been turned into Chuck's home office. A second bedroom was Helene Latham's sewing room, and the third was a guest bedroom.

When Chuck and Helene had bought the house, it had been with the expectation of having children. But they'd never had any.

Steven blinked, set aside his thoughts and moved. He headed toward Chuck's office. He pushed the door open, turned on the lights, and went inside.

He was too late. The drawers of Latham's desk were all open and empty. A tall file cabinet was empty as well. Steven backed out into the hallway and started toward the master bedroom. He was sure he'd find the same thing as in the office.

Carla followed, close on his heels. He paused at the partially opened door, and then stepped inside. He turned on the lights, and froze.

He heard Carla's startled gasp. Spinning to her, he clamped his hand over her mouth.

Carla's eyes were wide as she stared over his

shoulder. He watched her, waiting for her initial terror to lessen. When her eyes returned to normal he lowered his hand.

She was swallowing forcefully. Her skin was paper white. She looked as if she were going to be sick.

"Easy," he whispered.

She swallowed again and shook her head. "What in God's name is going on?"

Steven turned slowly, prepared by his first quick view, and started toward Helene Latham's naked body.

She lay in the center of the large brass bed. She was spread-eagled, her wrists and ankles tied to the corners of the curved headboard and footboard. Her dead and sightless eyes stared up at the ceiling. Her breasts and abdomen, all the way down to the joining of her torso and thighs, were covered with dried blood.

Her skin was lacerated with a hundred different cuts. Her mouth was partially open. It was as if she died in the middle of a scream.

Steven's stomach reacted violently. He turned, breaking away from the mutilated form, and took several calming breaths.

"How could he do this," Steven asked aloud, even as he realized that it didn't matter how Chuck could have killed his wife, only that he had. His friend was much sicker than he had at first believed. To kill his own wife like this told Steven that Chuck Latham had passed beyond any hope of sanity.

Steven became numb, physically and mentally. His emotions had been wiped away, pushed down to where they could no longer come into play. All that remained was logic, and the coldly analytical hatred that his logic brought forth.

He stepped close to Helene's body and closed her open and pleading eyes. Then he took the comforter that was crumpled on the floor and drew it slowly over her. "No more," he promised Helene. "No one else will be hurt by him."

Before covering her face, he bent and kissed Helene's forehead. "Chuck is sick, but he is still smart," Steven said, rejoining Carla. "I'll be blamed for this," he said, waving his arm toward Helene Latham. "Her abdomen was cut the same way as Ellie's."

"Steven," Carla began, but stopped at the sound of car doors closing.

They both spun at the same time and ran to the window. "Oh Jesus, not now," Steven whispered as Inspector Blayne and Special Agent Grodin walked toward the house.

Chapter Thirty-one

"How did they find us?" Carla asked, staring with disbelief at the two FBI agents who were heading for the front door.

"The same way Latham found us in Washington, and here. He knows the way I think."

Carla looked from the oncoming agents to Steven. "If he's the one who's been feeding Blayne his information, then—"

Steven cut her off with a sad shake of his head. "Then there's no way they'll let me talk myself out of this." Steven watched the two agents, thinking of the two times they had met before. He had no doubt that to face them meant to fight them. But he wouldn't take the chance of shooting one of them, and he sensed that shooting was the only way he would be able to stop them from arresting him.

"We do have a way," Carla said, withdrawing a thin leather case from her purse. "You forgot this." She opened the ID case and showed him her Secret Service identification card, complete with photograph. "Put your pistol away."

Exhaling in relief, Steven put on the safety and slid the weapon into his waistband. He looked over his shoulder, at the covered mound on the bed, and said, "Let's go."

Just as they reached the doorway, the sounds of gunshots rang out. Whirling, he raced to the window. He saw Blayne, face down on the snow-covered lawn. Grodin was next to him, turning and raising his weapon to the second floor. Another shot rang out. Grodin stiffened, and then crumpled backward. Blood spurted from his chest.

"He's up here!" Carla cried.

Steven pulled the Colt, Carla her nine-millimeter. They went to the hallway, and flattened themselves against opposite walls. Looking ahead, Steven saw that two of the three bedroom doors were open. The third, halfway down the wall he was on, was closed.

Holding the forty-five at shoulder level, he signalled Carla toward the door. When they reached the closed door, they pressed themselves against the walls on each side of door frame. Then Steven, his breathing coming in short gasps, stepped in front of the door and kicked it open.

Carla went in low, diving head first, her pistol held in front of her. Steven followed, jumping over her and then going to his knees in the center of the room. He spun in a circle, his arms fully extended.

The room was empty.

The window on the left was open. Cold air blustered through.

With the blood pounding through his temples, Steven went to the window. He saw a wide gouge in the snow of the roof, leading toward the ledge. Latham had slid down the roof after shooting the agents, and jumped to the ground. He saw Blayne and Grodin still on the ground. A deep scarlet pool was spreading around Grodin.

An engine started. Then the garage door shattered into a thousand pieces as a black four-by-four vehicle burst out of the garage and into the street. The four-by-four stopped and, in a sudden burst of acceleration, slammed backward into the FBI car, destroying the front end before taking off down the street.

Steven fired by instinct, emptying the nine-round clip before the black Jeep was out of sight.

"Goddamn him!" he shouted, slapping the window sill with his open palm.

He turned to Carla, but she was already on her way out of the room. He raced after her, hitting the front door a half second behind her. They reached the fallen agents at the same time.

Blayne was trying to sit up. He motioned to Carla to help Blayne while he went to Grodin. The man's features were twisted in a look of shock. A glistening pool of blood, from the fallen agent's chest, had spread out on the crusted snow. Steven knelt beside him. Before he touched Grodin's neck, he knew that the agent was dead. The lack of a pulse only confirmed it.

He stood slowly. Carla had helped Blayne to sit. Blood washed down the side of his face. A bullet had furrowed a nasty looking channel across Blayne's forehead. A second round had gone into his left shoulder. Blood was seeping out, onto his coat.

Blayne was staring at Carla, his eyes were without comprehension. Then Blayne turned and saw Steven.

The agent's face twisted with hatred. He pulled away from Carla and looked around frantically. He spotted his service piece five feet away. He half threw himself, half fell toward the weapon.

Carla reached it first and kicked it away. "Damn you," he snarled, levering himself up by his arm to stare at Steven. "I'm going to kill you Morrisy, you son of a bitch!"

Steven crossed the distance between them. He bent low and, when his face was inch from Blayne's, spoke in a level voice. "I'm not your enemy. It's time you accepted that."

Blayne snarled like a trapped animal.

Steven backed away. "Call Banacek," he told Carla. "Then report in. Tell them what happened, and tell them who the mole is."

"Where are you going?"

"After him," Steven said as he ran to their rental car.

"Wait!" Carla shouted, ignoring the wounded inspector and racing after him.

He stopped suddenly. "Help him!"

She gazed at him, her face lined with uncertainty. "Steven, I can't let you go alone."

"You don't have any choice. You have to get help for Blayne. Now!" he ordered before turning his back on her and walking the rest of the distance to the car.

As he walked, his eyes focused on the street where Latham had driven. He ejected the spent magazine and slammed a fresh one into the butt of the Colt.

But it was only when he was on the road with the Colt resting on the seat next to him that his breathing began to slow. It was almost over if he was right.

He turned the wheel hard when he reached the two lane blacktop highway, and floored the accelerator. The speedometer reached ninety, and hovered there. He couldn't get any more speed out of the four-cylinder rental.

The road was pitch black, the only light came from the beams of his headlights. When he reached a long and level stretch in the highway, he saw a set of tail lights in the distance. Once again he tried to coax more speed out of the car, but there was nothing left except his own frustration.

The tail lights disappeared over the crest of a hill. A minute and ten seconds later, Steven made the crest of the hill. On the downstroke, the car gained another ten miles an hour, but it didn't matter. The tail lights were gone.

Where? This section of the two lane highway crossed three minor hills, but was dead straight for five miles. Could he have made the next crest? No, not yet, Steven told himself.

A hundred yards later, his lights struck the remnants of an old billboard. Something clicked in his mind, and he knew exactly what had happened to the tail lights.

He hit the brakes hard. The car started to fishtail. He fought the wheel, getting the car under control as he slowed. When he was down to fifty, he took his foot off the brakes.

The billboard had triggered a memory, one he hadn't thought about in years. With the unexpected memory came the knowledge of where Chuck was going.

There was only one place between here and the interstate where Chuck could hide. It was a special place, a hideout for a half dozen pre-adolescent boys—at least that's what it had started out to be. But by the time they were fourteen, it had become their private place, their escape from parental authority, from school, and from the world in general.

They had used it to camp out in. They had used it to run away to. And when they had traded in their bicycles for cars, they had used it to pass more than one of the rites of manhood. It was *their* special place—his and Latham's and Savak's.

They had been ten years old, and out on a camping trip, when they'd discovered the old and forgotten hunting cabin. It was deep in the woods, on the side of Big Hand Mountain, which was part of the state's park system. To Steven's knowledge, then and now, they were the only ones ever to use it.

As they were growing up, they'd periodically worked on the cabin, repairing the roof with tar paper and the sides with lumber. They'd added discarded furniture, scavenged from the sidewalks of Greyton, and had even painted the interior once every few years.

With the disappearance of the tail lights from the open road, Steven's only alternative was to believe that Chuck was going there. It was the insane doctor's most feasible option. And just as he accepted the basis of his thought, he also knew that Latham would expect Steven to follow him.

He slowed the car down a half mile later, and turned onto a single lane gravel road that was partially hidden by the evergreens lining the road. He speeded up again, holding the car at fifty, until the twists and cutbacks became too much. He slowed to thirty, his anger and impatience building at the delay.

The four-wheel-drive vehicle would get Latham to the cabin ahead of Steven, but there was nothing he could do about it.

He drove for four more miles, until the gravel road was intersected by a path just wide enough to allow a car's passage. He stopped at the mouth of the dirt path, and used his headlights to give him a glimpse of what lay ahead. The first thing he saw were the fresh tire tracks in the crusted snow. He had been right. Latham had come this way.

He started onto the dirt road, realizing that with the passing of the years, the road had narrowed almost to the point of impassability. The leafless branches of the trees scratched the sides of the car with a sound like chalk being dragged against a blackboard. Uncaring, he continued on, using the tracks Latham had cut into the snow to give his lighter car more traction.

Seven minutes later, the headlights illuminated a three foot high white stake set off the side of the road. He hit the brakes and slowed to a stop.

Now he had a choice to make. The cabin was a quarter of a mile farther along the road. He could drive, or he could walk.

Latham was expecting him. Did the quiet really matter?

He leaned his head against the steering wheel. Latham had been a ranger scout in Nam, possibly the best ranger in the damned army.

Yes, it mattered.

Steven shut the engine off and sat quietly. His mind whirled with the day's events. Helene Latham's dead eyes stared at him. How could he have been so wrong about Chuck? He had never once thought of his friend as a psychotic—as a killer. Had Vietnam done so much more to him, than to Steven or Savak?

Speculation was pointless now, he told himself. When he was face to face with Chuck, he would have his answers. He took a deep preparatory breath, and got out of the car.

He took off his jacket and tossed it on the front seat. Then he pulled his shirt out of his pants and ripped off two strips. Bending, he secured his pant legs to his calves with the strips. When he stood again, he tucked in the ragged shirt tail, and took the Colt from the front seat.

He held the pistol in his right hand. He checked it, cocked it, and thumbed off the safety.

He waited another half minute, until his eyes were completely adjusted to the quarter moon's light. Momentarily, he flashed back to Nam, and his last mission. Once again, lies and false objectives had propelled him into combat. But at the core of this solitary mission would be justice.

He started into the woods. His only advantages were that he knew this piece of land, and he knew what his mission was, not what anyone else intended it to be.

"Enough," he told himself as he went deeper into the leafless world of the winter forest.

He went stealthily on, as he'd been trained to do a half world away and almost two decades before. He made no loud noises, avoided scraping against trees, and carefully skirted fallen branches. Loud noise carried for miles in the dead silence of a winter forest.

As he threaded his quiet and careful path to the cabin, Steven continually checked for footprints or anything else that might warn him of danger. Knowing what Latham had been in the war, and what he had become today, Steven was all too aware that the man he had called his friend might have set booby traps that would, if not kill him, warn Latham that Steven was closing in.

But despite his concern over possible traps, he found nothing in the eighteen minutes it took him to make the quarter mile. At last, when he stood behind the bole of a huge oak that he had climbed as a boy, he stared at the weak light coming from the crack between the bottom of the old warped door and the floor.

A hulking black Jeep was on the side of the cabin closest to him. Footprints led from the jeep to the front door.

Chuck was there.

But was he waiting for Steven inside, or was he

hiding somewhere within shooting distance, waiting for Steven to step into his line of fire?

Steven looked around, searching the trees at ground level, looking for any form of disturbance on the snow's surface. He scanned the branches above and saw nothing. But if Chuck was hiding in the trees, he would be impossible to spot.

He watched his white and misting breath float before him with each exhalation. He was getting cold now. The wounds on his back were hurting again, and he knew he had to move before the cold stiffened him too much.

Going into a low crouch and, using the trees and bushes for cover, Steven ran toward the cabin. He stopped at a tree ten feet from the cabin, and peered from behind it. The cabin was quiet. Nothing had changed during his slow run forward.

He pulled back, leaning his head against the tree. The sounds around him were normal and distant. He looked at the cabin again. The door was still closed. The windows were boarded up. He didn't remember if there were any openings large enough for a rifle or pistol barrel.

It didn't matter, he thought, moving forward in a crouched slow run. With every step, he expected to hear the sound of gunfire, and the feel the lethal bite of a bullet.

He made it to the cabin without a shot being fired.

Why? It didn't make sense. Did Chuck have something else planned for him?

His heart was racing, partially from fear, and

partially from the constant pumping of his adrenaline-saturated blood. He took a deep breath and stepped to the door. "Chuck!" he shouted. "Goddamn you, come out!"

He waited four seconds before repeating his order. When nothing happened, Steven knew the reason for it. Chuck wanted him inside.

The old fear and jitters from the war hit him as it always had just before he went into combat. In Nam, he never knew if he would return; but here, the reason was different—it was more than just his life that was on the line. Steven had to win, he had to survive so that others would live as well.

He made himself see Ellie again, the scars on her stomach and the emptiness of her eyes. He pictured Helene Latham's helplessness as her husband tortured her, and he listened to what he knew must have been Lomack and Londrigan's screams when their plane crashed.

Steven lunged at the door. He hit it on the run, using his left shoulder and ignoring the pain that erupted on his back. The old catch mechanism held, but the hinges didn't. The door crashed open loudly.

Steven kept his balance and spun inside. He aimed the Colt ahead of him, swinging it in short arcs around the room.

Just when he thought the room was empty, he caught a vision to his left. He turned hard, staring in shock.

Hanging from a rafter, his naked body suspended by a rope tied around his wrists, was

Chuck Latham.

He was dead.

Steven stared at his friend's disfigured abdomen. Drying blood had formed a second brownish red skin from his stomach to his feet. The floor beneath the hanging body was puddled with blood. A bucket of water was on the floor near Latham's left foot. Steven was certain it was salt water.

"Don't move, Steven."

Steven held himself still. The recognition of the voice sent his anger spiraling almost out of control.

Steven's shoulder's sagged. He didn't turn to face his killer. Instead, he lifted his head and looked at the suspended body of Chuck Latham. "Why?"

"Because you were changing. You were doubting. And then that stupid bitch you fell in love with was in the office when she shouldn't have been."

Steven's hands trembled with rage as he slipped the automatic into his belt. Slowly, with a taut casualness, he turned to face his killer.

"How could you have killed them? How could you have given Entente to the Soviets, and to the Chinese? It doesn't make any sense. Tell me why, Arnie."

Chapter Thirty-two

Every vision of the life he had led, and the life he had hoped to lead, crumpled when Savak spoke. All of Steven's beliefs were destroyed by the knowledge that his closest friend was a murderer, and worse.

"Why?" Steven repeated. The single word, coming husky and tight from his throat, hung heavily in the air between them.

Arnold Savak shrugged. "What difference does it make. You're a dead man now."

"It makes a difference to me. Arnie, if nothing else, you owe me an answer."

Cocking his head to the side, Savak gazed at Steven reflectively. His look was that of someone patiently deciding on whether or not to humor one who might not understand him. Slowly, he raised his left hand and double stroked the side of his nose with a bent finger. His eyes flicked to the pistol in his hand. The corner of his mouth curled into a sneer. "I don't owe you a fucking thing."

Seeing the insanity glowing in Savak's eyes,

Steven used the horror of what had happened to his friend to help him keep his anger in check. "You owe me a lot, Arnie. Without me, there would be no Entente," he said, his voice steady as he faced Savak without showing fear.

"Oh, no, Steven, you're wrong. With you or without you, there would be Entente. I'll grant that because of you, it came about a lot sooner. I needed you, Steven. I needed that clean-cut analytical mind of yours to push though all the debris and find the fastest and smoothest road to bringing Entente to life. No one else could have done it as quickly or as perfectly as you."

Steven continued to control his anger, smothering it with the knowledge that if he reacted strongly to Savak's barbs, he would force Savak's hand too soon. If that happened, and he died, Savak would walk away free. "Why did they have to die, Arnie? Why do I have to die?"

Savak's eyes narrowed into slits of hatred. "Because you were becoming a person I could no longer trust. And then Ellie overheard me."

Steven didn't flinch at the mention of Ellie's name. No matter what, he told himself, he had to appear strong before Savak. Reason and logic were the only weapons he could draw on. He had to use them precisely if he were to survive.

"When you realized that she had uncovered your scheme, you came up with the plan to kill her and plant her body in the lake. Did you really think that when spring came, I would be labeled as her killer?"

"Definitely," Savak said with a death's head grin. "And it also happened to be a convenient way to accomplish what I needed. I'd known for a while that I would have to take you out, and I'd already designed a plan to get rid of you, but this was too perfect an opportunity to waste," Savak said, waving the pistol with jerky up and down movements as he spoke.

Steven kept his eyes fastened on Savak's face, not on the pistol. "But I still don't understand what I did to turn you against me," Steven said quickly, fighting hard now to keep Savak's attention on his plans.

Savak shook his head. "I told you. You were starting to doubt. I knew that when the time came to use Entente properly, you wouldn't have the courage. You'd try to stop it. But I wasn't really worried, because once everything was in motion, there would be no way for you to prevent it from reaching the point which I intended."

Steven listened intently to his every word, measuring the tone, the inflection, and the unnaturally precise cadence of Savak's voice. All of it told him just how deeply unbalanced Savak had become. "I understand about Lomack and Londrigan. They would have been able to clear me. Why Chuck and Helene? They had nothing to do with Entente."

Savak's eyes momentarily flicked to Latham's hanging body. "You were better than I expected. Every time I thought I had worked out the perfect ploy, the ideal trap, you slipped by me. I just couldn't take the chance that you would get someone to believe you. By killing Chuck and Helene, I was able to add another solid piece of evidence. The FBI is convinced you're the mole who's leaking secrets to the Soviets, and that you're a killer as well."

Steven shook his head. "Not any more—not after what happened at Chuck's house."

Savak's smile was victorious. Triumph glistened in his eyes. "No one saw me. Blayne and his partner are dead. Dead men, even FBI agents, can't talk."

Steven didn't correct Savak about Blayne's death; rather, he concentrated on the job at hand—to keep Savak talking, and his mind off the pistol in his right hand. "Blayne doesn't matter. The Bureau will know who Blayne's informant is. He had to have been keeping some sort of records."

Savak's pupils dilated. His grin became obscene. "Actually, Steven, Blayne doesn't know who I am—he never has. His informant is a CIA operative."

"What?" Steven said, Savak's answer rocking him so much that the word slipped from his mouth before he could stop it. Now he understood why the CIA agent had been following him.

Then his mind sped up. "Jesus, Arnie, how in the hell could you have told the CIA about Entente?"

"You amaze me Steven. After everything we've been through. After . . . How can you still think in terms of black and white? A simple action requires a simple reaction? No, damn it all, the world doesn't work that way. When you want something, you take it, or you make things happen so you get what you want. There is no perfectly defined good or bad, no right way or wrong way. There is a middle ground, and it's a very big area. That's how I was able to use the CIA.

"But the CIA knows nothing about Entente except the usual rumors," Savak said before he paused to take a deep breath. "Remember Nam?"

Steven didn't bother to answer, he just stared hard into Savak's eyes and waited. Savak smiled. "Before we met up for that shit of a mission, I'd been assigned as a CIA liaison. I worked with the Company in Nam . . . for the Company. After we came home from the war, I stayed in contact with the people I'd known over there."

Steven searched Savak's face, looking for the friend he'd known almost all his life. What had happened to the boy whom he'd grown up with, and to the man he'd loved like a brother. In that man's place was a stranger whose life was dedicated to the death and destruction of everything he had once cherished.

"You had everything worked out from the very beginning, didn't you? Even before you enlisted me, you'd already made contact with the Soviets. Of course they never knew who you were. Clandestine meetings over the phone. How did you get it going? With a letter?"

Savak nodded thoughtfully. "You're close. When I finished school, and went to work for Pritman, I kept in contact with my friends at the Company. Every once in a while, I would feed them a tidbit that would help them with budget allocations, and the like. But everything I gave them, I got back with interest. I learned who the important operatives were for the Soviets, and for the Chinese. I spent years developing a deep cover for myself. A cover that could not be broken."

"Which is how you were able to borrow Anton from the Soviets."

"Good, Steven, you're catching on," Savak said with a sharp nod. "But Anton never met me. He took orders over the phone."

"But there were at least two people in the lake house with Ellie," Steven stated.

"Anton and his partner. But when they were there, I wasn't. I was alone with Ellie—that was my rule. They were there to watch her while I was in Washington. I didn't spend a lot of time with her—just enough to learn what I needed to know."

"How did you get the Soviets to go along with you? How could they not suspect you as a double, if you wouldn't meet them face to face?"

Again came the crazed smile. "Because I always gave them good information. I never once fed them anything false. And some of it was very important. After a while they accepted and believed. When staffs were changed, it became a habit, or even perhaps a tradition never to ask me to come in. I was a valuable source, one they could not risk losing."

The madness grew in Savak's eyes. Steven saw his hand tremble slightly, and strove to keep Savak's mind occupied. "Did you work the Chinese the same way?"

Savak gave one jerky bob of his head. "To a degree."

"To what purpose? Was this some weird game you were playing to see how much chaos you could cause?"

"Chaos? You can't even imagine the upheaval that will come. No, what I am doing is because I want them to be destroyed. Nixon opened diplomatic channels with China. The bastard wanted them to be our friends! Well they aren't our friends! They never have been and they never will, no more than the fucking Soviets are our friends!"

Steven looked at Chuck Latham's body, hanging five feet behind him. A shiver raced along his back. He shifted on his feet. Savak tensed at Steven's movement. His right hand jutted forward, the pistol rising toward Steven's face.

"Arnie," Steven pleaded. "Think about what you've told me. Think about what your actions mean."

"Think about it? That's all I've been doing since nineteen seventy-one! And now I'm finished thinking. I have no intention of proselytizing. This is *my* project. I don't need anyone else to believe in it but me."

Steven's blood was racing. Time was running out, and he sensed that Savak's words were about finished. Yet, from somewhere deep within him, he found the strength to wrap a mantle of calmness over himself and find a way to keep Savak's mind on the story. "So you fed information to the Chinese and the Soviets in order to gain their trust. And then you gave them Entente."

"Not right away," Savak said proudly. "I couldn't begin that phase of my plan until I was certain that I had Pritman ready to make a successful run for the Presidency. When we decided—all of us Steven, you, me, Simon Clarke, Pritman, and the rest of the team—that Pritman was ready, I started giving both sides information about our current administration's foreign policy plans. It was a necessary maneuver to make sure that whatever the administration attempted would be countered by the Soviets and the Chinese."

"Arnie," Steven whispered, his voice so choked with emotions that he could barely get his name out.

Savak laughed at Steven's abhorrence. "Then, as our not so great President's star began to tarnish, I leaked hints of Pritman's foreign policy plans. I told the Chinese that Pritman would want to sign a mutual protection treaty with them. Of course, I told the Soviets the exact same thing."

"That Pritman wanted to sign a treaty with the Soviets?"

Savak shook his head. His sandy hair whipped about wildly.

"No. That was the clincher. I told the Soviets that Pritman was planning to sign a treaty with the Chinese. That was the reason they began to mobilize."

Savak laughed. "When Pritman wins the election," he added, "the Soviets will start a full scale war with the Chinese. The Chinese think we'll come to their aid. But we won't, because I will make sure that the treaties will be stalled in congressional red tape, and we won't be able to commit ourselves to action without them."

Steven nodded his comprehension. "But even with all your intricate planning, Ellie was the unexpected. She found you out, and she made you push your timetable up. You didn't know she was Secret Service, did you?"

"No. Not at first. She was a lot like you Steven, she never broke. I worked on her like Lin worked on me. But she held fast. But then there came a point when she told me who she was." Savak paused, laughed, and said, "She even had the gall to tell me she'd reported in about me. But she was bluffing. I knew that."

Savak fell suddenly silent. He stared at Steven for several long seconds. "And now you'll have to die. Ellie will too, of course. And Ellie's sister. It will appear that you killed her after you killed Chuck and Helene. You went crazy. A post-war-induced schizophrenia sent your mind back to the prison camp. When you realized what you'd done, you killed yourself."

"It won't work, Arnie. Too many people know."

Savak's eyes went wild. The corners of his mouth turned white. "There's still a way. It will be harder now, but it can be done."

"I don't understand," Steven said, stalling again. "If you hate the Chinese and the Soviets so damned much, how could you have worked with them?"

"I told you I wasn't working with them!" Savak shouted. Spittle sprayed outward with each word. "I was setting them up. When Pritman is elected, Russia and China will destroy each other and we'll be the better for it. Entente will assure that."

"Entente? You're not talking about Entente. You're talking about using treason to gain political power! You corrupted our dream, Arnie, and turned it into some sort of a twisted scheme to get revenge for what was done to us. And the shame of it is, that the way we had originally envisioned Entente, it would have worked. We could have given the world something to grow on, and to become better with. But all you saw it for was a way to become powerful enough to hurt the people whose only crime was in the way they had been trained to think and act."

Savak drew in a sharp and ragged breath. The hand holding the pistol began to shake. Unable to stop himself this time, Steven watched Savak's hand. He saw Savak's finger tighten on the trigger. It held steady for a heartbeat, and then relaxed.

"Corrupted *our* dream?" he said. "You don't know what the hell you're talking about! Entente, as it is today, is exactly the way I planned it. Not your way, and certainly not the way those other asses who worked on it see it. What I've done is to implement what I set out to do from the moment you told me about our mission. It was then, in Nam, that I promised myself I would never be used again."

"Really?" Steven snapped angrily, unable to contain his rage. "But it's all right to do to other people what they did to us."

"That's right," Savak stated.

"You stupid bastard," Steven spat from between clenched teeth. He took a half step forward, but froze when Savak's hand jerked.

"Who's the stupid one, Steven? I've been planning this for years. And now it's within my grasp. After the election, I'm going to be Pritman's Chief of Staff. I'm going to be the second most important man in this country—perhaps in the world! When I reach that position, I'll have accomplished exactly what I've spent years working and planning for. And I'll have my revenge on the government who betrayed me during the war."

"Never."

"Absolutely!" Savak glanced at his watch. "Steven, in two hours, Pritman will sit with the committee, and put Entente on the table. They'll accept it, and they will accept him. In two months he'll win the first primary, and next January, I'll put Entente into action."

Savak stared past Steven to where Chuck Latham's body hung in bloody silence. Then he focused on Steven again. "When Pritman is elected, America will never be in a war again, because there won't be any countries strong enough to challenge us, once Russia and China have destroyed each other.

"Then the American government will slowly be changed. People like Colonel Botlin, along with the rest of the old line military leaders, will be removed. The government will once again be a government for the people, not for the armies and the old thinkers."

Listening to Savak's narrow-sighted philosophy, Steven saw that no amount of logic would be able to penetrate his sickened thoughts. What he had to do was get him angry enough to make him careless—just long enough for him to make a move.

Steven took a half step back, and said, "You're going to do nothing. The government will not be changed, at least not the way you foresee it."

"Perhaps you're right, Steven," Savak said in an all too calm manner, seemingly undisturbed by Steven's movement. "But, since you'll be dead, you'll never know, will you?"

Steven saw a telltale flicker cross his eyes and sensed that Savak was getting ready to pull the trigger. "Arnie, think! They'll know it was you."

Savak shook his head as if to rid himself of a bug on his face. "No. Everyone will think you went crazy. You failed when you tried to kill Ellie, but you were successful with Chuck and Helene and Latham and Londrigan. The FBI agents were closing in on you, so you killed them before ending your own haunted existence. Everyone will read the tragic story of your life, and some will even feel sorry for another deplorable example caused by our stupidity in Vietnam."

"Xzi Tao is still alive, and so is Carla. They know."

Savak laughed loudly. The sound grated on Steven's ears. "Xzi Tao knows nothing, because you knew nothing when you met with him. No, actually, the only thing Xzi Tao knows is that you saved his life. I still find it hard to believe that I missed both of you that night."

"How did you know I was meeting with him? The CIA agent?" Steven asked as he began to turn sideways.

Savak nodded. "He traced the call you made at the motel. Then I called my contact at the Chinese Embassy. They're just like the Soviets. Every call that comes in is monitored. He told me that Xzi Tao had a meeting arranged for that night, and the location as well."

"But—" Steven began.

Savak straightened his arm, pointing the pistol at Steven's head. "No buts. And Ellie's sister won't be alive much longer. If you're expecting her to come to your aid, don't bother. I blew the telephone grid junction box. The phones are out for a three mile radius. And I smashed up the FBI car. No, Steven, she'll still be at Latham's when I'm finished with you."

"It won't work. Carla isn't Ellie's sister, she's a

Secret Service agent."

"I'm not surprised. When there was no fallout from Treasury over Ellie, I knew that they must have already placed someone inside. But that just makes it better for me," Savak said, his eyes glazed, as he nodded forcefully. "She was watching you, Steven. Not only did the FBI suspect you of espionage, but the Secret Service did too."

"They know it wasn't me."

"They only think it wasn't you. In a few days more evidence pointing to you will surface. A note to Anton, instructing him to come after you and get you out of the agency safe house. I planned the scenario very carefully."

"But none of this was supposed to happen until the spring," Steven said as the final piece of the puzzle fell into place. "Isn't that the way you set it up. Ellie's body was to have been found after the lake thawed. Naturally, I would be arrested. I would also be proven to be a spy. Of course, I wouldn't still be working for Pritman. No, with Ellie missing, and my being—supposedly—the last person she was with, I'd have had to resign under a cloud of suspicion, long before spring.

"And Pritman would be heading for the first primary about then, assured of a victory because of his brilliant new foreign policy program ideas and the anxiety that Russia and China would soon be at war. No, you couldn't risk having me around. It would ruin your plans. But those plans are gone now, Arnie. It truly is over. You're supposed to be in California. If you're not there, then someone is going to wonder why."

"All taken care of. I called my friend at Langley. I told him you'd called me, and that you were in Greyton. He said he'd notify Blayne. I told him I was coming too, to help talk you into giving up."

"Awfully thin, Arnie," Steven said sarcastically.

"It's good enough," Savak said. Taking a step forward, Savak raised the pistol to Steven's temple.

Now! he ordered himself. Swinging his arm up, he threw himself sideways across Savak's tall frame, spilling them both to the ground.

They landed hard. Savak spun, twisting Steven under him. Steven screamed in fury and agony as the burns on his back were torn open by the rough wooden floor.

Using the barrel of his pistol, Savak slammed him in the injured cheek, and then raked the barrel across the barely healing gash, ripping it open. Agony burst through him. Blood splattered upward, blinding him in one eye.

And then Savak's weight was off him. He saw a blurry vision of Savak gaining his feet and arcing the pistol toward his head.

Steven rolled, ignoring the pain, and grabbed at the Colt in his waistband. When his fingers gripped the handle, he pulled it free.

They fired at the same moment. Steven felt a hot brand of pain slice across the back of his hand. His fingers opened in reflex and the pistol fell to the floor.

He scrambled backward, but stopped when he saw that Savak had fallen to his knees. Savak was holding his thigh. Blood spurted from under his hand. Steven had hit an artery in his thigh.

And then he saw that Savak's pistol was still in his hand. He threw himself forward, scrambling madly toward the Colt.

Savak raised his gun again, just as Steven's fingertips reached the handle. Even as he grasped the gun, he knew he was too late.

The shot came, loud. Steven jerked involuntarily. But there was no pain. And then he saw Savak's eyes fill with surprise. Savak opened his mouth, closed it, and fell face forward.

Savak's pistol hit the floor at the same time as his face. The gun went off, the bullet digging through the wooden floor.

Steven scrambled to his feet just as Carla and Blayne rushed in. Blayne had a hastily wrapped bandage tied around his head. His hand was tucked into the front of his jacket to support the useless arm. Carla's Browning was in her hand. Behind them, another group of men being led by Banacek entered the cabin.

Steven went over to Carla. "You have to call in. He didn't stop Pritman. Pritman must be stopped."

An unfamiliar man pushed through the group. Steven made him for one of the various government service branches. The newcomer, tall and thin and prematurely bald, came to a stop in front of Steven. "Ryan. Ken Ryan, I'm Paul

Grange's replacement. Mr. Morrisy, the Entente papers were confiscated from Senator Pritman earlier today. As of right now he's in the White House, meeting with the President. The threat to our government is over."

Steven looked at Carla, who shrugged. His eyes swept over Blayne's face and then locked on the agent's eyes. "Do you understand it now?"

Blayne nodded. "Not all of it. But I will. Miss Statler has been explaining things to me."

"Steven, your hand," Carla said, coming closer and reaching for him.

He turned from her and looked down at Savak. He bent and rolled Savak's body over. The look of surprise was still on Arnie's face. Steven thought that in death, Arnie looked more like himself.

"At least we got the traitorous bastard before he could do any more harm," Ken Ryan said as he came up behind Steven. "He won't be selling us out any more."

Steven whirled. The anger and hatred he'd felt for Savak, only moments before, had disappeared with Savak's death. The man lying dead on the floor was no longer an insane stranger who had tried to kill him; the dead man was his lifelong friend.

Grabbing Ryan by the lapel, Steven pulled him close. "You ignorant bastard! You have no idea of who this man was! And he wasn't a traitor. He wasn't selling out our country. He thought he was helping it. He thought he was saving this country from people like you!"

Steven abruptly released the Secret Service agent, and went to where Chuck was hanging from the ceiling. "Someone give me a knife."

One of Banacek's deputies started forward. Banacek stopped him and handed Steven his own knife. Steven pulled a chair over, stepped up on it, and cut his friend down.

When he came down from the chair, he bent and picked Latham up. The pain in his back and face was incredible, but he didn't care. He carried Chuck to where Arnie Savak lay and placed him next to Savak.

He gazed at his friends for several seconds, wishing that somehow he could turn back the clock and bring them to life again. He wanted to pretend that he didn't know how something like this could have happened, and how he could have been robbed of so many of the people he loved so deeply. But he did know. An unnecessary war, a lust for power, and an insanity born of revenge and hatred were responsible for their deaths.

Together, Arnie and Chuck and he had survived horrors that other people could not even imagine, much less live through. Together, they had been an invincible force that might have changed the course of history for the better. But only two of them were together now; and, Steven was alone, truly alone, for the first time in his life.

His vision blurred and his throat constricted. He'd lost his family tonight, and he'd lost the last vestiges of the idealism that he had somehow maintained through all the years. All that remained for him was Ellie, and he didn't know if she would ever remember who he was.

Steven felt the walls of the cabin closing in on him. He turned, pushed through the crowd of police and government agents, and stepped outside.

He took several deep breaths of the cold winter air. The grief that had begun to build inside the cabin finally came. Steven ignored his sadness and tears as he started toward the sheriff's car.

Banacek was at his side before he reached the car. "After you do whatever legal things are necessary, I want to bury Arnie, Chuck, and Helene. Will you arrange that?"

"I'll handle it," Banacek said, nodding. "After I get you to the hospital."

When they reached Banacek's car, Steven leaned against it, wiped his face, and stared up at the cloudless night sky. "At least it's over," he said.

Banacek looked curiously at Steven. "Until the next time someone thinks they have the answer to the world's problems."

"Not if I can help it," Steven said, his gaze straying passed Banacek's shoulder, to the people now milling in front of the cabin. He didn't like most of the people there. But he didn't hate them either. Then he saw Carla and Ken Ryan, the new field supervisor, break away from the group.

As he watched them approach, he said, "How did you find us?"

Banacek lighted a cigarette, and exhaled. "It was a hunch. I used to hunt in this area, before the Parks Department banned hunting on Big Hand. I found the cabin about ten years ago. You boys left personal stuff, books and such."

"I guess it was fortunate we did," Steven commented as Carla and Ryan stopped abreast of them.

Ryan, standing just out of Steven's reach, said, "Mr. Morrisy, Director Axelrod would like you to come back to Washington with us. He would like to speak with you about what happened."

Steven grunted. "When I'm ready to be debriefed, I'll be there."

"Mr. Morris—"

Steven cut him off. "You tell the director that after I've taken care of some personal matters I'll be in to see him. If that isn't good enough, then you may suggest that he come here to see me."

Ryan exhaled slowly. "You're making a mistake, but I'll give him the message."

As Ryan moved back, Carla stepped close to Steven. Her face was soft. Her eyes reflected emotions he wasn't sure he wanted to see. "I want to stay with you."

Steven closed his eyes, briefly. When he opened them, he shook his head slowly. It wasn't easy, but it was necessary. "Go back to Washington, Carla. I have things that have to be done. And I need to be alone right now."

"And Ellie?"

"She's part of those things. A very important part."

"Steven . . ."

"Carla, thank you for believing in me when no one else would."

She hung hesitant for a second, and then nodded. "Goodbye Steven. And be careful. They have long memories."

"So do I."